SEP 22 2015

D0250906

1919

Generously Donated By

Richard A. Freedman
Trust

Albuquerque / Bernalillo County
Libraries

SEP 2 2 2015

WithdrawnABCL

Books by John Dos Passos

Fiction

ONE MAN'S INITIATION

THREE SOLDIERS

STREETS OF NIGHT

MANHATTAN TRANSFER

THE 42ND PARALLEL

1919

THE BIG MONEY

U.S.A.

The 42nd Parallel

1919

The Big Money

ADVENTURES OF A YOUNG MAN

NUMBER ONE

THE GRAND DESIGN

CHOSEN COUNTRY

DISTRICT OF COLUMBIA

Adventures of a Young Man

Number One

The Grand Design

MOST LIKELY TO SUCCEED

THE GREAT DAYS

MIDCENTURY

CENTURY'S EBB

Drama

THE GARBAGE MAN

AIRWAYS, INC.

FORTUNE HEIGHTS

Poetry

A PUSHCART ON THE CURB

Nonfiction

ROSINANTE TO THE ROAD AGAIN

ORIENT EXPRESS

IN ALL COUNTRIES

JOURNEYS BETWEEN WARS

FACING THE CHAIR

THE GROUND WE STAND ON

STATE OF THE NATION

TOUR OF DUTY

THE PROSPECT BEFORE US

THE HEAD AND HEART OF THOMAS JEFFERSON

THE MEN WHO MADE THE NATION

PROSPECTS OF A GOLDEN AGE

MR. WILSON'S WAR

BRAZIL ON THE MOVE

OCCASIONS AND PROTESTS

THOMAS JEFFERSON: THE MAKING OF A PRESIDENT

THE PORTUGAL STORY: THREE CENTURIES
OF EXPLORATION AND DISCOVERY

THE BEST TIMES: AN INFORMAL MEMOIR

THE THEME IS FREEDOM

THE SHACKLES OF POWER

EASTER ISLAND

THE FOURTEENTH CHRONICLE: LETTERS
AND DIARIES OF JOHN DOS PASSOS

Poetry

A PUSHCART AT THE CURB

Nonfiction

ROSINANTE TO THE ROAD AGAIN

ORIENT EXPRESS

IN ALL COUNTRIES

JOURNEYS BETWEEN WARS

TAKING THE CHAIR

THE GROUND WE STAND ON

STATE OF THE NATION

TOUR OF DUTY

THE PROSPECT BEFORE US

THE HEAD AND HEART OF THOMAS JEFFERSON

THE MEN WHO MADE THE NATION

PROSPECTS OF A GOLDEN AGE

MR. WILSON'S WAR

BRAZIL ON THE MOVE

OCCASIONS AND PROTESTS

THOMAS JEFFERSON: THE MAKING OF A PRESIDENT

THE PORTUGAL STORY: THREE CENTURIES
OF EXPLORATION AND DISCOVERY

THE BEST TIMES: AN INFORMAL MEMOIR

THE THEME IS FREEDOM

THE SHACKLES OF POWER

EASTER ISLAND

THE FOURTEENTH CHRONICLE: LETTERS
AND DIARIES OF JOHN DOS PASSOS

Withdrawn/ABCL

JOHN DOS PASSOS

1919

VOLUME TWO OF THE

U.S.A. TRILOGY

A MARINER BOOK

HOUGHTON MIFFLIN COMPANY

Boston · New York

3 9075 04991339 2

First Mariner Books edition 2000

Copyright 1932 and © renewed 1959 by John Dos Passos

Grateful acknowledgment is made to E. L. Doctorow for permission to
reprint the foreword, previously published in *U.S.A.* by John Dos Passos,
copyright © 1991 by E. L. Doctorow.

Title page illustration by Reginald Marsh copyright 1946 by John Dos
Passos and Houghton Mifflin Company, copyright © renewed 1974
by Houghton Mifflin Company.

ALL RIGHTS RESERVED

For information about permission to reproduce selections from this
book, write to Permissions, Houghton Mifflin Harcourt Publishing
Company, 215 Park Avenue South, New York, New York 10003.

www.hmhco.com

Library of Congress Cataloging-in-Publication Data
Dos Passos, John, 1896–1970.
1919 / John Dos Passos.
p. cm. — (U.S.A. ; v. 2)
"A Mariner book."
ISBN 0-618-05682-3
1. United States — History — 1913–1921 — Fiction.
2. World War, 1914–1918—Influence—Fiction. I. Title:
Nineteen nineteen. II. Title.
PS3507.O743 N53 2000
813'.52 — dc21 00-027609

Printed in the United States of America

DOH 20 19 18 17 16

FOREWORD

Given neither to he-man esthetics, like Hemingway, nor to the romance of self-destruction, like Fitzgerald, John Dos Passos, their friend and contemporary — he was born in 1896 — was a modest self-effacing person, an inveterate wanderer who liked to hike through foreign places and sit down for a drink with strangers and listen to their stories. He saw literature as reportage. He admired the plain style of Defoe, and he read Thackeray's *Vanity Fair*, subtitled *A Novel Without a Hero*, all his life.

Dos Passos was born wandering, living out his lonely childhood with his unmarried mother, Lucy Madison, as she toured the European capitals to avoid scandal while, in the United States, his father, John R. Dos Passos, an eminent corporate lawyer and lobbyist, waited for his invalided first wife to die. When that event came about, in 1910, the mother, the father, and the boy, a strongly loving triad, were able finally to constitute themselves as a family. But the isolation of his early life left Dos Passos psychologically detached, with the feelings of a perpetual outsider.

The outside, of course, is a position of advantage for a writer. Reportage from the outside, and slightly above, is the working viewpoint of Dos Passos's masterpiece, *U.S.A.* It is a nice irony that not the era's big literary personalities, but this quiet inhibited young man, would produce the most vaultingly ambitious novel of all — a twelve-hundred-page chronicle of the historic and spiritual life of an entire country in the first three decades of the twentieth century. Not for him the portrait of a gangster, however metaphorically shimmering, or even the group portrait of a lost generation: Dos Passos goes wide — from the American incursion in the Philippines to the beginning of the talkies, from coast to coast and class to class. *U.S.A.* is the novel as mural, with society's heroes standing out from the flames of history while the small-figured masses toil at their feet.

In fact, the peripatetic Dos Passos landed one day in Mexico City and was much taken with the murals of Diego Rivera colorfully spreading, story after story, up the courtyard walls of the Secretariat of Education. In later years he indicated also his love of thirteenth- and fourteenth-century European tableaux — those with the saints painted big and the ordinary people painted small, filling up the background.

He published the first installment of *U.S.A.*, *The 42nd Parallel*, in 1929, having realized early on that what he was doing could not be contained in one volume. *1919* followed two years later, and the final volume, *The Big Money*, was published in 1936. He could have gone on — he had endless resources for the thing, having picked up its rhythm and much of the material from his own ambulating life. He'd gone up from Baltimore to Harvard, where he read and was impressed by the Imagist poets — Pound, Amy Lowell, Carl Sandburg. He also made his acquaintance with the work on James Joyce, the twentieth-century writer who, though hardly given to English plain speech, would have the most enduring influence on him. After Harvard he went back to his wandering, spending a year in Spain and studying architecture. But World War I was just over the border, and in 1916 he volunteered to drive for the Norton-Harjes Ambulance Service, the same organization for which Hemingway and E. E. Cummings drove. He served in France and Italy, and then with the entry of America into the conflict he enlisted in AEF and, all told, got as much of a dose of modern war as he would need for the inspiration to portray its soldier-victims in his first novel, *Three Soldiers* (1921).

The reticent writer was always disposed to the action. In the postwar twenties, he managed time and again to place himself in history's hotspots — whether the literary scene in New York and Paris, revolutionary Mexico after the death of Emiliano Zapata, the newly Communist Soviet Union, or the nativist city of Boston, where he marched for the two imprisoned and condemned immigrant anarchists Sacco and Vanzetti.

He was writing all the time, of course. He published *Rosinante to the Road Again* (1922), a book of essays about Spain, *Manhattan Transfer* (1925), a dark impressionist portrait of New York and technical precursor of the *U.S.A.* novels, and pieces in the *New Masses, The Dial, The Nation,* and *The New Republic* attesting to his leftist sensibility. He was a diarist and kept up an active correspondence with a variety of colleagues including Edmund Wilson, Malcolm Cowley,

Hemingway, and Fitzgerald — all of them worried in the world, all of them news junkies arguing politics and entangling themselves in the crises of civilization.

Not until the Spanish civil war would the profound difference between Dos Passos's humanist ideals and the doctrinaire idealism of many of his contemporaries become clear: the visible moment of separation seems to have occurred with the execution in Valencia of his friend José Robles, a Republican, by a Communist firing squad.

In his later life Dos Passos was as archly conservative as he had been radical. What remained constant, like a moral compass course that never veered, was his despair of the fate of the single human being bent into service of the institutions of modern industrial society, whatever those institutions might be.

In fact, the pervading vision of *U.S.A.* is of people dominated by institutions, which is to say trapped in history. The novel is without a hero. We are given narratives of the lives of a dozen men and women — Joe Williams, a seaman; Mac, a typesetter; J. Ward Moorehouse, a public relations man; Eleanor Stoddard, a stage designer; Dick Savage, a Harvard graduate and World War I ambulance driver; Charley Anderson, a wartime air ace and inventor; Margo Dowling, an actress; Ben Compton, a union organizer; and so on — and watch three decades pass through them as they reach their prime and then age and flounder, either to die or to simply disappear or, with one or two exceptions, to end in moral defeat. Living below the headlines, they're presented as ordinaries: their lives can intersect, they can sometimes be charming or sympathetic, but they are always seen from above, as in satire, and all their irresolution, self-deceit, and haplessness, and their failure to find empowerment in love or social rebellion, is unconsoled by the moral structure of a plot. *U.S.A.* has no plot, only the movement forward of its multiple narratives under the presiding circumstances of history.

The circumstances themselves are occasionally flashed to us by means of the so-called "Newsreels" that interrupt the text with actual headlines from newspapers of the time, fragments of news stories, advertising slogans, and popular song lyrics, all popping up in rat-a-tat fashion, like momentary garish illuminations, as from fireworks, of the American landscape.

Early readers were dazzled, as they should have been, by these collages. But Dos Passos does not stop there. A third mode is the minute biography, the periodic insertion into the text of highly editorialized brief lives of some of the paramount figures of each of the decades he covers, including Eugene Debs and William Jennings Bryan, Carnegie, Edison, John Reed and J. P. Morgan, Teddy Roosevelt, Woodrow Wilson, the Wright Brothers, Henry Ford, Isadora Duncan, and William Randolph Hearst — the secular saints of the Dos Passos tableau, often mocked, sometimes mourned, but in any event drawn big. Unlike the lives of his fictional characters, which flow incessantly, the breathless author saying *and then this happened and then that happened*, the biographies stand as firm in his annunciation as historical markers.

Through the fourth major mode of address of the book, those Joycean passages under the heading "The Camera Eye," Dos Passos records his own nameless life of sensations beginning with his early boyhood. These are perhaps the most enigmatic interludes. Like the Newsreels and brief biographies they give a topographical dimension to the text, as if points in the main narrative were being held under a higher lens magnification. They also implicate the narrator in the narrative, serving to underscore his moral commitment to the act of writing. But with his characteristic self-denigration, Dos Passos once justified these sections to an interviewer as planned lapses into "the subjective," a way of keeping this terrible contaminant out of the rest of the manuscript.

Here we should remember D. H. Lawrence's warning not to trust the writer but the book. As with Dos Passos's self-effacement, his objectivity, which is the literary form of self-effacement, masks an imperial intelligence, an acerbic wit, a great anger, and, above all, the audacity to write a novel that breathes in the excitements of all the revolutionary art of the early twentieth century — whether Joyce's compound word streams or Rivera's proletarian murals or D. W. Griffith's and Sergei Eisenstein's film montages.

The stature of *U.S.A.* was immediately recognized by the critics of the day. By the time of its publication as a completed one-volume trilogy in 1938, the novel was generally regarded as a major achievement, although displaying the characteristics of a highly controlled vision. Malcolm Cowley thought of it as a "collectivist novel" perversely lacking the celebrations of common humanity that would be expected from a collectivist novel. Edmund Wilson wondered why every one of the ordinary characters of the book went down to failure, why nobody took root, raised a family, established a worthwhile career, or found any of the satisfactions that were undeniably visible in actual middle-class American life. Others objected to the characters' lack of ideas, Dos Passos's refusal to give them any consequential thought or reflection not connected with their appetites. And it is true these are beings occupied almost entirely with their sensations and plagued by their longings, given mightily to drinking and fornication while their flimsy thought provides no anchor against the drift of their lives.

But for Jean-Paul Sartre, writing in 1938, it was exactly in the novel's refusal to redeem its characters that he found its greatness. Their lives are reported, their feelings and utterances put forth, says Sartre, in the style of a "statement to the Press." And we the readers accumulate endless catalogues of individual sensory adventures, from the outside, right up to the moment the character disappears or dies — and is dissolved in the collective consciousness. And to what purpose all those feelings, all that adventure? What is the individual life against history? "The pressure exerted by a gas on the walls of its container does not depend upon the individual histories of the molecules composing it," says the French existentialist philosopher.

But *U.S.A.* is an American novel after all, and we recognize the Americanness of the characters. They really do have a national specificity. In fact, the reader now, half a century further along, cannot help remark how current Dos Passos's characters are — how we could run into Margo Dowling or Ward Moorehouse or Charley Anderson today and recognize any one of them, and how they would fit right in without any trouble. How they do. *U.S.A.* is a useful book to us because it is far-seeing. It seems angrier and at the same time more hopeful than it might have seemed in 1938. A moral demand is implicit in its pages. Dos Passos says in his prologue that above all, "*U.S.A.* is the speech of the people." He heard our voice and recorded it, and we play it now for our solemn contemplation.

— E. L. Doctorow

CONTENTS

NEWSREEL XX *Oh the infantree the infantree* 1

JOE WILLIAMS 2

The Camera Eye (28) when the telegram came that she was
dying 6

       PLAYBOY 8

JOE WILLIAMS 12

NEWSREEL XXI *Goodby Broadway; Hello France* 53

The Camera Eye (29) the raindrops fall one by one out of the
horsechestnut tree 54

RICHARD ELLSWORTH SAVAGE 55

NEWSREEL XXII *Coming Year Promises Rebirth of*
Railroads 77

The Camera Eye (30) remembering the grey crooked fingers 78

      RANDOLPH BOURNE 79

NEWSREEL XXIII *If you dont like your Uncle Sammy* 82

EVELINE HUTCHINS 83

The Camera Eye (31) a mattress covered with something from
Vantine's 98

EVELINE HUTCHINS 99

NEWSREEL XXIV it is difficult to realize the colossal scale 108

The Camera Eye (32) à quatorze heures precisement 109

    THE HAPPY WARRIOR 110

The Camera Eye (33) 11,000 registered harlots 115

JOE WILLIAMS 117

The Camera Eye (34)   his voice was three thousand miles away 135

NEWSREEL XXV   General Pershing's forces today occupied 137

A HOOSIER QUIXOTE 138

NEWSREEL XXVI   Europe on Knife Edge 144

RICHARD ELLSWORTH SAVAGE 145

NEWSREEL XXVII   Her Wounded Hero of War a Fraud 168

The Camera Eye (35)   there were always two cats 170

EVELINE HUTCHINS 170

NEWSREEL XXVIII   *Oh the eagles they fly high* 181

JOE WILLIAMS 182

NEWSREEL XXIX   the arrival of the news 189

The Camera Eye (36)   when we emptied the rosies 190

MEESTER VEELSON 191

NEWSREEL XXX   Monster Guns Removed? 199

The Camera Eye (37)   *alphabetically according to rank* 200

NEWSREEL XXXI   washing and dressing hastily 203

DAUGHTER 203

NEWSREEL XXXII   Golden Voice of Caruso Swells in
Victory Song to Crowds on Streets 228

The Camera Eye (38)   sealed signed and delivered 229

NEWSREEL XXXIII   Can't Recall Killing Sister 231

EVELINE HUTCHINS 233

NEWSREEL XXXIV   Whole World Is Short of Platinum 266

THE HOUSE OF MORGAN 267

NEWSREEL XXXV   the Grand Prix de la Victoire 272

The Camera Eye (39)   daylight enlarges out of 273

NEWSREEL XXXVI   *To the Glory of France Eternal* 275

RICHARD ELLSWORTH SAVAGE 276

NEWSREEL XXXVII   Soviet Guards Displaced 317

The Camera Eye (40)   I walked all over town 319

NEWSREEL XXXVIII   *C'est la lutte finale* 321

DAUGHTER 322

NEWSREEL XXXIX   spectacle of ruined villages and tortured
earth 334

The Camera Eye (41)   arent you coming to the anarchist
picnic 335

NEWSREEL XL   Criminal in Pyjamas Saws Bars 337

   JOE HILL 338

BEN COMPTON 339

NEWSREEL XLI   in British Colonial Office quarters 362

The Camera Eye (42)   four hours we casuals pile up scrapiron 363

NEWSREEL XLII   it was a gala day for Seattle 365

   PAUL BUNYAN 366

RICHARD ELLSWORTH SAVAGE 370

NEWSREEL XLIII   the placards borne by the radicals 374

   THE BODY OF AN AMERICAN 375

1919

Newsreel XX

Oh the infantree the infantree
With the dirt behind their ears

ARMIES CLASH AT VERDUN IN GLOBE'S GREATEST BATTLE

150,000 MEN AND WOMEN PARADE

but another question and a very important one is raised. The New York Stock Exchange is today the only free securities market in the world. If it maintains that position it is sure to become perhaps the world's greatest center for the marketing of

BRITISH FLEET SENT TO SEIZE GOLDEN HORN

The cavalree artilleree
And the goddamned engineers
Will never beat the infantree
In eleven thousand years

TURKS FLEE BEFORE TOMMIES AT GALLIPOLI

when they return home what will our war veterans think of the American who babbles about some vague new order, while dabbling in the sand of shoal water? From his weak folly they who have lived through the spectacle will recall the vast new No Man's Land of Europe reeking with murder and the lust of rapine, aflame with the fires of revolution

STRIKING WAITERS ASK AID OF WOMEN

Oh the oak and the ash and the weeping willow tree
And green grows the grass in North Amerikee

coincident with a position of that kind will be the bringing from abroad of vast quantities of money for the purposes of maintaining balances in this country

When I think of the flag which our ships carry, the only touch of color about them, the only thing that moves as if it had a settled spirit in it, — in their solid structure; it seems to me I see alternate strips of parchment upon which are written the rights of liberty and justice and strips of blood spilt to vindicate these rights, and then, — in the corner a prediction of the blue serene into which every nation may swim which stands for these things.

Oh we'll nail Old Glory to the top of the pole
And we'll all reenlist in the pig's a—h—

Joe Williams

Joe Williams put on the secondhand suit and dropped his uniform, with a cobblestone wrapped up in it, off the edge of the dock into the muddy water of the basin. It was noon. There was nobody around. He felt bad when he found he didn't have the cigarbox with him. Back in the shed he found it where he'd left it. It was a box that had once held Flor de Mayo cigars he'd bought when he was drunk in Guantanamo. In the box under the goldpaper lace were Janey's high school graduation picture, a snapshot of Alec with his motorcycle, a picture with the signatures of the coach and all the players of the whole highschool junior team that he was captain of all in baseball clothes, an old pink almost faded snapshot of his Dad's tug, the *Mary B. Sullivan*, taken off the Virginia Capes with a fullrigged ship in tow, an undressed postcard picture of a girl named Antoinette he'd been with in Villefranche, some safetyrazor blades, a postcard photo of himself and two other guys, all gobs in white suits, taken against the background of a moorish arch in Malaga, a bunch of foreign stamps, a package of Merry Widows, and ten little pink and red shells he'd picked up on the beach at Santiago. With the box tucked right under his arm, feeling crummy in the baggy civies, he walked slowly out to the beacon and watched the fleet in formation steaming down the

River Plate. The day was overcast; the lean cruisers soon blurred into their trailing smokesmudges.

Joe stopped looking at them and watched a rusty tramp come in. She had a heavy list to port and you could see the hull below the waterline green and slimy with weed. There was a blue and white Greek flag on the stern and a dingy yellow quarantine flag halfway up the fore.

A man who had come up behind him said something to Joe in Spanish. He was a smiling ruddy man in blue denims and was smoking a cigar, but for some reason he made Joe feel panicky. "No savvy," Joe said and walked away and out between the warehouses into the streets back of the waterfront.

He had trouble finding Maria's place, all the blocks looked so much alike. It was by the mechanical violin in the window that he recognized it. Once he got inside the stuffy anise-smelling dump he stood a long time at the bar with one hand round a sticky beerglass looking out at the street he could see in bright streaks through the beadcurtain that hung in the door. Any minute he expected the white uniform and yellow holster of a marine to go past.

Behind the bar a yellow youth with a crooked nose leaned against the wall looking at nothing. When Joe made up his mind he jerked his chin up. The youth came over and craned confidentially across the bar, leaning on one hand and swabbing at the oilcloth with the rag he held in the other. The flies that had been grouped on the rings left by beerglasses on the oilcloth flew up to join the buzzing mass on the ceiling. "Say, bo, tell Maria I want to see her," Joe said out of the corner of his mouth. The youth behind the bar held up two fingers. "Dos pesos," he said. "Hell, no, I only want to talk to her."

Maria beckoned to him from the door in back. She was a sallow woman with big eyes set far apart in bluish sacks. Through the crumpled pink dress tight over the bulge of her breasts Joe could make out the rings of crinkled flesh round the nipples. They sat down at a table in the back room. "Gimme two beers," Joe yelled through the door.

"Watta you wan', iho de mi alma?" asked Maria. "You savvy Doc Sidner?" "Sure me savvy all yanki. Watta you wan' you no go wid beeg sheep?" "No go wid beeg sheep . . . Fight wid beeg sonofabeech, see?"

"Ché!" Maria breasts shook like jelly when she laughed. She put a fat hand at the back of his neck and drew his face towards hers. "Poor baby . . . black eye." "Sure he gave me a black eye." Joe pulled away from her. "Petty officer. I knocked him cold, see . . . Navy's no place for me after that . . . I'm through. Say, Doc said you knew a guy could fake A.B. certificates . . . able seaman savvy? Me for the Merchant Marine from now on, Maria."

Joe drank down his beer.

She sat shaking her head saying, "Ché . . . pobrecito . . . Ché." Then she said in a tearful voice, "'Ow much dollars you got?" "Twenty," said Joe. "Heem want fiftee." "I guess I'm f—d for fair then."

Maria walked round to the back of his chair and put a fat arm around his neck, leaning over him with little clucking noises. "Wait a minute, we tink . . . sabes?" Her big breast pressing against his neck and shoulder made him feel itchy; he didn't like her touching him in the morning when he was sober like this. But he sat there until she suddenly let out a parrot screech. "Paquito . . . ven acá."

A dirty pearshaped man with a red face and neck came in from the back. They talked Spanish over Joe's head. At last she patted his cheek and said, "Awright Paquito sabe where heem live . . . maybe heem take twenty, sabes?"

Joe got to his feet. Paquito took off the smudged cook's apron and lit a cigarette. "You savvy A.B. papers?" said Joe walking up and facing him. He nodded, "Awright," Joe gave Maria a hug and a little pinch. "You're a good girl, Maria." She followed them grinning to the door of the bar.

Outside Joe looked sharply up and down the street. Not a uniform. At the end of the street a crane tilted black above the cement warehouse buildings. They got on a streetcar and rode a long time without saying anything. Joe sat staring at the floor with his hands dangling between his knees until Paquito poked him. They got out in a cheaplooking suburban section of new cement houses already dingy. Paquito rang at a door like all the other doors and after a while a man with redrimmed eyes and big teeth like a horse came and opened it. He and Paquito talked Spanish a long while through the halfopen door. Joe stood first on one foot and then on the other. He could tell that they were sizing up how much they could get out of him by the way they looked at him sideways as they talked.

He was just about to break in when the man in the door spoke to him in cracked cockney. "You give the blighter five pesos for his trouble, mytey, an' we'll settle this hup between wahte men." Joe shelled out what silver he had in his pocket and Paquito went.

Joe followed the limey into the front hall that smelt of cabbage and frying grease and wash day. When he got inside he put his hand on Joe's shoulder and said, blowing stale whiskybreath in his face, "Well, mytey, 'ow much can you afford?" Joe drew away. "Twenty American dollars's all I got," he said through his teeth. The limey shook his head, "Only four quid . . . well, there's no 'arm in seein' what we can do, is there, mytey? Let's see it." While the limey stood looking at him Joe took off his belt, picked out a couple of stitches with the small blade of his jackknife and pulled out two orangebacked American bills folded long. He unfolded them carefully and was about to hand them over when he thought better of it and put them in his pocket. "Now let's take a look at the paper," he said grinning.

The limey's redrimmed eyes looked tearful; he said we ought to be 'elpful one to another and gryteful when a bloke risked a forger's hend to 'elp 'is fellow creatures. Then he asked Joe his name, age and birthplace, how long he'd been to sea and all that and went into an inside room, carefully locking the door after him.

Joe stood in the hall. There was a clock ticking somewhere. The ticks dragged slower and slower. At last Joe heard the key turn in the lock and the limey came out with two papers in his hand. "You oughter realize what I'm doin' for yez, mytey. . . ." Joe took the paper. He wrinkled his forehead and studied it; looked all right to him. The other paper was a note authorizing Titterton's Marine Agency to garnishee Joe's pay monthly until the sum of ten pounds had been collected. "But look here you," he said, "that makes seventy dollars I'm shelling out." The limey said think of the risk he was tyking and 'ow times was 'ard and that arfter all he could tyke it or leave it. Joe followed him into the paperlittered inside room and leaned over the desk and signed with a fountain pen.

They went downtown on the streetcar and got off at Rivadavia Street. Joe followed the limey into a small office back of a warehouse. "'Ere's a smart young 'and for you, Mr. McGregor," the limey said to a biliouslooking Scotchman who was walking up and down chewing his nails.

Joe and Mr. McGregor looked at each other. "American?" "Yes." "You're not expectin' American pay I'm supposin'?"

The limey went up to him and whispered something; McGregor looked at the certificate and seemed satisfied. "All right, sign in the book. . . . Sign under the last name." Joe signed and handed the limey the twenty dollars. That left him flat. "Well, cheeryoh, mytey." Joe hesitated a moment before he took the limey's hand. "So long," he said.

"Go get your dunnage and be back here in an hour," said McGregor in a rasping voice. "Haven't got any dunnage. I've been on the beach," said Joe, weighing the cigarbox in his hand. "Wait outside then and I'll take you aboard the *Argyle* by and by." Joe stood for a while in the warehouse door looking out into the street. Hell, he'd seen enough of B.A. He sat on a packingcase marked Tibbett & Tibbett, Enameled Ware, Blackpool, to wait for Mr. McGregor, wondering if he was the skipper or the mate. Time sure would drag all right till he got out of B.A.

The Camera Eye (28)

when the telegram came that she was dying (the streetcarwheels screeched round the bellglass like all the pencils on all the slates in all the schools) walking around Fresh Pond the smell of puddlewater willowbuds in the raw wind shrieking streecarwheels rattling on loose trucks through the Boston suburbs   grief isnt a uniform and go shock the Booch and drink wine for supper at the Lenox before catching the Federal

I'm so tired of violets
Take them all away

when the telegram came that she was dying the bellglass cracked in a screech of slate pencils (have you ever never been able to sleep for a week in April?)   and He met me in the grey trainshed my eyes were stinging with vermillion bronze and chromegreen inks that oozed from the spinning April hills   His moustaches were white the tired droop of an old man's cheeks   She's gone Jack grief isn't a uniform and the   in the parlor   the waxen odor of lilies in the parlor (He and I we must bury the uniform of grief)

then the riversmell the shimmering Potomac reaches the little choppysilver waves at Indian Head   there were mockingbirds in the graveyard and the roadsides steamed with spring   April enough to shock the world

*   *   *

when the cable came that He was dead I walked through the streets full of fiveoclock Madrid seething with twilight in shivered cubes of aguardiente redwine gaslampgreen sunsetpink tileochre   eyes lips red cheeks brown pillar of the throat climbed on the night train at the Norte station without knowing why

I'm so tired of violets
Take them all away

the shattered iridescent bellglass the carefully copied busts the architectural details the grammar of styles

it was the end of that book and I left the Oxford poets in the little noisy room that smelt of stale oliveoil in the Pension Boston   Ahora   Now   Maintenant   Vita   Nuova   but we

who had heard Copey's beautiful reading voice and read the handsomely bound books and breathed deep (breathe deep one two three four) of the waxwork lilies and the artificial parmaviolet scent under the ethercone and sat breakfasting in the library where the bust was of Octavius

were now dead at the cableoffice

on the rumblebumping wooden bench on the train slamming through midnight climbing up from the steerage to get a whiff of Atlantic on the lunging steamship (the ovalfaced Swiss girl and her husband were my friends) she had slightly popeyes and a little gruff way of saying *Zut alors* and throwing us a little smile a fish to a sealion that warmed our darkness   when the immigration officer came for her passport he couldn't send her to Ellis Island la grippe espagnole she was dead

washing those windows
K.P.
cleaning the sparkplugs with a pocketknife
A. W. O. L.
grinding the American Beauty roses to dust in that whore's bed (the foggy night flamed with proclamations of the League of the Rights of Man) the almond smell of high explosives sending singing éclats through the sweetish puking grandiloquence of the rotting dead

*   *   *

tomorrow I hoped would be the first day of the first month of the first year

Playboy

Jack Reed
was the son of a United States Marshal, a prominent citizen of Portland Oregon.
He was a likely boy
so his folks sent him east to school
and to Harvard.

Harvard stood for the broad *a* and those contacts so useful in later life and good English prose . . . if the hedgehog cant be cultured at Harvard the hedgehog cant
at all and the Lowells only speak to the Cabots and the Cabots and the Oxford Book of Verse.
Reed was a likely youngster, he wasnt a jew or a socialist and he didnt come from Roxbury; he was husky greedy had appetite for everything: a man's got to like many things in his life.
Reed was a man; he liked men he liked women he liked eating and writing and foggy nights and drinking and foggy nights and swimming and football and rhymed verse and being cheerleader ivy orator making clubs (not the very best clubs, his blood didn't run thin enough for the very best clubs)
and Copey's voice reading *The Man Who Would Be King,* the dying fall *Urnburial,* good English prose the lamps coming on across the Yard, under the elms in the twilight
dim voices in lecturehalls,
the dying fall the elms the Discobulus the bricks of the old buildings and the commemorative gates and the goodies and the deans and the instructors all crying in thin voices refrain,
refrain; the rusty machinery creaked, the deans quivered under their mortarboards, the cogs turned to Class Day, and Reed was out in the world:

*   *   *

Washington Square!

Conventional turns out to be a cussword;

Villon seeking a lodging for the night in the Italian tenements on Sullivan Street, Bleecker, Carmine;

research proves R.L.S. to have been a great cocksman, and as for the Elizabethans

to hell with them.

Ship on a cattleboat and see the world have adventures you can tell funny stories about every evening; a man's got to love . . . the quickening pulse the feel that today in foggy evenings footsteps taxi-cabs women's eyes . . . many things in his life.

Europe with a dash of horseradish, gulp Paris like an oyster;

but there's more to it than the Oxford Book of English Verse. Linc Steffens talked the cooperative commonwealth.

revolution in a voice as mellow as Copey's, Diogenes Steffens with Marx for a lantern going through the west looking for a good man, Socrates Steffens kept asking why not revolution?

Jack Reed wanted to live in a tub and write verses;

but he kept meeting bums workingmen husky guys he liked out of luck out of work why not revolution?

He couldn't keep his mind on his work with so many people out of luck;

in school hadnt he learned the Declaration of Independence by heart? Reed was a westerner and words meant what they said; when he said something standing with a classmate at the Harvard Club bar, he meant what he said from the soles of his feet to the waves of his untidy hair (his blood didnt run thin enough for the Harvard Club and the Dutch Treat Club and respectable New York freelance Bohemia).

Life, liberty, and the pursuit of happiness;

not much of that round the silkmills when

in 1913,

he went over to Paterson to write up the strike, textile workers parading beaten up by the cops, the strikers in jail; before he knew it he was a striker parading beaten up by the cops in jail;

he wouldn't let the editor bail him out, he'd learn more with the strikers in jail.

He learned enough to put on the pageant of the Paterson Strike in Madison Square garden.

He learned the hope of a new society where nobody would be out of luck,

why not revolution?

The Metropolitan Magazine sent him to Mexico
to write up Pancho Villa.

Pancho Villa taught him to write and the skeleton mountains and the tall organ cactus and the armored trains and the bands playing in little plazas full of dark girls in blue scarfs

and the bloody dust and the ping of rifleshots

in the enormous night of the desert, and the brown quietvoiced peons dying starving killing for liberty

for land for water for schools.

Mexico taught him to write.

Reed was a westerner and words meant what they said.

The war was a blast that blew out all the Diogenes lanterns;

the good men began to gang up to call for machineguns. Jack Reed was the last of the great race of warcorrespondents who ducked under censorships and risked their skins for a story.

Jack Reed was the best American writer of his time, if anybody had wanted to know about the war they could have read about it in the articles he wrote

about the German front,

the Serbian retreat,

Saloniki;

behind the lines in the tottering empire of the Czar,

dodging the secret police,

jail in Cholm.

The brasshats wouldnt let him go to France because they said one night in the German trenches kidding with the Boche guncrew he'd pulled the string on a Hun gun pointed at the heart of France . . . playboy stuff but after all what did it matter who fired the guns or

which way they were pointed? Reed was with the boys who were being blown to hell,
    with the Germans the French the Russians the Bulgarians the
seven little tailors in the Ghetto in Salonique,
    and in 1917
    he was with the soldiers and peasants
    in Petrograd in October:
    Smolny,
    Ten Days That Shook the World;

    no more Villa picturesque Mexico, no more Harvard Club play-
boy stuff, plans for Greek theatres, rhyming verse, good stories of an
oldtime warcorrespondent,
    this wasnt fun anymore
    this was grim.

    Delegate,
    back in the States indictments, the Masses trial, the Wobbly trial,
Wilson cramming the jails,
    forged passports, speeches, secret documents, riding the rods
across the cordon sanitaire, hiding in the bunkers on steamboats;
    jail in Finland all his papers stolen,
    no more chance to write verses now, no more warm chats with
every guy you met up with, the college boy with the nice smile talking
himself out of trouble with the judge;
    at the Harvard Club they're all in the Intelligence Service mak-
ing the world safe for the Morgan-Baker-Stillman combination of
banks;
    that old tramp sipping his coffee out of a tomatocan's a spy of
the General Staff.

    The world's no fun anymore,
    only machinegunfire and arson
    starvation lice bedbugs cholera typhus
    no lint for bandages no chloroform or ether thousands dead of
gangrened wounds cordon sanitaire and everywhere spies.
    The windows of Smolny glow whitehot like a bessemer,
    no sleep in Smolny,

Smolny the giant rollingmill running twentyfour hours a day
rolling out men nations hopes millenniums impulses fears,
   rawmaterial
   for the foundations
   of a new society.

A man has to do many things in his life.
Reed was a westerner words meant what they said.
He threw everything he had and himself into Smolny,
dictatorship of the proletariat;
U.S.S.R.
The first workers republic
was established and stands.
Reed wrote; undertook missions (there were spies everywhere),
worked till he dropped,
   caught typhus and died in Moscow.

Joe Williams

Twentyfive days at sea on the steamer *Argyle*, Glasgow, Captain
Thompson, loaded with hides, chipping rust, daubing red lead on
steel plates that were sizzling hot griddles in the sun, painting the
stack from dawn to dark, pitching and rolling in the heavy dirty swell;
bedbugs in the bunks in the stinking focastle, slumgullion for grub,
with potatoes full of eyes and mouldy beans, cockroaches mashed on
the messtable, but a tot of limejuice every day in accordance with the
regulations; then sickening rainy heat and Trinidad blue in the mist
across the ruddy water.

Going through the Boca it started to rain and the islands heaped
with ferny parisgreen foliage went grey under the downpour. By the
time they got her warped into the wharf at Port of Spain, everybody
was soaked to the skin with rain and sweat. Mr. McGregor, striding
up and down in a souwester purple in the face, lost his voice from the
heat and had to hiss out his orders in a mean whisper. Then the curtain of the rain lifted, the sun came out and everything steamed.
Apart from the heat everybody was sore because there was talk that
they were going up to the Pitch Lake to load asphaltum.

Next day nothing happened. The hides in the forward hold stank when they unbattened the hatches. Clothes and bedding, hung out to dry in the torrid glare of sun between showers, was always getting soaked again before they could get it in. While it was raining there was nowhere you could keep dry; the awning over the deck dripped continually.

In the afternoon, Joe's watch got off, though it wasn't much use going ashore because nobody had gotten any pay. Joe found himself sitting under a palm tree on a bench in a sort of a park near the waterfront staring at his feet. It began to rain and he ducked under an awning in front of a bar. There were electric fans in the bar; a cool whiff of limes and rum and whiskey in iced drinks wafted out through the open door. Joe was thirsty for a beer but he didn't have a red cent. The rain hung like a bead curtain at the edge of the awning.

Standing beside him was a youngish man in a white suit and a panama hat, who looked like an American. He glanced at Joe several times, then he caught his eye and smiled, "Are you an Am-m-merican," he said. He stuttered a little when he talked. "I am that," said Joe.

There was a pause. Then the man held out his hand. "Welcome to our city," he said. Joe noticed that he had a slight edge on. The man's palm was soft when he shook his hand. Joe didn't like the way his handshake felt. "You live here?" he asked. The man laughed. He had blue eyes and a round poutlipped face that looked friendly. "Hell no ... I'm only here for a couple of days on this West India cruise. Much b-b-better have saved my money and stayed home. I wanted to go to Europe but you c-c-can't on account of the war." "Yare, that's all they talk about on the bloody limejuicer I'm on, the war."

"Why they brought us to this hole I can't imagine and now there's something the matter with the boat and we can't leave for two days."

"That must be the *Monterey*."

"Yes. It's a terrible boat, nothing on board but women. I'm glad to run into a fellow I can talk to. Seems to be nothing but niggers down here."

"Looks like they had 'em all colors in Trinidad."

"Say, this rain isn't going to stop for a hell of a time. Come in and have a drink with me."

Joe looked at him suspiciously. "All right," he said finally, "but I might as well tell you right now I can't treat you back ... I'm flat and those goddam Scotchmen won't advance us any pay." "You're a sailor, aren't you?" asked the man when they got to the bar. "I work on a boat, if that's what you mean."

"What'll you have . . . They make a fine Planter's punch here. Ever tried that?" "I'll drink a beer . . . I usually drink beer." The barkeeper was a broadfaced chink with a heartbroken smile like a very old monkey's. He put the drinks down before them very gently as if afraid of breaking the glasses. The beer was cold and good in its dripping glass. Joe drank it off. "Say, you don't know any baseball scores, do you? Last time I saw a paper looked like the Senators had a chance for the pennant."

The man took off his panama hat and mopped his brow with a handkerchief. He had curly black hair. He kept looking at Joe as if he was making up his mind about something. Finally he said, "Say my name's . . . Wa-wa-wa- . . . Warner Jones." "They call me Yank on the *Argyle* . . . In the navy they called me Slim."

"So you were in the navy, were you? I thought you looked more like a jackie than a merchant seaman, Slim."

"That so?"

The man who said his name was Jones ordered two more of the same. Joe was worried. But what the hell, they can't arrest a guy for a deserter on British soil. "Say, did you say you knew anything about the baseball scores? The leagues must be pretty well underway by now."

"I got the papers up at the hotel . . . like to look at them?"

"I sure would."

The rain stopped. The pavement was already dry when they came out of the bar.

"Say, I'm going to take a ride around this island. Tell me you can see wild monkeys and all sorts of things. Why don't you come along? I'm bored to death of sightseeing by myself."

Joe thought a minute. "These clothes ain't fit. . . ."

"What the hell, this isn't Fifth Avenue. Come ahead." The man who said his name was Jones signalled a nicely polished Ford driven by a young chinaman. The chinaman wore glasses and a dark blue suit and looked like a college student; he talked with an English accent. He said he'd drive them round the town and out to the Blue Pool. As they were setting off the man who said his name was Jones said, "Wait a minute," and ran in the bar and got a flask of Planter's punch.

He talked a blue streak all the time they were driving out past the British bungalows and brick institution buildings and after that out along the road through rubbery blue woods so dense and steamy it seemed to Joe there must be a glass roof overhead somewhere. He said how he liked adventure and travel and wished he was free to ship on boats and bum around and see the world and that it must be wonderful to depend only on your own sweat and muscle the way Joe was doing. Joe said, "Yare?" But the man who said his name was Jones paid no attention and went right on and said how he had to take care of his mother and that was a great responsibility and sometimes he thought he'd go mad and he'd been to a doctor about it and the doctor had advised him to take a trip, but that the food wasn't any good on the boat and gave him indigestion and it was all full of old women with daughters they wanted to marry off and it made him nervous having women run after him like that. The worst of it was not having a friend to talk to about whatever he had on his mind when he got lonely. He wished he had a nice good looking fellow who'd been around and wasn't a softy and knew what life was and could appreciate beauty for a friend, a fellow like Joe in fact. His mother was awfully jealous and didn't like the idea of his having any intimate friends and would always get sick or try to hold out on his allowance when she found out about his having any friends, because she wanted him to be always tied to her apron strings but he was sick and tired of that and from now on he was going to do what he damn pleased, and she didn't have to know about everything he did anyway.

He kept giving Joe cigarettes and offering them to the chinaman who said each time, "Thank you very much, sir. I have forgone smoking." Between them they had finished the flask of punch and the man who said his name was Jones was beginning to edge over towards Joe in the seat, when the chinaman stopped the car at the end of a little path and said, "If you wish to view the Blue Pool you must walk up there almost seven minutes, sir. It is the principal attraction of the island of Trinidad."

Joe hopped out of the car and went to make water beside a big tree with shaggy red bark. The man who said his name was Jones came up beside him. "Two minds with but a single thought," he said. Joe said, "Yare," and went and asked the chinaman where they could see some monkeys.

"The Blue Pool," said the chinaman, "is one of their favorite resorts." He got out of the car and walked around it looking intently with his black beads of eyes into the foliage over their heads. Suddenly he pointed. Something black was behind a shaking bunch of foliage. A screechy giggle came from behind it and three monkeys went off flying from branch to branch with long swinging leaps. In a second they were gone and all you could see was the branches stirring at intervals through the woods where they jumped. One of them had a pinkish baby monkey hanging on in front. Joe was tickled. He'd never seen monkeys really wild like that before. He went off up the path, walking fast so that the man who said his name was Jones had trouble keeping up to him. Joe wanted to see some more monkeys.

After a few minutes' walk up hill he began to hear a waterfall. Something made him think of Great Falls and Rock Creek and he went all soft inside. There was a pool under a waterfall hemmed in by giant trees. "Dod gast it, I've a mind to take me a dip," he said. "Wouldn't there be snakes, Slim?" "Snakes won't bother you, 'less you bother 'em first."

But when they got right up to the pool they saw that there were people picnicking there, girls in light pink and blue dresses, two or three men in white ducks, grouped under striped umbrellas. Two Hindoo servants were waiting on them, bringing dishes out of a hamper. Across the pool came the chirp-chirp of cultivated English voices. "Shoot, we can't go swimmin' here and they won't be any monkeys either."

"Suppose we joined them . . . I might introduce myself and you would be my kid brother. I've got a letter to a Colonel Somebody but I felt too blue to present it."

"What the hell do they want to be fartin' around here for?" said Joe and started back down the path again. He didn't see any more monkeys and by the time he'd got back to the car big drops had started to fall.

"That'll spoil their goddam picnic," he said, grinning to the man who said his name was Jones when he came up, the sweat running in streams down his face. "My, you're a fast walker, Slim." He puffed and patted him on the back. Joe got into the car. "I guess we're goin' to get it." "Sirs," said the chinaman, "I will return to the city for I perceive that a downpour is imminent."

By the time they'd gone a half a mile it was raining so hard the chinaman couldn't see to drive. He ran the car into a small shed on the side of the road. The rain pounding on the tin roof overhead sounded loud as a steamboat letting off steam. The man who said his name was Jones started talking; he had to yell to make himself heard above the rain. "I guess you see some funny sights, Slim, leading the life you lead."

Joe got out of the car and stood facing the sudden curtain of rain; the spray in his face felt almost cool. The man who said his name was Jones sidled up to him holding out a cigarette. "How did you like it in the navy?"

Joe took the cigarette, lit it and said, "Not so good."

"I've been friends with lots of navy boys . . . I suppose you liked raising cain on shore leave, didn't you?" Joe said he didn't usually have much pay to raise cain with, used to play ball sometimes, that wasn't so bad. "But, Slim, I thought sailors didn't care what they did when they got in port." "I guess some of the boys try to paint the town red, but they don't usually have enough jack to get very far." "Maybe you and I can paint the town red in Port of Spain, Slim." Joe shook his head. "No, I gotta go back on board ship."

The rain increased till the tin roof roared so Joe couldn't hear what the man who said his name was Jones was trying to say, then slackened and stopped entirely. "Well, at least you come up to my room in the hotel, Slim, and we'll have a couple of drinks. Nobody knows me here. I can do anything I like." "I'd like to see the sports page of that paper from home if you don't mind."

They got into the car and rode back to town along roads brimmed with water like canals. The sun came out hot and everything was in a blue steam. It was late afternoon. The streets of the town were crowded; hindoos with turbans, chinks in natty Hart Schaffner and Marx clothes, redfaced white men dressed in white, raggedy shines of all colors.

Joe felt uncomfortable going through the lobby of the hotel in his dungarees, pretty wet at that, and he needed a shave. The man who said his name was Jones put his arm over his shoulders going up the stairs. His room was big with tall narrow shuttered windows and smelt of bay rum. "My, but I'm hot and wet," he said. "I'm going to take a shower . . . but first we'd better ring for a couple of gin fizzes. . . . Don't you want to take your clothes off and take it easy? His skin's about as much clothes as a fellow can stand in this weather." Joe shook his head, "They stink too much," he said. "Say, have you got them papers?"

The hindoo servant came with the drinks while the man who said his name was Jones was in the bathroom. Joe took the tray. There was something about the expression of the hindoo's thin mouth and black eyes looking at something behind you in the room that made Joe sore. He wanted to hit the tobaccocolored bastard. The man who said his name was Jones came back looking cool in a silk bathrobe.

"Sit down, Slim, and we'll have a drink and a chat." The man ran his fingers gently over his forehead as if it ached and through his curly black hair and settled in an armchair. Joe sat down in a straight chair across the room. "My, I think this heat would be the end of me if I stayed a week in this place. I don't see how you stand it, doing manual work and everything. You must be pretty tough!"

Joe wanted to ask about the newspapers but the man who said his name was Jones was talking again, saying how he wished he was tough, seeing the world like that, meeting all kinds of fellows, going to all kinds of joints, must see some funny sights, must be funny all these fellows bunking together all these days at sea, rough and tumble, hey? and then nights ashore, raising cain, painting the town red, several fellows with one girl. "If I was living like that, I wouldn't care what I did, no reputation to lose, no danger of somebody trying to blackmail you, only have to be careful to keep out of jail, hay? Why, Slim, I'd like to go along with you and lead a life like that." "Yare?" said Joe.

The man who said his name was Jones rang for another drink. When the hindoo servant had gone Joe asked again about the papers. "Honestly, Slim, I looked everywhere for them. They must have been thrown out." "Well, I guess I'll be gettin' aboard my bloody limejuicer." Joe had his hand on the door. The man who said his name was Jones came running over and took his hand and said, "No, you're not going. You said you'd go on a party with me. You're an awful nice boy. You won't be sorry. You can't go away like this, now that you've got me feeling all sort of chummy and you know amorous. Don't you ever feel that way, Slim? I'll do the handsome thing. I'll give you fifty dollars." Joe shook his head and pulled his hand away.

He had to give him a shove to get the door open; he ran down the white marble steps and out into the street.

It was about dark; Joe walked along fast. The sweat was pouring off him. He was cussing under his breath as he walked along. He felt rotten and sore and he'd wanted real bad to see some papers from home.

He loafed up and down in a little in the sort of park place where he'd sat that afternoon, then he started down towards the wharves. Might as well turn in. The smell of frying from eating joints reminded him he was hungry. He turned into one before he remembered he didn't have a cent in his pocket. He followed the sound of a mechanical piano and found himself in the red light district. Standing in the doorways of the little shacks there were nigger wenches of all colors and shapes, halfbreed Chinese and Indian women, a few faded fat German or French women; one little mulatto girl who reached her hand out and touched his shoulder as he passed was damn pretty. He stopped to talk to her, but when he said he was broke, she laughed and said, "Go long from here, Mister No-Money Man . . . no room here for a No-Money Man."

When he got back on board he couldn't find the cook to try and beg a little grub off him so he took a chaw and let it go at that. The focastle was like an oven. He went up on deck with only a pair of overalls on and walked up and down with the watchman who was a pinkfaced youngster from Dover everybody called Tiny. Tiny said he'd heard the old man and Mr. McGregor talking in the cabin about how they'd be off tomorrow to St. Luce to load limes and then 'ome to blighty and would 'e be glad to see the tight little hile an' get off this bleedin' crahft, not 'arf. Joe said a hell of a lot of good it'd do him, his home was in Washington, D.C. "I want to get out of the c——g life and get a job that pays something. This way every bastardly tourist with a little jack thinks he can hire you for his punk." Joe told Tiny about the man who said his name was Jones and he laughed like he'd split. "Fifty dollars, that's ten quid. I'd a 'ad 'arf a mind to let the toff 'ave a go at me for ten quid."

The night was absolutely airless. The mosquitoes were beginning to get at Joe's bare neck and arms. A sweet hot haze came up from the slack water round the wharves blurring the lights down the waterfront. They took a couple of turns without saying anything.

"My eye what did 'e want ye to do, Yank?" said Tiny giggling. "Aw to hell with him," said Joe. "I'm goin' to get out of this life. Whatever happens, wherever you are, the seaman gets the s——y end of the stick. Ain't that true, Tiny?"

"Not 'arf . . . ten quid! Why, the bleedin' toff ought to be ashaymed of hisself. Corruptin' morals, that's what 'e's after. Ought to go to 'is 'otel with a couple of shipmytes and myke him pay blackmyl. There's many an old toff in Dover payin' blackmyl for doin' less 'n 'e did. They comes down on a vacaytion and goes after the bath'ouse boys. . . . Blackmyl 'im, that's what I'd do, Yank."

Joe didn't say anything. After a while he said, "Jeez, an' when I was a kid I thought I wanted to go to the tropics."

"This ain't tropics, it's a bleedin' 'ell 'ole, that's what it is."

They took another couple of turns. Joe went and leaned over the side looking down into the greasy blackness. God damn these mosquitoes. When he spat out his plug of tobacco it made a light plunk in the water. He went down into the focastle again, crawled into his bunk and pulled the blanket over his head and lay there sweating. "Darn it, I wanted to see the baseball scores."

Next day they coaled ship and the day after they had Joe painting the officers' cabins while the *Argyle* nosed out through the Boca again between the slimegreen ferny islands, and he was sore because he had A.B. papers and here they were still treating him like an ordinary seaman and he was going to England and didn't know what he'd do when he'd get there, and his shipmates said they'd likely as not run him into a concentraytion camp; bein' an alien and landin' in England without a passport, wat wit' war on and 'un spies everywhere, an' all; but the breeze had salt in it now and when he peeked out of the porthole he could see blue ocean instead of the puddlewater off Trinidad and flying fish in hundreds skimming away from the ship's side.

The harbor at St. Luce's was clean and landlocked, white houses with red roofs under the coconutpalms. It turned out that it was bananas they were going to load; it took them a day and a half knocking up partitions in the afterhold and scantlings for the bananas to hang from. It was dark by the time they'd come alongside the bananawharf and had rigged the two gangplanks and the little derrick for lowering the bunches into the hold. The wharf was crowded with colored women laughing and shrieking and yelling things at the crew, and big buck niggers standing round doing nothing. The women did the loading. After a while they started coming up one gangplank, each one with a huge green bunch of bananas slung on her head and shoulders; there were old black mammies and pretty young mulatto girls; their faces shone with sweat under the big bunchlights, you could see their swinging breasts hanging down through their ragged clothes, brown flesh through a rip in a sleeve. When each woman got to the top of the gangplank two big buck niggers lifted the bunch tenderly off her shoulders, the foreman gave her a slip of paper and she ran down the other gangplank to the wharf again. Except for the donkeyengine men the deck crew had nothing to do. They stood around uneasy, watching the women, the glitter of white teeth and eyeballs, the heavy breasts, the pumping motion of their thighs. They stood around, looking at the women, scratching themselves, shifting their weight from one foot to the other; not even much smut was passed. It was a black still night, the smell of the bananas and the stench of niggerwoman sweat was hot around them; now and then a little freshness came in a whiff off some cases of limes piled on the wharf.

Joe caught on that Tiny was waving to him to come somewhere. He followed him into the shadow. Tiny put his mouth against his ear, "There's bleedin' tarts 'ere, Yank, come along." They went up the bow and slid down a rope to the wharf. The rope scorched their hands. Tiny spat into his hands and rubbed them together. Joe did the same. Then they ducked into the warehouse. A rat scuttled past their feet. It was a guano warehouse and stank of fertilizer. Outside a little door in the back it was pitch black, sandy underfoot. A little glow from streetlights hit the upper part of the warehouse. There were women's voices, a little laugh. Tiny had disappeared. Joe had his hand on a woman's bare shoulder. "But first you must give me a shilling," said a sweet cockney West India woman's voice. His voice had gone hoarse. "Sure, cutie, sure I will."

When his eyes got used to the dark he could see that they weren't the only ones. There were giggles, hoarse breathing all round them. From the ship came the intermittent whir of the winches, and a mixedup noise of voices from the women loading bananas.

The woman was asking for money. "Come on now, white boy, do like you say." Tiny was standing beside him buttoning up his pants. "Be back in a jiff, girls."

"Sure, we left our jack on board the boat."

They ran back through the warehouse with the girls after them, up the jacobsladder somebody had let down over the side of the ship and landed on deck out of breath and doubled up with laughing. When they looked over the side the women were running up and down the wharf spitting and cursing at them like wildcats. "Cheeryoh, laydies," Tiny called down to them, taking off his cap. He grabbed Joe's arm and pulled him along the deck; they stood round a while near the end of the gangplank. "Say, Tiny, yours was old enough to be your grandmother, damned if she wasn't," whispered Joe. "Granny me eye, it was the pretty un I 'ad." "The hell you say . . . She musta been sixty." "Wot a bleedin' wopper . . . it was the pretty un I 'ad," said Tiny, walking off sore.

A moon had come up red from behind the fringed hills. The bananabunches the women were carrying up the gangplank made a twisting green snake under the glare of the working lights. Joe suddenly got to feeling disgusted and sleepy. He went down and washed himself carefully with soap and water before crawling into his bunk. He went to sleep listening to the Scotch and British voices of his shipmates, talking about the tarts out back of the wharfhouse, 'ow many they'd 'ad, 'ow many times, 'ow it stacked up with the Argentyne or Durban or Singapore. The loading kept up all night.

By noon they'd cleared for Liverpool with the Chief stoking her up to make a fast passage and all hands talking about the blighty. They had bananas as much as they could eat that trip; every day the supercargo was bringing up overripe bunches and hanging them in the galley. Everybody was grousing about the ship not being armed, but the Old Man and Mr. McGregor seemed to take on more about the bananas than about the raiders. They were always peeping down under the canvas cover over the hatch that had been rigged with a ventilator on the peak of it, to see if they were ripening too soon. There was a lot of guying about the blahsted banahnas down in the focastle.

After crossing the tropic they ran into a nasty norther that blew four days, after that the weather was dirty right along. Joe didn't have much to do after his four hours at the wheel; in the focastle they were all grousing about the ship not being fumigated to kill the bugs and the cockroaches and not being armed and not picking up a convoy. Then word got around that there were German submarines cruising off the Lizard and everybody from the Old Man down got short tempered as hell. They all began picking on Joe on account of America's not being in the war and he used to have long arguments with Tiny and an old fellow from Glasgow they called Haig. Joe said he didn't see what the hell business the States had in the war and that almost started a fight.

After they picked up the Scilly Island lights, Sparks said they were in touch with a convoy and would have a destroyer all to themselves up through the Irish Sea that wouldn't leave them until they were safe in the Mersey. The British had won a big battle at Mons. The Old Man served out a tot of rum all round and everybody was in fine shape except Joe who was worried about what'd happen to him getting into England without a passport. He was chilly all the time on account of not having any warm clothes.

That evening a destroyer loomed suddenly out of the foggy twilight, looking tall as a church above the great wave of white water curling from her bows. It gave them a great scare on the bridge because they thought at first it was a Hun. The destroyer broke out the Union Jack and slowed down to the *Argyle's* speed, keeping close and abreast of her. The crew piled out on deck and gave the destroyer three cheers. Some of them wanted to sing *God Save the King* but the officer on the bridge of the destroyer began bawling out the Old Man through a megaphone asking him why in bloody f—g hell he wasn't steering a zigzag course and if he didn't jolly well know that it was prohibited making any kind of bloody f—g noise on a merchantship in wartime.

It was eight bells and the watches were changing and Joe and Tiny began to laugh coming along the deck just at the moment when they met Mr. McGregor stalking by purple in the face. He stopped square in front of Joe and asked him what he found so funny? Joe didn't answer. Mr. McGregor stared at him hard and began saying in his slow mean voice that he was probably not an American at all but a dirty 'un spy, and told him to report on the next shift in the stokehole. Joe said he'd signed on as an A.B. and they didn't have any right to work him as a stoker. Mr. McGregor said he'd never struck a man yet in thirty years at sea but if he let another word out he'd damn well knock him down. Joe felt burning hot but he stood still with his fists clenched without saying anything. For several seconds Mr. McGregor just stared at him, red as a turkey gobbler. Two of the watch passed along the deck. "Turn this fellow over to the bosun and put him in irons. He may be a spy. . . . You go along quiet now or it'll be worse for you."

Joe spent that night hunched up in a little cubbyhole that smelt of bilge with his feet in irons. The next morning the bosun let him out and told him fairly kindly to go get cookee to give him some porridge but to keep off the deck. He said they were going to turn him over to the aliens control as soon as they docked in Liverpool.

When he crossed the deck to go to the galley, his ankles still stiff from the irons, he noticed that they were already in the Mersey. It was a ruddy sunlit morning. In every direction there were ships at anchor, stumpylooking black sailboats and patrolboats cutting through the palegreen ruffled water. Overhead the great pall of brown smoke was shot here and there with crisp white steam that caught the sun.

The cook gave him some porridge and a mug of bitter barely warm tea. When he came out of the galley they were further up the river, you could see towns on both sides, the sky was entirely overcast with brown smoke and fog. The *Argyle* was steaming under one bell.

Joe went below to the focastle and rolled into his bunk. His shipmates all stared at him without speaking and when he spoke to Tiny who was in the bunk below him, he didn't answer. That made Joe feel worse than anything. He turned his face to the wall, pulled the blanket over his head and went to sleep.

Somebody shaking him woke him up. "Come on, my man," said a tall English bobby with a blue helmet and varnished chinstrap who had hold of his shoulder. "All right, just a sec," Joe said. "I'd like to get washed up." The bobby shook his head. "The quieter and quicker you come the better it'll be for you."

Joe pulled his cap over his eyes, took his cigarbox out from under his mattress, and followed the bobby out on deck. The *Argyle* was already tied up to the wharf. So without saying goodby to anybody or getting paid off, he went down the gangplank with the bobby half a step behind. The bobby had a tight grip on the muscle of his arm. They walked across a flagstoned wharf and out through some big iron gates to where the Black Maria was waiting. A small crowd of loafers, red faces in the fog, black grimy clothes. "Look at the filthy 'un," one man said. A woman hissed, there were a couple of boos and a catcall and the shiny black doors closed behind him; the car started smoothly and he could feel it speeding through the cobbled streets.

Joe sat hunched up in the dark. He was glad he was alone in there. It gave him a chance to get hold of himself. His hands and feet were cold. He had hard work to keep from shivering. He wished he was dressed decently. All he had on was a shirt and pants spotted with paint and a pair of dirty felt slippers. Suddenly the car stopped, two bobbies told him to get out and he was hustled down a whitewashed corridor into a little room where a police inspector, a tall longfaced Englishman, sat at a yellow varnished table. The inspector jumped to his feet, walked towards Joe with his fists clenched as if he was going to hit him and suddenly said something in what Joe thought must be German. Joe shook his head, it struck him funny somehow and he grinned. "No savvy," he said.

"What's in that box?" the inspector, who had sat down at the desk again, suddenly bawled out at the bobbies. "You'd oughter search these buggers before you bring 'em in here."

One of the bobbies snatched the cigarbox out from under Joe's arm and opened it, looked relieved when he saw it didn't have a bomb in it and dumped everything out on the desk. "So you pretend to be an American?" the man yelled at Joe. "Sure I'm an American," said Joe. "What the hell do you want to come to England in wartime for?" "I didn't want to come to . . ." "Shut up," the man yelled.

Then he motioned to the bobbies to go, and said, "Send in Corporal Eakins." "Very good, sir," said the two bobbies respectfully in unison. When they'd gone, he came towards Joe with his fists clenched again. "You might as well make a clean breast of it, my lad. . . . We have all the necessary information."

Joe had to keep his teeth clenched to keep them from chattering. He was scared.

"I was on the beach in B.A. you see . . . had to take the first berth I could get. You don't think anybody'd ship on a limejuicer if they could help it, do you?" Joe was getting sore; he felt warm again.

The plainclothes man took up a pencil and tapped with it threateningly on the desk. "Impudence won't help you, my lad . . . you'd better keep a civil tongue in your head." Then he began looking over the photographs and stamps and newspaper clippings that had come out of Joe's cigarbox. Two men in khaki came in. "Strip him and search him," the man at the desk said without looking up.

Joe looked at the two men without understanding; they had a little the look of hospital orderlies. "Sharp now," one of them said. "We don't want to 'ave to use force." Joe took off his shirt. It made him sore that he was blushing; he was ashamed because he didn't have any underwear. "All right, breeches next." Joe stood naked in his slippers while the men in khaki went through his shirt and pants. They found a bunch of clean waste in one pocket, a battered Prince Albert can with a piece of chewing tobacco in it and a small jackknife with a broken blade. One of them was examining the belt and pointed out to the other the place where it had been resewed. He slit it up with a knife and they both looked eagerly inside. Joe grinned, "I used to keep my bills in there," he said. They kept their faces stiff.

"Open your mouth." One of them put a heavy hand on Joe's jaw. "Sergeant, shall we take out the fillin's? 'E's got two or three fillin's in the back of 'is mouth." The man behind the desk shook his head. One of the men stepped out of the door and came back with an oiled rubber glove on his hand. "Lean hover," said the other man, putting his hand on Joe's neck and shoving his head down while the man with the rubber glove felt in his rectum. "Hay, for Chris' sake," hissed Joe through his teeth.

"All right, me lad, that's all for the present," said the man who held his head, letting go. "Sorry, but we 'ave to do it . . . part of the regulations."

The corporal walked up to the desk and stood at attention. "All right, sir . . . Nothin' of interest on the prisoner's person."

Joe was terribly cold. He couldn't keep his teeth from chattering.

"Look in his slippers, can't you?" growled the inspector. Joe didn't like handing over his slippers because his feet were dirty, but there was nothing he could do. The corporal slashed them to pieces with his penknife. Then both men stood at attention and waited for the inspector to lift his eye. "All right, sir . . . nothin' to report. Shall I get the prisoner a blanket, sir? 'E looks chilly."

The man behind the desk shook his head and beckoned to Joe, "Come over here. Now are you ready to answer truthfully and give us no trouble it won't be worse than a concentraytion camp for duraytion. . . . But if you give us trouble I can't say how serious it mightn't be. We're under the Defence of the Realm Act, Don't forget that. . . . What's your name?"

After Joe had told his name, birthplace, father's and mother's names, names of ships he's sailed on, the inspector suddenly shot a question in German at him. Joe shook his head, "Hay, what do you think I know German for?"

"Shut the bugger up. . . . We know all about him anyway."

"Shall we give him 'is kit, sir?" asked one of the men timidly.

"He won't need a kit if he isn't jolly careful."

The corporal got a bunch of keys and opened a heavy wooden door on the side of the room. They pushed Joe into a little cell with a bench and no window. The door slammed behind him and Joe was there shivering in the dark. Well, you're in the pig's a.h. for fair, Joe Williams, he said aloud. He found he could warm himself by doing exercises and rubbing his arms and legs, but his feet stayed numb.

After a while he heard the key in the lock; the man in khaki threw a blanket into the cell and slammed the door to, without giving him a chance to say anything.

Joe curled up in the blanket on the bench and tried to go to sleep.

He woke in a sudden nightmare fright. It was cold. The watch had been called. He jumped off the bench. It was blind dark. For a second he thought he'd gone blind in the night. Where he was, and everything since they sighted the Scilly Island lights came back. He had a lump of ice in his stomach. He walked up and down from wall to wall of the cell for a while and then rolled up in the blanket again. It was a good clean blanket and smelt of lysol or something like that. He went to sleep.

He woke up again hungry as hell, wanting to make water. He shuffled around the square cell for a long time until he found an enamelled pail under the bench. He used it and felt better. He was glad it had a cover on it. He began wondering how he'd pass the time. . He began thinking about Georgetown and good times he'd had with Alec and Janey and the gang that hung around Mulvaney's pool parlor and making pickups on moonlight trips on the *Charles Macalister* and went over all the good pitchers he'd ever seen or read about and tried to remember the batting averages of every man on the Washington ballteams.

He'd gotten back to trying to remember his highschool games, inning by inning, when the key was put into the lock. The corporal who'd searched him opened the door and handed him his shirt and pants. "You can wash up if you want to," he said. "Better clean up smart. Orders is to take you to Captain Cooper-Trahsk." "Gosh, can't you get me somethin' to eat or some water. I'm about starved. . . . Say, how long have I been in here, anyway?" Joe was blinking in the bright white light that came in from the other room. He pulled on his shirt and pants.

"Come along," said the corporal. "Can't ahnswer no question till

you've seen Captain Cooper-Trahsk." "But what about my slippers?"
"You keep a civil tongue in your mouth and ahnswer all questions
you're harsked and it'll be all the better for you. . . . Come along."

When he followed the corporal down the same corridor he'd come
in by all the English tommies stared at his bare feet. In the lavatory
there was a shiny brass tap of cold water and a hunk of soap. First Joe
took a long drink. He felt giddy and his knees were shaking. The cold
water and washing his hands and face and feet made him feel better.
The only thing he had to dry himself on was a roller towel already
grimy. "Say, I need a shave," he said. "You'll 'ave to come along now,"
said the corporal sternly. "But I got a Gillette somewheres. . . ."

The corporal gave him an angry stare. They were going in the door
of a nicely furnished office with a thick red and brown carpet on the
floor. At a mahogany desk sat an elderly man with white hair and a
round roastbeef face and lots of insignia on his uniform. "Is that . . .?"
Joe began, but he saw that the corporal after clicking his heels and saluting had frozen into attention.

The elderly man raised his head and looked at them with a fatherly
blue eye, "Ah . . . quite so . . ." he said. "Bring him up closer, corporal,
and let's have a look at him. . . . Isn't he in rather a mess, corporal?
You'd better give the poor beggar some shoes and stockings. . . ."
"Very good, sir," said the corporal in a spiteful tone, stiffening to attention again. "At ease, corporal, at ease," said the elderly man, putting on a pair of eyeglasses and looking at some papers on his desk.
"This is . . . er . . . Zentner . . . claim American citizenship, eh?" "The
name is Williams, sir." "Ah, quite so . . . Joe Williams, seaman. . . ." He
fixed his blue eyes confidentially on Joe. "Is that your name, me boy?"
"Yessir."

"Well, how do you come to be trying to get into England in wartime without passport or other identifying document?"

Joe told about how he had an American A.B. certificate and had
been on the beach at B.A. . . . Buenos Aires. "And why were you . . . er
. . . in this condition in the Argentine?" "Well, sir, I'd been on the
Mallory Line and my ship sailed without me and I'd been painting
the town red a little, sir, and the skipper pulled out ahead of schedule
so that left me on the beach."

"Ah . . . a hot time in the old town tonight . . . that sort of thing,
eh?" The elderly man laughed; then suddenly he puckered up his
brows. "Let me see . . . er . . . what steamer of the Mallory Line were

you travelling on?" "The *Patagonia*, sir, and I wasn't travellin' on her, I was a seaman on board of her."

The elderly man wrote a long while on a sheet of paper, then he lifted Joe's cigarbox out of the desk drawer and began looking through the clippings and photographs. He brought out a photograph and turned it out so that Joe could see it. "Quite a pretty girl . . . is that your best beloved, Williams?" Joe blushed scarlet. "That's my sister." "I say she looks like a ripping girl . . . don't you think so, corporal?" "Quite so, sir," said the corporal distantly. "Now, me boy, if you know anything about the activities of German agents in South America . . . many of them are Americans or impostors masquerading as Americans . . . it'll be much better for you to make a clean breast of it."

"Honestly, sir," said Joe, "I don't know a thing about it. I was only in B.A. for a few days." "Have you any parents living?" "My father's a pretty sick man. . . . But I have my mother and sisters in Georgetown." "Georgetown . . . Georgetown . . . let me see . . . isn't that in British Guiana?" "It's part of Washington, D.C." "Of course . . . ah, I see you were in the navy. . . ." The elderly man held off the picture of Joe and the two other gobs. Joe's knees felt so weak he thought he was going to fall down. "No, sir, that was in the naval reserve."

The elderly man put everything back in the cigarbox. "You can have these now, my boy. . . . You'd better give him a bit of breakfast and let him have an airing in the yard. He looks a bit weak on his pins, corporal."

"Very good, sir." The corporal saluted, and they marched out.

The breakfast was watery oatmeal, stale tea and two slices of bread with margarine on it. After it Joe felt hungrier than before. Still it was good to get out in the air, even if it was drizzling and the flagstones of the small courtyard where they put him were like ice to his bare feet under the thin slime of black mud that was over them.

There was another prisoner in the courtyard, a little fatfaced man in a derby hat and a brown overcoat, who came up to Joe immediately. "Say, are you an American?"

"Sure," said Joe.

"My name's Zentner . . . buyer in restaurant furnishings . . . from Chicago. . . . This is the tamnest outrage. Here I come to this tamned country to buy their tamned goods, to spend good American dollars. . . . Three days ago yet I placed a ten tousand dollar order in

Sheffield. And they arrest me for a spy and I been here all night yet and only this morning vill they let me telephone the consulate. It is outrageous and I hafe a passport and visa all they vant. I can sue for this outrage. I shall take it to Vashington. I shall sue the British government for a hundred tousand dollars for defamation of character. Forty years an American citizen and my fader he came not from Chermany but from Poland. . . . And you, poor boy, I see that you haf no shoes. And they talk about the atrocious Chermans and if this ain't an atrocity, vat is it?"

Joe was shivering and running round the court at a jogtrot to try to keep warm. Mr. Zentner took off his brown coat and handed it to him.

"Here, kid, you put that coat on." "But, jeez, it's too good; that's damn nice of you." "In adversity ve must help von anoder."

"Dod gast it, if this is their spring, I hate to think what their winter's like. . . . I'll give the coat back to you when I go in. Jeez, my feet are cold. . . . Say, did they search you?" Mr. Zentner rolled up his eyes. "Outrageous," he spluttered . . . "Vat indignities to a buyer from a neutral and friendly country. Vait till I tell the ambassador. I shall sue. I shall demand damages." "Same here," said Joe, laughing.

The corporal appeared in the door and shouted, "Williams." Joe gave back the coat and shook Mr. Zentner's fat hand. "Say, for Gawd's sake, don't forget to tell the consul there's another American here. They're talkin' about sendin' me to a concentration camp for duration." "Sure, don't vorry, boy. I'll get you out," said Mr. Zentner, puffing out his chest.

This time Joe was taken to a regular cell that had a little light and room to walk around. The corporal gave him a pair of shoes and some wool socks full of holes. He couldn't get the shoes on but the socks warmed his feet up a little. At noon they handed him a kind of stew that was mostly potatoes with eyes in them and some more bread and margarine.

The third day when the turnkey brought the noonday slum, he brought a brownpaper package that had been opened. In it was a suit of clothes, shirt, flannel underwear, socks and even a necktie.

"There was a chit with it, but it's against the regulaytions," said the turnkey. "That outfit'll make a bloomin' toff out of you."

Late that afternoon the turnkey told Joe to come along and he put on the clean collar that was too tight for his neck and the necktie and hitched up the pants that were much too big for him around the waist and followed along corridors and across a court full of tommies into a little office with a sentry at the door and a sergeant at a desk. Sitting on a chair was a busylooking young man with a straw hat on his knees. "'Ere's your man, sir," said the sergeant without looking at Joe. "I'll let you question him."

The busylooking young man got to his feet and went up to Joe. "Well, you've certainly been making me a lot of trouble, but I've been over the records in your case and it looks to me as if you were what you represented yourself to be. . . . What's your father's name?"

"Same as mine, Joseph P. Williams. . . . Say, are you the American consul?"

"I'm from the consulate. . . . Say, what the hell do you want to come ashore without a passport for? Don't you think we have anything better to do than to take care of a lot of damn fools that don't know enough to come in when it rains? Damn it, I was goin' to play golf this afternoon and here I've been here two hours waiting to get you out of the cooler."

"Jeez, I didn't come ashore. They come on and got me."

"That'll teach you a lesson, I hope. . . . Next time you have your pa pers in order."

"Yessirree . . . I shu will."

A half an hour later Joe was out on the street, the cigarbox and his old clothes rolled up in a ball under his arm. It was a sunny after-noon; the redfaced people in dark clothes, longfaced women in crummy hats, the streets full of big buses and the tall trolleycars; ev-erything looked awful funny, until he suddenly remembered it was England and he'd never been there before.

He had to wait a long time in an empty office at the consulate while the busylooking young man made up a lot of papers. He was hungry and kept thinking of beefsteak and frenchfried. At last he was called to the desk and given a paper and told that there was a berth all ready for him on the American steamer *Tampa*, out of Pensacola, and he'd better go right down to the agents and make sure about it and go on board and if they caught him around Liverpool again it would be the worse for him.

"Say, is there any way I can get anything to eat around here, Mr. Consul?" "What do you think this is, a restaurant? . . . No, we have no appropriations for any handouts. You ought to be grateful for what we've done already." "They never paid me off on the *Argyle* and I'm about starved in that jail, that's all." "Well, here's a shilling but that's absolutely all I can do." Joe looked at the coin, "Who's 'at — King George? Well, thank you, Mr. Consul."

He was walking along the street with the agent's address in one hand and the shilling in the other. He felt sore and faint and sick in his stomach. He saw Mr. Zentner the other side of the street. He ran across through the jammed up traffic and went up to him with his hand held out.

"I got the clothes, Mr. Zentner, it was damn nice of you to send them." Mr. Zentner was walking along with a small man in an officer's uniform. He waved a pudgy hand and said, "Glad to be of service to a fellow citizen," and walked on.

Joe went into a fried fish shop and spent sixpence on fried fish and spent the other sixpence on a big mug of beer in a saloon where he'd hoped to find free lunch to fill up on but there wasn't any free lunch. By the time he'd found his way to the agent's office it was closed and there he was roaming round the streets in the white misty evening without any place to go. He asked several guys around the wharves if they knew where the *Tampa* was docked, but nobody did and they talked so funny he could hardly understand what they said anyway.

Then just when the streetlights were going on, and Joe was feeling pretty discouraged, he found himself walking down a side street behind three Americans. He caught up to them and asked them if they knew where the *Tampa* was. Why the hell shouldn't they know, weren't they off'n her and out to see the goddam town and he'd better come along. And if he wasn't tickled to meet some guys from home after those two months on the limejuicer and being in jail and everything. They went into a bar and drank some whiskey and he told all about the jail and how the damn bobbies had taken him off the *Argyle* and he'd never gotten his pay nor nutten and they set him up to drinks and one of the guys who was from Norfolk, Virginia, named Will Stirp pulled out a five dollar bill and said to take that and pay him back when he could.

It was like coming home to God's country running into guys like that and they all had a drink all around; they were four of 'em Americans in this lousy limejuicer town and they each set up a round because they were four of 'em Americans ready to fight the world. Olaf was a Swede but he had his first papers so he counted too and the

other feller's name was Maloney. The hatchetfaced barmaid held back
on the change but they got it out of her; she'd only given 'em fifteen
shillings instead of twenty for a pound, but they made her give the
five shillings back. They went to another fried fish shop; couldn't
seem to get a damn thing to eat in this country except fried fish and
then they all had some more drinks and were the four of them Americans feeling pretty good in this lousy limejuicer town. A runner got
hold of them because it was closing time on account of the war and
there wasn't a damn thing open and very few streetlights and funny
little hats on the streetlights on account of the zeppelins. The runner
was a pale ratfaced punk and said he knowed a house where they
could 'ave a bit of beer and nice girls and a quiet social time. There
was a big lamp with red roses painted on it in the parlor of the house
and the girls were skinny and had horseteeth and there were some
bloody limejuicers there who were pretty well under way and they
were the four of them Americans. The limeys began to pick on Olaf
for bein' a bloody 'un. Olaf said he was a Swede but that he'd sooner
be a bloody 'un than a limejuicer at that. Somebody poked somebody
else and the first thing Joe knew he was fighting a guy bigger 'n he was
and police whistles blew and there was a whole crowd of them piled
up in the Black Maria.

Will Stirp kept saying they was the four of them Americans just
havin' a pleasant social time and there was no call for the bobbies to
interfere. But they were all dragged up to a desk and committed and
all four of 'em Americans locked up in the same cell and the limeys in
another cell. The police station was full of drunks yelling and singing.
Maloney had a bloody nose. Olaf went to sleep. Joe couldn't sleep; he
kept saying to Will Stirp he was scared they sure would send him to a
concentration camp for the duration of the war this time and each
time Will Stirp said they were the four of them Americans and wasn't
he a Freeborn American Citizen and there wasn't a damn thing they
could do to 'em. Freedom of the seas, God damn it.

Next morning they were in court and it was funny as hell except
that Joe was scared; it was solemn as Quakermeetin' and the magistrate wore a little wig and they were everyone of 'em fined three and
six and costs. It came to about a dollar a head. Darned lucky they still
had some jack on them.

And the magistrate in the little wig gave 'em a hell of a talking to
about how this was wartime and they had no right being drunk and

disorderly on British soil but had ought to be fighting shoulder to shoulder with their brothers, Englishmen of their own blood and to whom the Americans owed everything, even their existence as a great nation, to defend civilization and free institutions and plucky little Belgium against the invading huns who were raping women and sinking peaceful merchantmen.

When the magistrate had finished, the court attendants said, "Hear, hear," under their breath and they all looked very savage and solemn and turned the American boys loose after they'd paid their fines and the police sergeant had looked at their papers. They held Joe after the others on account of his paper being from the consulate and not having the stamp of the proper police station on it but after a while they let him go with a warning not to come ashore again and that if he did it would be worse for him.

Joe felt relieved when he'd seen the skipper and had been taken on and had rigged up his bunk and gone ashore and gotten his bundle that he'd left with the nice flaxenhaired barmaid at the first pub he'd gone to the night before. At last he was on an American ship. She had an American flag painted on either side of the hull and her name *Tampa*, Pensacola, Florida, in white letters. There was a colored boy cooking and first thing they had cornmeal mush and karo syrup, and coffee instead of that lousy tea and the food tasted awful good. Joe felt better than any time since he'd left home. The bunks were clean and a fine feeling it was when the *Tampa* left the dock with her whistle blowing and started easing down the slatecolored stream of the Mersey towards the sea.

Fifteen days to Hampton Roads, with sunny weather and a sea like glass every day up to the last two days and then a stiff northwesterly wind that kicked up considerable chop off the Capes. They landed the few bundles of cotton print goods that made up the cargo at the Union Terminal in Norfolk. It was a big day for Joe when he went ashore with his pay in his pocket to take a look around the town with Will Stirp, who belonged there.

They went to see Will Stirp's folks and took in a ball game and after that hopped the trolley down to Virginia Beach with some girls Will Stirp knew. One of the girls' names was Della; and she was very dark and Joe fell for her, kind of. When they were putting on their bathing suits in the bathhouse he asked Will would she . . .? And Will got sore and said, "Ain't you got the sense to tell a good girl from a hooker?" And Joe said well, you never could tell nowadays.

They went in swimming and fooled around the beach in their bathing suits and built a fire and toasted marshmallows and then they took the girls home. Della let Joe kiss her when they said good night and he began kinder planning that she'd be his steady girl.

Back in town they didn't know just what to do. They wanted some drinks and a couple of frails but they were afraid of getting tanked up and spending all their money. They went to a poolroom Will knew and shot some pool and Joe was pretty good and cleaned up the local boys. After that they went and Joe set up a drink but it was closing time and right away they were out on the street again. They couldn't find any hookers; Will said he knew a house but they soaked you too damn much, and they were just about going home to turn in when they ran into two high yellers who gave 'em the eye. They followed 'em down the street a long way and into a cross street where there weren't many lights. The girls were hot stuff but they were scared and nervous for fear somebody might see 'em. They found an empty house with a back porch where it was black as pitch and took 'em up there and afterwards they went back and slept at Will Stirp's folks' house.

The *Tampa* had gone into drydock at Newport News for repairs on a started plate. Joe and Will Stirp were paid off and hung round Norfolk all day without knowing what to do with themselves. Saturday afternoons and Sundays, Joe played a little baseball with a scratch team of boys who worked in the Navy Yard, evenings he went out with Della Matthews. She was a stenographer in the First National Bank and used to say she'd never marry a boy who went to sea, you couldn't trust 'em and that it was a rough kind of a life and didn't have any advancement in it. Joe said she was right but you were only young once and what the hell things didn't matter so much anyway. She used to ask him about his folks and why he didn't go up to Washington to see them especially as his dad was ill. He said the old man could choke for all he cared, he hated him, that was about the size of it. She said she thought he was terrible. That time he was setting her up to a soda after the movies. She looked cute and plump in a fluffy pink dress and her little black eyes all excited and flashing. Joe said not to talk about that stuff, it didn't matter, but she looked at him awful mean and mad and said she'd like to shake him and that everything mattered terribly and it was wicked to talk like that and that he was a nice boy and came from nice people and had been nicely raised and ought to be thinking of getting ahead in the world instead of being a bum and a loafer. Joe got sore and said was that so? and left her at her folks' house without saying another word. He didn't see her for four or five days after that.

Then he went by where Della worked, and waited for her to come out one evening. He'd been thinking about her more than he wanted to and what she'd said. First, she tried to walk past him but he grinned at her and she couldn't help smiling back. He was pretty broke by that tome but he took her and bought her a box of candy. They talked about how hot it was and he said they'd go to the ball game next week. He told her how the *Tampa* was pulling out for Pensacola to load lumber and then across to the other side.

They were waiting for the trolley to go to Virginia Beach, walking up and down fighting the mosquitoes. She looked all upset when he said he was going to the other side. Before Joe knew what he was doing he was saying that he wouldn't ship on the *Tampa* again, but that he'd get a job right here in Norfolk.

That night was full moon. They fooled around in their bathing suits a long while on the beach beside a little smudgefire Joe made to keep the mosquitoes off. He was sitting crosslegged and she lay with her head on his knees and all the time he was stroking her hair and leaning over and kissing her; she said how funny his face looked upside down when he kissed her like that. She said they'd get married as soon as he got a steady job and between the two of them they'd amount to something. Ever since she'd graduated from high school at the head of her class she'd felt she ought to work hard and amount to something. "The folks round here are awful no-account, Joe, don't know they're alive half the time."

"D'you know it, Del, you kinda remind me o' my sister Janey, honest you do. Dod gast it, she's amounting to something all right. . . . She's awful pretty too. . . ."

Della said she hoped she could see her some day and Joe said sure she would and he pulled her to her feet and drew her to him tight and hugged her and kissed her. It was late, and the beach was chilly and lonely under the big moon. Della got atrembling and said she'd have to get her clothes on or she'd catch her death. They had to run not to lose the last car.

The rails twanged as the car lurched through the moonlit pine barrens full of tambourining dryflies and katydids. Della suddenly crumpled up and began to cry. Joe kept asking her what the matter was but she wouldn't answer, only cried and cried. It was kind of a relief to leave her at her folks' house and walk alone through the empty airless streets to the boarding house where he had a room.

All the next week he hoofed it around Norfolk and Portsmouth looking for a job that had a future to it. He even went over to Newport News. Coming back on the ferry, he didn't have enough jack to pay his fare and had to get the guy who took tickets to let him work his way over sweeping up. The landlady began to ask for next week's rent. All the jobs Joe applied for needed experience or training or you'd ought to have finished high school and there weren't many jobs anyway, so in the end he had to go boating again, on a seagoing barge that was waiting for a towboat to take her down east to Rockport with a load of coal.

There were five barges in the tow; it wasn't such a bad trip, just him and an old man named Gaskin and his boy, a kid of about fifteen whose name was Joe too. The only trouble they had was in a squall off Cape Cod when the tow rope parted, but the towboat captain was right up on his toes and managed to get a new cable on board 'em before they'd straightened out on their anchor.

Up in Rockport they unloaded their coal and anchored out in the harbor waiting to be towed to another wharf to load granite blocks for the trip back. One night when Gaskin and his boy had gone ashore and Joe was on watch the second engineer of the tug, a thinfaced guy named Hart came under the stern in a skiff and whispered to Joe did he want some c——t. Joe was stretched out on the house smoking a pipe and thinking about Della. The hills and the harbor and the rocky shore were fading into a warm pink twilight. Hart had a nervous stuttering manner. Joe held off at first but after a while he said, "Bring 'em along." "Got any cards?" said Hart. "Yare I got a pack."

Joe went below to clean up the cabin. He'd just kid 'em along, he was thinking. He'd oughtn't to have a rough time with girls and all that now that he was going to marry Della. He heard the sound of the oars and went out on deck. A fogbank was coming in from the sea. There was Hart and his two girls under the stern. They tripped and giggled and fell hard against him when he helped 'em over the side.

They'd brought some liquor and a couple of pounds of hamburger and some crackers. They weren't much for looks but they were pretty good sorts with big firm arms and shoulders and they sure could drink liquor. Joe'd never seen girls like that before. They were sports all right. They had four quarts of liquor between 'em and drank it in tumblers.

The other two barges were sounding their claxons every two minutes, but Joe forgot all about his. The fog was white like canvas nailed across the cabin ports. They played strip poker but they didn't get very far with it. Him and Hart changed girls three times that night. The girls were cookoo, they never seemed to have enough, but round twelve the girls were darned decent, they cooked up the hamburger and served up a lunch and ate all old man Gaskin's bread and butter.

Then Hart passed out and the girls began to get worried about getting home on account of the fog and everything. All of 'em laughing like loons they hauled Hart up on deck and poured a bucket of water on him. That Maine water was so cold that he came to like sixty sore as a pup and wanting to fight Joe. The girls quieted him down and got him into the boat and they went off into the fog singing *Tipperary*.

Joe was reeling himself. He stuck his head in a bucket of water and cleaned up the cabin and threw the bottles overboard and started working on the claxon regularly. To hell with 'em, he kept saying to himself, he wouldn't be a plaster saint for anybody. He was feeling fine, he wished he had something more to do than spin that damn claxon.

Old man Gaskin came on board about day. Joe could see he'd gotten wind of something because after that he never would speak to him except to give orders and wouldn't let his boy speak to him; so that when they'd unloaded the granite blocks in East New York, Joe asked for his pay and said he was through. Old man Gaskin growled out it was a good riddance and that he wouldn't have no boozin' and whorin' on his barge. So there was Joe with fortyfive dollars in his pocket walking through Red Hook looking for a boarding house.

After he'd been a couple of days reading want ads and going around Brooklyn looking for a job he got sick. He went to a sawbones an oldtimer at the boarding house told him about. The doc who was a little kike with a goatee told him it was the gonawria and he'd have to come every afternoon for treatment. He said he'd guarantee to cure him up for fifty dollars, half payable in advance, and that he'd advise him to have a bloodtest taken to see if he had syphilis too and that would cost him fifteen dollars. Joe paid down the twentyfive but said he'd think about the test. He had a treatment and went out onto the street. The doc had told him to be sure to walk as little as possible, but he couldn't seem to go home to the stinking boardinghouse and wandered aimlessly round the clattering Brooklyn streets. It was a hot afternoon. The sweat was pouring off him as he walked. If you catch it right the first day or two it ain't so bad, he kept saying to himself. He came out on a bridge under the elevated; must be Brooklyn Bridge.

It was cooler walking across the bridge. Through the spiderwebbing of cables, the shipping and the pack of tall buildings were black against the sparkle of the harbor. Joe sat down on a bench at the first pier and stretched his legs out in front of him. Here he'd gone to work and caught a dose. He felt terrible and how was he going to write Del now; and his board to pay, and a job to get and these damn treatments to take. Jesus, he felt lousy.

A kid came by with an evening paper. He bought a *Journal* and sat with the paper on his lap looking at the headlines: RUSH MORE TROOPS TO MEX BORDER. What the hell could he do? He couldn't even join the national guard and go to Mexico; they wouldn't take you if you were sick and even if they did it would be the goddam navy all over again. He sat reading the want ads, the ads about adding to your income with two hours' agreeable work at home evenings, the ads of Pelmanism and correspondence courses. What the hell could he do? He sat there until it was dark. Then he took a car to Atlantic Avenue and went up four flights to the room where he had a cot under the window and turned in.

That night a big thundersquall came up. There was a lot of thunder and lightning damned close. Joe lay flat on his back watching the lightning so bright it dimmed the streetlights flicker on the ceiling. The springs rattled every time the guy in the other cot turned in his sleep. It began to rain in, but Joe felt so weak and sick it was a long time before he had the gumption to sit up and pull down the window.

In the morning the landlady, who was a big raw-boned Swedish woman with wisps of flaxen hair down over her bony face, started bawling him out about the bed's being wet. "I can't help it if it rains, can I?" he grumbled, looking at her big feet. When he caught her eye, it came over him that she was kidding him and they both laughed. She was a swell woman, her name was Mrs. Olsen and she'd raised six children, three boys who'd grown up and gone to sea, a girl who was a school teacher in St. Paul and a pair of girl twins about seven or eight who were always getting into mischief. "Yust one year more and I send them to Olga in Milwaukee. I know sailormen." Pop Olsen had been on the beach somewhere in the South Seas for years. "Yust as well he stay there. In Brooklyn he been always in de lockup. Every week cost me money to get him outa yail."

Joe got to helping her round the house with the cleaning and did odd painting and carpentering jobs for her. After his money ran out she let him stay on and even lent him twentyfive bucks to pay the doctor when he told her about being sick. She slapped him on the back when he thanked her; "Every boy I ever lend money to, he turn out yust one big bum," she said and laughed. She was a swell woman.

It was nasty sleety winter weather. Mornings Joe sat in the steamy kitchen studying a course in navigation he'd started getting from the Alexander Hamilton Institute. Afternoons he fidgeted in the dingy doctor's office that smelt of carbolic, waiting for his turn for treatment, looking through frayed copies of the *National Geographic* for 1909. It was a glum looking bunch waited in there. Nobody ever said anything much to anybody else. A couple of times he met guys on the street he'd talked with a little waiting in there, but they always walked right past him as if they didn't see him. Evenings he sometimes went over to Manhattan and played checkers at the Seamen's Institute or hung around the Seaman's Union getting the dope on ships he might get a berth on when the doc dried him up. It was a bum time except that Mrs. Olsen was darn good to him and he got fonder of her than he'd ever been of his own mother.

The darn kike sawbones tried to hold him up for another twentyfive bucks to complete the cure but Joe said to hell with it and shipped as an A.B. on a brandnew Standard Oil tanker, the *Montana*, bound light for Tampico and then out east, some of the boys said, to Aden and others said to Bombay. He was sick of the cold and the sleet and the grimy Brooklyn streets and the logarithm tables in the course on navigation he couldn't get through his head and Mrs. Olsen's bullying jollying voice; she was beginning to act like she wanted to run his life for him. She was a swell woman but it was about time he got the hell out.

The *Montana* rounded Sandy Hook in a spiteful lashing snowstorm out of the northwest, but three days later they were in the Gulf

Stream south of Hatteras rolling in a long swell with all the crew's denims and shirts drying on lines rigged from the shrouds. It was good to be on blue water again.

Tampico was a hell of a place; they said that mescal made you crazy if you drank too much of it; there were big dance halls full of greasers dancing with their hats on and with guns on their hips, and bands and mechanical pianos going full tilt in every bar, and fights and drunk Texans from the oilwells. The doors of all the cribhouses were open so that you could see the bed with white pillows and the picture of the Virgin over it and the lamps with fancy shades and the colored paper trimming; the broadfaced brown girls sat out in front in lace slips. But everything was so damned high that they spent up all their jack first thing and had to go back on board before it was hardly midnight. And the mosquitoes got into the focastle and the sandflies about day and it was hot and nobody could sleep.

When the tanks had been pumped full the *Montana* went out into the Gulf of Mexico into a norther with the decks awash and the spray lashing the bridge. They hadn't been out two hours before they'd lost a man overboard off the monkeywalk and a boy named Higgins had had his foot smashed lashing the starboard anchor that had broken loose. It made 'em pretty sore down in the focastle that the skipper wouldn't lower a boat, though the older men said that no boat could have lived in a sea like that. As it was the skipper cruised in a wide curve and took a couple of seas on his beam that like to stove in the steel decks.

Nothing much else happened on that trip except that one night when Joe was at the wheel and the ship was dead quiet except for the irregular rustle of broken water as she ploughed through the long flat seas eastward, he suddenly smelt roses or honeysuckle maybe. The sky was blue as a bowl of curdled milk with a waned scrap of moon bobbing up from time to time. It was honeysuckle, sure enough, and manured garden patches and moist foliage like walking past the open door of a florist's in winter. It made him feel soft and funny inside like he had a girl standing right beside him on the bridge, like he had Del there with her hair all smelly with some kind of perfume. Funny, the smell of dark, girls' hair. He took down the binoculars but he couldn't see anything on the horizon only the curdled scud drifting west in the faint moonlight. He found he was losing his course, good thing the mate hadn't picked out that moment to look aft at the wake. He got her back to E.N.E. by ½E. When his trick was over and he rolled into his bunk he lay awake a long time thinking of Del. God, he wanted money and a good job and a girl of his own instead of all these damn floosies when you got into port. What he ought to do was go down to Norfolk and settle down and get married.

Next day about noon they sighted the grey sugarloaf of Pico with a band of white clouds just under the peak and Fayal blue and irregular to the north. They passed between the two islands. The sea got very blue; it smelled like the country lanes outside of Washington when there was honeysuckle and laurel blooming in the runs. The bluegreen yellowgreen patchwork fields covered the steep hills like an oldfashioned quilt. That night they raised other islands to the eastward.

Five days of a heavy groundswell and they were in the Straits of Gibraltar. Eight days of dirty sea and chilly driving rain and they were off the Egyptian coast, a warm sunny morning, going into the port of Alexandria under one bell while the band of yellow mist ahead thickened up into masts, wharves, buildings, palmtrees. The streets smelt like a garbage pail, they drank arrack in bars run by Greeks who'd been in America and paid a dollar apiece to see three Jewishlooking girls dance a belly dance naked in a back room. In Alexandria they saw their first camouflaged ships, three British scoutcruisers striped like zebras and a transport all painted up with blue and green watermarkings. When they saw them, all the watch on deck lined up along the rail and laughed like they'd split.

When he got paid off in New York a month later it made him feel pretty good to go to Mrs. Olsen and pay her back what he owed her. She had another youngster staying with her at the boarding house, a towheaded Swede who didn't know any English, so she didn't pay much attention to Joe. He hung around the kitchen a little while and asked her how things were and told her about the bunch on the *Montana,* then he went over to the Penn Station to see when he could catch a train to Washington. He sat dozing in the smoker of the daycoach half the night thinking of Georgetown and when he'd been a kid at school and the bunch in the poolroom on 4½ Street and trips on the river with Alec and Janey.

It was a bright wintry sunny morning when he piled out at the Union Station. He couldn't seem to make up his mind to go over to Georgetown to see the folks. He loafed around the Union Station, got a shave and a shine and a cup of coffee, read the Washington *Post*, counted his money; he still had more'n fifty iron men, quite a roll of lettuce for a guy like him. Then he guessed he'd wait and see Janey first, he'd wait around and maybe he'd catch her coming out from where she worked at noon. He walked around the Capitol Grounds and down Pennsylvania Avenue to the White House. On the Avenue he saw the same enlistment booth where he'd enlisted for the navy. Kinder gave him the creeps. He went and sat in the winter sunlight in Lafayette Square, looking at the little dressed up kids playing and the nursemaids and the fat starlings hopping round the grass and the statue of Andrew Jackson, until he thought it was time to go catch Janey. His heart was beating so he could hardly see straight. It must have been later than he thought because none of the girls coming out of the elevator was her, though he waited about an hour in the vestibule of the Riggs Building until some lousy dick or other came up to him and asked him what the hell we was loitering around for.

So Joe had to go over to Georgetown after all to find out where Janey was. Mommer was in and his kid sisters and they were all talking about how they were going to have the house remodeled with the ten thousand dollars from the Old Man's insurance and they wanted him to go up to Oak Hill to see the grave, but Joe said what was the use and got away as soon as he could. They asked all kinds of questions about how he was getting on and he didn't know what the hell to tell 'em. They told him where Janey lived but they didn't know when she got out of her office.

He stopped at the Belasco and bought some theatre tickets and then went back to the Riggs Building. He got there just as Janey was stepping out of the elevator. She was nicely dressed and had her chin up with a new little cute independent tilt. He was so glad to see her he was afraid he was going to bawl. Her voice was different. She had a quick chilly way of talking and a kidding manner she'd never had before. He took her to supper and to the theatre and she told him all about how well she was getting on at Dreyfus and Carroll and what interesting people she was getting to know. It made him feel like a bum going around with her.

Then he left her at the apartment she had with a girl friend and took the car back to the station. He settled down and smoked a cigar in the smoker of the daycoach. He felt pretty blue. Next day in New York he looked up a guy he knew and they went out and had a few drinks and found 'em some skirts and the day after that he was sitting on a bench in Union Square with a headache and not a red cent in his jeans. He found the stubs of the tickets to the show at the Belasco theatre he'd taken Janey to and put them carefully in the cigarbox with the other junk.

Next boat he shipped on was the *North Star* bound for St. Nazaire with a cargo listed as canned goods that everybody knew was shell caps, and bonuses for the crew on account of the danger of going through the zone. She was a crazy whaleback, had been an oreboat on the Great Lakes, leaked so they had to have the pumps going half the time, but Joe liked the bunch and the chow was darn good and old Cap'n Perry was as fine an old seadog as you'd like to see, had been living ashore for a couple of years down at Atlantic Highlands but had come back on account of the big money to try to make a pile for his daughter; she'd get the insurance anyway, Joe heard him tell the mate with a wheezy laugh. They had a smooth winter crossing, the wind behind them all the way right till they were in the Bay of Biscay. It was very cold and the sea was dead calm when they came in sight of the French coast, low and sandy at the mouth of the Loire.

They had the flag up and the ship's name signal and Sparks was working overtime and they sure were nervous on account of mines until the French patrol boat came out and led the way through the winding channel into the river between the minefields.

When they saw the spires and the long rows of grey houses and the little clustered chimney pots of St. Nazaire in the smoky dusk the boys were going round slapping each other on the back and saying they sure would get cockeyed this night.

But what happened was that they anchored out in the stream and Cap'n Perry and the First Mate went ashore in the dingy and they didn't dock till two days later on account of there being no room at the wharves. When they did get ashore to take a look at the mademosels and the vin rouge, they all had to show their seaman's passports when they left the wharf to a redfaced man in a blue uniform trimmed with red who had a tremendous pair of pointed black moustaches. Blackie Flannagan had crouched down behind him and somebody was just going to give him a shove over his back when the Chief yelled at them from across the street, "For Chris' sake, can't you c——s see that's a frog cop? You don't want to get run in right on the wharf, do you?"

Joe and Flannagan got separated from the others and walked around to look the town over. The streets were paved with cobblestones and awful little and funny and the old women all wore tight white lace caps and everything looked kinder falling down. Even the dogs looked like frog dogs. They ended up in a place marked American Bar but it didn't look like any bar they'd ever seen in the States. They bought a bottle of cognac for a starter. Flannagan said the town looked like Hoboken, but Joe said it looked kinder like Villefranche where he'd been when he was in the navy. American dollars went pretty far if you knew enough not to let 'em gyp you.

Another American came in to the dump and they got to talking and he said he'd been torpedoed on the *Oswego* right in the mouth of the Loire river. They gave him some of the cognac and he said how it had been, that Uboat had blowed the poor old *Oswego* clear outa the water and when smoke cleared away she'd split right in two and closed up like a jackknife. They had another bottle of cognac on that and then the feller took them to a house he said he knew and there they found some more of the bunch drinking beer and dancing around with the girls.

Joe was having a good time parleyvooing with one of the girls, he'd point to something and she'd tell him how to say it in French, when a fight started someway and the frog cops came and the bunch had to run for it. They all got back aboard ship ahead of the cops but they came and stood on the dock and jabbered for about a half an hour until old Cap'n Perry, who'd just gotten back from town in a horsecab, told 'em where to get off.

The trip back was slow but pretty good. They were only a week in Hampton Roads, loaded up with a cargo of steel ingots and explosives, and cleared for Cardiff. It was nervous work. The Cap'n took a northerly course and they got into a lot of fog. Then after a solid week of icy cold weather with a huge following sea they sighted Rockall. Joe was at the wheel. The green hand in the crowsnest yelled out, "Battleship ahead," and old Cap'n Perry stood on the bridge laughing, looking at the rock through his binoculars.

Next morning they raised the Hebrides to the south. Cap'n Perry was just pointing out the Butt of Lewis to the mate when the lookout in the bow gave a scared hail. It was a submarine all right. You could see first the periscope trailing a white feather of foam, then the dripping conning tower. The submarine had hardly gotten to the surface when she started firing across the *North Star*'s bows with a small gun that the squareheads manned while decks were still awash. Joe went running aft to run up the flag, although they had the flag painted amidships on either side of the boat. The engineroom bells jingled as Cap'n Perry threw her into full speed astern. The jerries stopped firing and four of them came on board in a collapsible punt. All hands had their life preservers on and some of the men were going below for their duffle when the fritz officer who came aboard shouted in English that they had five minutes to abandon the ship. Cap'n Perry handed over the ship's papers, the boats were lowered like winking as the blocks were well oiled. Something made Joe run back up to the boat deck and cut the lashings on the liferafts with his jackknife, so he and Cap'n Perry and the ship's cat were the last to leave the *North Star*. The jerries had planted bombs in the engine room and were rowing back to the submarine like the devil was after them. The Cap'n's boat had hardly pushed off when the explosion lammed them a blow on the side of the head. The boat swamped and before they knew what had hit them they were swimming in the icy water among all kinds of planking and junk. Two of the boats were still afloat. The old *North Star* was sinking quietly with the flag flying and the signalflags blowing out prettily in the light breeze. They must have been half an hour or an hour in the water. After the ship had sunk they managed to get onto the liferafts and the mate's boat and the Chief's boat took them in tow. Cap'n Perry called the roll. There wasn't a soul missing. The submarine had submerged and gone some time ago. The men in the boats started pulling towards shore. Till nightfall the strong tide was carrying them in fast towards the Pentland Firth. In the last dusk they could see the tall headlands of the Orkneys. But when the tide changed they couldn't make headway against it. The men in the boats and the men in the rafts took turn and turn about at the oars but they couldn't buck the terrible ebb. Somebody said the tide ran eight knots an hour in there. It was a pretty bad night. With the first dawn they caught sight of a scoutcruiser bearing down on them. Her searchlight glared suddenly in their faces making everything look black again. The Britishers took 'em on board and hustled them down into the engineroom to get warm. A redfaced steward came down with a bucket of steaming tea with rum in it and served it out with a ladle.

The scoutcruiser took 'em into Glasgow, pretty well shaken up by the chop of the Irish Sea, and they all stood around in the drizzle on the dock while Cap'n Perry went to find the American consul. Joe was getting numb in the feet standing still and tried to walk across to the iron gates opposite the wharf house to take a squint down the street, but an elderly man in a uniform poked a bayonet at his belly and he stopped. Joe went back to the crowd and told 'em how they were prisoners there like they were fritzes. Jez, it made 'em sore. Flannagan started telling about how the frogs had arrested him one time for getting into a fight with an orangeman in a bar in Marseilles and had been ready to shoot him because they said the Irish were all pro German. Joe told about how the limeys had run him in Liverpool. They were all grousing about how the whole business was a lousy deal when Ben Tarbell the mate turned up with an old guy from the consulate and told 'em to come along.

They had to troop half across town through streets black dark for fear of airraids and slimy with rain, to a long tarpaper shack inside a barbedwire enclosure. Ben Tarbell told the boys he was sorry but they'd have to stay there for the present, and that he was trying to get the consul to do something about it and the old man had cabled the owners to try to get 'em some pay. Some girls from the Red Cross brought them grub, mostly bread and marmalade and meatpaste, nothing you could really sink your teeth into, and some thin blankets. They stayed in that damn place for twelve days, playing poker and yarning and reading old newspapers. Evenings sometimes a frousy halfdrunk woman would get past the old guard and peek in the door of the shack and beckon one of the men out into the foggy darkness behind the latrines somewhere. Some of the guys were disgusted and wouldn't go.

They'd been shut up in there so long that when the mate finally came around and told 'em they were going home they didn't have enough spunk left in 'em to yell. They went across the town packed with traffic and gasflare in the fog again and on board a new 6000 ton freighter, the *Vicksburg*, that had just unloaded a cargo of cotton. It felt funny being a passenger and being able to lay around all day on the trip home.

Joe was lying out on the hatchcover the first sunny day they'd had when old Cap'n Perry came up to him. Joe got to his feet. Cap'n Perry said he hadn't had a chance to tell him what he thought of him for having the presence of mind to cut the lashings on those rafts and that half the men on the boat owed their lives to him. He said Joe was a bright boy and ought to start studying how to get out of the focastle and that the American merchant marine was growing every day on account of the war and young fellers like him were just what they needed for officers. "You remind me, boy," he said, "when we get to Hampton Roads and I'll see what I can do on the next ship I get. You could get your third mate's ticket right now with a little time in shore school." Joe grinned and said he sure would like to. It made him feel good the whole trip. He couldn't wait to go and see Del and tell her he wasn't in the focastle any more. Dod gast it, he was tired of being treated like a jailbird all his life.

The *Vicksburg* docked at Newport News. Hampton Roads was fuller of shipping than Joe had ever seen it. Along the wharves everybody was talking about the *Deutschland* that had just unloaded a cargo of dyes in Baltimore. When Joe got paid off he wouldn't even take a drink with his shipmates but hustled down to the ferry station to get the ferry for Norfolk. Jez, the old ferry seemed slow. It was about five o'clock a Saturday afternoon when he got into Norfolk. Walking down the street he was scared she wouldn't be home yet.

Del was home and seemed glad to see him. She said she had a date that night but he teased her into breaking it off. After all, weren't they engaged to be married? They went out and had a sundae at an icecream parlor and she told him all about her new job with the Duponts and how she was getting ten more a week and how all the boys she knew and several girls were working in the munition factories and how some of 'em were making fifteen dollars a day and they were buying cars and the boy she'd had a date with that night had a Packard. It took a long time for Joe to get around to tell her about what old Cap'n Perry had said and she was all excited about his having been torpedoed and said why didn't he go and get a job over at Newport News in the shipyard and make real money, she didn't like the idea of his being torpedoed every minute, but Joe said he hated to leave the sea now that there was a chance of getting ahead. She asked him how much he'd make as third mate on a freighter and he said a hundred and twentyfive a month but there'd always be bonuses for the zone and there were a lot of new ships being built and he thought the prospects pretty good all around.

Del screwed her face up in a funny way and said she didn't know how she'd like having a husband who was away from home all the time, but she went into a phone booth and called the other boy up and broke off the date she had with him. They went back to Del's house and she cooked up a bite of supper. Her folks had gone over to Fortress Monroe to eat with an aunt of hers. It made Joe feel good to see her with an apron on bustling around the kitchen. She let him kiss her a couple of times but when he went up behind her and hugged her and pulled her face back and kissed her, she said not to do that, it made her feel all out of breath. The dark smell of her hair and the feel of her skin that was white like milk against his lips made him feel giddy. It was a relief when they went out on the street in the keen northwest wind again. He bought her a box of Saturday night candies at a drugstore. They went to see a bill of vaudeville and movies at the Colonial. The Belgian war pictures were awful exciting and Del said wasn't it terrible and Joe started to tell her about what a guy he knew had told him about being in an air raid in London but she didn't listen.

When he kissed her goodnight in the hall, Joe felt awful hot and pressed her up in the corner by the hatrack and tried to get his hand under her skirt but she said not till they were married and he said with his mouth against hers, when would they get married and she said they'd get married as soon as he got his new job.

Just then they heard the key in the latch just beside them and she pulled him into the parlor and whispered not to say anything about their being engaged just yet. It was Del's old man and her mother and her two kid sisters and the old man gave Joe a mean look and the kid sisters giggled and Joe went away feeling fussed. It was early yet but Joe felt too het up to sleep so he walked around a little and then went by the Stirps' house to see if Will was in town. Will was in Baltimore looking for a job, but old Mrs. Stirp said if he didn't have nowhere to go and wanted to sleep in Will's bed he was welcome, but he couldn't sleep for thinking of Del and how smart she was and how she felt in his arms and how the smell of her hair made him feel crazy and how much he wanted her.

First thing he did Monday morning was to go over to Newport

News and see Cap'n Perry. The old man was darn nice to him, asked him about his schooling and his folks. When Joe said he was old Cap'n Joe Williams' son, Cap'n Perry couldn't do enough for him. Him and Joe's old man had been on the *Albert and Mary Smith* together in the old clipper ship days. He said he'd have a berth for Joe as junior officer on the *Henry B. Higginbotham* as soon as she'd finished repairs and he must go to work at shore school over in Norfolk and get ready to go before the licensing board and get his ticket. He'd coach him up on the fine points himself. When he left the old man said, "Ma boy, if you work like you oughter, bein' your Dad's son, an' this war keeps up, you'll be master of your own vessel in five years, I'll guarantee it."

Joe couldn't wait to get hold of Del and tell her about it. That night he took her to the movies to see the Four Horsemen. It was darned exciting, they held hands all through and he kept his leg pressed against her plump little leg. Seeing it with her and the war and everything flickering on the screen and the music like in church and her hair against his cheek and being pressed close to her a little sweaty in the warm dark like to went to his head. When the picture was over he felt he'd go crazy if he couldn't have her right away. She was kinder kidding him along and he got sore and said God damn it, they'd have to get married right away or else he was through. She'd held out on him just about long enough. She began to cry and turned her face up to him all wet with tears and said if he really loved her he wouldn't talk like that and that that was no way to talk to a lady and he felt awful bad about it. When they got back to her folks' house, everybody had gone to bed and they went out in the pantry back of the kitchen without turning the light on and she let him love her up. She said honestly she loved him so much she'd let him do anything he wanted only she knew he wouldn't respect her if she did. She said she was sick of living at home and having her mother keep tabs on her all the time, and she'd tell her folks in the morning about how he'd got a job as a ship's officer and they had to get married before he left and that he must get him his uniform right away.

When Joe left the house to look around and find a flop, he was walking on air. He hadn't planned to get married that soon but what the hell, a man had to have a girl of his own. He began doping out what he'd write Janey about it, but he decided she wouldn't like it and that he'd better not write. He wished Janey wasn't getting so kind of uppish, but after all she was making a big success of business. When he was skipper of his own ship she'd think it was all great.

Joe was two months ashore that time. He went to shore school every day, lived at the Y.M.C.A. and didn't take a drink or shoot pool or anything. The pay he had saved up from the two trips on the *North Star* was just about enough to swing it. Every week or so he went over to Newport News to talk it over with old Cap'n Perry who told him what kind of questions the examining board would ask him and what kind of papers he'd need. Joe was pretty worried about his original A.B. certificate, but he had another now and recommendations from captains of ships he'd been on. What the hell, he'd been at sea four years, it was about time he knew a little about running a ship. He almost worried himself sick over the examination, but when he was actually there standing before the old birds on the board it wasn't as bad as he thought it ud be. When he actually got the third mate's license and showed it to Del, they were both of them pretty tickled.

Joe bought his uniform when he got an advance of pay. From then on he was busy all day doing odd jobs round the drydock for old Cap'n Perry who hadn't gotten a crew together yet. Then in the evenings he worked painting up the little bedroom, kitchenette and bath he'd rented for him and Del to live in when he was ashore. Del's folks insisted on having a church wedding and Will Stirp, who was making fifteen dollars a day in a shipyard in Baltimore, came down to be best man.

Joe felt awful silly at the wedding and Will Stirp had gotten hold of some whiskey and had a breath like a distillery wagon and a couple of the other boys were drunk and that made Del and her folks awful sore and Del looked like she wanted to crown him all through the service. When it was over Joe found he'd wilted his collar and Del's old man began pulling a lot of jokes and her sisters giggled so much in their white organdy dresses, he could have choked 'em. They went back to the Matthews' house and everybody was awful stiff except Will Stirp and his friends who brought in a bottle of whiskey and got old man Matthews cockeyed. Mrs. Matthews ran 'em all out of the house and all the old cats from the Ladies Aid rolled their eyes up and said, "Could you imagine it?" And Joe and Del left in a taxicab a feller he knew drove and everybody threw rice at them and Joe found he had a sign reading Newlywed pinned on the tail of his coat and Del cried and cried and when they got to their apartment Del locked herself in

the bathroom and wouldn't answer when he called and he was afraid
she'd fainted.

Joe took off his new blue serge coat and his collar and necktie and
walked up and down not knowing what to do. It was six o'clock in the
evening. He had to be aboard ship at midnight because they were sailing for France as soon as it was day. He didn't know what to do. He
thought maybe she'd want something to eat so he cooked up some
bacon and eggs on the stove. By the time everything was cold and Joe
was walking up and down cussing under his breath, Del came out of
the bathroom looking all fresh and pink like nothing had happened.
She said she couldn't eat anything but let's go to a movie . . . "But,
honeybug," said Joe, "I've got to pull out at twelve." She began to cry
again and he flushed and felt awful fussed. She snuggled up to him
and said, "We won't stay for the feature. We'll come back in time." He
grabbed her and started hugging her but she held him off firmly and
said, "Later."

Joe couldn't look at the picture. When they got back to the apartment it was ten o'clock. She let him pull off her clothes but she
jumped into bed and wrapped the bedclothes around her and whim-
pered that she was afraid of having a baby, that he must wait till she
found out what to do to keep from having a baby. All she let him do
was rub up against her through the bedclothes and then suddenly it
was ten of twelve and he had to jump into his clothes and run down
to the wharf. An old colored man rowed him out to where his ship lay
at anchor. It was a sweetsmelling spring night without any moon. He
heard honking overhead and tried to squint up his eyes to see the
birds passing against the pale stars. "Them's geese, boss," said the old
colored man in a soft voice. When he climbed onboard everybody
started kidding him and declared he looked all wore out. Joe didn't
know what to say so he talked big and kidded back and lied like a fish.

Newsreel XXI

Goodby Broadway
Hello France
We're ten million strong

8 YEAR OLD BOY SHOT BY LAD WITH RIFLE

the police have already notified us that any entertainment in Paris must be brief and quietly conducted and not in public view and that we have already had more dances than we ought

capitalization grown 104% while business expands 520%

HAWAIIAN SUGAR CONTROL LOST BY GERMANS

efforts of the Bolshevik Government to discuss the withdrawal of the U.S. and allied forces from Russia through negotiation for an armistice are attracting no serious attention

BRISTISH AIRMAN FIGHTS SIXTY FOES

SERBIANS ADVANCE 10 MILES; TAKE 10 TOWNS; MENACE PRILEP

Good morning
Mr. Zip Zip Zip
You're surely looking fine
Good morning
Mr. Zip Zip Zip
With your hair cut just as short as
With your hair cut just as short as
With your hair cut just as short as mine

LENINE REPORTED ALIVE

AUDIENCE AT HIPPODROME TESTIMONIALS MOVED TO CHEERS AND TEARS

several different stories have come to me well authenticated concerning the depth of Hindenburg's brutality; the details are too horrible for print.   They relate to outraged womanhood and girlhood, suicide and blood of the innocent that wet the feet of Hindenburg

WAR DECREASES MARRIAGES AND BIRTHS

Oh ashes to ashes
And dust to dust
If the shrapnel dont get you
Then the eightyeights must

The Camera Eye (29)

the raindrops fall one by one out of the horsechestnut tree over the arbor onto the table in the abandoned beergarden and the puddly gravel and my clipped skull where my fingers move gently forward and back over the fuzzy knobs and hollows

spring and we've just been swimming in the Marne way off somewhere beyond the fat clouds on the horizon they are hammering on a tin roof   in the rain in the spring after a swim in the Marne with that hammering to the north pounding the thought of death into our ears

the winey thought of death stings in the spring blood that throbs in the sunburned neck   up and down the belly under the tight belt   hurries like cognac into the tips of my toes and the lobes of my ears and my fingers stroking the fuzzy closecropped skull

shyly tingling fingers feel out the limits of the hard immortal skull under the flesh   a deathshead and skeleton sits wearing glasses in the arbor under the lucid occasional raindrops inside the new khaki uniform inside my twentyoneyearold body that's been swimming in the Marne in red and whitestriped trunks in Chalons in the spring

Richard Ellsworth Savage

The years Dick was little he never heard anything about his Dad, but when he was doing his homework evenings up in his little room in the attic he'd start thinking about him sometimes; he'd throw himself on the bed and lie on his back trying to remember what he had been like and Oak Park and everything before Mother had been so unhappy and they had had to come east to live with Aunt Beatrice. There was the smell of bay rum and cigarsmoke and he was sitting on the back of an upholstered sofa beside a big man in a panama hat who shook the sofa when he laughed; he held on to Dad's back and punched his arm and the muscle was hard like a chair or a table and when Dad laughed he could feel it rumble in his back, "Dicky, keep your dirty feet off my palm beach suit," and he was on his hands and knees in the sunlight that poured through the lace curtains of the window trying to pick the big purple roses off the carpet; they were all standing in front of a red automobile and Dad's face was red and he smelt of armpits and white steam was coming out around, and people were saying Safetyvalve. Downstairs Dad and Mummy were at dinner and there was company and wine and a new butler and it must be awful funny because they laughed so much and the knives and forks went click click all the time; Dad found him in his nightgown peeking through the portières and came out awful funny and excited smelling like wine and whaled him and mother came out and said, "Henry, don't strike the child," and they stood hissing at one another in low voices behind the portières on account of company and Mummy had picked Dick up and carried him upstairs crying in her evening dress all lacy and frizzly and with big puffy silk sleeves; touching silk put his teeth on edge, made him shudder all down his spine. He and Henry had had tan overcoats with pockets in them like grownup overcoats and tan caps and he'd lost the button off the top of his. Way back there it was sunny and windy; Dick got tired and sickyfeeling when he tried to remember back like that and it got him so he couldn't keep his mind on tomorrow's lessons and would pull out "Twenty Thousand Leagues Under the Sea" that he had under the mattress because Mother took books away when they weren't just about the lessons and would read just a little and then he'd forget everything reading and wouldn't know his lessons the next day.

All the same he got along very well at school and the teachers liked him, particularly Miss Teazle, the English teacher, because he had nice manners and said little things that weren't fresh but that made them laugh. Miss Teazle said he showed real feeling for English composition. One Christmas he sent her a little rhyme he made up about the Christ Child and the Three Kings and she declared he had a gift.

The better he liked it in school the worse it was at home. Aunt Beatrice was always nag nag nag from morning till night. As if he didn't know that he and mother were eating her bread and sleeping under her roof; they paid board, didn't they? even if they didn't pay as much as Major and Mrs. Glen or Dr. Kern did, and they certainly did enough work to pay for their keep anyway. He'd heard Mrs. Glen saying when Dr. Atwood was calling and Aunt Beatrice was out of the room how it was a shame that poor Mrs. Savage, such a sweet woman, and a good churchwoman too, and the daughter of a general in the army, had to work her fingers to the bone for her sister who was only a fussy old maid and overcharged so, though of course she did keep a very charming house and set an excellent table, not like a boarding house at all, more like a lovely refined private home, such a relief to find in Trenton, that was such a commercial city so full of working people and foreigners; too bad that the daughters of General Ellsworth should be reduced to taking paying guests. Dick felt Mrs. Glen might have said something about his carrying out the ashes and shovelling snow and all that. Anyway he didn't think a highschool student ought to have to take time from his studies to do the chores.

Dr. Atwood was the rector of the St. Gabriel's Episcopal Church where Dick had to sing in the choir every Sunday at two services while mother and his brother Henry S., who was three years older than he was and worked in a drafting office in Philadelphia and only came home weekends, sat comfortably in a pew. Mother loved St. Gabriel's because it was so highchurch and they had processions and even incense. Dick hated it on account of choirpractice and having to keep his surplice clean and because he never had any pocketmoney to shoot craps with behind the bench in the vestry and he was always the one who had to stand at the door and whisper, "Cheeze it," if anybody was coming.

One Sunday, right after his thirteenth birthday, he'd walked home from church with his mother and Henry feeling hungry and wondering all the way if they were going to have fried chicken for dinner.

They were all three stepping up onto the stoop, Mother leaning a little on Dick's arm and the purple and green poppies on her wide hat jiggling in the October sunlight, when he saw Aunt Beatrice's thin face looking worriedly out through the glass panel of the front door. "Leona," she said in an excited reproachful voice, "he's here." "Who, Beatrice dear?" "You know well enough . . . I don't know what to do . . . he says he wants to see you. I made him wait in the lower hall on account of . . . er . . . our friends."

"Oh, God, Beatrice, haven't I borne enough from that man?"

Mother let herself drop onto the bench under the stagshorn coatrack in the hall. Dick and Henry stared at the white faces of the two women. Aunt Beatrice pursed up her lips and said in a spiteful tone, "You boys had better go out and walk round the block. I can't have two big hulks like you loafing round the house. You be back for Sunday dinner at one thirty sharp . . . run along now."

"Why, what's the matter with Aunt Beatrice?" asked Dick as they walked off down the street. "Got the pip I guess . . . she gives me a pain in the neck," Henry said in a superior tone.

Dick walked along kicking at the pavement with his toes.

"Say, we might go around and have a soda . . . they have awful good sodas at Dryer's."

"Got any dough?"

Dick shook his head.

"Well, you needn't think I'm goin' to treat you. . . . Jimminy criskets, Trenton's a rotten town. . . . In Philadelphia I seen a drugstore with a sodafountain half a block long."

"Aw, you."

"I bet you don't remember when we lived in Oak Park, Dick. . . . Now Chicago's a fine town." "Sure I do . . . and you an' me going to kindergarden and Dad being there and everything."

"Hell's bells, I wanta smoke."

"Mother'll smell it on you."

"Don't give a damn if she does."

When they got home Aunt Beatrice met them at the front door looking sore as a crab and told them to go down to the basement. Mother wanted to see them. The back stairs smelt of Sunday dinner and sage chickenstuffing. They hobbled down as slowly as possible, it must be about Henry's smoking. She was in the dark basement hall. By the light of the gasjet against the wall Dick couldn't make out who the man was. Mother came up to them and they could see that her eyes were red. "Boys, it's your father," she said in a weak voice. The tears began running down her face.

The man had a grey shapeless head and his hair was cut very short, the lids of his eyes were red and lashless and his eyes were the same color as his face. Dick was scared. It was somebody he'd known when he was little; it couldn't be Dad.

"For God's sake, no more waterworks, Leona," the man said in a whining voice. As he stood staring into the boys' faces his body wabbled a little as if he was weak in the knees. "They're good lookers both of them, Leona . . . I guess they don't think much of their poor old Dad."

They all stood there without saying anything in the dark basement hall in the rich close smell of Sunday dinner from the kitchen. Dick felt he ought to talk but something had stuck in his throat. He found he was stuttering, "Ha-ha-hav-have you been sick?"

The man turned to Mother. "You'd better tell them all about it when I'm gone . . . don't spare me . . . nobody's ever spared me. . . . Don't look at me as if I was a ghost, boys, I won't hurt you." A nervous tremor shook the lower part of his face. "All my life I've always been the one has gotten hurt. . . . Well, this is a long way from Oak Park . . . I just wanted to take a look at you, good-by. . . . I guess the likes of me had better go out the basement door . . . I'll meet you at the bank at eleven sharp, Leona, and that'll be the last thing you'll ever have to do for me."

The gasjet went red when the door opened and flooded the hall with reflected sunlight. Dick was shaking for fear the man was going to kiss him, but all he did was give them each a little trembly pat on the shoulder. His suit hung loose on him and he seemed to have trouble lifting his feet in their soft baggy shoes up the five stone steps to the street.

Mother closed the door sharply.

"He's going to Cuba," she said. "That's the last time we'll see him. I hope God can forgive him for all this, your poor mother never can . . . at least he's out of that horrible place." "Where was he, Mom?" asked Henry in a business like voice. "Atlanta."

Dick ran away and up to the top floor and into his own room in the attic and threw himself on the bed sobbing.

They none of them went down to dinner although they were hungry and the stairs were rich with the smell of roast chicken. When Pearl was washing up Dick tiptoed into the kitchen and coaxed a big heaping plate of chicken and stuffing and sweetpotatoes out of her; she said to run along and eat it in the back yard because it was her day out and she had the dishes to do. He sat on a dusty stepladder in the laundry eating. He could hardly get the chicken down on account of the funny stiffness in his throat. When he'd finished, Pearl made him help her wipe.

That summer they got him a job as bellboy in a small hotel at Bay Head that was run by a lady who was a parishioner of Dr. Atwood's. Before he left Major and Mrs. Glen, who were Aunt Beatrice's star boarders, gave him a fivedollar bill for pocket money and a copy of the "Little Shepherd of Kingdom Come" to read on the train. Dr. Atwood asked him to stay after the bibleclass his last Sunday and told him the parable of the talent, that Dick knew very well already because Dr. Atwood preached on it as a text four times every year, and showed him a letter from the headmaster of Kent accepting him for the next year as a scholarship pupil and told him that he must work hard because God expected from each of us according to our abilities. Then he told him a few things a growing boy ought to know and said he must avoid temptations and always serve God with a clean body and a clean mind, and keep himself pure for the lovely sweet girl he would some day marry, and that anything else led only to madness and disease. Dick went away with his cheeks burning.

It wasn't so bad at the Bayview, but the guests and help were all old people; about his own age there was only Skinny Murray the other bellhop, a tall sandyhaired boy who never had anything to say. He was a couple of years older than Dick. They slept on two cots in a small airless room right up under the roof that would still be so hot from the sun by bedtime they could hardly touch it. Through the thin partition they could hear the waitress in the next room rustling about and giggling as they went to bed. Dick hated that sound and the smell of girls and cheap facepowder that drifted in through the crack in the wall. The hottest nights he and Skinny would take the screen out of the window and crawl out along the gutter to a piece of flat roof there was over one of the upper porches. There the mosquitoes would torment them, but it was better than trying to sleep on their cots. Once the girls were looking out of the window and saw them crawling along the gutter and made a great racket that they were peeping and that they'd report them to the manageress, and they were scared to death and made plans all night about what they'd do if they were fired, they'd go to Barnegat and get work on fishing boats; but the next day the girls didn't say anything about it. Dick was kinda disappointed because he hated waiting on people and running up and down stairs answering bells.

It was Skinny who got the idea they might make some extra money selling fudge, because when Dick got a package of fudge from his mother he sold it to one of the waitresses for a quarter. So Mrs. Savage sent a package of fresh fudge and panocha every week by parcel post that Dick and Skinny sold to the guests in little boxes. Skinny bought the boxes and did most of the work but Dick convinced him it wouldn't be fair for him to take more than ten percent of the profits because he and his mother put up the original capital.

The next summer they made quite a thing of the fudgeselling. Skinny did the work more than ever because Dick had been to a private school and had been hobnobbing with rich boys all winter whose parents had plenty of money. Luckily none of them came to Bay Head for the summer. He told Skinny all about the school and recited ballads about St. John Hospitaller and Saint Christopher he'd made up and that had been published in the school paper; he told him about serving at the altar and the beauty of the Christian Faith and about how he'd made the outfield in the junior baseball team. Dick made Skinny go to church with him every Sunday to the little Episcopal chapel called St. Mary's-by-the-Sea. Dick used to stay after the service and discuss points of doctrine and ceremony with Mr. Thurlow the young minister and was finally invited to come home with him to dinner and meet his wife.

The Thurlows lived in an unpainted peakedroofed bungalow in the middle of a sandlot near the station. Mrs. Thurlow was a dark girl with a thin aquiline nose and bangs, who smoked cigarettes and hated Bay Head. She talked about how bored she was and how she shocked the old lady parishioners and Dick thought she was wonderful. She was a great reader of the *Smart Set* and *The Black Cat* and books that were advanced, and poked fun at Edwin's attempts to restore primitive Christianity to the boardwalk, as she put it. Edwin Thurlow would look at her from under the colorless lashes of his pale eyes and whisper meekly, "Hilda, you oughtn't to talk like that"; then he'd turn mildly to Dick and say, "Her bark is worse than her bite, you know." They got to be great friends and Dick took to running around to their house whenever he could get away from the hotel. He took Skinny around a couple of times but Skinny seemed to feel that their talk was too deep for him and would never stay long but would shuffle off after explaining that he had to sell some fudge.

The next summer it was mostly the hope of seeing the Thurlows that made Dick not mind going to work at the Bayview where Mrs. Higgins gave him the job of the roomclerk with an increase of pay on account of his gentlemanly manners. Dick was sixteen and his voice was changing; he had dreams about things with girls and thought a lot about sin and had a secret crush on Spike Culbertson, the yellowhaired captain of his school ballteam. He hated everything about his life, his aunt and the smell of her boarding house, the thought of his father, his mother's flowergarden hats, not having enough money to buy good clothes or go to fashionable summer-resorts like the other fellows did. All kinds of things got him terribly agitated so that it was hard not to show it. The wabble of the wait-resses' hips and breasts while they were serving meals, girls' under-wear in store windows, the smell of the bathhouses and the salty tin-gle of a wet bathingsuit and the tanned skin of fellows and girls in bathingsuits lying out in the sun on the beach.

He'd been writing Edwin and Hilda long letters all winter about anything that came into his head, but when he actually saw them he felt funny and constrained. Hilda was using a new kind of perfume that tickled his nose; even when he was sitting at the table at lunch with them, eating cold ham and potato salad from the delicatessen and talking about the primitive litanies and gregorian music he couldn't help undressing them in his mind, thinking of them in bed naked; he hated the way he felt.

Sunday afternoons Edwin went to Elberon to conduct services in another little summer chapel. Hilda never went and often invited Dick to go out for a walk with her or come to tea. He and Hilda began to have a little world between them that Edwin had nothing to do with, where they only talked about him to poke fun at him. Dick be-gan to see Hilda in his queer horrid dreams. Hilda began to talk about how she and Dick were really brother and sister, how passionless peo-ple who never really wanted anything couldn't understand people like them. Those times Dick didn't get much chance to say anything. He and Hilda would sit on the back stoop in the shade smoking Egyptian Deities until they felt a little sick. Hilda'd say she didn't care whether the damn parishioners saw her or not and talk and talk about how she wanted something to happen in her life, and smart clothes and to travel to foreign countries and to have money to spend and not to have to fuss with the housekeeping and how she felt sometimes she could kill Edwin for his mild calfish manner.

Edwin usually got back on a train that got in at 10:53 and, as Dick had Sunday evenings off from the hotel, he and Hilda would eat supper alone together and then take a walk along the beach. Hilda would take his arm and walk close to him; he'd wonder if she felt him tremble whenever their legs touched.

All week he'd think about those Sunday evenings. Sometimes he'd tell himself that he wouldn't go another time. He'd stay up in his room and read Dumas or go out with fellows he knew; being alone with Hilda like that made him feel too rotten afterwards. Then one moonless night, when they'd walked way down the beach beyond the rosy fires of the picnickers, and were sitting side by side on the sand talking about India's Love Lyrics that Hilda had been reading aloud that afternoon, she suddenly jumped on him and mussed up his hair and stuck her knees into his stomach and began to run her hands over his body under his shirt. She was strong for a girl, but he'd just managed to push her off when he had to grab her by the shoulders and pull her down on top of him. They neither of them said anything but lay there in the sand breathing hard. At last she whispered, "Dick, I mustn't have a baby . . . We can't afford it. . . . That's why Edwin won't sleep with me. Damn it, I want you, Dick. Don't you see how awful it all is?" While she was talking her hands were burning him, moving down across his chest, over his ribs, around the curve of his belly. "Don't, Hilda, don't." There were mosquitoes around their heads. The long hissing invisible wash of the surf came almost to their feet.

That night Dick couldn't go down to the train to meet Edwin the way he usually did. He went back to the Bayview with his knees trembling, and threw himself on his bed in his stuffy little room under the roof. He thought of killing himself but he was afraid of going to hell; he tried to pray, at least to remember the Lord's Prayer. He was terribly scared when he found he couldn't even remember the

Lord's Prayer. Maybe that was the sin against the Holy Ghost they had committed.

The sky was grey and the birds were chirping outside before he got to sleep. All next day, as he sat holloweyed behind the desk, passing on the guests' demands for icewater and towels, answering inquiries about rooms and traintimes, he was turning a poem over in his mind about the scarlet of my sin and the scarlet of thy sin and dark birds above the surging seawaves crying and damned souls passionately sighing. When it was finished he showed the poem to the Thurlows, Edwin wanted to know where he got such morbid ideas, but was glad that faith and the church triumphed in the end. Hilda laughed hysterically and said he was a funny boy but that maybe he'd be a writer someday.

When Skinny came down for a two weeks' vacation to take the place of one of the new bellhops that was sick, Dick talked very big to him about women and sin and about how he was in love with a married woman. Skinny said that wasn't right because there were plenty of easy women around who'd give a feller all the loving he wanted. But when Dick found out that he'd never been with a girl although he was two years older, he put on so many airs about experience and sin, that one night when they'd gone down to the drugstore for a soda, Skinny picked up a couple of girls and they walked down the beach with them. The girls were thirtyfive if they were a day and Dick didn't do anything but tell his girl about his unhappy love affair and how he had to be faithful to his love even though she was being unfaithful to him at the very moment. She said he was too young to take things serious like that and that a girl ought to be ashamed of herself who made a nice boy like him unhappy. "Jez, I'd make a feller happy if I had the chance," she said and burst out crying.

Walking back to the Bayview, Skinny was worried for fear he might have caught something, but Dick said physical things didn't matter and that repentance was the key of redemption. It turned out that Skinny did get sick because later in the summer he wrote Dick that he was paying a doctor five dollars a week to cure him up and that he felt terrible about it. Dick and Hilda went on sinning Sunday evenings when Edwin was conducting services in Elberon and when Dick went back to school that fall he felt very much the man of the world.

In the Christmas vacation he went to stay with the Thurlows in

East Orange where Edwin was the assistant to the rector of the church of St. John, Apostle. There, at tea at the rector's he met Hiram Halsey Cooper, a Jersey City lawyer and politician who was interested in High Church and first editions of Huysmans and who asked Dick to come to see him. When Dick called Mr. Cooper gave him a glass of sherry, showed him first editions of Beardsley and Huysmans and Austin Dobson, sighed about his lost youth and offered him a job in his office as soon as school was over. It turned out that Mr. Cooper's wife, who was dead, had been an Ellsworth and a cousin of Dick's mother's. Dick promised to send him copies of all his poems, and the articles he published in the school paper.

All the week he was with the Thurlows he was trying to get to see Hilda alone, but she managed to avoid him. He'd heard about French letters and wanted to tell her about them, but it wasn't until the last day that Edwin had to go out and make parochial calls. This time it was Dick who was the lover and Hilda who tried to hold him off, but he made her take off her clothes and they laughed and giggled together while they were making love. This time they didn't worry so much about sin and when Edwin came home to supper he asked them what the joke was, they seemed in such a good humor. Dick started telling a lot of cock and bull stories about his Aunt Beatrice and her boarders and they parted at the train in a gale of laughter.

That summer was the Baltimore convention. Mr. Cooper had rented a house there and entertained a great deal. Dick's job was to stay in the outer office and be polite to everybody and take down people's names. He wore a blue serge suit and made a fine impression on everybody with his wavy black hair that Hilda used to tell him was like a raven's wing, his candid blue eyes and his pink and white complexion. What was going on was rather over his head, but he soon discovered what people Mr. Cooper really wanted to see and what people were merely to be kidded along. Then when he and Mr. Cooper found themselves alone, Mr. Copper would get out a bottle of Amontillado and pour them each a glass and sit in a big leather chair rubbing his forehead as if to rub the politics out of his mind and start talking about literature and the nineties and how he wished he was young again. It was understood that he was going to advance Dick the money to go through Harvard with.

Dick had hardly gotten back to school as a senior the next fall when he got a telegram from his mother: Come home at once darling your poor father is dead. He didn't feel sorry but kind of ashamed, afraid of meeting any of the masters or fellows who might ask him questions. At the railway station it seemed as if the train would never come. It was Saturday and there were a couple of fellows in his class at the station. Until the train came he thought of nothing else but dodging them. He sat stiff on his seat in the empty daycoach looking out at the russet October hills, all keyed up for fear somebody would speak to him. It was a relief to hurry out of the Grand Central Station into the crowded New York streets where nobody knew him, where he knew nobody. Crossing on the ferry he felt happy and adventurous. He began to dread getting home and deliberately missed the first train to Trenton. He went into the old dining room of the Pennsylvania Station and ate fried oysters and sweet corn for lunch and ordered a glass of sherry, half afraid the colored waiter wouldn't serve him. He sat there a long time reading *The Smart Set* and drinking the sherry feeling like a man of the world, a traveller on his own, but underneath it all was the memory of that man's trembling white hurt face, the way he'd walked up the area steps that day. The restaurant gradually emptied. The waiter must be thinking it was funny his sitting there that long. He paid his check, and before he wanted to found himself on the train for Trenton.

At Aunt Beatrice's house everything looked and smelt the same. His mother was lying on the bed with the shades down and a handkerchief soaked in eau de cologne on her forehead. She showed him a photograph that he'd sent from Havana, a withered man who looked too small for his palm beach suit and panama hat. He'd been working in the consulate as a clerk and had left a ten thousand dollar life insurance in her favor. While they were talking Henry came in looking worried and sore. The two of them went out in the back yard and smoked cigarettes together. Henry said he was going to take Mother to live with him in Philadelphia, get her away from Aunt Beatrice's nagging and this damn boardinghouse. He wanted Dick to come too and go to the U. of P. Dick said no, he was going to Harvard. Henry asked him how he was going to get the money. Dick said he'd make out all right, he didn't want any of the damned insurance. Henry said he wasn't going to touch it, that was Mother's, and they went back upstairs feeling about ready to sock each other in the jaw. Dick felt better though, he could tell the fellows at school that his father had been consul at Havana and had died of a tropical fever.

That summer Dick worked for Mr. Cooper at $25 a week getting up a prospectus for an art museum he wanted to found in Jersey City and delighted him so by dedicating to him a verse translation of Horace's poem about Maecenas that he worked up with the help of the trot, that Mr. Cooper made him a present of a thousand dollars to take him through college; for the sake of form and so that Dick should feel his responsibilities he put it in the form of a note maturing in five years at four percent interest.

He spent his two weeks' vacation with the Thurlows at Bay Head. He'd hardly been able to wait going down on the train to see how Hilda would be, but everything was different. Edwin didn't have the paperwhite look he used to have; he'd had a call as assistant in a rich church on Long Island where the only thing that worried him was that part of the congregation was low and wouldn't allow chanting or incense. He was comforting himself with the thought that they did allow candles on the altar. Hilda was changed too. Dick was worried to see that she and Edwin held hands during supper. When they got alone she told him that she and Edwin were very happy now and that she was going to have a baby and that bygones must be bygones. Dick stalked up and down and ran his hands through his hair and talked darkly about death and hellonearth and going to the devil as fast as he could but Hilda just laughed and told him not to be silly, that he was a goodlooking attractive boy and would find many nice girls crazy to fall in love with him. Before he left they had a long talk about religion and Dick told them with a bitter stare at Hilda, that he'd lost his faith and only believed in Pan and Bacchus, the old gods of lust and drink. Edwin was quite startled, but Hilda said it was all nonsense and only growing pains. After he'd left he wrote a very obscure poem full of classical references that he labelled, To a Common Prostitute and sent to Hilda, adding a postscript that he was dedicating his life to Beauty and Sin.

Dick had an exam to repeat in Geometry which he'd flunked in the spring and one in Advanced Latin that he was taking for extra credits, so he went up to Cambridge a week before college opened. He sent his trunk and suitcase out by the transfer company from the South Station and went out on the subway. He had on a new grey suit and a new grey felt hat and was afraid of losing the certified cheque he had in his pocket for deposit in the Cambridge bank. The glimpse of redbrick Boston and the state house with its gold dome beyond the slatecolored Charles as the train came out into the air to cross the bridge looked like the places in foreign countries he and Hilda had talked about going to. Kendall Square ... Central Square ... Harvard Square. The train didn't go any further; he had to get out. Something about the sign on the turnstile *Out To The College Yard* sent a chill down his spine. He hadn't been in Cambridge two hours before he discovered that his felt hat ought to have been brown and old instead of new and that getting a room in the Yard had been a grave mistake for a freshman.

Perhaps it was the result of living in the Yard that he got to know all the wrong people, a couple of socialist Jews in first year law, a graduate student from the middlewest who was taking his Ph.D. in Gothic, a Y.M.C.A. addict out from Dorchester who went to chapel every morning. He went out for Freshman rowing but didn't make any of the crews and took to rowing by himself in a wherry three afternoons a week. The fellows he met down at the boathouse were pleasant enough to him, but most of them lived on the Gold Coast or in Beck and he never got much further than hello and solong with them. He went to all the football rallies and smokers and beer nights but he never could get there without one of his Jewish friends or a graduate student so he never met anybody there who was anybody.

One Sunday morning in the spring he ran into Freddy Wigglesworth in the Union just as they were both going in to breakfast; they say down at the same table. Freddy, and old Kent man, was a junior now. He asked Dick what he was doing and who he knew, and appeared horrified by what he heard. "My dear boy," he said, "there's nothing to do now but go out for the *Monthly* or the *Advocate*. ... I don't imagine the *Crime* would be much in your line, would it?"

"I was thinking of taking some of my stuff around, but I hardly had the nerve."

"I wish you'd come around to see me last fall. ... Goodness, we owe it to the old school to get you started right. Didn't anybody tell you that nobody lived in the Yard except seniors?" Freddy shook his head sadly as he drank his coffee.

Afterwards they went around to Dick's room and he read some poems out loud. "Why, I don't think they're so bad," said Freddy Wigglesworth, between puffs at a cigarette. "Pretty purple I'd say, though. ... You get a few of them typed and I'll take them around to

R.G. . . . Meet me at the Union at eight o'clock a week from Monday night and we'll go around to Copey's. . . . Well, so long, I must be going." After he'd gone Dick walked up and down his room, his heart thumping hard. He wanted to talk to somebody, but he was sick of all the people he knew around Cambridge, so he sat down and wrote Hilda and Edwin a long letter with rhyming inserts about how well he was getting on at college.

Monday night finally came around. Already trying to tell himself not to be disappointed if Freddy Wigglesworth forgot about the date, Dick was on his way to the Union a full hour before the time. The cavernous clatter and smell of Mem, the funny stories of the boneheads at his table, and Mr. Kanrich's sweaty bald head bobbing above the brass instruments of the band in the gallery seemed particularly dreary that evening.

There were tulips in the trim Cambridge gardens, and now and then a whiff of lilacs on the wind. Dick's clothes irked him; his legs were heavy as he walked around and around the blocks of yellow frame houses and grass dooryards that he already knew too well. The blood pounding through his veins seemed too fast and too hot to stand. He must get out of Cambridge or go crazy. Of course at eight sharp when he walked slowly up the Union steps Wigglesworth hadn't come yet. Dick went upstairs to the library and picked up a book, but he was too nervous to even read the title. He went downstairs again and stood around in the hall. A fellow who worked next to him in Physics 1 lab. came up and started to talk about something, but Dick could hardly drag out an answer. The fellow gave him a puzzled look and walked off. It was twenty past eight. Of course he wasn't coming, God damn him, he'd been a fool to expect he'd come, a stuck up snob like Wigglesworth wouldn't keep a date with a fellow like him.

Freddy Wigglesworth was standing in front of him, with his hands in his pockets. "Well, shall we Copify?" he was saying.

There was another fellow with him, a dreamy looking boy with fluffy light gold hair and very pale blue eyes. Dick couldn't help staring at him he was so handsome. "This is Blake. He's my younger brother. . . . You're in the same class." Blake Wigglesworth hardly looked at Dick when they shook hands, but his mouth twisted up into a lopsided smile. When they crossed the Yard in the early summer dusk fellows were leaning out the windows yelling "Rinehart O

Rinehart" and grackles were making a racket in the elms, and you could hear the screech of streetcar wheels from Mass. Avenue; but there was a complete hush in the lowceiling room lit with candles where a scrubbylooking little man was reading aloud a story that turned out to be Kipling's "The Man Who Would be King." Everybody sat on the floor and was very intent. Dick decided he was going to be a writer.

Sophomore year Dick and Blake Wigglesworth began to go around together. Dick had a room in Ridgely and Blake was always there. Dick suddenly found he liked college, that the weeks were flying by. The *Advocate* and the *Monthly* each published a poem of his that winter; he and Ned, as he took to calling Blake Wigglesworth, had tea and conversation about books and poets in the afternoons and lit the room with candles. They hardly ever ate at Mem any more, though Dick was signed up there. Dick had no pocketmoney at all once he'd paid for his board and tuition and the rent at Ridgely but Ned had a pretty liberal allowance that went for both. The Wigglesworths were well off; they often invited Dick to have Sunday dinner with them at Nahant. Ned's father was a retired art critic and had a white Vandyke beard; there was an Italian marble fireplace in the drawingroom over which hung a painting of a madonna, two angels and some lilies that the Wigglesworths believed to be by Botticelli, although B.B., out of sheer malice, Mr. Wigglesworth would explain, insisted that it was by Botticini.

Saturday nights Dick and Ned took to eating supper at the Thorndike in Boston and getting a little tight on sparkling nebbiolo. Then they'd go to the theatre or the Old Howard.

The next summer Hiram Halsey Cooper was campaigning for Wilson. In spite of Ned's kidding letters, Dick found himself getting all worked up about the New Freedom, Too Proud to Fight, Neutrality in Mind and Deed, Industrial Harmony between capital and labor, and worked twelve hours a day typing releases, jollying smalltown newspaper editors into giving more space to Mr. Cooper's speeches, branding Privilege, flaying the Interests. It was a letdown to get back to the dying elms of the Yard, lectures that neither advocated anything, nor attacked anything, *The Hill of Dreams* and tea in the afternoons. He'd gotten a scholarship from the English department and he and Ned had a room together in a house on Garden Street. They had quite a bunch of friends who were interested in English and Fine

Arts and things like that, who'd gather in their room in the late afternoon, and sit late in the candlelight and the cigarettesmoke and the incense in front of a bronze Buddha Ned had bought in Chinatown when he was tight once, drinking tea and eating cake and talking. Ned never said anything unless the talk came around to drinking or sailingships; whenever politics or the war or anything like that came up he had a way of closing his eyes and throwing back his head and saying Blahblahblahblah.

Election Day Dick was so excited he cut all his classes. In the afternoon he and Ned took a walk round the North End, and out to the end of T wharf. It was a bitterly raw grey day. They were talking about a plan they had, that they never spoke about before people, of getting hold of a small yawl or ketch after they'd graduated and following the coast down to Florida and the West Indies and then through the Panama Canal and out into the Pacific. Ned had bought a book on navigation and started to study it. That afternoon Ned was sore because Dick couldn't seem to keep his mind on talk about sailing and kept wondering out loud how this state and that state was going to vote. They ate supper grumpily at the Venice, that was crowded for once, of cold scallopini and spaghetti; the service was wretched. As soon as they'd finished one bottle of white orvieto, Ned would order another; they left the restaurant walking stiffly and carefully, leaning against each other a little. Disembodied faces swirled past them against the pinkishgold dark of Hanover Street. They found themselves on the Common in the fringes of the crowd watching the bulletin board on the Boston *Herald* building. "Who's winning? Batter up. . . . Hurray for our side," Ned kept yelling. "Don't you know enough to know it's election night?" a man behind them said out of the corner of his mouth. "Blahblahblahblah," brayed Ned in the man's face.

Dick had to drag him off among the trees to avoid a fight. "We'll certainly be pinched if you go on like this," Dick was whispering earnestly in his ear. "And I want to see the returns. Wilson might be winning."

"Let's go to Frank Locke's and have a drink."

Dick wanted to stay out with the crowd and see the returns; he was excited and didn't want to drink any more. "It means we won't go to war." "Razer have a war," said Ned thickly, "be zo amuzing . . . but war or no war lez have a lil drink on it."

The barkeep at Frank Locke's wouldn't serve them, though he'd often served them before, and they were disgruntedly on their way down Washington Street to another bar when a boy ran past with an extra in four inch black type HUGHES ELECTED. "Hurray," yelled Ned. Dick put his hand over his mouth and they wrestled there in the street while a hostile group of men gathered around them. Dick could hear the flat unfriendly voices, "College boys . . . Harvard men." His hat fell off. Ned let go his hold to let him pick it up. A cop was elbowing his way through toward them. They both straightened up and walked off soberly, their faces red. "It's all blahblahblahblah," whispered Ned under his breath. They walked along toward Scollay Square. Dick was sore.

He didn't like the looks of the crowd around Scollay Square either and wanted to go home to Cambridge, but Ned struck up a conversation with a thuggylooking individual and a sailor whose legs were weaving. "Say, Chub, let's take 'em along to Mother Bly's," said the thuggylooking individual, poking the sailor in the ribs with his elbow. "Take it easy now, feller, take it easy," the sailor kept muttering unsteadily.

"Go anywhere they don't have all this blahblahblahblah," Ned was shouting, seesawing from one foot to the other. "Say, Ned, you're drunk, come along back to Cambridge," Dick whined desperately in his ear and tugged at his arm, "They want to get you drunk and take your money."

"Can't get me drunk, I am drunk . . . blahblahblahblah," whinnied Ned and took the sailor's white cap and put it on his head instead of his own hat.

"Well, do what you damn please, I'm going." Dick let go Ned's arm suddenly and walked away as fast as he could. He walked along across Beacon Hill, his ears ringing, his head hot and thumping. He walked all the way to Cambridge and got to his room shivering and tired, on the edge of crying. He went to bed but he couldn't sleep and lay there all night cold and miserable even after he'd piled the rug on top of the blankets, listening for every sound in the street.

In the morning he got up with a headache and a sour burntout feeling all through him. He was having some coffee and a toasted roll at the counter under the *Lampoon* Building when Ned came in looking fresh and rosy with his mouth all twisted up in a smile, "Well, my young politico, Professor Wilson was elected and we've missed out on the sabre and epaulettes." Dick grunted and went on eating. "I was worried about you," went on Ned airily, "where did you disappear to?" "What do you think I did? I went home and went to bed," snapped Dick. "That Barney turned out to be a very amusing fellow, a boxing instructor, if he didn't have a weak heart he'd be welterweight champion of New England. We ended up in a Turkish Bath . . . a most curious place." Dick felt like smashing him in the face. "I've got a lab period," he said hoarsely and walked out of the lunchcounter.

It was dusk before he went back to Ridgely. There was somebody in the room. It was Ned moving about the room in the blue dusk. "Dick," he began to mumble as soon as the door closed behind him, "never be sore." He stood in the middle of the room with his hands in his pockets swaying. "Never be sore, Dick, at things fellows do when they're drunk. . . . Never be sore at anything fellows do. Be a good fellow and make me a cup of tea." Dick filled the kettle and lit the alcohol flame under it. "Fellow has to do lotta damn fool things, Dick."

"But people like that . . . picking up a sailor in Scollay Square . . . so damn risky," he said weakly.

Ned swung around towards him laughing easily and happily, "And you always told me I was a damn Backbay snob."

Dick didn't answer. He had dropped into the chair beside the table. He wasn't sore any more. He was trying to keep from crying. Ned had lain down on the couch and was lifting first one leg and then the other above his head. Dick sat staring at the blue alcohol flame of the lamp listening to the purring of the teakettle until the last dusk faded to darkness and ashy light from the street began to filter into the room.

That winter Ned was drunk every evening. Dick made the *Monthly* and *The Advocate,* had poems reprinted in *The Literary Digest* and *The Conning Tower,* attended meetings of the Boston Poetry Society, and was invited to dinner by Amy Lowell. He and Ned argued a good deal because Dick was a pacifist and Ned said what the hell he'd join the Navy, it was all a lot of Blah anyway.

In the Easter vacation, after the Armed Ship Bill had passed Dick had a long talk with Mr. Copper who wanted to get him a job in Washington, because he said a boy of his talent oughtn't to endanger his career by joining the army and already there was talk of conscription. Dick blushed becomingly and said he felt it would be against his conscience to help in the war in any way. They talked a long time without getting anywhere about duty to the state and party leader-

ship and highest expediency. In the end Mr. Cooper made him promise not to take any rash step without consulting him. Back in Cambridge everybody was drilling and going to lectures on military
science. Dick was finishing up the four year course in three years and
had to work hard, but nothing in the courses seemed to mean anything any more. He managed to find time to polish up a group of
sonnets called Morituri Te Salutant that he sent to a prize competi-
tion run by *The Literary Digest*. It won the prize but the editors wrote
back that they would prefer a note of hope in the last sestet. Dick put
in the note of hope and sent the hundred dollars to Mother to go to
Atlantic City with. He discovered that if he went into war work he
could get his degree that spring without taking any exams and went
in to Boston one day without saying anything to anybody and signed
up in the volunteer ambulance service.

The night he told Ned that he was going to France they got very
drunk on orvieto wine in their room and talked a great deal about
how it was the fate of Youth and Beauty and Love and Friendship to
be mashed out by an early death, while the old fat pompous fools
would make merry over their carcasses. In the pearly dawn they went
out and sat with a last bottle on one of the old tombstones in the
graveyard, on the corner of Harvard Square. They sat on the cold
tombstone a long time without saying anything, only drinking, and
after each drink threw their heads back and softly bleated in unison
Blahblahblahblah.

Sailing for France on the *Chicago* in early June was like suddenly
having to give up a book he'd been reading and hadn't finished. Ned
and his mother and Mr. Cooper and the literary lady considerably
older than himself he'd slept with several times rather uncomfortably
in her doubledecker apartment on Central Park South, and his poetry
and his pacifist friends and the lights of the Esplanade shakily reflected in the Charles, faded in his mind like paragraphs in a novel
laid by unfinished. He was a little seasick and a little shy of the boat
and the noisy boozing crowd and the longfaced Red Cross women
workers giving each other gooseflesh with stories of spitted Belgian
babies and Canadian officers crucified and elderly nuns raped; inside
he was coiled up tight as an overwound clock with wondering what it
would be like over there.

Bordeaux, the red Garonne, the pastelcolored streets of old tall mansardroofed houses, the sunlight and shadow so delicately blue and yellow, the names of the stations all out of Shakespeare, the yellowbacked novels on the bookstands, the bottles of wine in the buvettes, were like nothing he'd imagined. All the way to Paris the faintly bluegreen fields were spattered scarlet with poppies like the first lines of a poem; the little train jogged along in dactyls; everything seemed to fall into rhyme.

They got to Paris too late to report at the Norton-Harjes office. Dick left his bag in the room assigned him with two other fellows at the Hotel Mont Thabor and walked around the streets. It wasn't dark yet. There was almost no traffic but the boulevards were full of strollers in the blue June dusk. As it got darker women leaned out towards them from behind all the trees, girls' hands clutched their arms, here and there a dirty word in English burst like a thrown egg above the nasal singsong of French. The three of them walked arm in arm, a little scared and very aloof, their ears still ringing from the talk on the dangers of infection with syphilis and gonorrhea a medical officer had given the last night on the boat. They went back to the hotel early.

Ed Schuyler, who knew French on account of having been to boarding school in Switzerland, shook his head as he was cleaning his teeth at the washstand and spluttered out through his toothbrush, "C'est la guerre." "Well, the fist five years 'll be the hardest," said Dick, laughing. Fred Summers was an automobile mechanic from Kansas. He was sitting up in bed in his woolly underwear. "Fellers," he said, solemnly looking from one to the other, "This ain't a war. . . . It's a goddam whorehouse."

In the morning they were up early and hurried through their coffee and rolls and rushed out hot and cold with excitement to the rue François Premier to report. They were told where to get their uniforms and cautioned to keep away from wine and women and told to come back in the afternoon. In the afternoon they were told to come back next morning for their identity cards. The identity cards took another day's waiting around. In between they drove around the Bois in horsecabs, went to see Nôtre Dâme and the Conciérgerie and the Sainte Chapelle and out on the street car to Malmaison. Dick was furbishing up his prepschool French and would sit in the mild sunlight among the shabby white statues in the Tuileries Gardens reading *Les Dieux Ont Soif* and *L'Ile des Pinguins*. He and Ed Schuyler and Fred stuck together and after dining exceeding well every night for fear it might be their last chance at a Paris meal, took a turn around the boulevards in the crowded horizonblue dusk; they'd gotten to the point of talking to the girls now and kidding them along a little. Fred Summers had bought himself a prophylactic kit and a set of smutty postalcards. He said the last night before they left he was going to tear loose. When they got to the front he might get killed and then what? Dick said he liked talking to the girls but that the whole business was too commercial and turned his stomach. Ed Schuyler, who'd been nicknamed Frenchie and was getting very continental in his ways, said that the street girls were too naïve.

The last night before they left was bright moonlight, so the Gothas came over. They were eating in a little restaurant in Montmartre. The cashlady and the waiter made them all go down into the cellar when the sirens started wailing for the second time. There they met up with three youngish women named Suzette, Minette and Annette. When the little honking fireengine went by to announce that the raid was over it was already closing time and they couldn't get any more drinks at the bar; so the girls took them to a closely shuttered house where they were ushered into a big room with livercolored wallpaper that had green roses on it. An old man in a green baize apron brought up champagne and the girls began to sit on knees and ruffle up hair. Summers got the prettiest girl and hauled her right into the alcove where the bed was with a big mirror above the whole length of it. Then he pulled the curtain. Dick found himself stuck with the fattest and oldest one and got disgusted. Her flesh felt like rubber. He gave her ten francs and left.

Hurrying down the black sloping street outside he ran into some Australian officers who gave him a drink of whiskey out of a bottle and took him into another house where they tried to get a show put on, but the madam said the girls were all busy and the Australians were too drunk to pay attention anyway and started to wreck the place. Dick just managed to slip out before the gendarmes came. He was walking in the general direction of the hotel when there was another alerte and he found himself being yanked down into a subway by a lot of Belgians. There was a girl down there who was very pretty and Dick was trying to explain to her that she ought to go to a hotel with him when the man she was with, who was a colonel of Spahis in a red cloak covered with gold braid, came up, his waxed mustaches bristling with fury. Dick explained that it was all a mistake and there were apologies all around and they were all braves alliés. They walked around several blocks looking for some place to have a drink together, but everything was closed, so they parted regretfully at the door of Dick's hotel. He went up to the room in splendid humor; there he found the other two glumly applying argyrol and Metchnikoff paste. Dick made a good tall story out of his adventures. But the other two said he'd been a hell of a poor sport to walk out on a lady and hurt her sensitive feelings. "Fellers," began Fred Summers, looking in each of their faces with his round eyes, "it ain't a war, it's a goddam . . ." He couldn't think of a word for it so Dick turned out the light.

Newsreel XXII

COMING YEAR PROMISES REBIRTH OF RAILROADS

DEBS IS GIVEN 30 YEARS IN PRISON

> *There's a long long trail awinding*
> *Into the land of my dreams*
> *Where the nightingales are singing*
> *And the white moon beams*

future generations will rise up and call those men blessed who have the courage of their convictions, a proper appreciation of the value of human life as contrasted with material gain, and who, imbued with the spirit of brotherhood will lay hold of the great opportunity

BONDS BUY BULLETS BUY BONDS

COPPERS INFLUENCED BY UNCERTAIN OUTLOOK

WOMEN VOTE LIKE VETERAN POLITICIANS

restore time honored meat combination dishes such as hash, goulash, meat pies and liver and bacon. Every German soldier carries a little clothesbrush in his pocket; first thing he does when he lands in a prisoncage is to get out this brush and start cleaning his clothes

EMPLOYER MUST PROVE WORKER IS ESSENTIAL

> *There's a long long night of waiting*
> *Until my dreams all come true*

AGITATORS CAN'T GET AMERICAN PASSPORTS

the two men out of the Transvaal district during the voyage expressed their opinion that the British and American flags expressed nothing and, as far as they were concerned could be sunk to the bottom of the Atlantic, and acknowledged that they were socalled Nationalists, a type much resembling the I.W.W. here. "I have no intention" wrote Hearst, "of meeting Governor Smith either publicly, privately, politically, or socially, as I do not find any satisfaction

KILLS HERSELF AT SEA; CROWDER IN CITY AFTER SLACKERS

> *Oh old Uncle Sam*
> > *He's got the infantree*
> *He's got the cavalree*
> > *He's got artilleree*
> *And then by God we'll all go to Chermanee*
> *God Help Kaiser Bill!*

The Camera Eye (30)

remembering the grey crooked fingers the thick drip of blood off the canvas the bubbling when the lungcases try to breathe the muddy scraps of flesh you put in the ambulance alive and haul out dead

three of us sit in the dry cement fountain of the little garden with the pink walls in Récicourt

No   there must be some way   they taught us Land of the Free   conscience   Give me liberty or give me   Well they give us death

sunny afternoon   through the faint aftersick of mustardgas I smell the box the white roses and the white phlox with a crimson eye   three brownandwhitestriped snails hang with infinite delicacy from a honeysucklebranch overhead   up in the blue a sausageballoon grazes drowsily like a tethered cow   there are drunken wasps clinging to the tooripe pears that fall and squash whenever the near guns spew their heavy shells that go off rumbling through the sky

with a whir that makes you remember walking in the woods and starting a woodcock

welltodo country people carefully built the walls and the little backhouse with the cleanscrubbed seat and the quartermoon in the

door like the backhouse of an old farm at home   carefully planted
the garden and savored the fruit and the flowers and carefully
planned this war

    *to hell with 'em   Patrick Henry in khaki submits to shortarm in-
spection and puts all his pennies in a Liberty Loan   or give me*

arrivés   shrapnel twanging its harps out of tiny powderpuff
clouds invites us delicately to glory   we happy watching the careful
movements of the snails in the afternoon sunlight talking in low
voices about

    *La Libre Belgique   The Junius papers   Areopagitica Milton
went blind for freedom of speech   If you hit the words Democracy
will   understand   even   the   bankers   and   the   clergy-
men   I   you   we   must*

            *When three men hold together
            The kingdoms are less by three*

    we are happy talking in low voices in the afternoon sunlight
about après la guerre that our fingers our blood our lungs our flesh
under the dirty khaki feldgrau bleu horizon might go on sweeten
grow until we fall from the tree ripe like the tooripe pears   the
arrivés know and singing éclats sizzling gas shells   theirs is the
power and the glory

    or give me death

Randolph Bourne

Randolph Bourne
came as an inhabitant of this earth
without the pleasure of choosing his dwelling or his career.

    He was a hunchback, grandson of a congregational minister,
born in 1886 in Bloomfield, New Jersey; there he attended grammar-
school and highschool.

    At the age of seventeen he went to work as secretary to a Morris-
town businessman.

    He worked his way through Columbia working in a pianola re-
cord factory in Newark, working as proofreader, pianotuner, accom-
panist in a vocal studio in Carnegie Hall.

At Columbia he studied with John Dewey,
    got a travelling fellowship that took him to England Paris Rome
Berlin Copenhagen,
    wrote a book on the Gary schools.
    In Europe he heard music, a great deal of Wagner and Sciabine
    and bought himself a black cape.

This little sparrowlike man,
    tiny twisted bit of flesh in a black cape,
    always in pain and ailing,
    put a pebble in his sling
    and hit Goliath square in the forehead with it.

War, he wrote, *is the health of the state.*

Half musician, half educational theorist (weak health and being
poor and twisted in body and on bad terms with his people hadn't
spoiled the world for Randolph Bourne; he was a happy man, loved
die Meistersinger and playing Bach with his long hands that stretched
so easily over the keys and pretty girls and good food and evenings of
talk. When he was dying of pneumonia a friend brought him an egg-
nog; Look at the yellow, it's beautiful, he kept saying as his life ebbed
into delirium and fever. He was a happy man.) Bourne seized with feverish intensity on the ideas then going around at Columbia, he
picked rosy glasses out of the turgid jumble of John Dewey's teaching
through which he saw clear and sharp
    the shining capitol of reformed democracy,
    Wilson's New Freedom;
    but he was too good a mathematician; he had to work the equa-
tions out;
    with the result
    that in the crazy spring of 1917 he began to get unpopular where
his bread was buttered at the New Republic;
    for *New Freedom* read *Conscription*, for *Democracy, Win the War*,
for *Reform, Safeguard the Morgan Loans*
    for *Progress Civilization Education Service*,
    Buy a Liberty Bond,
    Straff the Hun,
    Jail the Objectors.

He resigned from *The New Republic*; only *The Seven Arts* had the nerve to publish his articles against the war. The backers of *The Seven Arts* took their money elsewhere; friends didn't like to be seen with Bourne, his father wrote him begging him not to disgrace the family name. The rainbowtinted future of reformed democracy went pop like a pricked soapbubble.

The liberals scurried to Washington;

some of his friends plead with him to climb up on Schoolmaster Wilson's sharabang; the war was great fought from the swivel chairs of Mr. Creel's bureau in Washington.

He was cartooned, shadowed by the espionage service and the counter-espionage service; taking a walk with two girl friends at Wood's Hole he was arrested, a trunk full of manuscript and letters was stolen from him in Connecticut. (Force to the utmost, thundered Schoolmaster Wilson)

He didn't live to see the big circus of the Peace of Versailles or the purplish normalcy of the Ohio Gang.

Six weeks after the armistice he died planning an essay on the foundations of future radicalism in America.

If any man has a ghost
Bourne has a ghost,
a tiny twisted unscared ghost in a black cloak
hopping along the grimy old brick and brownstone streets still
left in downtown New York,
crying out in a shrill soundless giggle:
War is the health of the state.

Newsreel XXIII

If you dont like your Uncle Sammy
If you dont like the red white and blue

smiles of patriotic Essex County will be concentrated and recorded at Branch Brook Park, Newark, N.J., tomorrow afternoon. Bands will play while a vast throng marches happily to the rhythm of wartime anthems and airs. Mothers of the nation's sons will be there; wives, many of them carrying babes born after their fathers sailed for the front, will occupy a place in Essex County's graphic pageant; relatives and friends of the heroes who are carrying on the message of Freedom will file past a battery of cameras and all will smile a message recording installment no. 7 of Smiles Across the Sea. The hour for these folks to start smiling is 2:30.

MOBS PLUNDER CITIES

NEWSPAPERMAN LEADS THROUGH BARRAGE

it was a pitiful sight at dusk every evening when the whole population evacuated the city, going to sleep in the fields until daylight. Old women and tiny children, cripples drawn in carts or wheeled in barrows men carrying chairs bring those too feeble and old to walk

JERSEY TROOPS TAKE WOMAN GUNNERS

the trouble had its origin with the demand of the marine workers for an eight hour day

If you dont like the stars in Old Glory
Then go back to your land across the sea
To the land from which you came
Whatever be its name

G.O.P. LEADER ACCUSED OF DRAFT FRAUDS

If you dont like the red white and blue
Then dont act like the cur in the story
Dont bite the hand that's feeding you

Eveline Hutchins

Little Eveline and Arget and Lade and Gogo lived on the top floor of a yellowbrick house on the North Shore Drive. Arget and Lade were little Eveline's sisters. Gogo was her little brother littler than Eveline; he had such nice blue eyes but Miss Mathilda had horrid blue eyes. On the floor below was Dr. Hutchins' study where Yourfather mustn't be disturbed, and Dearmother's room where she stayed all morning painting dressed in a lavender smock. On the groundfloor was the drawingroom and the diningroom, where parishioners came and little children must be seen and not heard, and at dinnertime you could smell good things to eat and hear knives and forks and tinkly companyvoices and Yourfather's booming scary voice and when Yourfather's voice was going all the companyvoices were quiet. Your-father was Dr. Hutchins but Our Father art in heaven. When Your-father stood beside the bed at night to see that little girls said their prayers Eveline would close her eyes tightscared. It was only when she'd hopped into bed and snuggled way down so that the covers were right across her nose that she felt cosy.

George was a dear although Adelaide and Margaret teased him and said he was their Assistant like Mr. Blessington was Father's assis-tant. George always caught things first and then they all had them. It was lovely when they had the measles and the mumps all at once. They stayed in bed and had hyacinths in pots and guinea pigs and Dearmother used to come up and read the Jungle Book and do funny pictures and Yourfather would come up and make funny birdbeaks that opened out of paper and tell stories he made up right out of his head and Dearmother said he had said prayers for you children in church and that made them feel fine and grownup.

When they were all up and playing in the nursery George caught something again and had monia on account of getting cold on his chest and Yourfather was every solemn and said not to grieve if God called little brother away. But God brought little George back to them only he was delicate after that and had to wear glasses, and when Dearmother let Eveline help bathe him because Miss Mathilda was having the measles too Eveline noticed he had something funny there where she didn't have anything. She asked Dearmother if it was a mump, but Dearmother scolded her and said she was a vulgar little girl to have looked. "Hush, child, don't ask questions." Eveline got red all over and cried and Adelaide and Margaret wouldn't speak to her for days on account of her being a vulgar little girl.

Summers they all went to Maine with Miss Mathilda in a drawingroom. George and Eveline slept in the upper and Adelaide and Margaret slept in the lower; Miss Mathilda was trainsick and didn't close her eyes all night on the sofa opposite. The train went rumblebump chug chug and the trees and houses ran by, the front ones fast and those way off very slow and at night the engine wailed and the children couldn't make out why the strong nice tall conductor was so nice to Miss Mathilda who was so hateful and trainsick. Maine smelt all woodsy and mother and father were there to meet them and they all put on khaki jumpers and went camping with Father and the guides. It was Eveline who learned to swim quicker than anybody.

Going back to Chicago it would be autumn and Mother loved the lovely autumn foliage that made Miss Mathilda feel so traurig on account of winter coming on, and the frost on the grass beyond the shadows of the cars out of the trainwindow in the morning. At home Sam would be scrubbing the enamel paint and Phoebe and Miss Mathilda would be putting up curtains and the nursery would smell traurig of mothballs. One fall Father started to read aloud a little of the *Ideals of the King* every night after they were all tucked into bed. All that winter Adelaide and Margaret were King Arthur and Queen Whenever. Eveline wanted to be Elaine the Fair, but Adelaide said she couldn't because her hair was mousy and she had a face like a pie, so she had to be the Maiden Evelina.

The Maiden Evelina used to go into Miss Mathilda's room when she was out and look at herself for a long time in the lookingglass. Her hair wasn't mousy, it was quite fair if only they would let her have it curly instead of in pigtails and even if her eyes weren't blue like George's they had little green specks in them. Her forehead was noble. Miss Mathilda caught her staring like that into the mirror one day.

"Look at yourself too much and you'll find you're looking at the devil," said Miss Mathilda in her nasty stiff German way.

When Eveline was twelve years old they moved to a bigger house over on Drexel Boulevard. Adelaide and Margaret went east to boardingschool at New Hope and Mother had to go spend the winter with friends at Santa Fé on account of her health. It was fun eating breakfast every morning with just Dad and George and Miss Mathilda, who was getting elderly and paid more attention to running the house and to reading Sir Gilbert Parker's novels than to the children. Eveline didn't like school but she liked having Dad help her with her Latin evenings and do algebra equations for her. She thought he was wonderful when he preached so kind and good from the pulpit and was proud of being the minister's daughter at Sunday afternoon bibleclass. She thought a great deal about the fatherhood of God and the woman of Samaria and Joseph of Arimathea and Baldur the beautiful and the Brotherhood of Man and the apostle that Jesus loved. That Christmas she took around a lot of baskets to poor people's houses. Poverty was dreadful and the poor were so scary and why didn't God do something about the problems and evils of Chicago, and the conditions, she'd ask her father. He'd smile and say she was too young to worry about those things yet. She called him Dad now and was his Pal.

On her birthday Mother sent her a beautiful illustrated book of the Blessed Damosel by Dante Gabriel Rossetti with colored illustrations from his paintings and those of Burne Jones. She used to say the name Dante Gabriel Rossetti over and over to herself like traurig she loved it so. She started painting and writing little verses about choirs of angels and little poor children at Christmastime. The first picture she did in oils was a portrait of Elaine, the Fair, that she sent her mother for Christmas. Everybody said it showed great talent. When friends of Dad's came to dinner they'd say when they were introduced to her, "So this is the talented one, is it?"

Adelaide and Margaret were pretty scornful about all that when they came home from school. They said the house looked dowdy and nothing had any style to it in Chicago, and wasn't it awful being ministers' daughters, but of course Dad wasn't like an ordinary minister in a white tie, he was a Unitarian and very broad and more like a prominent author or scientist. George was getting to be a sulky little boy with dirty fingernails who never could keep his necktie straight and was always breaking his glasses. Eveline was working on a portrait of him the way he had been when he was little with blue eyes and gamboge curls. She used to cry over her paints she loved him so and little poor children she saw on the street. Everybody said she ought to study art.

It was Adelaide who first met Sally Emerson. One Easter they were going to put on *Aglavaine and Selizette* at the church for charity. Miss Rodgers the French teacher at Dr. Grant's school was going to coach them and said that they ought to ask Mrs. Philip Payne Emerson, who had seen the original production abroad, about the scenery and costumes; and that besides her interest would be invaluable to make it *go*; everything that Sally Emerson was interested in *went*. The Hutchins girls were all excited when Dr. Hutchins called up Mrs. Emerson on the telephone and asked if Adelaide might come over some morning and ask her advice about some amateur theatricals. They'd already sat down to lunch when Adelaide came back, her eyes shining. She wouldn't say much except that Mrs. Philip Payne Emerson knew Matterlink intimately and that she was coming to tea, but kept declaring, "She's the most stylish woman I ever met."

Aglavaine and Selizette didn't turn out quite as the Hutchins girls and Miss Rodgers had hoped, though everybody said the scenery and costumes Eveline designed showed real ability, but the week after the performance, Eveline got a message one morning that Mrs. Emerson had asked her to lunch that day and only her. Adelaide and Margaret were so mad they wouldn't speak to her. She felt pretty shaky when she set off into the icybright dusty day. At the last minute Adelaide had lent her a hat and Margaret her fur neckpiece, so that she wouldn't disgrace them they said. By the time she got to the Emersons' house she was chilled to the bone. She was ushered into a little dressing room with all kinds of brushes and combs and silver jars with powder and even rouge and toiletwaters in purple, green and pink bottles and left to take off her things. When she saw herself in the big mirror she almost screamed she looked so young and piefaced and her dress was so horrid. The only thing that looked any good was the foxfur so she kept that on when she went into the big upstairs lounge with its deep grey carpet soft underfoot and the sunlight pouring in through French windows onto bright colors and the black polished grandpiano. There were big bowls of freezias on every table and yellow and pink French and German books of reproductions of paintings. Even the sootbitten blocks of Chicago houses flattened under the wind and the zero sunlight looked faintly exciting and foreign through the big pattern of the yellow lace curtains. In the rich smell of the freezias there was a little expensive whisp of cigarettesmoke.

Sally Emerson came in smoking a cigarette and said, "Excuse me, my dear," some wretched woman had had her impaled on the telephone like a butterfly on a pin for the last halfhour. They ate lunch at a little table the elderly colored man brought in all set and Eveline was treated just like a grownup woman and a glass of port poured out for her. She only dared take a sip but it was delicious and the lunch was all crispy and creamy with cheese grated on things and she would have eaten a lot if she hadn't felt so shy. Sally Emerson talked about how clever Eveline's costumes had been for the show and said she must keep up her drawing and talked about how there were as many people with artistic ability in Chicago as anywhere in the world and what was lacking was the milieu, the atmosphere my dear, and that the social leaders were all vicious numbskulls and that it was up to the few people who cared about art to stick together and create the rich beautiful milieu they needed, and about Paris, and about Mary Garden, and Debussy. Eveline went home with her head reeling with names and pictures, little snatches out of operas and in her nose the tickling smell of the freezias mixed with toasted cheese and cigarettesmoke. When she got home everything looked so cluttered and bare and ugly she burst out crying and wouldn't answer any of her sisters' questions; that made them madder than ever.

That June after school was over, they all went out to Santa Fé to see her mother. She was awfully depressed out at Santa Fé, the sun was so hot and the eroded hills were so dry and dusty and Mother had gotten so washedout looking and was reading theosophy and talking about God and the beauty of soul of the Indians and Mexicans in a way that made the children uncomfortable. Eveline read a great many books that summer and hated going out. She read Scott and Thackeray and W. J. Locke and Dumas and when she found an old copy of *Trilby* in the house she read it three times running. That started her seeing things in Du Maurier illustrations instead of in knights and ladies.

When she wasn't reading she was lying flat on her back dreaming out long stories about herself and Sally Emerson. She didn't feel well most of the time and would drop into long successions of horrid thoughts about people's bodies that made her feel nauseated. Adelaide and Margaret told her what to do about her trouble every month but she didn't tell them how horrid it made her feel inside. She read the Bible and looked up *uterus* and words like that in encyclopaedias and dictionaries. Then one night she decided she wouldn't stand it any more and went through the medicine chest in the bathroom till she found a bottle marked POISON that had some kind of laudenum compound in it. But she wanted to write a poem before she died, she felt so lovely musically traurig about dying, but she couldn't seem to get the rhymes right and finally fell asleep with her head on the paper. When she woke up it was dawn and she was hunched up over the table by her window, stiff and chilly in her thin nightgown. She slipped into bed shivering. Anyway she promised herself that she'd keep the bottle and kill herself whenever things seemed too filthy and horrid. That made her feel better.

That fall Margaret and Adelaide went to Vassar. Eveline would have liked to go east too but everybody said she was too young though she'd passed most of her college board exams. She stayed in Chicago and went to artclasses and lectures of one sort or another and did churchwork. It was an unhappy winter. Sally Emerson seemed to have forgotten her. The young people around the church were so stuffy and conventional. Eveline got to hate the evenings at Drexel Boulevard, and all the vague Emerson her father talked in his rich preacher's boom. What she liked best was the work she did at Hull House. Eric Egstrom gave drawingclasses there in the evenings and she used to see him sometimes smoking a cigarette in the back passage, leaning against the wall, looking very Norse, she thought, in his grey smock full of bright fresh dabs of paint. She'd sometimes smoke a cigarette with him exchanging a few words about Manet or Claude Monet's innumerable haystacks, all the time feeling uneasy because the conversation wasn't more interesting and clever and afraid somebody would come and find her smoking.

Miss Mathilda said it was bad for a girl to be so dreamy and wanted her to learn to sew.

All Eveline thought about that winter was going to the Art Institute and trying to paint pictures of the Lake Front that would be colored like Whistlers but be rich and full like Millet drawings. Eric didn't love her or else he wouldn't be so friendly and aloof. She'd had her great love; now her life was over and she must devote herself to art. She began to wear her hair screwed up in a knot at the nape of her neck and when her sisters said it was unbecoming she said she wanted it to be unbecoming. It was at the Art Institute that her beautiful friendship with Eleanor Stoddard began. Eveline was wearing her new grey hat that she thought looked like something in a Manet portrait and got to talking with such an interesting girl. When she went home she was so excited she wrote George, who was at boarding school, about it, saying she was the first girl she'd met who really seemed to *feel* painting, that she could *really* talk about things with. And then too she was *really* doing something, and so independent and told things so comically. After all if love was going to be denied her she could build her life on a *beautiful friendship*.

Eveline was getting to like to so much in Chicago, she was really disappointed when the time came to leave for the year's trip abroad that Dr. Hutchins had been planning for his family for so many years. But New York and getting on the *Baltic* and making out the tags for their baggage and the funny smell of the staterooms made her forget all about that. They had a rough trip and the boat rolled a good deal, but they sat at the captain's table and the captain was a jovial Englishman and kept their spirits up so that they hardly missed a meal. They landed in Liverpool with twentythree pieces of baggage but lost the shawlstrap that had the medicinechest in it on the way down to London and had to spend their first morning getting it from the Lost and Found Office at St. Pancras. In London it was very foggy. George and Eveline went to see the Elgin marbles and the Tower of London and ate their lunches in A B C restaurants and had a fine time riding in the tube. Dr. Hutchins only let them stay ten days in Paris and most of that time they were making side trips to see cathedrals. Notre Dame and Rheims and Beauvais and Chartres with their bright glass and their smell of incense in cold stone and the tall grey longfaced statues nearly made Eveline a Catholic. They had a first class compartment reserved all the way to Florence and a hamper with cold chicken in it and many bottles of Saint Galmier mineral water and they made tea on a little alcohol lamp.

That winter it rained a lot and the villa was chilly and the girls squabbled among themselves a good deal and Florence seemed to be full of nothing but old English ladies; still Eveline drew from life and read Gordon Craig. She didn't know any young men and she hated the young Italians with names out of Dante that hung around Adelaide and Margaret under the delusion that they were rich heiresses. On the whole she was glad to go home with mother a little earlier than the others who were going to take a trip to Greece. They sailed from Antwerp on the *Kroonland*. Eveline thought it was the happiest moment of her life when she felt the deck tremble under her feet as the steamer left the dock and the long rumble of the whistle in her ears.

Her mother didn't go down to the diningsaloon the first night out so that Eveline was a little embarrassed going in to table all alone and had sat down and started eating her soup before she noticed that the young man opposite her was an American and goodlooking. He had blue eyes and crisp untidy tow hair. It was too wonderful when he turned out to be from Chicago. His name was Dirk McArthur. He'd been studying a year at Munich, but said he was getting out before they threw him out. He and Eveline got to be friends right away; they owned the boat after that. It was a balmy crossing for April. They played shuffleboard and decktennis and spent a lot of time in the bow watching the sleek Atlantic waves curl and break under the lunge of the ship.

One moonlight night when the moon was plunging westward through scudding spindrift the way the *Kroonland* was plunging through the uneasy swell, they climbed up to the crowsnest. This was an adventure; Eveline didn't want to show she was scared. There was no watch and they were alone a little giddy in the snug canvas socket that smelt a little of sailors' pipes. When Dirk put his arm around her shoulders Eveline's head began to reel. She oughtn't to let him. "Gee, you're a good sport, Eveline," he said in a breathless voice. "I never knew a nice girl who was a good sport before." Without quite meaning to she turned her face towards his. Their cheeks touched and his mouth slid around and kissed her hard on the mouth. She pushed him away with a jerk.

"Hey, you're not trying to throw me overboard, are you?" he said, laughing. "Look, Eveline, won't you give me a little tiny kiss to show there's no hard feeling. There's just you and me tonight on the whole broad Atlantic."

She kissed him scaredly on the chin. "Say, Eveline, I like you so much. You're the swellest girl." She smiled at him and suddenly he was hugging her tight, his legs hard and strong against her legs, his hands spread over her back, his lips trying to open her lips. She got her mouth away from him. "No, no, please don't," she could hear her little creaky voice saying.

"All right, I'm sorry. . . . No more caveman stuff, honest injun, Eveline. But you mustn't forget that you're the most attractive girl on the boat. . . . I mean in the world, you know how a feller feels."

He started down first. Letting herself down through the opening in the bottom of the crowsnest she began to get dizzy. She was falling. His arms tightened around her.

"That's all right, girly, your foot slipped," he said gruffly in her ear. "I've got you."

Her head was swimming, she couldn't seem to make her arms and legs work; she could hear her little moaning voice, "Don't drop me, Dirk, don't drop me."

When they finally got down the ladder to the deck Dirk leaned against the mast and let out a long breath, "Whee . . . you certainly give me a scare, young lady."

"I'm so sorry," she said. "It was silly of me to suddenly get girlish like that. . . . I must have fainted for a minute."

"Gosh, I oughtn't to have taken you up there."

"I'm glad you did," Eveline said; then she found herself blushing and hurried off down the main deck to the first class entrance and the stateroom, where she had made up a story to explain to mother how she'd torn her stocking.

She couldn't sleep that night but lay awake in her bunk listening to the distant rhythm of the engines and the creaking of the ship and the seethe of churned seas that came in through the open porthole. She could still feel the soft brush of his cheek and the sudden tightening muscles of his arms around her shoulder. She knew now she was terribly in love with Dirk and wished he'd propose to her. But next morning she was really flattered when Judge Ganch, a tall whitehaired lawyer from Salt Lake City with a young red face and a breezy manner sat on the end of her deckchair and talked to her by the hour about his early life in the west and his unhappy marriage and politics and Teddy Roosevelt and the progressive party. She'd rather have been with Dirk, but it made her feel pretty and excited to see Dirk walk past with his nose out of joint while she listened to Judge Ganch's stories. She wished the trip would never end.

Back in Chicago she saw a lot of Dirk McArthur. He always kissed her when he brought her home and he held her very tight when he danced with her and sometimes used to hold her hand and tell her what a nice girl she was, but he never would say anything about getting married. Once she met Sally Emerson at a dance she'd gone to with Dirk she had to admit that she wasn't doing any painting, and Sally Emerson looked so disappointed that Eveline felt quite ashamed and started talking fast about Gordon Craig and an exhibition of Matisse she'd seen in Paris. Sally Emerson was just leaving. A young man was waiting to dance with Eveline. Sally Emerson took her hand and said: "But, Eveline, you mustn't forget that we have high hopes of you." And while she was dancing everything that Sally Emerson stood for and how wonderful she used to think her came sweeping through Eveline's head; but driving home with Dirk all these thoughts were dazzled out of her in the glare of his headlights, the strong leap forward of the car on the pickup, the purr of the motor, his arm around her, the great force pressing her against him when they went around curves.

It was a hot night, he drove west through endless identical suburbs out into the prairie. Eveline knew that they ought to go home, everybody was back from Europe now and they'd notice how late she got in, but she didn't say anything. It was only when he stopped the car that she noticed that he was very drunk. He took out a flask and offered her a drink. She shook her head. They'd stopped in front of a white barn. In the reflection of the headlights his shirtfront and his face and his mussed up hair all looked chalky white. "You don't love me, Dirk," she said. "Sure I do, love you better'n anybody . . . except myself . . . that's a trouble with me . . . love myself best." She rubbed her knuckles through his hair, "You're pretty silly, do you know it?" "Ouch," he said. It was starting to rain so he turned the car around and made for Chicago.

Eveline never knew exactly where it was they smashed up, only that she was crawling out from under the seat and that her dress was ruined and she wasn't hurt only the rain was streaking the headlights of the cars that stopped along the road on either side of them. Dirk was sitting on the mudguard of the first car that had stopped. "Are you all right, Eveline?" he called shakily. "It's only my dress," she said. He was bleeding from a gash in his forehead and he was holding his arm against his body as if he were cold. Then it was all nightmare, telephoning Dad, getting Dirk to the hospital, dodging the reporters, calling up Mr. McArthur to get him to set to work to keep it out of the morning papers. It was eight o'clock of a hot spring morning when she got home wearing a raincoat one of the nurses had lent her over her ruined evening dress.

The family was all at breakfast. Nobody said anything. Then Dad got to his feet and came forward, with his napkin in his hand, "My dear, I shan't speak of your behavior now, to say nothing of the pain and mortification you have caused all of us. . . . I can only say it would have served you right if you had sustained serious injuries in such an escapade. Go up and rest if you can." Eveline went upstairs, doublelocked her door and threw herself sobbing on the bed.

As soon as they could, her mother and sisters hurried her off to Santa Fé. It was hot and dusty there and she hated it. She couldn't stop thinking of Dirk. She began telling people she believed in free love and lay for hours on the bed in her room reading Swinburne and Laurence Hope and dreaming Dirk was there. She got so she could almost feel the insistent fingers of his hands spread over the small of her back and his mouth like that night in the crowsnest on the *Kroonland*. It was a kind of relief when she came down with scarlet fever and had to lie in bed for eight weeks in the isolation wing of the hospital. Everybody sent her flowers and she read a lot of books on design and interior decorating and did watercolors.

When she went up to Chicago for Adelaide's wedding in October she had a pale mature look. Eleanor cried out when she kissed her, "My dear, you've grown stunningly handsome." She had one thing on her mind, to see Dirk and get it over with. It was several days before they could arrange to meet because Dad had called him up and forbidden him to come to the house and they had a scene over the telephone. They met in the lobby of The Drake. She could see at a glance that Dirk had been hitting it up since she'd seem him. He was a little drunk now. He had a sheepish boyish look that made her feel like crying. "Well, how's Barney Oldfield?" she said, laughing. "Rotten, gee you look stunning, Eveline. . . . Say *The Follies of 1914* are in town, a big New York hit. . . . I got tickets, do you mind if we go?" "No, it'll be bully."

He ordered everything most expensive he could find on the bill of fare, and champagne. She had something in her throat that kept her from swallowing. She had to say it before he got too drunk.

"Dirk . . . this doesn't sound very ladylike, but like this it's too tiresome. . . . The way you acted last spring I thought you liked me . . . well, how much do you? I want to know?"

Dirk put his glass down and turned red. Then he took a deep breath and said, "Eveline, you know I'm not the marrying kind . . . love 'em and leave 'em 's more like it. I can't help how I am."

"I don't mean I want you to marry me," her voice rose shrilly out of control. She began to giggle. "I don't mean I want to be made an honest woman. Anyway, there's no reason." She was able to laugh more naturally. "Let's forget it. . . . I won't tease you anymore."

"You're a good sport, Eveline. I always knew you were a good sport."

Going down the aisle of the theatre he was so drunk she had to put her hand under his elbow to keep him from staggering. The music and cheap colors and jiggling bodies of the chorus girls all seemed to hit on some raw place inside her, so that everything she saw hurt like sweet on a jumpy tooth. Dirk kept talking all through, "See that girl . . . second from the left on the back row, that's Queenie Frothingham. . . . You understand, Eveline. But I'll tell you one thing, I never made a girl take the first misstep. . . . I haven't got that to reproach myself with." The usher came down and asked him to quit talking so loud, he was spoiling others' enjoyment of the show. He gave her a dollar and said he'd be quiet as a mouse, as a little dumb mouse and suddenly went to sleep.

At the end of the first act Eveline said she had to go home, said the doctor had told her she'd have to have plenty of sleep. He insisted on taking her to her door in a taxicab and then went off to go back to the show and to Queenie. Eveline lay awake all night staring at her window. Next morning she was the first one down to breakfast. When Dad came down she told him she'd have to go to work and asked him to lend her a thousand dollars to start an interior decorating business.

The decorating business she started with Eleanor Stoddard in Chicago didn't make as much money as Eveline had hoped, and Eleanor was rather trying on the whole; but they met such interesting people and went to parties and first nights and openings of art exhibitions, and Sally Emerson saw to it that they were very much in the vanguard of things in Chicago socially. Eleanor kept complaining that the young men Eveline collected were all so poor and certainly more of a liability than an asset to the business. Eveline had great faith in their all making names for themselves, so that when Freddy Seargeant, who'd been such a nuisance and had had to be lent money various times, came through with an actual production of *Tess of the d'Urbervilles* in New York, Eveline felt so triumphant she almost fell in love with him. Freddy was very much in love with her and Eveline couldn't decide what to do about him. He was a dear and she was very fond of him, but she couldn't imagine marrying him and this would be her first love affair and Freddy just didn't seem to carry her off her feet.

What she did like was sitting up late talking to him over Rhine wine and seltzer in the Brevoort café that was full of such interesting people. Eveline would sit there looking at him through the crinkling cigarettesmoke wondering whether she was going to have a love affair. He was a tall thin man of about thirty with some splashes of white in his thick black hair and a long pale face. He had a distinguished rather literary manner, used the broad "a" so that people often thought he was from Boston, one of the Back Bay Seargeants.

One night they got to making plans for themselves and the American theater. If they could get backing they'd start a repertory theatre and do real American plays. He'd be the American Stanislavsky and she'd be the American Lady Gregory, and maybe the American Bakst too. When the café closed she told him to go around by the other staircase and go up to her room. She was excited by the idea of being alone in a hotel room with a young man and thought how shocked Eleanor would be if she knew about it. They smoked cigarettes and talked about the theatre a little distractedly, and at last Freddy put his arm around her waist and kissed her and asked if he could stay all night. She let him kiss her but she could only think of Dirk and told him please not this time, and he was very contrite and begged her with tears in his eyes to forgive him for sullying a beautiful moment. She said she didn't mean that and to come back and have breakfast with her.

After he'd gone she half wished she'd made him stay. Her body tingled all over the way it used to when Dirk put his arms around her and she wanted terribly to know what making love was like. She took a cold bath and went to bed. When she woke up and saw Freddy again she'd decide whether she was in love with him. But the next morning she got a telegram calling her home. Dad was seriously ill with diabetes. Freddy put her on the train. She'd expected that the parting would carry her off her feet, but it didn't somehow.

Dr. Hutchins got better and Eveline took him down to Santa Fé to recuperate. Her mother was sick most of the time too, and as Margaret and Adelaide were both married and George had gotten a job abroad with Hoover's Belgian Relief, it seemed to be up to her to take care of the old people. She spent a dreamy unhappy year in spite of the great skeleton landscape and horsebacktrips and working at watercolors of Mexicans and Indian penitentes. She went around the house ordering meals, attending to housekeeping, irritated by the stupidity of servantgirls, making out laundry lists.

The only man she met there who made her seem alive was José O'Riely. He was a Spaniard in spite of his Irish name, a slender young man with a tobaccocolored face and dark green eyes, who had somehow gotten married to a stout Mexican woman who brought out a new squalling brown infant every nine months. He was a painter and lived by doing odd carpenter jobs and sometimes posing as a model. Eveline got to talk to him one day when he was painting the garage doors and asked him to pose for her. He kept looking at the pastel she was doing of him and telling her it was wretched, until she broke down and cried. He apologized in his stiff English and said she must not be upset, that she had talent and that he'd teach her to draw himself. He took her down to his house, an untidy little shack in the Mexican part of town, where he introduced her to Lola, his wife, who looked at her with scared suspicious black eyes, and showed her his paintings, big retablos painted on plaster that looked like Italian primitives. "You see I paint martires," he said, "but not Christian. I paint the martires of the working class under exploitation. Lola does not understand. She want me to paint rich ladies like you and make plenty money. Which you think is best?" Eveline flushed; she didn't like being classed with the rich ladies. But the pictures thrilled her and she said she would advertise them among her friends; she decided she'd discovered a genius.

O'Riely was grateful and wouldn't take any money for posing or criticizing her paintings after that, instead he sometimes borrowed small sums as a friend. Even before he started making love to her, she decided that this time it must be a real affair. She'd go crazy if something didn't happen to her soon.

The main difficulty was finding somewhere they could go. Her studio was right back of the house and there was the danger that her father or mother or friends coming to call might break in on them any time. Then too Santa Fé was a small place and people were already noticing how often he went to her studio.

One night when the Hutchins' chauffeur was away, they climbed up to his room above the garage. It was pitch black there and smelled of old pipes and soiled clothes. Eveline was terrified to find she'd lost control of her own self; it was like going under ether. He was surprised to find she was a virgin and was very kind and gentle, almost apologetic. But she felt none of the ecstasy she had expected lying in his arms on the chauffeur's bed; it was almost as if it had all happened before. Afterwards they lay on the bed talking a long time in low intimate voices. His manner had changed; he treated her gravely and indulgently, like a child. He said he hated things to be secret and sordid like that, it was brutalizing to them both. He would find a place where they could meet in the open, in the sun and air, not like criminals this way. He wanted to draw her, the beautiful slenderness of her body would be the inspiration of his painting and her lovely little round breasts. Then he looked her over carefully to see if her dress looked mussed and told her to run over to the house and go to bed; and to take precautions if she didn't want to have a baby, though he would be proud to have her bear a child of his, particularly as she was rich enough to support it. The idea horrified her and she felt it was coarse and unfeeling of him to talk about it lightly that way.

They met all that winter a couple of times a week in a little deserted cabin that lay off the trail in the basin of a small stony cañon back of the town. She would ride over and he would walk by a different road. They called it their desert island. Then one day Lola looked in his portfolios and found hundreds of drawings of the same naked girl; she came up to the Hutchins' house shaking and screaming with the hair streaming down her face, looking for Eveline and crying that she was going to kill her. Dr. Hutchins was thunderstruck; but though she was terribly frightened inside, Eveline managed to keep cool and tell her father that she had let O'Riely do drawings of her but that there'd been nothing else between them, and that his wife was a stupid ignorant Mexican and couldn't imagine a man and a woman being alone in a studio together without thinking something disgusting. Although he scolded her for being so imprudent Dad believed her and they managed to keep the whole thing from Mother, but she only managed to see Pepe once more after that. He shrugged his shoulders and said what could he do, he couldn't abandon his wife and children to starve, poor as he was he had to live with them, and a man had to have a woman to work for him and cook; he couldn't live on romantic lifeclasses, he had to eat, and Lola was a good woman but stupid and untidy and had made him promise not to see Eveline again. Eveline turned on her heel and left him before he was through talking. She was glad she had a horse she could jump on and ride away.

The Camera Eye (31)

a matrass covered with something from Vantine's makes a divan in the ladyphotographer's studio   we sit on the divan and on cushions on the floor and the longnecked English actor reads the Song of Songs in rhythms

and the ladyphotographer in breastplates and silk bloomers dances the Song of Songs in rhythms

the little girl in pink is a classical dancer with panpipes but the hennahaired ladyphotographer dances the Song of Songs in rhythms with winking bellybutton and clash of breastplates in more oriental style

stay muh with flahgons comfort muh with ahpples
for I am sick of loeuve

his left hand is under muh head and his rahght hand doth embrace muh

the semiretired actress who lived upstairs let out a yell and then another   Burglars secondstory men   Good god she's being attacked   we men run up the stairs poor woman she's in hysterics   Its the wrong flat   the stairs are full of dicks outside they're backing up the waggon   All right men on one side girls on the other what the hell kind of place is this anyway? Dicks coming in all the windows dicks coming out of the kitchenette

the hennahaired ladyphotographer holds them at bay draped in a portière waving the telephone   Is this Mr. Wickersham's office?   District Attorney   trying experience   a few friends   a little dance recital in the most brutal manner prominent actress upstairs in hysterics   allright officer talk to the District Attorney he'll tell you who I am who our friends are

Dicks slink away waggon jangles to another street the English actor is speaking   Only by the greatest control I kept muh temper the swine I'm terrible when I'm aroused terrible

and the Turkish consul and his friend who were there incog belligerent nation Department of Justice Espionage hunting radicals proGermans slipped quietly out and the two of us ran down the stairs   and walked fast downtown and crossed to Weehawken on the ferry

it was a night of enormous fog through which moved blunderingly the great blind shapes of steamboat sirens from the lower bay

in the bow of the ferry we breathed the rancid riverbreeze talking loud in a shouting laugh

out of the quiet streets of Weehawken incredible slanting viaducts lead up into the fog

Eveline Hutchins

She felt half crazy until she got on the train to go back east. Mother and Dad didn't want her to go, but she showed them a telegram she'd wired Eleanor to send her offering her a high salary in her decorating business. She said it was an opening that wouldn't come again and she had to take it, and anyway, as George was coming home for a vacation, they wouldn't be entirely alone. The night she left she lay awake in her lower berth tremendously happy in the roar of the air and the swift pound of the wheels on the rails. But after St. Louis she began to worry: she'd decided she was pregnant.

She was terribly frightened. The Grand Central Station seemed so immense, so full of blank faces staring at her as she passed following the redcap who carried her bag. She was afraid she'd faint before she got to the taxicab. All the way downtown the jolting of the cab and the jangling throb of the traffic in her ears made her head swim with nausea. At the Brevoort she had some coffee. Ruddy sunlight was coming in the tall windows, the place had a warm restaurant smell;

she began to feel better. She went to the phone and called Eleanor. A French maid answered that Mademoiselle was still asleep, but that she would tell her who had called as soon as she woke up. The she called Freddy who sounded very much excited and said he'd be there as soon as he could get over from Brooklyn.

When she saw Freddy it was just as if she hadn't been away at all. He almost had a backer for the Maya ballet and he was mixed up in a new musical show he wanted Eveline to do costumes for. But he was very gloomy about the prospects of war with Germany, said he was a pacifist and would probably have to go to jail, unless there was a revolution. Eveline told him about her talks with José O'Riely and what a great painter he was, and said she thought maybe she was an anarchist. Freddy looked worried and asked her if she was sure she hadn't fallen in love with him, and she blushed and smiled and said no, and Freddy said she was a hundred times better looking than last year.

They went together to see Eleanor whose house in the east thirties was very elegant and expensivelooking. Eleanor was sitting up in bed answering her mail. Her hair was carefully done and she had on a pink satin dressing gown with lace and ermine on it. They had coffee with her and hot rolls that the Martinique maid had baked herself. Eleanor was delighted to see Eveline and said how well she looked and was full of mysteries about her business and everything. She said she was on the edge of becoming a theatrical producer and spoke about "my financial adviser" this and that, until Eveline didn't know what to think; still it was evident that things were going pretty well with her. Eveline wanted to ask her what she knew about birthcontrol, but she never got around to it, and perhaps it was just as well, as, when they got on the subject of the war they quarrelled at once.

That afternoon Freddy took her to tea with him at the house of a middleaged lady who lived on West 8th Street and was an enthusiastic pacifist. The house was full of people arguing and young men and young women wagging their heads together in important whispers. There she got to talking with a haggardlooking brighteyed young man named Don Stevens. Freddy had to go off to a rehearsal and she stayed there talking to Don Stevens. Then all of a sudden they found that everybody had gone and that they were alone with the hostess, who was a stout puffy eager woman that Eveline decided was just too tiresome. She said Goodnight and left. She had hardly gotten down the front steps to the street when Stevens was after her with his lanky stride dragging his overcoat behind him; "Where are you going to eat supper, Eveline Hutchins?" Eveline said she hadn't thought and before she knew it was eating with him in an Italian restaurant on 3rd Street. He ate a lot of spaghetti very fast and drank a lot of red wine and introduced her to the waiter, whose name was Giovanni. "He's a maximalist and so am I," he said. "This young woman seems to be a philosophic anarchist, but we'll get her over that."

Don Stevens came from South Dakota and had worked on small town papers ever since his highschool days. He'd also worked as a harvest hand back home and been in on several I.W.W. scraps. He showed Eveline his red card with considerable pride. He'd come to New York to work on *The Call,* but had just resigned because they were too damn lilylivered, he said. He also wrote for the *Metropolitan Magazine* and the *Masses,* and spoke at antiwar meetings. He said that there wasn't a chinaman's chance that the U.S. would keep out of the war; the Germans were winning, the working class all over Europe was on the edge of revolt, the revolution in Russia was the beginning of the worldwide social revolution and the bankers knew it and Wilson knew it; the only question was whether the industrial workers in the east and the farmers and casual laborers in the middle west and west would stand for war. The entire press was bought and muzzled. The Morgans had to fight or go bankrupt. "It's the greatest conspiracy in history."

Giovanni and Eveline listened holding their breath. Giovanni occasionally looking nervously around the room to see if any of the customers at the other tables looked like detectives. "God damn it, Giovanni, let's have another bottle of wine," Don would cry out in the middle of a long analysis of Kuhn, Loeb and Company's foreign holdings. Then suddenly he'd turn to Eveline filling up her glass, "Where have you been all these years? I've so needed a lovely girl like you. Let's have a splendid time tonight, may be the last good meal we ever get, we may be in jail or shot against a wall a month from now, isn't that so, Giovanni?"

Giovanni forgot to wait on his other tables and was bawled out by the proprietor. Eveline kept laughing. When Don asked her why, she said she didn't know except that he was so funny.

"But it really is Armageddon, God damn it." Then he shook his head: "What's the use, there never was a woman living who could understand political ideas."

"Of course I can . . . I think it's terrible. I don't know what to do."

"I don't know what to do," he said savagely, "I don't know whether to fight the war and got to jail, or to get a job as a war correspondent and see the goddam mess. If you could rely on anybody to back you up it ud be another thing . . . Oh, hell, let's get out of here."

He charged the cheque, and asked Eveline to lend him half a dollar to leave for Giovanni, said he didn't have a cent in his jeans. She found herself drinking a last glass of wine with him in a chilly littered room up three flights of dirty wooden stairs in Patchin Place. He began to make love to her and when she objected that she'd just known him for seven hours he said that was another stupid bourgeois idea she ought to get rid of. When she asked him about birthcontrol, he sat down beside her and talked for half an hour about what a great woman Margaret Sanger was and how birthcontrol was the greatest single blessing to mankind since the invention of fire. When he started to make love to her again in a businesslike way she laughing and blushing let him take off her clothes. It was three o'clock when feeling weak and guilty and bedraggled she got back to her room at the Brevoort. She took a huge dose of castor oil and went to bed where she lay awake till daylight wondering what she could say to Freddy. She'd had a date to meet him at eleven for a bite of supper after his rehearsal. Her fear of being pregnant had disappeared, like waking up from a nightmare.

That spring was full of plans for shows and decorating houses with Eleanor and Freddy, but nothing came of them, and after a while Eveline couldn't keep her mind on New York, what with war declared, and the streets filling with flags and uniforms, and everybody going patriotic crazy around her and seeing spies and pacifists under every bed. Eleanor was getting herself a job in the Red Cross. Don Stevens had signed up with the Friends' Relief. Freddy announced a new decision every day, but finally said he wouldn't decide what to do till he was called for the draft. Adelaide's husband had a job in Washington in the new Shipping Board. Dad was writing her every few days that Wilson was the greatest president since Lincoln. Some days she felt that she must be losing her mind, people around her seemed so cracked. When she began talking about it to Eleanor, Eleanor smiled in a superior way and said she'd already asked to have her as assistant in her office in Paris.

"Your office in Paris, darling?" Eleanor nodded. "I don't care what kind of work it is, I'll do it gladly," said Eveline. Eleanor sailed one Saturday on the *Rochambeau*, and two weeks later Eveline herself sailed on the *Touraine*.

It was a hazy summer evening. She'd been almost rude cutting short the goodby of Margaret and Adelaide and Margaret's husband Bill who was a Major by this time and teaching sharpshooting out on Long Island, she was so anxious to cut loose from this America she felt was just too tiresome. The boat was two hours late in sailing. The band kept playing *Tipperary* and *Auprès de ma Blonde* and *La Madelon*. There were a great many young men around in various uniforms, all rather drunk. The little French sailors with their red pompons and baby faces yelled back and forth in rolling twangy bordelais. Eveline walked up and down the deck until her feet were tired. It seemed as if the boat would never sail. And Freddy, who had turned up late, kept waving to her from the dock and she was afraid Don Stevens would come and she was sick of all her life in these last years.

She went down to her cabin and started reading Barbusse's *Le Feu* that Don had sent her. She fell asleep, and when the greyhaired skinny woman who was her cabinmate woke her up bustling around, the first thing she felt was the trembling pound of the ship's engines. "Well, you missed dinner," said the greyhaired woman.

Her name was Miss Eliza Felton and she was an illustrator of children's books. She was going to France to drive a truck. At first Eveline thought she was just too tiresome, but as the warm quiet days of the crossing wore on she got to like her. Miss Felton had a great crush on Eveline and was a nuisance, but she was fond of wine and knew a great deal about France, where she'd lived for many years. In fact she'd studied painting at Fontainebleau in the old days of the impressionists. She was bitter against the Huns on account of Rheims and Louvain and the poor little Belgian babies with their hands cut off, but she didn't have much use for any male government, called Wilson a coward, Clemenceau a bully and Lloyd George a sneak. She laughed at the precautions against submarine attack and said she knew the French line was perfectly safe because all the German spies travelled by it. When they landed in Bordeaux she was a great help to Eveline.

They stayed over a day to see the town instead of going up to Paris with all the other Red Cross people and Relief workers. The rows of grey eighteenth century houses were too lovely in the endless rosy summer twilight, and the flowers for sale and the polite people in the shops and the delicate patterns of the ironwork, and the fine dinner they had at the Chapon Fin.

The only trouble with going around with Eliza Felton was that she kept all the men away. They went up to Paris on the day train next day and Eveline could hardly keep from tears at the beauty of the country and the houses and the vines and the tall ranks of poplars. There were little soldiers in pale blue at every station and the elderly and deferential conductor looked like a collegeprofessor. When the train finally slid smoothly through the tunnel and into the Orleans station her throat was so tight she could hardly speak. It was as if she'd never been to Paris before.

"Now where are you going, dear? You see we have to carry our own traps," said Eliza Felton in a businesslike way.

"Well, I suppose I should go to the Red Cross and report."

"Too late for tonight, I can tell you that."

"Well, I might try to call up Eleanor."

"Might as well try to wake the dead as try to use the Paris telephone in wartime . . . what you'd better do, dear, is come with me to a little hotel I know on the Quai and sign up with the Red Cross in the morning; that's what I'm going to do."

"I'd hate to get sent back home."

"They won't know you're here for weeks. . . . I know those dumbbells."

So Eveline waited with their traps while Eliza Felton fetched a little truck. They piled their bags on it and rolled them out of the station and through the empty streets in the last faint mauve of twilight to the hotel. There were very few lights and they were blue and hooded with tin hats so that they couldn't be seen from above. The Seine, the old bridges, and the long bulk of the Louvre opposite looked faint and unreal; it was life walking through a Whistler.

"We must hurry and get something to eat before everything closes up. . . . I'll take you to Adrienne's," said Miss Felton.

They left their bags to be taken up to their rooms at the hôtel du Quai Voltaire and walked fast through a lot of narrow crisscross fastdarkening streets. They ducked into the door of the little restaurant just as some one was starting to pull the heavy iron shutter down, "Tiens, c'est Madmoiselle Elise," cried a woman's voice from the back of the heavily upholstered little room. A short Frenchwoman with a very large head and very large popeyes ran forward and hugged Miss Felton and kissed her a number of times. "This is Miss Hutchins," said Miss Felton in her dry voice. "Verry plised . . . she is so prretty . . . beautiful eyes, hein?" It made Eveline uncomfortable the way the woman looked at her, the way her big powdered face was set like an egg in a cup in the frilly highnecked blouse. She brought out some soup and cold veal and bread, with many apologies on account of not having butter or sugar, complaining in a singsong voice about how severe the police were and how the profiteers were hoarding food and how bad the military situation was. Then she suddenly stopped talking; all their eyes lit at the same moment on the sign on the wall:

MEFIEZ VOUS LES OREILLES ENEMIES
VOUS ECOUTENT

"Enfin c'est la guerre," Adrienne said. She was sitting beside Miss Felton, patting Miss Felton's thin hand with her pudgy hand all covered with paste rings. She had made them coffee. They were drinking little glasses of Cointreau. She leaned over and patted Eveline on the neck. "Faut pas s'en faire, hein?" Then she threw back her head and let out a shrill hysterical laugh. She kept pouring out more little glasses of Cointreau and Miss Felton seemed to be getting a little tipsy. Adrienne kept patting her hand. Eveline felt her own head swimming in the stuffy dark closedup little room. She got to her feet and said she was going back to the hotel, that she had a headache and was sleepy. They tried to coax her to stay but she ducked out under the shutter.

Half the street outside was lit up by moonlight, the other half was in pitchblack shadow. All at once Eveline remembered that she didn't know the way back to the hotel, still she couldn't go into that restaurant again and that woman gave her the horrors, so she walked along fast, keeping in the moonlight, scared of the silence and the few shadowy people and the old gaunt houses with their wide inky doorways. She came out on a boulevard at last where there were men and women strolling, voices and an occasional automobile with blue lights running silently over the asphalt. Suddenly the nightmare scream of a siren started up in the distance, then another and another. Somewhere lost in the sky was a faint humming like a bee, louder then fainter, then louder again. Eveline looked at the people around her. Nobody seemed alarmed or to hurry their strolling pace.

"Les avions . . . les boches . . ." she heard people saying in unstartled tones. She found herself standing at the curb staring up into the milky sky that was fast becoming rayed with searchlights. Next to her was a fatherlylooking French officer with all kinds of lace on his kepi and drooping moustaches. The sky overhead began to sparkle like with mica; it was beautiful and far away like fireworks seen across the lake on the Fourth. Involuntarily she said aloud, "What's that?" "C'est le shrapnel, mademoiselle. It is ourr ahnt-aircrahft cannons," he said carefully in English, and then gave her his arm and offered to take her home. She noticed that he smelt rather strongly of cognac but he was very nice and paternal in his manner and made funny gestures of things coming down on their heads and said they must get under cover. She said please to go to the hôtel du Quai Voltaire as she'd lost her way.

"Ah charmant, charmant," said the elderly French officer. While they had stood there talking everybody else on the street had melted out of sight. Guns were barking in every direction now. They were going down through the narrow streets again, keeping close to the wall. Once her pulled her suddenly into a doorway and something landed whang on the pavement opposite. "It is the fragments of shrapnel, not good," he said, tapping himself on the top of the kepi. He laughed and Eveline laughed and they got along famously. They had come out on the riverbank. It seemed safe for some reason under the thickfoliaged trees. From the door of the hotel he suddenly pointed to the sky, "Look, c'est les fokkers, ils s'en fichent de nous." As he spoke the Boche planes wheeled overhead so that their wings caught the moonlight. For a second they were like seven tiny silver dragonflies, then they'd vanished. At the same moment came the rending snort of a bomb from somewhere across the river. "Permettez, mademoiselle." They went into the pitchblack hall of the hotel and felt their way down into the cellar. As he handed Eveline down the last step of the dusty wooden stairs the officer gravely saluted the mixed group of people in bathrobes or overcoats over their nightclothes who were grouped around a couple of candles. There was a waiter there and the officer tried to order a drink, but the waiter said, "Ah, mon colonel, s'est defendu," and the colonel made a wry face. Eveline sat up on a sort of table. She was so excited looking at the people and listening to the distant snort of the bombs that she hardly noticed that colonel was squeezing her knee a little more than was necessary. The colonel's hands became a problem. When the airraid was over something went by on the street making a funny seesaw noise between the quacking of a duck and a burro's bray. It struck Eveline so funny she laughed and laughed so that the colonel didn't seem to know what to make of her. When she tried to say goodnight to him to go up to her room and get some sleep, he wanted to go up too. She didn't know what to do. He'd been so nice and polite she didn't want to be rude to him, but she couldn't seem to make him understand that she wanted to go to bed and to sleep; he'd answer that so did he. When she tried to explain that she had a friend with her, he asked if the friend was as charming as mademoiselle, in that case he'd be delighted. Eveline's French broke down entirely. She wished to heavens Miss Felton would turn up, she couldn't make the concièrge understand that she wanted the key to her room and that mon colonel wasn't coming up and was ready to break down and cry when a young American in civilian clothes with a red face and a turnedup nose appeared from somewhere out of the shadows and said with a flourish in very bad French, "Monsieur, moi frère de madmosel, can't you see that the little girl is fatiguee and wants to say bon-soir?" He linked his arm in the colonel's and said, "Vive la France. . . . Come up to my room and have a drink." The colonel drew himself up and looked very angry. Without waiting to see what happened Eveline ran up the stairs to her room, rushed in and doublelocked the door.

Newsreel XXIV

it is difficult to realize the colossal scale upon which Europe will have to borrow in order to make good the destruction of war

BAGS 28 HUNS SINGLEHANDED

Peace Talk Beginning To Have Its Effect On Southern Iron Market

LOCAL BOY CAPTURES OFFICER

ONE THIRD WAR ALLOTMENTS FRAUDULENT

There are smiles that make us happy
There are smiles that make us blue

again let us examine into the matter of rates; let it be assumed that the United States is operating fleets aggregating 3000 freight and passenger vessels between U.S. and foreign ports

GANG LEADER SLAIN IN STREET

There are smiles that wipe away the teardrops
Like the sunbeams dry away the dew
There are smiles that have a tender meaning
That the eyes of love alone can see

SOLDIER VOTE CARRIED ELECTION

suppose now that into this delicate medium of economic law there is thrust the controlling factor of an owner of a third of the world's tonnage, who regards with equanimity both profit and loss, who does not count as a factor in the cost of operation the interest on capital investment, who builds vessels whether they may be profitably operated or not and who charges rates commensurate in no certain measure with the laws of supply and demand; how long would it be before the ocean transport of the whole world had broken down completely?

CROWN PRINCE ON THE RUN

But the smiles that fill my heart with sunshine
Are
the
smiles
you
give
to
me

persistent talk of peace is an unsettling factor and the epidemic of influenza has deterred country buyers from visiting the larger centers

The Camera Eye (32)

à quatorze heures precisement the Boche diurnally shelled that bridge with their wellknown precision as to time and place   à quatorze heures precisement Dick Norton with his monocle in his eye lined up his section at a little distance from the bridge to turn it over to the American Red Cross

the Red Cross majors looked pudgy and white under their new uniforms in their shined Sam Browne belts in their shined tight leather puttees   so this was overseas

so this was the front   well   well

Dick Norton adjusted his monocle and began to talk about how as gentlemen volunteers he had signed us up and as gentlemen volunteers he bade us farewell   Wham the first arrivé the smell of almonds the sunday feeling of no traffic on the road not a poilu in sight   Dick Norton adjusted his monocle   the Red Cross majors felt the showering mud   sniffed the lyddite   swift whiff of latrines and of huddled troops

Wham Wham Wham like the Fourth of July   the shellfragments sing our ears ring
　　the bridge is standing and Dick Norton adjusting his monocle is
standing talking at length about gentlemen volunteers and ambulance service and la belle France

　　The empty staffcar is standing
　　but where are the majors taking over command
　　who were to make a speech in the name of the Red Cross? The
slowest and pudgiest and whitest of the majors is still to be seen on
his hands and knees with mud all over his puttees crawling into the
abris and that's the last we saw of the Red Cross Majors
　　and the last we heard of gentlemen
　　or volunteers

The Happy Warrior

　　The Roosevelts had lived for seven righteous generations on
Manhattan Island; they owned a big brick house on 20th Street, an es-
tate up at Dobbs Ferry, lots in the city, a pew in the Dutch Reformed
Church, interests, stocks and bonds, they felt Manhattan was theirs,
they felt America was theirs. Their son,
　　Theodore,
　　was a sickly youngster, suffered from asthma, was very near-
sighted; his hands and feet were so small it was hard for him to learn
to box; his arms were very short;
　　his father was something of a humanitarian, gave Christmas
dinners to newsboys, deplored conditions, slums the East Side, Hell's
Kitchen.
　　Young Theodore had ponies, was encouraged to walk in the
woods, to go camping, was instructed in boxing and fencing (an
American gentleman should know how to defend himself) taught Bible Class, did mission work (an American gentleman should do his
best to uplift those not so fortunately situated);
　　righteousness was his by birth;
　　he had a passion for nature study, for reading about birds and

wild animals, for going hunting; he got to be a good shot in spite of his glasses, a good walker in spite of his tiny feet and short legs, a fair horseman, an aggressive scrapper in spite of his short reach, a crack politician in spite of being the son of one of the owning Dutch families of New York.

In 1876 he went up to Cambridge to study at Harvard, a wealthy talkative erratic young man with sidewhiskers and definite ideas about everything under the sun.

at Harvard he drove around in a dogcart, collected stuffed birds, mounted specimens he'd shot on his trips in the Adirondacks; in spite of not drinking and being somewhat of a christer, having odd ideas about reform and remedying abuses, he made Porcellian and the Dickey and the clubs that were his right as the son of one of the owning Dutch families of New York.

He told his friends he was going to devote his life to social service: *I wish to preach not the doctrine of ignoble ease, but the doctrine of the strenuous life, the life of toil and effort, of labor and strife.*

From the time he was eleven years old he wrote copiously, filled diaries, notebooks, loose leaves with a big impulsive scrawl about everything he did and thought and said;

naturally he studied law.

He married young and went to Switzerland to climb the Matterhorn; his first wife's early death broke him all up. He went out to the badlands of western Dakota to become a rancher on the Little Missouri River;

when he came back to Manhattan he was Teddy, the straight shooter from the west, the elkhunter, the man in the Stetson hat, who'd roped steers, fought a grizzly hand to hand, acted as Deputy Sheriff,

(a Roosevelt has a duty to his country; the duty of a Roosevelt is to uplift those not so fortunately situated, those who have come more recently to our shores)

in the west, Deputy Sheriff Roosevelt felt the white man's burden, helped to arrest malefactors, bad men; service was bully.

All this time he'd been writing, filling the magazines with stories of his hunts and adventures, filling political meetings with his opinions, his denunciations, his pat phrases: Strenuous Life, Realizable

Ideals, Just Government, *when men fear work or fear righteous war, when women fear motherhood, they tremble on the brink of doom, and well it is that they should vanish from the earth, where they are fit subjects for the scorn of all men and women who are themselves strong and brave and highminded.*

T.R. married a wealthy woman and righteously raised a family at Sagamore Hill.

He served a term in the New York Legislature, was appointed by Grover Cleveland to the unremunerative job of Commissioner for Civil Service Reform,

was Reform Police Commissioner of New York, pursued malefactors, stoutly maintained that white was white and black was black,

wrote the Naval History of the War of 1812,

was appointed Assistant Secretary of the Navy,

and when the *Maine* blew up resigned to lead the Rough Riders, Lieutenant-Colonel.

This was the Rubicon, the Fight, the Old Glory, the Just Cause. The American public was not kept in ignorance of the Colonel's bravery when the bullets sang, how he charged without his men up San Juan Hill and had to go back to fetch them, how he shot a running Spaniard in the tail.

It was too bad that the regulars had gotten up San Juan Hill first from the other side, that there was no need to get up San Juan Hill at all. Santiago was surrendered. It was a successful campaign. T.R. charged up San Juan Hill into the governorship of the Empire State;

but after the fighting, volunteers warcorrespondents magazinewriters began to want to go home;

it wasn't bully huddling under puptents in the tropical rain or scorching in the morning sun of the seared Cuban hills with malaria mowing them down and dysentery and always yellowjack to be afraid of.

T.R. got up a round robin to the President and asked for the amateur warriors to be sent home and leave the dirtywork to the regulars

who were digging trenches and shovelling crap and fighting malaria and dysentery and yellowjack

to make Cuba cosy for the Sugar Trust

and the National City Bank.

*   *   *

When he landed at home, one of his first interviews was with Lemuel Quigg, emissary of Boss Platt who had the votes of upstate New York sewed into the lining of his vest;

he saw Boss Platt too, but he forgot about that afterwards. Things were bully. He wrote a life of Oliver Cromwell whom people said he resembled. As Governor he doublecrossed the Platt machine (a righteous man may have a short memory); Boss Platt thought he'd shelved him by nominating him for the Vice-Presidency in 1900;

Czolgocz made him president.

T.R. drove like a fiend in a buckboard over the muddy roads through the driving rain from Mt. Marcy in the Adirondacks to catch the train to Buffalo where McKinley was dying.

As President

he moved Sagamore Hill, the healthy happy normal American home, to the White House, took foreign diplomats and fat armyofficers out walking in Rock Creek Park where he led them a terrible dance through brambles, hopping across the creek on steppingstones, wading the fords, scrambling up the shaly banks,

and shook the Big Stick at malefactors of great wealth.

Things were bully.

He engineered the Panama revolution under the shadow of which took place the famous hocuspocus of juggling the old and new canal companies by which forty million dollars vanished into the pockets of the international bankers,

but Old Glory floated over the Canal Zone

and the canal was cut through.

He busted a few trusts,

had Booker Washington to lunch at the White House,

and urged the conservation of wild life.

He got the Nobel Peace Prize for patching up the Peace of Portsmouth that ended the Russo-Japanese war,

and sent the Atlantic Fleet round the world for everybody to see that America was a firstclass power. He left the presidency to Taft after his second term leaving to that elephantine lawyer the congenial task of pouring judicial oil on the hurt feelings of the moneymasters

and went to Africa to hunt big game.

Big game hunting was bully.

Every time a lion or an elephant went crashing down into the jungle underbrush, under the impact of a wellplaced mushroom bullet

the papers lit up with headlines;

when he talked with the Kaiser on horseback

the world was not ignorant of what he said, or when he lectured the Nationalists at Cairo telling them that this was a white man's world.

He went to Brazil where he travelled through the Matto Grosso in a dugout over waters infested with the tiny maneating fish, the piranha,

shot tapirs,

jaguars,

specimens of the whitelipped peccary.

He ran the rapids of the River of Doubt

down to the Amazon frontiers where he arrived sick, an infected abscess in his leg, stretched out under an awning in a dugout with a tame trumpeterbird beside him.

Back in the States he fought his last fight when he came out for the republican nomination in 1912 a progressive, champion of the Square Deal, crusader for the Plain People; the Bull Moose bolted out from under the Taft steamroller and formed the Progressive Party for righteousness' sake at the Chicago Colosseum while the delegates who were going to restore democratic government rocked with tears in their eyes as they sang

> On   ward Christian so   old   gers
> March   ing as to war

Perhaps the River of Doubt had been too much for a man of his age; perhaps things weren't so bully any more; T.R. lost his voice during the triangular campaign. In Duluth a maniac shot him in the chest, his life was saved only by the thick bundle of manuscript of the speech he was going to deliver. T.R. delivered the speech with the bullet still in him, heard the scared applause, felt the plain people praying for his recovery but the spell was broken somehow.

The Democrats swept in, the world war drowned out the righteous voice of the Happy Warrior in the roar of exploding lyddite.

Wilson wouldn't let T.R. lead a division, this was no amateur's

war (perhaps the regulars remembered the round robin at Santiago).
All he could do was write magazine articles against the Huns, send his
sons; Quentin was killed.

It wasn't the bully amateur's world any more. Nobody knew
that on armistice day, Theodore Roosevelt, happy amateur warrior
with the grinning teeth, the shaking forefinger, naturalist, explorer,
magazinewriter, Sundayschool teacher, cowpuncher, moralist, politician, righteous orator with a short memory, fond of denouncing liars
(the Ananias Club) and having pillowfights with his children, was
taken to the Roosevelt hospital gravely ill with inflammatory rheu-
matism.

Things weren't bully any more;

T.R. had grit;

he bore the pain, the obscurity, the sense of being forgotten as he
had borne the grilling portages when he was exploring the River of
Doubt, the heat, the fetid jungle mud, the infected abscess in his leg,

and died quietly in his sleep

at Sagamore Hill

on January 6, 1919

and left on the shoulders of his sons

the white man's burden.

The Camera Eye (33)

11,000 registered harlots said the Red Cross Publicity Man infest
the streets of Marseilles

the Ford stalled three times in the Rue de Rivoli   in Fontainebleau we had our café au lait in bed   the Forest was so achingly red
yellow novemberbrown under the tiny lavender rain   beyond the
road climbed through dovecolored hills   the air smelt of apples

Nevers (Dumas nom de dieu) Athos Porthos and d'Artagnan
had ordered a bisque at the inn   we wound down slowly into red
Macon that smelt of wineless and the vintage   fais ce que
voudras   saute Bourgignon in the Rhone valley the first straw-
colored sunlight streaked the white road with shadows of skeleton
poplars   at every stop we drank wine strong as beefsteaks rich
as the palace of François Premier bouquet of the last sleetlashed

roses   we didn't cross the river to Lyon where Jean-Jacques suffered from greensickness as a youngster   the landscapes of Provence were all out of the Gallic Wars the towns were dictionaries of latin roots Orange Tarascon Arles where Van Gogh cut off his ears   the convoy became less of a conducted tour   we stopped to play craps in the estaminets   boys we're going south   to drink the red wine the popes loved best   to eat fat meals in oliveoil and garlic   bound south   cêpes provençale the north wind was shrilling over the plains of the Camargue hustling us into Marseilles where the eleven thousand were dandling themselves in the fogged mirrors of the promenoir at the Apollo

oysters and vin de Cassis petite fille tellement brune tête de lune qui amait les veentair sports   in the end they were all slot machines undressed as Phocean figurines posted with their legs apart around the scummy edges of the oldest port

the Riviera was a letdown but there was a candy-colored church with a pointed steeple on every hill beyond San Remo   Porto Maurizio blue seltzerbottles standing in the cinzanocolored sunlight beside a glass of VERMOUTH TORINO   Savona was set for the Merchant of Venice painted by Veronese Ponte Decimo   in Ponte Decimo ambulances were parked in a moonlit square of bleak stone workingpeople's houses   hoarfrost covered everything   in the little bar the Successful Story Writer taught us to drink cognac and maraschino half and half

havanuzzerone

it turned out he was not writing what he felt he wanted to be writing What can you tell them at home about the war? it turned out he was not wanting what he wrote he wanted to be feeling   cognac and maraschino   was no longer young   (It made us damn sore we greedy for what we felt we wanted tell 'em all they lied see new towns go to Genoa)   havanuzzerone?   it turned out that he wished he was a naked brown shepherd boy sitting on a hillside playing a flute in the sunlight

going to Genoa was easy enough the streetcar went there Genoa the new town we'd never seen full of marble doges and breakneck stairs marble lions in the moonlight   Genoa   was the ancient ducal city burning? all the marble palaces and the square stone houses and the campaniles topping hills had one marble wall on fire

bonfire under the moon

the bars were full of Britishers overdressed civilians strolling under porticoes outside the harbor under the Genoa moon the sea was on fire the member of His Majesty's Intelligence Service said it was a Yankee tanker had struck a mine? been torpedoed? why don't they scuttle her?

Genoa   eyes   flared   with   the   light   of   the   burning tanker   Genoa   what are you looking for? the flare in the blood under the moon down the midnight streets in boys' and girls' face   Genoa   eyes the question in their eyes

through the crumbling stone courts under the Genoa moon up and down the breakneck stairs eyes on fire under the moon round the next corner full in your face the flare of the bonfire on the sea

11,000 registered harlots said the Red Cross Publicity Man infest the streets of Marseilles

Joe Williams

It was a lousy trip. Joe was worried all the time about Del and about not making good and the deckcrew was a bunch of soreheads. The engines kept breaking down. The *Higginbotham* was built like a cheesebox and so slow there were days when they didn't make more'n thirty or forty miles against moderate head winds. The only good times he had was taking boxing lessons from the second engineer, a fellow named Glen Hardwick. He was a little wiry guy, who was a pretty good amateur boxer, though he must have been forty years old. By the time they got to Bordeaux Joe was able to give him a good workout. He was heavier and had a better reach and Glen said he'd a straight natural right that would take him far as a lightweight.

In Bordeaux the first port official that came on board tried to kiss Cap'n Perry on both cheeks. President Wilson had just declared war on Germany. All over the town nothing was too good for Les Americains. Evenings when they were off Joe and Glen Hardwick cruised around together. The Bordeaux girls were damn pretty. They met up with a couple one afternoon in the public garden that weren't hookers at all. They were nicely dressed and looked like they came of good families, what the hell it was wartime. At first Joe thought he ought to lay off that stuff now that he was married, but hell, hadn't

Del held out on him. What did she think he was, a plaster saint? They ended by going to a little hotel the girls knew and eating supper and drinking a beaucoup wine and champagne and having a big party. Joe had never had such a good time with a girl in his life. His girl's name was Marceline and when they woke up in the morning the help at the hotel brought them in coffee and rolls and they ate breakfast, both of 'em sitting up in bed and Joe's French began to pick up and he learned how to say C'est la guerre and On les aura and Je m'en fiche and Marceline said she'd always be his sweetie when he was in Bordeaux and called him petit lapin.

They only stayed in Bordeaux the four days it took 'em to wait their turn to go up to the dock and unload, but they drank wine and cognac all the time and the food was swell and nobody could do enough for them on account of America having come into the war and it was a great old four days.

On the trip home the *Higginbotham* sprung leaks so bad the old man stopped worrying about submarines altogether. It was nip and tuck if they'd make Halifax. The ship was light and rolled like a log so that even with fiddles on they couldn't keep dishes on the messtable. One dirty night of driving fog somewhere south of Cape Race, Joe with his chin in his peajacket was taking a turn on the deck amidship when he was suddenly thrown flat. They never knew what hit 'em, a mine or a torpedo. It was only that the boats were in darn good order and the sea was smooth that they got off at all. As it was the four boats got separated. The *Higginbotham* faded into the fog and they never saw her sink, though the last they could make out her maindeck was awash.

They were cold and wet. In Joe's boat nobody said much. The men at the oars had to work hard to keep her bow into the little chop that came up. Each sea a little bigger than the others drenched them with spray. They had on wool sweaters and lifepreservers but the cold seeped through. At last the fog greyed a little and it was day. Joe's boat and the captain's boat managed to keep together until late that afternoon they were picked up by a big fishing schooner, a banker bound for Boston.

When they were picked up old Cap'n Perry was in a bad way. The master of the fishing schooner did everything he could for him, but he was unconscious when they reached Boston four days later and died on the way to the hospital. The doctors said it was pneumonia.

Next morning Joe and the mate went to the office of the agent of Perkins and Ellerman, the owners, to see about getting themselves and the crew paid off. There was some kind of damn monkeydoodle business about the vessel's having changed owners in midAtlantic, a man named Rosenberg had bought her on a speculation and now he couldn't be found and the Chase National Bank was claiming owner-ship and the underwriters were raising cain. The agent said he was sure they'd be paid all right, because Rosenberg had posted bond, but it would be some time. "And what the hell do they expect us to do all that time, eat grass?" The clerk said he was sorry but they'd have to take it up direct with Mr. Rosenberg.

Joe and the first mate stood side by side on the curb outside the of-fice and cursed for a while, then the mate went over to South Boston to break the news to the chief who lived there.

It was a warm June afternoon. Joe started to go around the ship-ping offices to see what he could do in the way of a berth. He got tired of that and went and sat on a bench on the Common, staring at the sparrows and the gobs loafing around and the shop girls coming home from work, their little heels clattering on the asphalt paths.

Joe hung around Boston broke for a couple of weeks. The Salvation Army took care of the survivors, serving 'em beans and watery soup and a lot of hymns off key that didn't appeal to Joe the way he felt just then. He was crazy to get enough jack to go to Norfolk and see Del. He wrote her every day but the letters he got back to General Delivery seemed kinder cool. She was worried about the rent and wanted some spring clothes and was afraid they wouldn't like it at the office if they found out about her being married.

Joe sat on the benches on the Common and roamed around among the flowerbeds in the Public Garden, and called regularly at the agent's office to ask about a berth, but finally he got sick of hang-ing around and went down and signed on as quartermaster, on a United Fruit boat, the *Callao*. He thought it ud be a short run and by the time he got back in a couple of weeks he'd be able to get his money.

On the home trip they had to wait several days anchored outside in the roads at Roseau in Dominica, for the limes they were going to load to be crated. Everybody was sore at the port authorities, a lot of damn British niggers, on account of the quarantine and the limes not being ready and how slow the lighters were coming off from the shore. The last night in port Joe and Larry, one of the other quarter-masters, got kidding some young coons in a bumboat that had been selling fruit and liquor to the crew under the stern; first thing they knew they'd offered 'em a dollar each to take 'em ashore and land 'em down the beach so's the officers wouldn't see them. The town smelt of niggers. There were no lights in the streets. A little coalblack young-ster ran up and asked did they want some mountain chicken. "I guess that means wild women, sure," said Joe. "All bets are off tonight." The little dinge took 'em into a bar kept by a stout mulatto woman and said something to her in the island lingo they couldn't understand, and she said they'd have to wait a few minutes and they sat down and had a couple of drinks of corn and oil. "I guess she must be the madam," said Larry. "If they ain't pretty good lookers they can go to hell for all I care. I'm not much on the dark meat." From out back came a sound of sizzling and a smell of something frying. "Dod gast it, I could eat something," said Joe. "Say, boy, tell her we want something to eat." "By and by you eat mountain chicken." "What the hell?" They finished their drinks just as the woman came back with a big platter of something fried up. "What's that?" asked Joe. "That's mountain chicken, mister; that's how we call froglegs down here but they ain't like the frogs you all has in the states. I been in the states and I know. We wouldn't eat them here. These here is clean frogs just like chicken. You'll find it real good if you eat it." They roared. "Jesus, the drinks are on us," said Larry, wiping the tears out of his eyes.

Then they thought they'd go pick up some girls. They saw a couple leaving the house where the music was and followed 'em down the dark street. They started to talk to 'em and the girls showed their teeth and wriggled in their clothes and giggled. But three or four nigger men came up sore as hell and began talking in the local lingo. "Jez, Larry, we'd better watch our step," said Joe through his teeth. "These bozos got razors." They were in the middle of a yelling bunch of big black men when they heard an American voice behind them, "Don't say another word, boys, I'll handle this." A small man in khaki riding breeches and a panama hat was pushing his way through the crowd talking in the island lingo all the time. He was a little man with a gray triangular face tufted with a goatee. "My name's Henderson, DeBuque Henderson of Bridgeport, Connecticut." He shook hands with both of them.

"Well, what's the trouble, boys? It's all right now, everybody knows me here. You have to be careful on this island, boys, they're touchy, these people, very touchy. . . . You boys better come along with me and have a drink. . . ." He took them each by the arm and walked them hurriedly up the street. "Well, I was young once . . . I'm still young . . . sure, had to see the island . . . damn right too, the most interesting island in the whole Caribbean only lonely . . . never see a white face."

When they got to his house he walked them through a big white-washed room onto a terrace that smelt of vanilla flowers. They could see the town underneath with its few lights, the dark hills, the white hull of the *Callao* with the lighters around her lit up by the working lights. At intervals the rattle of winches came up to them and a crazy jigtune from somewhere.

The old feller poured them each a glass of rum; then another. He had a parrot on a perch that kept screeching. The landbreeze had come up full of heavy flowersmells off the mountains and blew the old feller's stringy white hair in his eyes. He pointed at the *Callao* all lit up with its ring of lighters. "United Fruit . . . United Thieves Company . . . it's a monopoly . . . if you won't take their prices they let your limes rot on the wharf; it's a monopoly. You boys are working for a bunch of thieves, but I know it ain't your fault. Here's lookin' at you."

Before they knew it Larry and Joe were singing. The old man was talking about cotton spinning machinery and canecrushers and pouring out drinks from a rumbottle. They were pretty goddam drunk. They didn't know how they got aboard. Joe remembered the dark focastle and the sound of snoring from the bunks spinning around, then sleep hitting him like a sandbag and the sweet, sicky taste of rum in his mouth.

A couple of days later Joe came down with a fever and horrible pains in his joints. He was out of his head when they put him ashore at St. Thomas's. It was dengue and he was sick for two months before he had the strength even to write Del to tell her where he was. The hospital orderly told him he'd been out of his head five days and they'd given him up for a goner. The doctors had been sore as hell about it because this was post hospital; after all he was a white man and unconscious and they couldn't very well feed him to the sharks.

It was July before Joe was well enough to walk around the steep little coraldust streets of the town. He had to leave the hospital and would have been in a bad way if one of the cooks at the marina barracks hadn't looked out for him and found him a flop in an unused section of the building. It was hot and there was never a cloud in the sky and he got pretty sick of looking at the niggers and the bare hills and the blue shutin harbor. He spent a lot of time sitting out on the old coalwharf in the shade of a piece of corrugated iron roof looking through the planking at the clear deep bluegreen water, watching shoals of snappers feeding around the piles. He got to thinking about Del and that French girl in Bordeaux and the war and how the United Fruit was a bunch of thieves and then the thoughts would go round and round in his head like the little silver and blue and yellow fish round the swaying weeds on the piles and he'd find he'd dropped off to sleep.

When a northbound fruitsteamer came into the harbor he got hold of one of the officers on the wharf and told him his sad story. They gave him passage up to New York. First thing he did was try to get hold of Janey; maybe if she thought he ought to, he'd give up this dog's life and take a steady job ashore. He called up the J. Ward Moorehouse advertising office where she worked but the girl at the other end of the line told him she was the boss's secretary and was out west on business.

He went over and got a flop at Mrs. Olsen's in Redhook. Everybody over there was talking about the draft and how they rounded you up for a slacker if they picked you up on the street without a registration card. And sure enough, just as Joe was stepping out of the subway at Wall Street one morning a cop came up to him and asked him for his card. Joe said he was a merchant seaman and had just got back from a trip and hadn't had time to register yet and that he was exempt, but the cop said he'd have to tell that to the judge. They were quite a bunch being marched down Broadway; smart guys in the crowd of clerks and counterjumpers along the sidewalks yelled "Slackers" at them and the girls hissed and booed.

In the Custom House they were herded into some of the basement rooms. It was a hot August day. Joe elbowed his way through the sweating, grumbling crowd towards the window. Most of them were foreigners, there were longshoremen and waterfront loafers; a lot of the group were talking big but Joe remembered the navy and kept his mouth shut and listened. He was in there all day. The cops wouldn't let anybody telephone and there was only one toilet and they had to go to that under guard. Joe felt pretty weak on his pins, he hadn't gotten over the effect of that dengue yet. He was about ready to pass out when he saw a face he knew. Damned if it wasn't Glen Hardwick.

Glen had been picked up by a Britisher and taken into Halifax. He'd signed as second on the *Chemang*, taking out mules to Bordeaux and a general cargo to Genoa, going to be armed with a threeinch gun and navy gunners, Joe ought to come along. "Jesus, do you think I could get aboard her?" Joe asked. "Sure, they're crazy for navigation officers; they'd take you on even without a ticket." Bordeaux sounded pretty good, remember the girlfriends there? They doped out that when Glen got out he'd phone Mrs. Olsen to bring over Joe's license that was in a cigarbox at the head of his bed. When they finally were taken up to the desk to be questioned the guy let Glen go right away and said Joe could go as soon as they got his license over but that they must register at once even if they were exempt from the draft. "After all, you boys ought to remember that there's a war on," said the inspector at the desk. "Well, we sure ought to know," said Joe.

Mrs. Olsen came over all in a flurry with Joe's papers and Joe hustled over to the office in East New York and they took him on as bosun. The skipper was Ben Tarbell who'd been first mate on the *Higginbotham*. Joe wanted to go down to Norfolk to see Del, but hell this was no time to stay ashore. What he did was to send her fifty bucks he borrowed from Glen. He didn't have time to worry about it anyway because they sailed the next day with sealed orders as to where to meet the convoy.

It wasn't so bad steaming in convoy. The navy officers on the destroyers and the *Salem* that was in command gave the orders, but the merchant captains kidded back and forth with wigwag signals. It was some sight to see the Atlantic Ocean full of long strings of freighters all blotched up with gray and white watermarkings like barberpoles by the camouflage artists. There were old tubs in that convoy that a man wouldn't have trusted himself in to cross to Staten Island in peacetime and one of the new wooden Shipping Board boats leaked so bad, jerrybuilt out of new wood — somebody musta been making money — that she had to be abandoned and scuttled half way across.

Joe and Glen smoked their pipes together in Glen's cabin and chewed the fat a good deal. They decided that everything ashore was the bunk and the only place for them was blue water. Joe got damn fed up with bawling out the bunch of scum he had for a crew. Once they got in the zone, all the ships started steering a zigzag course and everybody began to get white around the gills. Joe never cussed so much in his life. There was a false alarm of submarines every few hours and seaplanes dropping depth bombs and excited gun crews firing at old barrels, bunches of seaweed, dazzle in the water. Steaming into the Gironde at night with the searchlights crisscrossing and the blinker signals and the patrolboats scooting around, they sure felt good.

It was a relief to get the dirty trampling mules off the ship and their stench out of everything, and to get rid of the yelling and cussing of the hostlers. Glen and Joe only got ashore for a few hours and couldn't find Marceline and Loulou. The Garonne was beginning to look like the Delaware with all the new Americanbuilt steel and concrete piers. Going out they had to anchor several hours to repair a leaky steampipe and saw a patrol boat go by towing five ships' boats crowded to the gunnels, so they guessed the fritzes must be pretty busy outside.

No convoy this time. They slipped out in the middle of a foggy night. When one of the deckhands came up out of the focastle with a cigarette in the corner of his mouth, the mate knocked him flat and said he'd have him arrested when he got back home for a damn German spy. They coasted Spain as far as Finisterre. The skipper had just changed the course to southerly when they saw a sure enough periscope astern. The skipper grabbed the wheel himself and yelled down the tube to the engine room to give him everything they'd got, that wasn't much to be sure, and the gun crew started blazing away.

The periscope disappeared but a couple of hours later they overhauled a tubby kind of ketch, must be a Spanish fishingboat, that was heading for the shore, for Vigo probably, scudding along wing and wing in the half a gale that was blowing up west northwest. They'd no sooner crossed the wake of the ketch than there was a thud that shook the ship and a column of water shot up that drenched them all on the bridge. Everything worked like clockwork. No. 1 was the only compartment flooded. As luck would have it, the crew was all out of the focastle standing on deck amidships in their life preservers. The *Chemang* settled a little by the bow, that was all. The gunners were certain it was a mine dropped by the old black ketch that had crossed their bow and let them have a couple of shots, but the ship was rolling so in the heavy sea that the shots went wild. Anyway, the ketch went out of sight behind the island that blocks the mouth of the roadstead of Vigo. The *Chemang* crawled on in under one bell.

By the time they got into the channel opposite the town of Vigo, the water was gaining on the pumps in No. 2, and there was four feet of water in the engineroom. They had to beach her on the banks of hard sand to the right of the town.

So they were ashore again with their bundles standing around outside the consul's office, waiting for him to find them somewhere to flop. The consul was a Spaniard and didn't speak as much English as he might have but he treated them fine. The Liberal Party of Vigo invited officers and crew to go to a bullfight there was going to be that afternoon. More monkeydoodle business, the skipper got a cable to turn the ship over to the agents of Gomez and Ca. of Bilboa who had bought her as she stood and were changing her registry.

When they got to the bullring half the crowd cheered them and yelled, "Viva los Aliados," and the rest hissed and shouted, "Viva Maura." They thought there was going to be a fight right there but the bull came out and everybody quieted down. The bullfight was darn bloody, but the boys with the spangles were some steppers and the people sitting around made them drink wine all the time out of little black skins and passed around bottles of cognac so that the crew got pretty cockeyed and Joe spent most of his time keeping the boys in order. Then the officers were tendered a banquet by the local proallied society and a lot of bozos with mustachios made fiery speeches that nobody could understand and the Americans cheered and sang, *The Yanks are Coming* and *Keep the Home Fires Burning* and *We're Bound for the Hamburg Show.* The chief, an old fellow named McGillicudy, did some card tricks, and the evening was a big success. Joe and Glen bunked together at the hotel. The maid there was awful pretty but wouldn't let 'em get away with any foolishness. "Well, Joe," said Glen, before they went to sleep, "it's a great war." "Well, I guess that's strike three," said Joe. "That was no strike, that was a ball," said Glen.

They waited two weeks in Vigo while the officials quarreled about their status and they got pretty fed up with it. Then they were all loaded on a train to take them to Gibraltar where they were to be taken on board a Shipping Board boat. They were three days on the train with nothing to sleep on but hard benches. Spain was just one set of great dusty mountains after another. They changed cars in Madrid and in Seville and a guy turned up each time from the consulate to take care of them. When they got to Seville they found it was Algeciras they were going to instead of Gib.

When they got to Algeciras they found that nobody had ever heard of them. They camped out in the consulate while the consul telegraphed all over the place and finally chartered two trucks and sent them over to Cadiz. Spain was some country, all rocks and wine and busty black eyed women and olive trees. When they got to Cadiz the consular agent was there to meet them with a telegram in his hand. The tanker *Gold Shell* was waiting in Algeciras to take them on board there, so it was back again cooped up on the trucks, bouncing on the hard benches with their faces powdered with dust and their mouths full of it and not a cent in anybody's jeans left to buy a drink with. When they got on board the *Gold Shell* around three in the morning a bright moonlight night some of the boys were so tired they fell down and went to sleep right on the deck with their heads on their seabags.

The *Gold Shell* landed 'em in Perth Amboy in late October. Joe drew his back pay and took the first train connections he could get for Norfolk. He was fed up with bawling out that bunch of pimps in the focastle. Damn it, he was through with the sea; he was going to settle down and have a little married life.

He felt swell coming over on the ferry from Cape Charles, passing the Ripraps, out of the bay full of whitecaps into the smooth brown water of Hampton Roads crowded with shipping; four great battlewaggons at anchor, subchasers speeding in and out and a white revenue cutter, camouflaged freighters and colliers, a bunch of red munitions barges anchored off by themselves. It was a sparkling fall day. He felt good; he had three hundred and fifty dollars in his pocket. He had a good suit on and he felt sunburned and he'd just had a good meal. God damn it, he wanted a little love now. Maybe they'd have a kid.

Things sure were different in Norfolk. Everybody in new uniforms, twominute speakers at the corner of Main and Granby, liberty loan posters, bands playing. He hardly knew the town walking up from the ferry. He'd written Del that he was coming but he was worried about seeing her, hadn't had any letters lately. He still had a latch key to the apartment but he knocked before opening the door. There was nobody there.

He'd always pictured her running to the door to meet him. Still it was only four o'clock, she must be at her work. Must have another girl with her, don't keep the house so tidy. . . . Underwear hung to dry on a line, bits of clothing on all the chairs, a box of candy with halfeaten pieces in it on the table. . . . Jez, they must have had a party last night. There was a half a cake, glasses that had had liquor in them, a plate full of cigarette butts and even a cigar butt. Oh, well, she'd probably had some friends in. He went to the bathroom and shaved and cleaned up a little. Sure Del was always popular, she probably had a lot of friends in all the time, playing cards and that. In the bathroom there was a pot of rouge and lipsticks, and facepowder spilt over the faucets. It made Joe feel funny shaving among all these women's things.

He heard her voice laughing on the stairs and a man's voice; the key clicked in the lock. Joe closed his suitcase and stood up. Del had bobbed her hair. She flew up to him and threw her arms around his neck. "Why, I declare it's my hubby." Joe could taste rouge on her lips. "My, you look thin, Joe. Poor Boy, you musta been awful sick. . . . If I'd had any money at all I'd have jumped on a boat and come on down. . . . This is Wilmer Tayloe . . . I mean Lieutenant Tayloe, he just got his commission yesterday."

Joe hesitated a moment and then held out his hand. The other fellow had red hair clipped close and a freckled face. He was all dressed up in a whipcord uniform, shiny Sam Browne belt and puttees. He had a silver bar on each shoulder and spurs on his feet.

"He's just going overseas tomorrow. He was coming by to take me out to dinner. Oh, Joe, I've got so much to tell you, honey."

Joe and Lieutenant Tayloe stood around eyeing each other uncomfortably while Del bustled around tidying the place up, talking to Joe all the time. "It's terrible I never get any chance to do anything and neither does Hilda . . . You remember Hilda Thompson, Joe? Well, she's been livin' with me to help make up the rent but we're both of us doin' war work down at the Red Cross canteen every evening and then I sell Liberty bonds. . . . Don't you hate the huns, Joe. Oh, I just hate them, and so does Hilda. . . . She's thinking of changing her name on account of its being German. I promised to call her Gloria but I always forget. . . . You know, Wilmer, Joe's been torpedoed twice."

"Well, I suppose the first six times is the hardest," stammered Lieutenant Tayloe. Joe grunted.

Del disappeared into the bathroom and closed the door. "You boys make yourselves comfortable. I'll be dressed in a minute."

Neither of them said anything. Lieutenant Tayloe's shoes creaked as he shifted his weight from one foot to the other. At last he pulled a flask out of his pocket. "Have a drink," he said. "Ma outfit's goin' overseas any time after midnight." "I guess I'd better," said Joe, without smiling. When Della came out of the bathroom all dressed up she certainly looked snappy. She was much prettier than last time Joe had seen her. He was all the time wondering if he ought to go up and hit that damn shavetail until at last he left, Del telling him to come by and get her at the Red Cross canteen.

When he'd left she came and sat on Joe's knee and asked him about everything and whether he'd got his second mate's ticket yet and whether he'd missed her and how she wished he could make a little more money because she hated to have another girl in with her this way but it was the only way she could pay the rent. She drank a little of the whiskey that the lieutenant had forgotten on the table and ruffled his hair and loved him up. Joe asked her if Hilda was coming in soon and she said no she had a date and she was going to meet her at the canteen. But Joe went and bolted the door anyway and for the first time they were really happy hugged in each other's arms on the bed.

Joe didn't know what to do with himself around Norfolk. Del was at the office all day and at the Red Cross canteen all the evening. He'd usually be in bed when she came home. Usually there'd be some damn army officer or other bringing her home, and he'd hear them talking and kidding outside the door and lie there in bed imagining that the guy was kissing her or loving her up. He'd be about ready to hit her when she'd come in and bawl her out and they'd quarrel and yell at each other and she'd always end by saying that he didn't understand her and she thought he was unpatriotic to be interfering with her war work and sometimes they'd make up and he'd feel crazy in love with her and she'd make herself little and cute in his arms and give him little tiny kisses that made him almost cry they made him feel so happy. She was getting better looking every day and she sure was a snappy dresser.

Sunday mornings she'd be too tired to get up and he'd cook breakfast for her and they'd sit up in bed together and eat breakfast like he had with Marceline that time in Bordeaux. Then she'd tell him she was crazy about him and what a smart guy he was and how she wanted him to get a good shore job and make a lot of money so that she wouldn't have to work any more and how Captain Barnes whose folks were worth a million had wanted her to get a divorce from Joe and marry him and Mr. Canfield in the Dupont office who made a cool 50,000 a year had wanted to give her a pearl necklace but she hadn't taken it because she didn't think it was right. Talk like that made Joe feel pretty rotten. Sometimes he'd start to talk about what they'd do if they had some kids, but Del ud always make a funny face and tell him not to talk like that.

Joe went around looking for work and almost landed the job of foreman in one of the repair shops over at the shipyard in Newport News, but at the last minute another berry horned in ahead of him and got it. A couple of times he went out on parties with Del and Hilda Thompson, and some army officers and a midshipman off a destroyer, but they all highhatted him and Del let any boy who wanted to kiss her and would disappear into a phone booth with anything she could pick up so long as it had a uniform on and he had a hell of a time. He found a poolroom where some boys he knew hung out and where he could get corn liquor and started tanking up a good deal. It made Del awful sore to come home and find him drunk but he didn't care any more.

Then one night when Joe had been to a fight with some guys and had gotten an edge on afterward, he met Del and another damn shavetail walking on the street. It was pretty dark and there weren't many people around and they stopped in every dark doorway and the shavetail was kissing and hugging her. When he got them under a street light so's he made sure it was Del he went up to them and asked them what the hell they meant. Del must have had some drinks because she started tittering in a shrill little voice that drove him crazy and he hauled off and let the shavetail have a perfect left right on the bottom. The spurs tinkled and the shavetail went to sleep right flat on the little grass patch under the streetlight. It began to hit Joe kinder funny but Del was sore as the devil and said she'd have him arrested for insult to the uniform and assault and battery and that he was nothing but a yellow sniveling slacker and what was he doing hanging around home when all the boys were at the front fighting the huns. Joe sobered up and pulled the guy up to his feet and told them both they could go straight to hell. He walked off before the shavetail, who musta been pretty tight, had time to do anything but splutter, and went straight home and packed his suitcase and pulled out.

Will Stirp was in town so Joe went over to his house and got him up out of bed and said he'd busted up housekeeping and would Will lend him twentyfive bucks to go up to New York with. Will said it was a damn good thing and that love 'em and leave 'em was the only thing for guys like them. They talked till about day about one thing and another. Then Joe went to sleep and slept till late afternoon. He got up in time to catch the Washington boat. He didn't take a room but roamed around on deck all night. He got to cracking with one of the officers and went and sat in the pilot house that smelt comfortably of old last year's pipes. Listening to the sludge of water from the bow and watching the wabbly white finger of the searchlight pick up buoys and lighthouses he began to pull himself together. He said he was going up to New York to see his sister and try for a second mate's ticket with the Shipping Board. His stories about being torpedoed went big because none of them on the *Dominion City* had even been across the pond.

It felt like old times standing in the bow in the sharp November morning, sniffing the old brackish smell of the Potomac water, passing redbrick Alexandria and Anacostia and the Arsenal and the Navy Yard, seeing the Monument stick up pink through the mist in the early light. The wharves looked about the same, the yachts and power boats anchored opposite, the Baltimore boat just coming in, the ramshackle excursion steamers, the oystershells underfoot on the wharf, the nigger roustabouts standing around. Then he was hopping the Georgetown car and too soon he was walking up the redbrick street. While he rang the bell he was wondering why he'd come home.

Mommer looked older but she was in pretty good shape and all taken up with her boarders and how the girls were both engaged. They said that Janey was doing so well in her work, but that living in New York had changed her. Joe said he was going down to New York to try to get his second mate's ticket and that he sure would look her up. When they asked him about the war and the submarines and all that he didn't know what to tell 'em so he kinder kidded them along. He was glad when it was time to go over to Washington to get his train, though they were darn nice to him and seemed to think that he was making a big success getting to be a second mate so young. He didn't tell 'em about being married.

Going down on the train to New York Joe sat in the smoker looking out of the window at farms and stations and billboards and the grimy streets of factory towns through Jersey under a driving rain and everything he saw seemed to remind him of Del and places outside of Norfolk and good times he'd had when he was a kid. When he got to the Penn Station in New York first thing he did was check his bag, then he walked down Eighth Avenue all shiny with rain to the corner of the street where Janey lived. He guessed he'd better phone her first and called from a cigarstore. Her voice sounded kinder stiff; she said she was busy and couldn't see him till tomorrow. He came out of the phonebooth and walked down the street not knowing where to go. He had a package under his arm with a couple of Spanish shawls he'd bought for her and Del on the last trip. He felt so blue he wanted to drop the shawls and everything down a drain, but he thought better of it and went back to the checkroom at the station and left them in his suitcase. Then he went and smoked a pipe for a while in the waitingroom.

God damn it to hell he needed a drink. He went over to Broadway and walked down to Union Square, stopping in every place he could find that looked like a saloon but they wouldn't serve him anywhere. Union Square was all lit up and full of navy recruiting posters. A big wooden model of battleship filled up one side of it. There was a crowd standing around and a young girl dressed like a sailor was making a speech about patriotism. The cold rain came on again and the crowd scattered. Joe went down a street and into a ginmill called The Old Farm. He must have looked like somebody the barkeep knew because he said hello and poured him out a shot of rye.

Joe got to talking with two guys from Chicago who were drinking whiskey and beer chasers. They said this wartalk was a lot of bushwa propaganda and that if working stiffs stopped working in munition factories making shells to knock other working stiffs' blocks off with, there wouldn't be no goddam war. Joe said they were goddam right but look at the big money you made. The guys from Chicago said they'd been working in a munitions factory themselves but they were through, goddam it, and that if the working stiffs made a few easy dollars it meant that the war profiteers were making easy millions. They said the Russians had the right idea, make a revolution and shoot the goddam profiteers and that ud happen in this country if they didn't watch out and a damn good thing too. The barkeep leaned across the bar and said they'd oughtn't to talk thataway, folks ud take 'em for German spies.

"Why, you're a German yourself, George," said one of the guys.

The barkeep flushed and said, "Names don't mean nothin'... I'm a patriotic American. I vas talking yust for your good. If you vant to land in de hoosgow it's not my funeral." But he set them up to drinks on the house and it seemed to Joe that he agreed with 'em.

They drank another round and Joe said it was all true but what the hell could you do about it? The guys said what you could do about it was join the I.W.W. and carry a red card and be a classconscious worker. Joe said that stuff was only for foreigners, but if somebody started a white man's party to fight the profiteers and the goddam bankers he'd be with 'em. The guys from Chicago began to get sore and said the wobblies were just as much white men as he was and that political parties were the bunk and that all southerners were scabs. Joe backed off and was looking at the guys to see which one of 'em he'd hit first when the barkeep stepped around from the end of the bar and came between them. He was fat but he had shoulders and a meanlooking pair of blue eyes.

"Look here, you bums," he said, "you listen to me, sure I'm a Cherman but am I for de Kaiser? No, he's a schweinhunt, I am sokialist unt I live toity years in Union City unt own my home unt pay taxes unt I'm a good American, but dot don't mean dot I vill foight for Banker Morgan, not vonce. I know American vorkman in de sokialist party toity years unt all dey do is foight among each oder. Every sonofabitch denk him better den de next sonofabitch. You loafers geroutahere... closin' time... I'm goin' to close up an' go home."

One of the guys from Chicago started to laugh, "Well, I guess the drinks are on us, Oscar... it'll be different after the revolution."

Joe still wanted to fight but he paid for a round with his last green-back and the barkeep who was still red in the face from his speech, lifted a glass of beer to his mouth. He blew the foam off it and said, "If I talk like dot I lose my yob."

They shook hands all around and Joe went out into the gusty northeast rain. He felt lit but he didn't feel good. He went up to Union Square again. The recruiting speeches were over. The model battleship was dark. A couple of ragged looking youngsters were huddled in the lee of the recruiting tent. Joe felt lousy. He went down into the subway and waited for the Brooklyn train.

At Mrs. Olsen's everything was dark. Joe rang and in a little while she came down in a padded pink dressing gown and opened the door. She was sore at being waked up and bawled him out for drinking, but she gave him a flop and next morning lent him fifteen bucks to tide him over till he got work on a Shipping Board boat. Mrs. Olsen looked tired and a lot older, she said she had pains in her back and couldn't get through her work any more.

Next morning Joe put up some shelves in the pantry for her and carried out a lot of litter before he went over to the Shipping Board recruiting office to put his name down for the officer's school. The little kike behind the desk had never been to sea and asked him a lot of damnfool questions and told him to come around next week to find out what action would be taken on his application. Joe got sore and told him to f—k himself and walked out.

He took Janey out to supper and to a show, but she talked just like everybody else did and bawled him out for cussing and he didn't have a very good time. She liked the shawls though and he was glad she was making out so well in New York. He never did get around to talking to her about Della.

After taking her home he didn't know what the hell to do with himself. He wanted a drink, but taking Janey out and everything had cleaned up the fifteen bucks he'd borrowed from Mrs. Olsen. He walked west to a saloon he knew on Tenth Avenue, but the place was closed: wartime prohibition. Then he walked back towards Union Square, maybe that feller Tex he'd seen when he was walking across the square with Janey would still be sitting there and he could chew the rag a while with him. He sat down on a bench opposite the cardboard battleship and began sizing it up: not such a bad job. Hell, I wisht I'd never seen the inside of a real battleship, he was thinking, when Tex slipped into the seat beside him and put his hand on his knee. The minute he touched him Joe knew he'd never liked the guy, eyes too close together: "What you lookin' so blue about, Joe? Tell me you're getting' your ticket."

Joe nodded and leaned over and spat carefully between his feet.

"What do you think of that for a model battleship, pretty nifty, ain't it? Jez, us guys is lucky not to be overseas fightin' the fritzes in the trenches."

"Oh, I'd just as soon," growled Joe. "I wouldn't give a damn."

"Say, Joe, I got a job lined up. Guess I oughtn't to blab around about it, but you're regular. I know you won't say nothin'. I been on the bum for two weeks, somethin' wrong with my stomach. Man, I'm sick, I'm tellin' you. I can't do no heavy work no more. A punk I know works in a whitefront been slippin' me my grub, see. Well, I was sittin' on a bench right here on the square, a feller kinda well dressed sits down an' starts to chum up. Looked to me like one of these here sissies lookin' for rough trade, see, thought I'd roll him for some jack, what the hell, what can you do if you're sick an' can't work?"

Joe sat leaning back with his legs stuck out, his hands in his pockets staring hard at the outline of the battleship against the buildings. Tex was talking fast, poking his face into Joe's: "Turns out the sonofabitch was a dick. S—t I was scared pissless. A secret service agent. Burns is his big boss . . . but what he's lookin' for's reds, slackers, German spies, guys that can't keep their traps shut . . . an' he turns around and hands me out a job, twentyfive smackers a week if little Willy makes good. All I got to do's bum around and listen to guys talk, see? If I hears anything that ain't 100 per cent I slips the word to the boss and he investigates. Twentyfive a week and servin' my country besides, and if I gets in any kind of jam, Burns gets me out. . . . What do you think of that for the gravy, Joe?"

Joe got to his feet. "Guess I'll go back to Brooklyn." "Stick around . . . look here, you've always treated me white . . . you belong, I know that Joe . . . I'll put you next to this guy if you want. He's a good scout, educated feller an' all that and he knows where you can get plenty liquor an' women if you want 'em." "Hell, I'm goin" to sea and get out of all this s—t," said Joe, turning his back and walking towards the subway station.

The Camera Eye (34)

his voice was three thousand miles away   all the time he kept wanting to get up outa bed   his cheeks were bright pink and the choky breathing   No kid you better lay there quiet we dont want you catching more cold that's why they sent me down to stay with you to keep you from getting up outa bed

the barrelvaulted room all smells fever and whitewash carbolic sick wops outside the airraid siren's got a nightmare

(Mestre's a railhead and its moonlight over the Brenta and the basehospital and the ammunition dump

carbolic blue moonlight)

all the time he kept trying to get up outa bed   Kiddo you better lay there quiet   his voice was in Minnesota but dontjaunerstandafellersgottogetup   I got a date animportantengagementtoseeabout those lots ought nevertohavestayedinbedsolate I'll lose my deposit   For chrissake dont you think I'm broke enough as it is?

Kiddo you gotto lay there quiet   we're in the hospital in Mestre you got a little fever makes things seem funny

Cant you letafellerbe? You're in cahoots withem thaswhassematteris I know theyreouttorookme they think Imagoddamsucker tomadethatdeposit I'll showem Illknockyergoddamblockoff

my shadow on the vault bulkyclumsily staggering and swaying from the one candle spluttering red in the raw winterhospital carbolic night above the shadow on the cot gotto keep his shoulders down to the cot Curley's husky inspite of

(you can hear their motors now the antiaircraft batteries are letting loose must be great up there in the moonlight out of the smell of carbolic and latrines and sick wops)

sit back and light a macedonia by the candle he seems to be asleep his breathing's so tough pneumonia breathing   can hear myself breathe   and the water tick in the faucet   doctors and orderlies all down in the bombproof cant even hear a sick wop groan

Jesus is the guy dying?

they've cut off their motors   the little drums in my ears sure that's why they call em drums (up there in the blue moonlight the Austrian observer's reaching for the string that dumps the applecart) the candleflame stands up still

not that time but wham in the side of the head woke Curley and the glass tinkling in the upstairs windows the candle staggered but didnt go out the vault sways with my shadow and Curley's shadow dammit he's strong head's full of the fever reek Kiddo you gotto stay in bed (they dumped the applecart allright) shellfragments hailing around outside Kiddo you gotto get back to bed

But I gotadate oh christohsweetjesus cant you tell me how to get back to the outfit haveaheart dad I didntmeannoharm itsonlyaboutthose lots

the voice dwindles into a whine I'm pulling the covers up to his chin again light the candle again smoke a macedonia again look at my watch again must be near day ten o'clock they dont relieve me till eight

way off a voice goes up and up and swoops like the airraid siren ayayooo TO

Newsreel XXV

General Pershing's forces today occupied Belle Joyeuse Farm and the southern edges of the Bois des Loges. The Americans encountered but little machinegun opposition. The advance was in the nature of a linestraightening operation. Otherwise the activity along the front today consisted principally of artillery firing and bombing. Patrols are operating around Belluno having preceded the flood of allies pouring through the Quero pass in the Grappa region

REBEL SAILORS DEFY ALLIES

> *Bonjour ma cherie*
> *Comment allez vous?*
> *Bonjour ma cherie*
> *how do you do?*

after a long conference with a secretary of war and the secretary of state President Wilson returned to the White House this afternoon apparently highly pleased that events are steadily pursuing the course which he had felt they would take

> *Avez vous fiancé? cela ne fait rien*
> *Voulez vous couchez avec moi ce soir?*
> *Wee, wee, combien?*

HELP THE FOOD ADMINISTRATION BY REPORTING
WAR PROFITEERS

Lord Robert, who is foreign minister Balfour's right hand man added, "When victory comes the responsibility for America and Great Britain will rest not on statesmen but on the people." The display of the red flag in our thoroughfares seems to be emblematic of unbridled license and an insignia for lawhating and anarchy, like the black flag it represents everything that is repulsive

LENINE FLEES TO ENGLAND

here I am snug as a bug in a rug on this third day of October. It was Sunday I went over and got hit in the left leg with a machinegun bullet above the knee. I am in a base hospital and very comfortable. I am writing with my left hand as my right one is under my head

STOCK MARKET STRONG BUT NARROW

Some day I'm going to murder the bugler
Some day they're going to find him dead
I'll dislocate his reveille
And step upon it heavily
And spend
the rest of my life in bed

A Hoosier Quixote

Hibben, Paxton, journalist, Indianapolis, Ind., Dec. 5, 1880, s. Thomas Entrekin and Jeannie Merrill (Ketcham) H.; A.B. Princeton 1903, A.M. Harvard 1904

Thinking men were worried in the middle west in the years Hibben was growing up there, something was wrong with the American Republic, was it the Gold Standard, Privilege, The Interests, Wall Street?

The rich were getting richer, the poor were getting poorer, small farmers were being squeezed out, workingmen were working twelve hours a day for a bare living; profits were for the rich, the law was for the rich, the cops were for the rich;

was it for that the pilgrims had bent their heads into the storm, filled the fleeing Indians with slugs out of their blunderbusses
and worked the stony farms of New England;
was it for that the pioneers had crossed the Appalachians,
long squirrelguns slung across lean backs,

a fistful of corn in the pocket of the buckskin vest,

was it for that the Indiana farmboys had turned out to shoot down Johnny Reb and make the black man free?

Paxton Hibben was a small cantankerous boy, son of one of the best families (the Hibbens had a wholesale dry goods business in Indianapolis); in school the rich kids didn't like him because he went around with the poor kids and the poor kids didn't like him because his folks were rich,

but he was the star pupil of Short Ridge High

ran the paper,

won all the debates.

At Princeton he was the young collegian, editor of the Tiger, drank a lot, didn't deny that he ran around after girls, made a brilliant scholastic record and was a thorn in the flesh of the godly. The natural course for a bright young man of his class and position was to study law, but Hibben wanted

travel and romance à la Byron and de Musset, wellgroomed adventures in foreign lands,

so

as his family was one of the best in Indiana and friendly with Senator Beveridge he was gotten a post in the diplomatic service:

3rd sec and 2nd sec American Embassy St. Petersburg and Mexico City 1905–6, sec Legation and Chargé d'affaires, Bogotá, Colombia, 1908–9; The Hague and Luxemburg 1909–12, Santiago de Chile 1912 (retired).

Pushkin for de Musset; St. Petersburg was a young dude's romance:

goldencrusted spires under a platinum sky,

the icegrey Neva flowing swift and deep under bridges that jingled with sleighbells;

riding home from the Islands with the Grand Duke's mistress, the more beautiful most amorous singer of Neapolitan streetsongs;

staking a pile of rubles in a tall room glittering with chandeliers, monocles, diamonds dripped on white shoulders;

white snow, white tableclothes, white sheets,

Kakhetian wine, vodka fresh as newmown hay, Astrakhan caviar, sturgeon, Finnish salmon, Lapland ptarmigan, and the most beautiful women in the world;

but it was 1905, Hibben left the embassy one night and saw a
flare of red against the trampled snow of the Nevsky
and red flags,
blood frozen in the ruts, blood trickling down the cartracks;
he saw the machineguns on the balconies of the Winter Palace,
the cossacks charging the unarmed crowds that wanted peace and
food and a little freedom,
heard the throaty roar of the Russian Marseillaise;
some stubborn streak in the old American blood flared in revolt,
he walked the streets all night with the revolutionists, got in wrong at
the embassy
and was transferred to Mexico City where there was no revolution yet, only peons and priests and the stillness of the great volcanos.

The Cientificos made him a member of the Jockey Club
where in the magnificent building of blue Puebla tile he lost all
his money at roulette and helped them drink up the last few cases of
champagne left over from the plunder of Cortez.

Chargé d'Affaires in Colombia (he never forgot he owed his career to Beveridge; he believed passionately in Roosevelt, and righteousness and reform, and the antitrust laws, the Big Stick that was going to scare away the grafters and malefactors of great wealth and get the common man his due) he helped wangle the revolution that stole the canal zone from the bishop of Bogotá; later he stuck up for Roosevelt in the Pulitzer libel suit; he was a progressive, believed in the Canal and T.R.

He was shunted to the Hague where he went to sleep during the vague deliberations of the International Tribunal.

In 1912 he resigned from the Diplomatic Service and went home to campaign for Roosevelt.

got to Chicago in time to hear them singing *Onward Christian Soldiers* at the convention in the Colosseum; in the closepacked voices and the cheers, he heard the trample of the Russian Marseillaise, the sullen silence of Mexican peons, Colombian Indians waiting for a deliverer, in the reverberançe of the hymn he heard the measured cadences of the Declaration of Independence.

The talk of social justice petered out; T.R. was a windbag like the rest of 'em, the Bull Moose was stuffed with the same sawdust as the G.O.P.

Paxton Hibben ran for Congress as a progressive in Indiana but the European war had already taken people's minds off social justice.

Warr Corr Collier's Weekly 1914–15, staff corr Associated Press in Europe, 1915–17; war corr Leslie's Weekly in Near East and see Russian commn for Near East Relief, June–Dec, 1921

In those years he forgot all about the diplomat's mauve silk bathrobe and the ivory toilet sets and the little tête-à-têtes with grandduchesses,

he went to Germany as Beveridge's secrètary, saw the German troops goosestepping through Brussels,

saw Poincaré visiting the long doomed galleries of Verdun between ranks of bitter halfmutinous soldiers in blue,

saw the gangrened wounds, the cholea, the typhus, the little children with their bellies swollen with famine, the maggoty corpses of the Serbian retreat, drunk Allied officers chasing sick naked girls upstairs in the brothels in Saloniki, soldiers looting stores and churches, French and British sailors fighting with beerbottles in the bars;

walked up and down the terrace with King Constantine during the bombardment of Athens, fought a duel with a French commission agent who got up and left when a German sat down to eat in the diningroom at the Grande Bretagne; Hibben thought the duel was a joke until all his friends began putting on silk hats; he stood up and let the Frenchman take two shots at him and then fired into the ground; in Athens as everywhere he was always in hot water, a slightly built truculent man, always standing up for his friends, for people out of luck, for some idea, too reckless ever to lay down the careful steppingstones of a respectable career.

Commd 1st lieut F.A. Nov 27–1917; capt May 31–1919; served at war coll camp Grant; in France with 332nd E.A.; Finance Bureau S.O.S.; at G.H.Q. in office of Insp Gen of A.E.F.; discharged Aug. 21–1919; capt O.R.C. Feb. 7th 1920; recommend Feb 7–1925

The war in Europe was bloody and dirty and dull, but the war in New York revealed such slimy depths of vileness and hypocrisy that no man who saw it can ever feel the same again; in the army training camps it was different, the boys believed in a world safe for Democracy; Hibben believed in the Fourteen Points, he believed in The War To End War.

With mil Mission to Armenia Aug–Dec 1919; staff corr in Europe for the Chicago Tribune; with the Near East Relief 1920–22; sec Russian Red Cross commn in American 1922; v dir for U.S. Nansen Relief Mission 1923; sec AM Commn Relief Russian Children Apr 1922

In the famineyear the cholera year the typhusyear Paxton Hibben went to Moscow with a relief commission.

In Paris they were still haggling over the price of blood, squabbling over toy flags, the riverfrontiers on reliefmaps, the historical destiny of peoples, while behind the scenes the good contractplayers, the Deterdings, the Zahkaroffs, the Stinnesses sat quiet and possessed themselves of the raw materials.

In Moscow there was order,

in Moscow there was work,

in Moscow there was hope;

the *Marseillaise* of 1905, *Onward Christian Soldiers* of 1912, the sullen passiveness of American Indians, of infantrymen waiting for death at the front was part of the tremendous roar of the Marxian *Internationale*.

Hibben believed in the new world.

Back in America

somebody got hold of a photograph of Captain Paxton Hibben laying a wreath on Jack Reed's grave; they tried to throw him out of the O.R.C.;

at Princeton at the twentieth reunion of his college class his classmates started to lynch him; they were drunk and perhaps it was just a collegeboy prank twenty years too late but they had a noose around his neck,

lynch the goddam red,

no more place in America for change, no more place for the old gags: social justice, progressivism, revolt against oppression, democracy; put the reds on the skids,

no money for them,
no jobs for them.

Mem Authors League of America, Soc of Colonial Wars, Vets Foreign Wars, Am Legion, fellow Royal and Am Geog Socs. Decorated chevalier Order of St. Stanislas (Russian), Officer Order of the Redeemer (Greek), Order of the Sacred Treasure (Japan). Clubs Princeton, Newspaper, Civic (New York)

Author: Constantine and the Greek People 1920, The Famine in Russia 1922, Henry Ward Beecher an American Portrait 1927.

d. 1929.

Newsreel XXVI

EUROPE ON KNIFE EDGE

Tout le long de la Thamise
Nous sommes allés tout les deux
Gouter l'heure exquise.

in such conditions is it surprising that the Department of Justice looks with positive affection upon those who refused service in the draft, with leniency upon convicted anarchists and with something like indifference upon the overwhelming majority of them still out of jail or undeported for years after the organization of the U.S. Steel Corporation Wall Street was busy on the problem of measuring the cubic yards of water injected into the property

FINISHED STEEL MOVES RATHER MORE FREELY

Where do we go from here boys
Where do we go from here?

WILD DUCKS FLY OVER PARIS

FERTILIZER INDUSTRY STIMULATED BY WAR

Anywhere from Harlem
To a Jersey City pier

the winning of the war is just as much dependent upon the industrial workers as it is upon the soldiers. Our wonderful record of launching one hundred ships on independence day shows what can be done when we put our shoulders to the wheel under the spur of patriotism

SAMARITAINE BATHS SINK IN
SWOLLEN SEINE

I may not know
What the war's about
But you bet by gosh
I'll soon find out
And so my sweetheart
Don't you fear
I'll bring you a king
For a souvenir
And I'll get you a Turk
And the Kaiser too
And that's about all
One feller can do

AFTER-WAR PLANS OF AETNA EXPLOSIVES

ANCIENT CITY IN GLOOM EVEN THE CHURCH BELLS ON SUNDAY BEING STILLED

Where do we go from here boys
Where do we go from here?

Richard Ellsworth Savage

It was at Fontainebleau lined up in the square in front of Francis I's palace they first saw the big grey Fiat ambulances they were to drive. Schuyler came back from talking with the French drivers who were turning them over with the news that they were sore as hell because it meant they had to go back into the front line. They asked why the devil the Americans couldn't stay home and mind their own business instead of coming over here and filling up all the good embusqué jobs. That night the section went into cantonment in tarpaper barracks that stank of carbolic, in a little town in Champagne. It turned out to be the Fourth of July, so the maréchale-de-logis served out champagne with supper and a general with white walrus whiskers came and made a speech about how with the help of Amérique héroique la victoire was certain, and proposed a toast to le président Veelson. The chef of the section, Bill Knickerbocker, got up a little nervously and toasted la France héroique, l'héroique Cinquième

Armée and la victorie by Christmas. Fireworks were furnished by the
Boches who sent over an airraid that made everybody scuttle for the
bombproof dugout.

Once they got down there Fred Summers said it smelt too bad and
anyway he wanted a drink and he and Dick went out to find an
estaminet, keeping close under the eaves of the houses to escape the
occasional shrapnel fragments from the antiaircraft guns. They found
a little bar all full of tobacco smoke and French poilus singing *la
Madelon.* Everybody cheered when they came in and a dozen glasses
were handed to them. They smoked their first caporal ordinaire and
everybody set them up to drinks so that at closing time, when the
bugles blew the French equivalent of taps, they found themselves
walking a little unsteadily along the pitchblack streets arm in arm
with two poilus who'd promised to find them their cantonment. The
poilus said la guerre was une saloperie and la victoire was une sale
blague and asked eagerly if les americains knew anything about la
revolution en Russie. Dick said he was a pacifist and was for anything
that would stop the war and they all shook hands very significantly
and talked about la revolution mondiale. When they were turning in
on their folding cots, Fred Summers suddenly sat bolt upright with
his blanket around him and said in a solemn funny way he had, "Fellers, this ain't a war, it's a goddam madhouse."

There were two other fellows in the section who liked to drink
wine and chatter bad French; Steve Warner, who'd been a special student at Harvard, and Ripley who was a freshman at Columbia. The
five of them went around together, finding places to get omelettes and
pommes frites in the villages within walking distance, making the
rounds of the estaminets every night; they got to be known as the
grenadine guards. When the section moved up onto the Voie Sacrée
back of Verdun and was quartered for three rainy weeks in a little ruined village called Erize la Petite, they set up their cots together in the
same corner of the old brokendown barn they were given for a cantonment. It rained all day and all night; all day and all night camions
ground past through the deep liquid putty of the roads carrying men
and munitions to Verdun. Dick used to sit on his cot looking out
through the door at the jiggling mudspattered faces of the young
French soldiers going up for the attack, drunk and desperate and yelling à bas la guerre, mort au vaches, à bas la guerre. Once Steve came
in suddenly, his face pale above the dripping poncho, his eyes snap-

ping, and said in a low voice, "Now I know what the tumbrils were like in the Terror, that's what they are, tumbrils."

Dick was relieved to find out, when they finally moved up within range of the guns, that he wasn't any more scared than anybody else. The first time they went on post he and Fred lost their way in the shellshredded woods and were trying to turn the car around on a little rise naked as the face of the moon when three shells from an Austrian eightyeight went past them like three cracks of a whip. They never knew how they got out of the car and into the ditch, but when the sparse blue almondsmelling smoke cleared they were both lying flat in the mud. Fred went to pieces and Dick had to put his arm around him and keep whispering in his ear, "Come on, boy, we got to make it. Come on, Fred, we'll fool 'em." It all hit him funny and he kept laughing all the way back along the road into the quieter section of the woods where the dressing station had been cleverly located right in front of a battery of 405s so that the concussion almost bounced the wounded out of their stretchers every time a gun was fired. When they got back to the section after taking a load to the triage they were able to show three jagged holes from shellfragments in the side of the car.

Next day the attack began and continual barrages and counterbarrages and heavy gasbombardments; the section was on twentyfour hour duty for three days, at the end of it everybody had dysentery and bad nerves. One fellow got shellshock, although he'd been too scared to go on post, and had to be sent back to Paris. A couple of men had to be evacuated for dysentery. The grenadine guards came through the attack pretty well, except that Steve and Ripley had gotten a little extra sniff of mustard gas up at P2 one night and vomited whenever they ate anything.

In their twentyfour hour periods off duty they'd meet in a little garden at Récicourt that was the section's base. No one else seemed to know about it. The garden had been attached to a pink villa but the villa had been mashed to dust as if a great foot had stepped on it. The garden was untouched, only a little weedy from neglect, roses were in bloom there and butterflies and bees droned around the flowers on sunny afternoons. At first they took the bees for distant arrivés and went flat on their bellies when they heard them. There had been a cement fountain in the middle of the garden and there they used to sit when the Germans got it into their heads to shell the road and the nearby bridge. There was regular shelling three times a day and a little scattering between times. Somebody would be detailed to stand in line at the Copé and buy south of France melons and four franc fifty champagne. Then they'd take off their shirts to toast their backs and shoulders if it was sunny and sit in the dry fountain eating the melons and drinking the warm cidery champagne and talk about how they'd go back to the States and start an underground newspaper like *La Libre Belgique* to tell people what the war was really like.

What Dick liked best in the garden was the little backhouse, like the backhouse in a New England farm, with a clean scrubbed seat and a half moon in the door, through which on sunny days the wasps who had a nest in the ceiling hummed busily in and out. He'd sit there with his belly aching listening to the low voices of his friends talking in the driedup fountain. Their voices made him feel happy and at home while he stood wiping himself on a few old yellowed squares of a 1914 *Petit Journal* that still hung on the nail. Once he came back buckling his belt and saying, "Do you know? I was thinking how fine it would be if you could reorganize the cells of your body into some other kind of life . . . it's too damn lousy being a human . . . I'd like to be a cat, a nice comfortable housecat sitting by the fire."

"It's a hell of a note," said Steve, reaching for his shirt and putting it on. A cloud had gone over the sun and it was suddenly chilly. The guns sounded quiet and distant. Dick felt suddenly chilly and lonely. "It's a hell of a note when you have to be ashamed of belonging to your own race. But I swear I am, I swear I'm ashamed of being a man . . . it will take some huge wave of hope like a revolution to make me feel any selfrespect ever again. . . . God, we're a lousy cruel vicious dumb type of tailless ape." "Well, if you want to earn your selfrespect, Steve, and the respect of us other apes, why don't you go down, now that they're not shelling, and buy us a bottle of champagny water?" said Ripley.

After the attack on hill 304 the division went en repos back of Barle-Duc for a couple of weeks and then up into a quiet section of the Argonne called le Four de Paris where the French played chess with the Boches in the front line and where one side always warned the other before setting off a mine under a piece of trench. When they were off duty they could go into the inhabited and undestroyed town of Sainte Ménéhoulde and eat fresh pastry and pumpkin soup and roast chicken. When the section was disbanded and everybody sent back to Paris Dick hated to leave the mellow autumn woods of the Argonne. The U. S. army was to take over the ambulance service attached to the French. Everybody got a copy of the section's citation; Dick Norton made them a speech under shellfire, never dropping the monocle out of his eye, dismissing them as gentlemen volunteers and that was the end of the section.

Except for an occasional shell from the Bertha, Paris was quiet and pleasant that November. It was too foggy for airraids. Dick and Steve Warner got a very cheap room back of the Pantheon; in the daytime they read French and in the evenings roamed round cafés and drinking places. Fred Summers got himself a job with the Red Cross at twentyfive dollars a week and a steady girl the second day they hit Paris. Ripley and Ed Schuyler took lodgings in considerable style over Henry's bar. They all ate dinner together every night and argued themselves sick about what they ought to do. Steve said he was going home and C.O. and to hell with it; Ripley and Schuyler said they didn't care what they did as long as they kept out of the American army, and talked about joining the Foreign Legion or the Lafayette Escadrille.

Fred Summers said, "Fellers, this war's the most gigantic cockeyed graft of the century and me for it and the cross red nurses." At the end of first week he was holding down two Red Cross jobs, each at twentyfive a week, and being kept by a middleaged French marraine who owned a big house in Neuilly. When Dick's money gave out Fred borrowed some for him from his marraine, but he never would let any of the others see her. "Don't want you fellers to know what I'm in for," he'd say.

At lunchtime one day Fred Summers came round to say that everything was fixed up and that he had jobs for them all. The wops, he explained, were pretty well shot after Caporetto and couldn't get out of the habit of retreating. It was thought that sending the American Red Cross ambulance section down would help their morale. He was in charge of recruiting for the time being and had put all their names down. Dick immediately said he spoke Italian and felt he'd be a great help to the morale of the Italians, so the next morning they were all at the Red Cross office when it opened and were duly enrolled in Section 1 of the American Red Cross for Italy. There followed a couple more weeks waiting around during which Fred Summers took on a mysterious Serbian lad he picked up in a café back of the Place St. Michel who wanted to teach them to take hashish, and Dick became friends with a drunken Montenegran who'd been a barkeep in New York and who promised to get them all decorated by King Nicholas of Montenegro. But the day they were going to be received at Neuilly to have the decorations pinned on, the section left.

The convoy of twelve Fiats and eight Fords ran along the smooth macadam roads south through the Forest of Fontainebleau and wound east through the winecolored hills of central France. Dick was driving a Ford alone and was so busy trying to remember what to do with his feet he could hardly notice the scenery. Next day they went over the mountains and down into the valley of the Rhone, into a rich wine country with planetrees and cypresses, smelling of the vintage and late fall roses and the south. By Montélimar, the war, the worry about jail and protest and sedition all seemed a nightmare out of another century.

They had a magnificent supper in the quiet pink and white town with cêpes and garlic and strong red wine. "Fellers," Fred Summers kept saying, "this ain't a war, it's a goddam Cook's tour." They slept in style in the big brocadehung beds at the hotel, and when they left in the morning a little schoolboy ran after Dick's car shouting Vive l'Amerique and handed him a box of nougat, the local specialty; it was the land of Cockaigne.

That day the convoy fell to pieces running to Marseilles; discipline melted away; drivers stopped at all the wineshops along the sunny roads to drink and play craps. The Red Cross publicity man and the Saturday Evening Post correspondent who was the famous writer, Montgomery Ellis, got hideously boiled and could be heard whooping and yelling in the back of the staffcar, while the little fat lieutenant ran up and down the line of cars at every stop red and hysterically puffing. Eventually they were all rounded up and entered Marseilles in formation. They'd just finished parking in a row in the main square and the boys were settling back into the bars and cafés round about, when a man named Ford got the bright idea of looking into his gasoline tank with a match and blew his car up. The local firedepartment came out in style and when car No. 8 was properly incinerated turned their highpressure hose on the others, and Schuyler, who spoke the best French in the section, had to be dragged away from a conversation with the cigarette girl at the corner café to beg the firechief for chrissake to lay off.

With the addition of a fellow named Sheldrake who was an expert on folkdancing and had been in the famous section 7, the grenadine guards dined in state at the Bristol. They continued the evening at the promenoire at the Apollo, that was so full of all the petite femmes in the world, they never saw the show. Everything was cockeyed and full of women, the shrill bright main streets with their cafés and cabarets, and the black sweaty tunnels of streets back of the harbor full of rumpled beds and sailors and black skin and brown skin, wriggling bellies, flopping purplewhite breasts, grinding thighs.

Very late Steve and Dick found themselves alone in a little restaurant eating ham and eggs and coffee. They were drunk and sleepy and quarrelling drowsily. When they paid, the middleaged waitress told them to put the tip on the corner of the table and blew them out of their chairs by calmly hoisting her skirts and picking up the coins between her legs.

"It's a hoax, a goddam hoax. . . . Sex is a slotmachine," Steve kept saying and it seemed gigantically funny, so funny that they went into an early morning bar and tried to tell the man behind the counter about it, but he didn't understand them and wrote out on a piece of paper the name of an establishment where they could faire rigajig, une maison, propre, convenable, et de haute moralité. Hooting with laughter they found themselves reeling and stumbling as they climbed endless stairways. The wind was cold as hell. They were in front of a crazylooking cathedral looking down on the harbor, steamboats, great expanses of platinum sea hemmed in by ashen mountains. "By God, that's the Mediterranean."

They sobered up in the cold jostling wind and the wide metallic flare of dawn and got back to their hotel in time to shake the others out of their drunken slumbers and be the first to report for duty at the parked cars. Dick was so sleepy he forgot what he ought to do with his feet and ran his Ford into the car ahead and smashed his headlights. The fat lieutenant bawled him out shrilly and took the car away from him and put him on a Fiat with Sheldrake, so he had nothing to do all day but look out of his drowse at the Corniche and the Mediterranean and the redroofed towns and the long lines of steamboats bound east hugging the shore for fear of Uboats, convoyed by an occasional French destroyer with its smokestacks in all the wrong places.

Crossing the Italian border they were greeted by crowds of school-children with palmleaves and baskets of oranges, and a movie opera-tor. Sheldrake kept stroking his beard and bowing and saluting at the cheers of evviva gli americani, until zowie, he got an orange be-tween the eyes that pretty near gave him a nosebleed. Another man down the line came within an inch of having his eye put out by a palmbranch thrown by a delirious inhabitant of Vintimiglia. It was a great reception. That night in San Remo enthusiastic wops kept run-ning up to the boys on the street, shaking their hands and congratu-lating them on il Presidente Veelson; somebody stole all the spare tires out of the camionette and the Red Cross Publicity Man's suitcase that had been left in the staffcar. They were greeted effusively and shortchanged in the bars. Evviva gli aleati.

Everybody in the section began to curse out Italy and the rubber spaghetti and the vinegary wine, except Dick and Steve, who sud-denly became woplovers and bought themselves grammars to learn the language. Dick already gave a pretty good imitation of talking Italian, especially before the Red Cross officers, by putting an *o* on the end of all the French words he knew. He didn't give a damn about anything any more. It was sunny, vermouth was a great drink, the towns and the toy churches on the tops of hills and the vineyards and the cypresses and the blue sea were like a succession of backdrops for an oldfashioned opera. The buildings were stagy and ridiculously magnificent; on every blank wall the damn wops had painted win-dows and colonnades and balconies with fat Titianhaired beauties leaning over them and clouds and covies of dimpletummied cupids.

That night they parked the convoy in the main square of a godfor-saken little burg on the outskirts of Genoa. They went with Sheldrake to have a drink in a bar and found themselves drinking with the *Sat-urday Evening Post* correspondent who soon began to get tight and to say how he envied them their good looks and their sanguine youth and idealism. Steve picked him up about everything and argued bit-terly that youth was the lousiest time in your life, and that he ought to be goddam glad he was forty years old and able to write about the war instead of fighting in it. Ellis goodnaturedly pointed out that they weren't fighting either. Steve made Sheldrake sore by snapping out, "No, of course not, we're goddamned embusqués." He and Steve left the bar and ran like deer to get out of sight before Sheldrake could follow them. Around the corner they saw a streetcar marked Genoa and Steve hopped it without saying a word. Dick didn't have anything to do but follow.

The car rounded a block of houses and came out on the water-front. "Judas Priest, Dick," said Steve, "the goddam town's on fire." Beyond the black hulks of boats drawn up on the shore a rosy flame like a gigantic lampflame sent a broad shimmer towards them across the water. "Gracious, Steve, do you suppose the Austrians are in there?"

The car went whanging along; the conductor who came and got their fare looked calm enough. "Inglese?" he asked. "Americani," said Steve. He smiled and clapped them on the back and said something about the Presidente Veelson that they couldn't understand.

They got off the car in a big square surrounded by huge arcades that a raw bittersweet wind blew hugely through. Dressedup people in overcoats were walking up and down on the clean mosaic pave-ment. The town was all marble. Every façade that faced the sea was pink with the glow of the fire. "Here the tenors and the baritones and the sopranos all ready for the show to begin," said Dick. Steve grunted, "Chorus'll probably be the goddam Austrians."

They were cold and went into one of the shiny nickel and plateglass cafés to have a grog. The waiter told them in broken English that the fire was on an American tanker that had hit a mine and that she'd been burning for three days. A longfaced English officer came over from the bar and started to tell them how he was on a secret mission; it was all bloody awful about the retreat; it hadn't stopped yet; in Mi-lan they were talking about falling back on the Po; the only reason the bloody Austrians hadn't overrun all bloody Lombardy was they'd been so disorganized by their rapid advance they were in almost as bad shape as the bloody Italians were. Damned Italian officers kept talking about their quadrilateral, and if it wasn't for the French and British troops behind the Italian lines they'd have sold out long ago. French morale was pretty shaky, at that. Dick told him about how the tools got swiped every time they took their eyes off their cars. The Englishman said the thievery in these parts was extraordinary; that was what his secret mission was about; he was trying to trace an en-tire carload of boots that had vanished between Vintimiglia and San Raphael, "Whole bloody luggage van turns into thin air overnight . . .

extraordinary. . . . See those blighters over there at that table, they're bloody Austrian spies every mother's son of them . . . but try as I can I can't get them arrested . . . extraordinary. It's a bloody melodrama that's what it is, just like Drury Lane. A jolly good thing you Americans have come in. If you hadn't you'd see the bloody German flag flying over Genoa at this minute." He suddenly looked at his wristwatch, advised them to buy a bottle of whiskey at the bar if they wanted another bit of drink, because it was closing time, said cheeryoh, and hustled out.

They plunged out again into the empty marble town, down dark lanes and streets of stone steps with always the glare on some jutting wall overhead brighter and redder as they neared the waterfront. Time and again they got lost; at last they came out on wharves and bristle of masts of crowded feluccas and beyond the little crimsontipped waves of the harbor, the breakwater, and outside the breakwater the mass of flame of the burning tanker. Excited and drunk they walked on and on through the town: "By God, these towns are older than the world," Dick kept saying.

While they were looking at a marble lion, shaped like a dog, that stood polished to glassy smoothness by centuries of hands at the bottom of a flight of steps, an American voice hailed them, wanting to know if they knew their way around this goddam town. It was a young fellow who was a sailor on an American boat that had come over with a carload of mules. They said sure they knew their way and gave him a drink out of the bottle of cognac they'd bought. They sat there on the stone balustrade beside the lion that looked like a dog and swigged cognac out of the bottle and talked. The sailor showed them some silk stockings he'd salvaged off the burning oilship and told them about how he'd been jazzing an Eyetalian girl only she'd gone to sleep and he'd gotten disgusted and walked out on her. "This war's hell ain't it de truth?" he said; they all got to laughing.

"You guys seem to be a couple of pretty good guys," the sailor said. They handed him the bottle and he took a gulp. "You fellers are princes," he added spluttering, "and I'm goin' to tell you what I think, see. . . . This whole goddam war's a gold brick, it ain't on the level, its crooked from A to Z. No matter how it comes out fellers like us gets the s—y end of the stick, see? Well, what I say is all bets is off . . . every man go to hell in his own way . . . and three strikes is out, see?" They finished up the cognac.

Singing out savagely, "To hell wid 'em I say," the sailor threw the bottle with all his might against the head of the stone lion. The Genoese lion went on staring ahead with glassy doglike eyes.

Sourlooking loafers started gathering around to see what the trouble was so they moved on, the sailor waving his silk stockings as he walked. They found him his steamer tied up to the dock and shook hands again and again at the gangplank.

Then it was up to Dick and Steve to get themselves back across the ten miles to Ponte Decimo. Chilly and sleepy they walked until their feet were sore, then hopped a wop truck the rest of the way. The cobbles of the square and the roofs of the cars were covered with hoarfrost when they got there. Dick made a noise getting into the stretcher beside Sheldrake's and Sheldrake woke up, "What the hell?" he said. "Shut up," said Dick, "don't you see you're waking people up?"

Next day they got to Milan, huge wintry city with its overgrown pincushion cathedral and its Galleria jammed with people and restaurants and newspapers and whores and Cinzano and Campari Bitters. There followed another period of waiting during which most of the section settled down to an endless crapgame in the back room at Cova's; then they moved out to a place called Dolo on a frozen canal somewhere in the Venetian plain. To get to the elegant carved and painted villa where they were quartered they had to cross the Brenta. A company of British sappers had the bridge all mined and ready to blow up when the retreat began again. They promised to wait till Section 1 had crossed before blowing the bridge up. In Dolo there was very little to do; it was raw wintry weather; while most of the section sat around the stove and swapped their jack at poker, the grenadine guards made themselves hot rum punches over a gasoline burner, read Boccaccio in Italian and argued with Steve about anarchism.

Dick spent a great deal of his time wondering how he was going to get to Venice. It turned out that the fat lieutenant was worried by the fact that the section had no cocoa and that the Red Cross commissary in Milan hadn't sent the section any breakfast foods. Dick suggested that Venice was one of the world's great cocoamarkets, and that somebody who knew Italian ought to be sent over there to buy cocoa; so one frosty morning Dick found himself properly equipped with papers and seals boarding the little steamboat at Mestre.

There was a thin skim of ice on the lagoon that tore with a sound of silk on either side of the narrow bow where Dick stood leaning forward over the rail, tears in his eyes from the raw wind, staring at the long rows of stakes and the light red buildings rising palely out of the green water to bubblelike domes and square pointedtipped towers that etched themselves sharper and sharper against the zinc sky. The hunchback bridges, the greenslimy steps, the palaces. the marble quays were all empty. The only life was in a group of torpedoboats anchored in the Grand Canal. Dick forgot all about the cocoa walking through sculptured squares and the narrow streets and quays along the icefilled canals of the great dead city that lay there on the lagoon frail and empty as a cast snakeskin. To the north he could hear the tomtomming of the guns fifteen miles away on the Piave. One the way back it began to snow.

A few days later they moved up to Bassano behind Monte Grappa into a late renaissance villa all painted up with cupids and angels and elaborate draperies. Back of the villa the Brenta roared day and night under a covered bridge. There they spent their time evacuating cases of frozen feet, drinking hot rum punches at Citadella where the base hospital and the whorehouses were, and singing *The Foggy Foggy Dew* and *The Little Black Bull Came Down From the Mountain* over the rubber spaghetti at chow. Ripley and Steve decided they wanted to learn to draw and spent their days off drawing architectural details or the covered bridge. Schuyler practiced his Italian talking about Nietzsche with the Italian Lieut. Fred Summers had gotten a dose off a Milanese lady who he said must have belonged to one of the best families because she was riding in a carriage and picked him up, not he her, and spent most of his spare time brewing himself home remedies like cherry stems in hot water. Dick got to feeling lonely and blue, and in need of privacy, and wrote a great many letters home. The letters he got back made him feel worse than not getting any.

"You must understand how it is," he wrote the Thurlows, answering an enthusiastic screed of Hilda's about the "war to end war," "I don't believe in Christianity any more and can't argue from that standpoint, but you do, or at least Edwin does, and he ought to realize that in urging young men to go into his cockeyed lunatic asylum of war he's doing everything he can to undermine all the principles and ideals he most believes in. As the young fellow we had that talk with in Genoa that night said, it's not on the level, it's a dirty goldbrick game put over by governments and politicians for their own selfish interests, it's crooked from A to Z. If it wasn't for the censorship I could tell you things that would make you vomit."

Then he'd suddenly snap out of his argumentative mood and all the phrases about liberty and civilization steaming up out of his head would seem damn silly too, and he'd light the gasoline burner and make a rum punch and cheer up chewing the rag with Steve about books or painting or architecture. Moonlight nights the Austrians made things lively by sending bombing planes over. Some nights Dick found that staying out of the dugout and giving them a chance at him gave him a sort of bitter pleasure, and the dugout wasn't any protection against a direct hit anyway.

Sometime in February Steve read in the paper that the Empress Taitu of Abyssinia had died. They held a wake. They drank all the rum they had and keened until the rest of the section thought they'd gone crazy. They sat in the dark round the open moonlit window wrapped in blankets and drinking warm zabaglione. Some Austrian planes that had been droning overhead suddenly cut off their motors and dumped a load of bombs right in front of them. The antiaircraft guns had been barking for some time and shrapnel sparkling in the moonhazy sky overhead but they'd been too drunk to notice. One bomb fell geflump into the Brenta and the others filled the space in front of the window with red leaping glare and shook the villa with three roaring snorts. Plaster fell from the ceiling. They could hear the tiles skuttering down off the roof overhead.

"Jesus, that was almost good night," said Summers. Steve started singing, *Come away from that window, my light and my life,* but the rest of them drowned it out with an out of tune *Deutschland Deutschland Uber Alles.* They suddenly all felt crazy drunk.

Ed Schuyler was standing on a chair giving a recitation of the *Erlkönig* when Feldmann, the Swiss hotelkeeper's son who was now head of the section, stuck his head in the door and asked what in the devil they thought they were doing. "You'd better go down in the abris, one of the Italian mechanics was killed and a soldier walking up the road had his legs blown off . . . no time for monkeyshines." They offered him a drink and he went off in a rage. After that they drank marsala. Sometime in the early dawn greyness Dick got up and staggered to the window to vomit; it was raining pitchforks, the foaming rapids of the Brenta looked very white through the shimmering rain.

Next day it was Dick's and Steve's turn to go on post to Rova. They drove out of the yard at six with their heads like fireballoons, damn glad to be away from the big scandal there'd be at the section. At Rova the lines were quiet, only a few pneumonia or venereal cases to evacuate, and a couple of poor devils who'd shot themselves in the foot and were to be sent to the hospital under guard; but at the officers' mess where they ate things were very agitated indeed. Tenente Sardinaglia was under arrest in his quarters for saucing the Coronele and had been up there for two days making up a little march on his mandolin that he called the march of the medical colonels. Serrati told them about it giggling behind his hand while they were waiting for the other officers to come to mess. It was all on account of the macchina for coffee. There were only three macchine for the whole mess, one for the colonel, one for the major, and the other went around to the junior officers in rotation; well, one day last week they'd been kidding that bella ragazza, the niece of the farmer on whom they were quartered; she hadn't let any of the officers kiss her and had carried on like a crazy woman when they pinched her behind, and the colonel had been angry about it, and angrier yet when Sardinaglia had bet him five lira that he could kiss her and he'd whispered something in her ear and she'd let him and that had made the colonel get purple in the face and he'd told the ordinanza not to give the macchina to the tenente when his turn came round; and Sardinaglia had slapped the ordinanza's face and there'd been a row and as a result Sardinaglia was confined to his quarters and the Americans would see what a circus it was. They all had to straighten their faces in a hurry because the colonel and the major and the two captains came jingling in at that moment.

The ordinanza came and saluted, and said pronto spaghetti in a cheerful tone, and everybody sat down. For a while the officers were quiet sucking in the long oily tomatocoated strings of spaghetti, the wine was passed around and the colonel had just cleared his throat to begin one of his funny stories that everybody had to laugh at, when from up above there came the tinkle of a mandolin. The colonel's face got red and he put a forkful of spaghetti in his mouth instead of saying anything. As it was Sunday the meal was unusually long: at dessert the coffee macchina was awarded to Dick as a courtesy to gli americani and somebody produced a bottle of strega. The colonel told the ordinanza to tell the bella ragazza to come and have a glass of strega with him; he looked pretty sour at the idea, Dick thought; but he went and got her. She turned out to be a handsome stout oliveskinned countrygirl. Her cheeks burning she went timidly up to the colonel and said, thank you very much but please she never drank strong drinks. The colonel grabbed her and made her sit on his knee and tried to make her drink his glass of strega, but she kept her handsome set of ivory teeth clenched and wouldn't drink it. It ended by several of the officers holding her and tickling her and the colonel pouring the strega over her chin. Everybody roared with laughter except the ordinanza, who turned white as chalk, and Steve and Dick who didn't know where to look. While the senior officers were teasing and tickling her and running their hands into her blouse, the junior officers were holding her feet and running their hands up her legs. Finally the colonel got control of his laughter enough to say, "Basta, now she must give me a kiss." But the girl broke loose and ran out of the room.

"Go and bring her back," the colonel said to the ordinanza. After a moment the ordinanza came back and stood at attention and said he couldn't find her. "Good for him," whispered Steve to Dick. Dick noticed that the ordinanza's legs were trembling. "You can't can't you?" roared the colonel, and gave the ordinanza a push; one of the lieutenants stuck his foot out and the ordinanza tripped over it and fell. Everybody laughed and the colonel gave him a kick; he had gotten to his hands and knees when the colonel gave him a kick in the seat of his pants that sent him flat to the floor again. The officers all roared, the ordinanza crawled to the door with the colonel running after him giving him little kicks first on one side and then on the other, like a soccerplayer with a football. That put everybody in a good humor and they had another drink of strega all around. When they got outside Serrati, who'd been laughing with the rest, grabbed Dick's arm and hissed in his ear, "Bestie, . . . sono tutti bestie."

When the other officers had gone, Serrati took them up to see Sardinaglia who was a tall longfaced young man who liked to call himself a futurista. Serrati told him what had happened and said he was afraid the Americans had been disgusted. "A futurist must be disgusted at nothing except weakness and stupidity," said Sardinaglia sententiously. Then he told them he'd found out who the bella ragazza was really sleeping with . . . with the ordinanza. That he said disgusted him; it showed that women were all pigs. Then he said to sit down on his cot while he played them the march of the medical colonels. They declared it was fine. "A futurist must be strong and disgusted with nothing," he said, still trilling on the mandolin, "that's why I admire the Germans and American millionaires." They all laughed.

Dick and Steve went out to pick up some feriti to evacuate to the hospital. Behind the barn where they parked the cars, they found the ordinanza sitting on a stone with his head in his hands, tears had made long streaks on the dirt of his face. Steve went up to him and patted him on the back and gave him a package of Mecca cigarettes, that had been distributed to them by the Y.M.C.A. The ordinanza squeezed Steven's hand, looked as if he was going to kiss it. He said after the war he was going to America where people were civilized, not bestie like here. Dick asked him where the girl had gone. "Gone away," he said. "Andata via."

When they got back to the section they found there was hell to pay. Orders had come for Savage, Warner, Ripley and Schuyler to report to the head office in Rome in order to be sent back to the States. Feldmann wouldn't tell them what the trouble was. They noticed at once that the other men in the section were looking at them suspiciously and were nervous about speaking to them, except for Fred Summers who said he didn't understand it, the whole frigging business was a madhouse anyway. Sheldrake, who'd moved his dufflebag and cot into another room in the villa, came around with an I told you so air and said he'd heard the words seditious utterances and that an Italian intelligence officer had been around asking about them. He wished them good luck and said it was too bad. They left the section without saying goodby to anybody. Feldmann drove them and their dufflebags and bedrolls down to Vicenza in the camionette. At the railroad station he handed them their orders of movement to Rome, said it was too bad, wished them good luck, and went off in a hurry without shaking hands.

"The sons of bitches," growled Steve, "you might think we had leprosy." Ed Schuyler was reading the military passes, his face beaming. "Men and brethren," he said, "I am moved to make a speech . . . this is the greatest graft yet . . . do you gentlemen realize that what's happening is that the Red Cross, otherwise known as the goose that lays the golden egg, is presenting us with a free tour of Italy? We don't have to get to Rome for a year." "Keep out of Rome till the revolution," suggested Dick. "Enter Rome with the Austrians," said Ripley.

A train came into the station. They piled into a first class compartment; when the conductor came and tried to explain that their orders read for second class transportation, they couldn't understand Italian, so finally he left them there. At Verona they piled off to check their dufflebags and cots to Rome. It was suppertime so they decided to walk around the town and spend the night. In the morning they went to see the ancient theatre and the great peachcolored marble church of San Zeno. Then they sat around the café at the station until a train came by for Rome. The train was jampacked with officers in pale blue and pale green cloaks; by Bologna they'd gotten tired of sitting on the floor of the vestibule and decided they must see the leaning towers. Then they went to Pistoja, Lucca, Pisa and back to the main line at Florence. When the conductors shook their heads over the orders of movement they explained that they'd been misinformed and due to ignorance of the language had taken the wrong train. At Florence, where it was rainy and cold and the buildings all looked like the replicas of them they'd seen at home, the station master put them forcibly on the express for Rome, but they sneaked out the other side after it had started and got into the local for Assisi. From there they got to Siena by way of San Gimignano, as full of towers as New York, in a hack they hired for the day, and ended up one fine spring morning full up to the neck with painting and architecture and oil and garlic and scenery, looking at the Signorelli frescoes in the cathedral at Orvieto. They stayed there all day looking at the great fresco of the Last Judgment, drinking the magnificent wine and basking in the sunny square outside. When the got to Rome, to the station next to the baths of Diocletian, they felt pretty bad at the prospect of giving up their passes; they were amazed when the employee merely stamped them and gave them back, saying, "Per il ritorno."

They went to a hotel and cleaned up, and then pooling the last of their money went on a big bust with a highclass meal, Frascati wine and asti for dessert, a vaudeville show and a cabaret on the Via Roma where they met an American girl they called the baroness who promised to show them the town. By the end of the evening nobody had enough money left to got home with the baroness or any of her charming ladyfriends, so they hired a cab with their last ten lire to take them out to see the Colosseum by moonlight. The great masses of ruins, the engraved stones, the names, the stately Roman names, the old cabdriver with his oilcloth stovepipe hat and his green soupstrainers recommending whorehouses under the last quarter of the ruined moon, the great masses of masonry full of arches and columns piled up everywhere into the night, the boom of the word Rome dying away in pompous chords into the past, sent them to bed with their heads whirling, Rome throbbing in their ears so that they could not sleep.

Next morning Dick got up while the others were still dead to the world and went round to the Red Cross; he was suddenly nervous and worried so that he couldn't eat his breakfast. At the office he saw a stoutish Bostonian Major who seemed to be running things, and asked him straight out what the devil the trouble was. The Major hemmed and hawed and kept the conversation in an agreeable tone, as one Harvard man to another. He talked about indiscretions and the oversensitiveness of the Italians. As a matter of fact the censor didn't like the tone of certain letters, etcetera, etcetera. Dick said he felt he ought to explain his position, and that if the Red Cross felt he hadn't done his duty they ought to give him a courtmartial, he said he felt there were many men in his position who had pacifist views but now that the country was at war were willing to do any kind of work they could to help, but that didn't mean he believed in the war, he felt he ought to be allowed to explain his position. The major said Ah well he quite understood, etcetera, etcetera, but that the young should realize the importance of discretion, etcetera, etcetera, and that the whole thing had been satisfactorily explained as an indiscretion; as a matter of fact the incident was closed. Dick kept saying, he ought to be allowed to explain his position, and the major kept saying the incident was closed, etcetera, etcetera, until it all seemed a little silly and he left the office. The major promised him transportation to Paris if he wanted to take it up with the office there. Dick went back to the hotel feeling baffled and sore.

The other two had gone out, so he and Steve walked around the town, looking at the sunny streets, that smelt of frying oliveoil and wine and old stones, and the domed baroque churches and the columns and the Pantheon and the Tiber. They didn't have a cent in their pockets to buy lunch or a drink with. They spent the afternoon hungry, napping glumly on the warm sod of the Pincian, and got back to the room famished and depressed to find Schuyler and Ripley drinking vermouth and soda and in high spirits. Schuyler had run into an old friend of his father's, Colonel Anderson, who was on a mission investigating the Red Cross, and had poured out his woes and given him dope about small graft at the office in Milan. Major Anderson had set him up to lunch and highballs at the Hotel de Russie, lent him a hundred dollars and fixed him up with a job in the publicity department. "So men and brethren, evviva Italia and the goddamned Alleati, we're all set." "What about the dossier?" Steve asked savagely. "Aw forget it, siamo tutti Italiani . . . who's a defeatist now?"

Schuyler set them all up to meals, took them out to Tivoli and the Lake of Nemi in a staff car, and finally put them on the train to Paris with the rating of captain on their transport orders.

The first day in Paris Steve went off to the Red Cross office to get shipped home. "To hell with it, I'm going to C.O.," was all he'd say. Ripley enlisted in the French artillery school at Fontainebleau Dick got himself a cheap room in a little hotel on the Ile St. Louis and spent his days interviewing first one higher up and then another in the Red Cross; Hiram Halsey Cooper had suggested the names in a very guarded reply to a cable Dick sent him from Rome. The higherups sent him from one to the other. "Young man," said one baldheaded official in a luxurious office at the Hotel Crillon, "your opinions, while showing a senseless and cowardly turn of mind, don't matter. The American people is out to get the kaiser. We are bending every nerve and every energy towards that end; anybody who gets in the way of the great machine the energy and devotion of a hundred million patriots is building towards the stainless purpose of saving civilization from the Huns will be mashed like a fly. I'm surprised that a collegebred man like you hasn't more sense. Don't monkey with the buzzsaw."

Finally he was sent to the army intelligence service where he found a young fellow named Spaulding he'd known in college who greeted him with a queazy smile. "Old man," he said, "in a time like this we can't give in to our personal feelings can we . . .? I think it's perfectly criminal to allow yourself the luxury of private opinions, perfectly criminal. It's war time and we've all got to do our duty, it's people like you that are encouraging the Germans to keep up the fight, people like you and the Russians." Spaulding's boss was a captain and wore spurs and magnificently polished puttees; he was a sternlooking young man with a delicate profile. he strode up to Dick, put his face close to his and yelled, "What would you do if two Huns attacked your sister? You'd fight, wouldn't you? . . . if you're not a dirty yellow dawg. . . ." Dick tried to point out that he was anxious to keep on doing the work he had been doing, he was trying to get back to the front with the Red Cross, he wanted an opportunity to explain his position. The captain strode up and down, bawling him out, yelling that any man who was still a pacifist after the President's declaration of war was a moron or what was worse a degenerate and that they didn't want people like that in the A.E.F. and that he was going to see to it that Dick would be sent back to the States and that he would not be allowed to come back in any capacity whatsoever. "The A.E.F. is no place for a slacker."

Dick gave up and went to the Red Cross office to get his transportation; they gave him an order for the *Touraine* sailing from Bordeaux in two weeks. His last two weeks in Paris he spent working as a volunteer stretcherbearer at the American hospital on the Avenue du Bois de Boulogne. It was June. There were airraids every clear night and when the wind was right you could hear the guns on the front. The German offensive was on, the lines were so near Paris the ambulances were evacuating wounded directly on the basehospitals. All night the stretcher cases would spread along the broad pavements under the trees in fresh leaf in front of the hospital; Dick would help carry them up the marble stairs into the reception room. One night they put him on duty outside the operating room and for twelve hours he had the job of carrying out buckets of blood and gauze from which protruded occasionally a shattered bone or a piece of an arm or a leg. When he went off duty he'd walk home achingly tired through the strawberryscented early Parisian morning, thinking of the faces and the eyes and the sweatdrenched hair and the clenched fingers clotted with blood and dirt and the fellows kidding and pleading for cigarettes and the bubbling groans of the lung cases.

One day he saw a pocket compass in a jeweller's window on the Rue de Rivoli. He went in and bought it; there was suddenly a fullformed plan in his head to buy a civilian suit, leave his uniform in a heap on the wharf at Bordeaux and make for the Spanish border. With luck and all the old transport orders he had in his inside pocket he was sure he could make it; hop across the border and then, once in a country free from nightmare, decide what to do. He even got ready a letter to send his mother.

All the time he was packing his books and other junk in his dufflebag and carrying it on his back up the quais to the Gare d'Orleans, Swinburne's *Song in Time of Order* kept going through his head:

> While three men hold together
> The kingdoms are less by three.

By gum, he must write some verse: what people needed was stirring poems to nerve them for revolt against their cannibal governments. Sitting in the secondclass compartment he was so busy building a daydream of himself living in a sunscorched Spanish town, sending out flaming poems and manifestoes, calling young men to revolt against their butchers, poems that would be published by secret presses all over the world, that he hardly saw the suburbs of Paris or the bluegreen summer farmlands sliding by.

> Let our flag run out straight in the wind
> The old red shall be floated again
> When the ranks that are thin shall be thinned
> When the names that were twenty are ten

Even the rumblebump rumblebump of the French railroad train seemed to be chanting as if the words were muttered low in unison by a marching crowd:

> While three men hold together
> The kingdoms are less by three.

At noon Dick got hungry and went to the diner to eat a last deluxe meal. He sat down at a table opposite a goodlooking young man in a French officer's uniform. "Good God, Ned, is that you?" Blake Wigglesworth threw back his head in the funny way he had and laughed. "Garçon," he shouted, "un verre pour le monsieur."

"But how long were you in the Lafayette Escadrille?" stammered Dick.

"Not long . . . they wouldn't have me."

"And how about the Navy?"

"Threw me out too, the damn fools think I've got T.B. . . . garçon, une bouteille de champagne. . . . Where are you going?"

"I'll explain."

"Well, I'm going home on the *Touraine*." Ned threw back his head laughing again and his lips formed the syllables blahblahblahblah. Dick noticed that although his face was very pale and thin his skin under his eyes and up onto the temples was flushed and his eyes looked a little too bright. "Well, so am I," he heard himself say.

"I got into hot water," said Ned.

"Me too," said Dick. "Very."

They lifted their glasses and looked into each other's eyes and laughed. They sat in the diner all afternoon talking and drinking and got to Bordeaux boiled as owls. Ned had spent all his money in Paris and Dick had very little left, so they had to sell their bedrolls and equipment to a couple of American lieutenants just arrived they met in the Café de Bordeaux. It was almost like old days in Boston going around from bar to bar and looking for places to get drinks after closing. They spent most of the night in an elegant maison publique all upholstered in pink satin, talking to the madam, a driedup woman with a long upper lip like a llama's wearing a black spangled evening dress, who took a fancy to them and made them stay and eat onion soup with her. They were so busy talking they forgot about the girls. She'd been in the Transvaal during the Boer War and spoke a curious brand of South African English. "Vous comprennez ve had very fine clientele, every man jack officers, very much elegance, decorum. These johnnies off the veldt . . . get the hell outen here . . . bloody select don't you know. Ve had two salons, one salon English officers, one salon Boer officers, very select, never in all the war make any bloody row, no fight. . . . Vos compatriotes les Americains ce n'est pas comme ça, mes amis. Beaucoup sonofabeetch, make drunk, make bloody row, make sick, naturellement il y a aussi des gentils garçons comme vous, mes mignons, des veritables gentlemens," and she patted them both on the cheeks with her horny ringed hands. When they left she wanted to kiss them and went with them to the door saying, "Bonsoi mes jolis petits gentlemens."

All the crossing they were never sober after eleven in the morning;

it was calm misty weather; they were very happy. One night when he was standing alone in the stern beside the small gun, Dick was searching his pocket for a cigarette when his fingers felt something hard in the lining of his coat. It was the little compass he had bought to help him across the Spanish border. Guiltily, he fished it out and dropped it overboard.

Newsreel XXVII

HER WOUNDED HERO OF WAR A FRAUD
SAYS WIFE IN SUIT

Mid the wars great coise
Stands the red cross noise
She's the rose of no man's land

according to the thousands who had assembled to see the launching and were eyewitnesses of the disaster the scaffold simply seemed to turn over like a gigantic turtle precipitating its occupants into twentyfive feet of water. This was exactly four minutes before the launching was scheduled

Oh that battle of Paree
It's making a bum out of me

BRITISH BEGIN OPERATION ON AFGHAN FRONTIER

the leading part in world trade which the U.S. is now confidently expected to take, will depend to a very great extent upon the intelligence and success with which its harbors are utilized and developed

I wanta go home I wanta go home
The bullets they whistle the cannons they roar
I dont want to go to the trenches no more
Oh ship me over the sea
Where the Allemand cant get at me

you have begun a crusade against toys, but if all the German toys were commandeered and destroyed the end of German importations would not yet have been reached

HOLDS UP 20 DINERS IN CAFE

LAWHATING GATHERINGS NOT TO BE ALLOWED IN CRITICAL TIME THREATENING SOCIAL UPHEAVAL

Oh my   I'm too young to die
I wanta go home

Nancy Enjoys Nightlife Despite Raids

TATTOOED WOMAN SOUGHT BY POLICE IN TRUNK MURDER

ARMY WIFE SLASHED BY ADMIRER

Young Man Alleged to Have Taken Money to Aid in Promotion of a Reserve Office. It appears that these men were Chinese merchants from Irkutsk, Chita and elsewhere who were proceeding homeward to Harbin carrying their profits for investment in new stocks

Oh that battle of Paree
Its making a bum out of me
Toujours la femme et combien

300,000 RUSSIAN NOBLES SLAIN BY BOLSHEVIKI

Bankers of This Country, Britain and France to Safeguard Foreign Investors

these three girls came to France thirteen months ago and were the first concertparty to entertain at the front. They staged a show for the American troops from a flatcar base of a large naval gun three kilometers behind the line on the day of the evening of the drive at Chateau Thierry. After that they were assigned to the Aix-les-Bains leave area where they acted during the day as canteen girls and entertained and danced at night

You never knew a place that was so short of men
Beaucoup rum   beaucoup fun
Mother'd never know her loving son
Oh, if you want to see   that statue of Libertee
Keep away from that battle of Paree

The Camera Eye (35)

there were always two cats the color of hot milk with a little coffee in it with aquamarine eyes and sootblack faces in the window of the laundry opposite the little creamery where we ate breakfast on the Montagne St. Geneviève huddled between the old squeezedup slategrey houses of the Latin Quarter leaning over steep small streets cosy under the fog   minute streets lit with different-colored chalks cluttered with infinitesimal bars restaurants paintships and old prints beds bidets faded perfumery microscopic sizzle of frying butter

the Bertha made a snapping noise no louder than a cannon-cracker near the hotel where Oscar Wilde died we all ran up stairs to see if the house was on fire but the old woman whose lard was burning was sore as a crutch

all the big new quarters near the Arc de Triomphe were deserted but in the dogeared yellowbacked Paris of the Carmagnole the Faubourg St Antoine the Commune we were singing

'suis dans l'axe
'suis dans l'axe
'suis dans l'axe du gros canon

when the Bertha dropped in the Seine there was a concours de pêche in the little brightgreen skiffs among all the old whiskery fishermen scooping up in nets the minnows the concussion had stunned

Eveline Hutchins

Eveline went to live with Eleanor in a fine apartment Eleanor had gotten hold of somehow on the quai de la Tournelle. It was the mansard floor of a grey peelingfaced house built at the time of Richelieu and done over under Louis Quinze. Eveline never tired of looking out the window, through the delicate tracing of the wroughtiron balcony, at the Seine where toy steamboats bucked the current, towing shinyvarnished barges that had lace curtains and geraniums in the windows of their deckhouses painted green and red, and at the island opposite where the rocketing curves of the flying buttresses shoved the apse of Nôtre Dâme dizzily upwards out of the trees of a little park. They had tea at a small Buhl table in the window almost every evening when they got home from the office on the Rue de Rivoli, after spending the day pasting pictures of ruined French farms and orphaned children and starving warbabies into scrapbooks to be sent home for use in Red Cross drives.

After tea she'd go out in the kitchen and watch Yvonne cook. With the groceries and sugar they drew at the Red Cross commissary, Yvonne operated a system of barter so that their food hardly cost them anything. At first Eveline tried to stop her but she'd answer with a torrent of argument: did Mademoiselle think that President Poincaré or the generals or the cabinet ministers, ces salots de profiteurs, ces salots d'embusqués, went without their brioches? It was the systme D, ils s'en fichent des particuliers, des pauvres gens... very well her ladies would eat as well as any old camels of generals, if she had her way she'd have all the generals line up before a firingsquad and the embusqué ministers and the ronds de cuir too. Eleanor said her sufferings had made the old woman a little cracked but Jerry Burnham said it was the rest of the world that was cracked.

Jerry Burnham was the little redfaced man who'd been such a help with the colonel the first night Eveline got to Paris. They often laughed about it afterwards. He was working for the U.P. and appeared every few days in her office on his rounds covering Red Cross activities. He knew all the Paris restaurants and would take Eveline out to dinner at the Tour d'Argent or to lunch at the Taverne Nicholas Flamel and they'd walk around the old streets of the Marais afternoons and get late to their work together. When they'd settle in the evening at a good quiet table in a café where they couldn't be overheard (all the waiters were spies he said), he'd drink a lot of cognac and soda and pour out his feelings, how his work disgusted him, how a correspondent couldn't get to see anything anymore, how he had three or four censorships on his neck all the time and had to send out prepared stuff that was all a pack of dirty lies every word of it, how a man lost his selfrespect doing things like that year after year, how a newspaperman had been little better than a skunk before the war, but that now there wasn't anything low enough you could call him. Eveline would try to cheer him up telling him that when the war was over he ought to write a book like *Le Feu* and really tell the truth about it. "But the war won't ever be over . . . too damn profitable, do you get me? Back home they're coining money, the British are coining money; even the French, look at Bordeaux and Toulouse and Marseilles coining money and the goddam politicians, all of 'em got bank accounts in Amsterdam or Barcelona, the sons of bitches." Then he'd take her hand and get a crying jag and promise that if it did end he'd get back his selfrespect and write the great novel he felt he had in him.

Late that fall Eveline came home one evening tramping through the mud and the foggy dusk to find that Eleanor had a French soldier to tea. She was glad to see him, because she was always complaining that she wasn't getting to know any French people, nothing but professional relievers and Red Cross women who were just too tiresome; but it was some moments before she realized it was Maurice Millet. She wondered how she could have fallen for him even when she was a kid, he looked so middleaged and pasty and oldmaidish in his stained blue uniform. His large eyes with their girlish long lashes had heavy violet rings under them. Eleanor evidently thought he was wonderful still, and drank up his talk about l'élan suprème du sacrifice and l'harmonie mysterieuse de la mort. He was a stretcherbearer in a basehospital at Nancy, had become very religious and had almost forgotten his English. When they asked him about his painting he shrugged his shoulders and wouldn't answer. At supper he ate very little and drank only water. He stayed till late in the evening telling them about miraculous conversions of unbelievers, extreme unction on the firing line, a vision of the young Christ he'd seen walking among the wounded in a dressingstation during a gasattack. Après la guerre he was going into a monastery. Trappist perhaps. After he left Eleanor said it had been the most inspiring evening she'd ever had in her life; Eveline didn't argue with her.

Maurice came back one other afternoon before his perme expired bringing a young writer who was working at the Quai d'Orsay, a tall young Frenchman with pink cheeks who looked like an English publicschool boy, whose name was Raoul Lemonnier. He seemed to refer to speak English than French. He'd been at the front for two years in the Chasseurs Alpins and had been reformé on account of his lungs or his uncle who was a minister he couldn't say which. It was all very boring, he said. He thought tennis was ripping, though, and went out to St. Cloud to row every afternoon. Eleanor discovered that what she'd been wanting all fall had been a game of tennis. He said he liked English and American women because they liked sport. Here every woman thought you wanted to go to bed with her right away; "Love is very boring," he said. He and Eveline stood in the window talking about cocktails (he adored American drinks) and looked out at the last purple shreds of dusk settling over Nôtre Dâme and the Seine, while Eleanor and Maurice sat in the dark in the little salon talking about St. Francis of Assisi. She asked him to dinner.

The next morning Eleanor said she thought she was going to become a Catholic. On their way to the office she made Eveline stop into Nôtre Dâme with her to hear mass and they both lit candles for Maurice's safety at the front before what Eveline thought was a just too tiresomelooking virgin near the main door. But it was impressive all the same, the priests moaning and the lights and the smell of chilled incense. She certainly hoped poor Maurice wouldn't be killed.

For dinner that night Eveline invited Jerry Burnham, Miss Felton who was back from Amiens and Major Appleton who was in Paris doing something about tanks. It was a fine dinner, duck roasted with oranges, although Jerry, who was sore about how much Eveline talked to Lemonnier, had to get drunk and use a lot of bad language and tell about the retreat at Caporetto and say that the Allies were in a bad way. Major Appleton said he oughtn't to say it even if it was true and got quite red in the face. Eleanor was pretty indignant and said he ought to be arrested for making such a statement, and after everybody had left she and Eveline had quite a quarrel. "What will that young Frenchman be thinking of us? You're a darling, Eveline dear, but you have the vulgarest friends. I don't know where you pick them up, and that Felton woman drank four cocktails, a quart of beaujolais and three cognacs, I kept tabs on her myself;" Eveline started to laugh and they both got to laughing. But Eleanor said that their life was getting much too bohemian and that it wasn't right with the war on and things going so dreadfully in Italy and Russia and the poor boys in the trenches and all that.

That winter Paris gradually filled up with Americans in uniform, and staffcars, and groceries from the Red Cross supply store; and Major Moorehouse who, it turned out, was an old friend of Eleanor's, arrived straight from Washington to take charge of the Red Cross publicity. Everybody was talking about him before he came because he'd been one of the best known publicity experts in New York before the war. There was no one who hadn't heard of J. Ward Moorehouse.

There was a lot of scurry around the office when word came around that he'd actually landed in Brest and everybody was nervous worrying where there axe was going to fall.

The morning he arrived the first thing Eveline noticed was that Eleanor had had her hair curled. Then just before noon the whole publicity department was asked into Major Wood's office to meet Major Moorehouse. He was a biggish man with blue eyes and hair so light it was almost white. His uniform fitted well and his Sam Browne belt and his puttees shone like glass. Eveline thought at once that there was something sincere and appealing about him, like about her father, that she liked. He looked young too, in spite of the thick jowl, and he had a slight southern accent when he talked. He made a little speech about the importance of the work the Red Cross was doing to keep up the morale of civilians and combatants, and that their publicity ought to have two aims, to stimulate giving among the folks back home and to keep people informed of the progress of the work. The trouble now was that people didn't know enough about what a valuable effort the Red Cross workers were making and were too prone to listen to the criticisms of proGermans working under the mask of pacifism and knockers and slackers always ready to carp and criticize; and that the American people and the warwracked populations of the Allied countries must be made to know the splendid sacrifice the Red Cross workers were making, as splendid in its way as the sacrifice of the dear boys in the trenches.

"Even at this moment, my friends, we are under fire, ready to make the supreme sacrifice that civilization shall not perish from the earth." Major Wood leaned back in his swivelchair and it let out a squeak that made everybody look up with a start and several people looked out of the window as if they expected to see a shell from big Bertha hurtling right in on them. "You see," said Major Moorehouse eagerly, his blue eyes snapping, "that is what we must make people feel . . . the catch in the throat, the wrench to steady the nerves, the determination to carry on."

Eveline felt stirred in spite of herself. She looked a quick sideways look at Eleanor, who looked cool and lilylike as she had when she was listening to Maurice tell about the young Christ of the gasattack. Can't ever tell what she's thinking, though, said Eveline to herself.

That afternoon when J.W., as Eleanor called Major Moorehouse, came down to have a cup of tea with them, Eveline felt that she was being narrowly watched and minded her P's and Q's as well as she could; it is the financial adviser; she was giggling about inside. He looked a little haggard and didn't say much, and winced noticeably when they talked about airraids moonlight nights, and how President Poincaré went around in person every morning to visit the ruins and condole with the survivors. He didn't stay long and went off someplace in a staffcar to confer with some high official or other. Eveline thought he looked nervous and uneasy and would rather have stayed with them. Eleanor went out on the landing of the stairs with him and was gone some time. Eveline watched her narrowly when she came back into the room but her face had its accustomed look of finely chiselled calm. It was on the tip of Eveline's tongue to ask her if Major Moorehouse was her . . . her . . . but she couldn't think of a way of putting it.

Eleanor didn't say anything for some time; then she shook her head and said, "Poor Gertrude." "Who's that?" Eleanor's voice was just a shade tinny, "J.W.'s wife . . . she's in a sanitarium with a nervous breakdown . . . the strain, darling, this terrible war."

Major Moorehouse went down to Italy to reorganize the publicity of the American Red Cross there, and a couple of weeks later Eleanor got orders from Washington to join the Rome office. That left Eveline alone with Yvonne in the apartment.

It was a chilly, lonely winter and working with all these relievers was just too tiresome, but Eveline managed to hold her job and to have some fun sometimes in the evening with Raoul, who would come around and take her out to some petite boite or other that he'd always say was very boring. He took her to the Noctambules where you could sometimes get drinks after the legal hour; or up to a little restaurant on the Butte of Montmartre where one cold moonlit January night they stood on the porch of the Sacré Coeur and saw the Zeppelins come over. Paris stretched out cold and dead as if all the tiers of roofs and domes were carved out of snow and the shrapnel sparkled frostily overhead and the searchlights were antennae of great insects moving through the milky darkness. At intervals came red snorting flares of the incendiary bombs. Just once they caught sight of two tiny silver cigars overhead. They looked higher than the moon.

Eveline found that Raoul's arm that had been around her waist had slipped up and that he had his hand over her breast. "C'est fou tu sais . . . c'est fou tu sais," he was saying in a singsong voice, he seemed to have forgotten his English. After that they talked French and Eveline thought she loved him terribly much. After the breloque had gone through the streets they walked home across dark silent Paris. At one corner a gendarme came up and asked Lemonnier for his papers. He read them through painfully in the faint blue glow of a corner light, while Eveline stood by breathless, feeling her heart pound. The gendarme handed back the papers, saluted, apologized profusely and walked off. Neither of them said anything about it, but Raoul seemed to be taking it for granted he was going to sleep with her at her apartment. They walked home briskly through the cold black streets, their footsteps clacking sharply on the cobbles. She hung on his arm; there was something tight and electric and uncomfortable in the way their hips occasionally touched as they walked.

Her house was one of the few in Paris that didn't have a concièrge. She unlocked the door and they climbed shivering together up the cold stone stairs. She whispered to him to be quiet, because of her maid. "It is very boring," he whispered; his lips brushed warm against her ear. "I hope you won't think it's too boring."

While he was combing his hair at her dressingtable, taking little connoisseur's sniffs at her bottles of perfume, preening himself in the mirror without haste and embarrassment, he said, "Charmante Eveline, would you like to be my wife? It could be arranged, don't you know. My uncle who is the head of the family is very fond of Americans. Of course it would be very boring, the contract and all that." "Oh, no, that wouldn't be my idea at all," she whispered giggling and shivering from the bed. Raoul gave her a furious offended look, said good night very formally and left.

When the trees began to bud outside her window and the flowerwomen in the markets began to sell narcissuses and daffodils, the feeling that it was spring made her long months alone in Paris seem drearier than ever. Jerry Burnham had gone to Palestine; Raoul Lemonnier had never come to see her again; whenever he was in town Major Appleton came around and paid her rather elaborate attentions, but he was just too tiresome. Eliza Felton was driving an ambulance attached to a U.S. basehospital on the Avenue du Bois de Boulogne and would come around those Sundays when she was off duty and make Eveline's life miserable with her complaints that Eveline was not the free pagan soul she'd thought at first. She said that nobody loved her and that she was praying for the Bertha with her number on it that would end it all. It got so bad that Eveline wasn't able to stay in the house at all on Sunday and often spent the afternoon in her office reading Anatole France.

Then Yvonne's crotchets were pretty trying; she tried to run Eveline's life with her tightlipped comments. When Don Stevens turned up for a leave, looking more haggard than ever in the grey uniform of the Quaker outfit, it was a godsend, and Eveline decided maybe she'd been in love with him after all. She told Yvonne he was her cousin and that they'd been brought up like brother and sister and put him up in Eleanor's room.

Don was in a tremendous state of excitement about the success of the Bolsheviki in Russia, ate enormously, drank all the wine in the house, and was full of mysterious references to underground forces he was in touch with. He said all the armies were mutinous and that what had happened at Caporetto would happen on the whole front, the German soldiers were ready for revolt too and that would be the beginning of the world revolution. He told her about the mutinies at Verdun, about long trainloads of soldiers he'd seen going up to an attack crying, "A bas la guerre," and shooting at the gendarmes as they went.

"Eveline, we're on the edge of gigantic events. . . . The working classes of the world won't stand for this nonsense any longer . . . damn it, the war will have been almost worth while if we get a new socialist civilization out of it." He leaned across the table and kissed her right under the thin nose of Yvonne who was bringing in pancakes with burning brandy on them. He wagged his finger at Yvonne and almost got a smile out of her by the way he said, "Après la guerre finie."

That spring and summer things certainly did seem shaky, almost as if Don were right. At night she could hear the gigantic surf of the guns in continuous barrage on the crumbling front. The office was full of crazy rumors: the British Fifth army had turned and run, the Canadians had mutinied and seized Amiens, spies were disabling all the American planes, the Austrians were breaking through in Italy again. Three times the Red Cross office had orders to pack up their records and be ready to move out of Paris. In the face of all that it was hard for the publicity department to keep up the proper cheer-

ful attitude in their releases, but Paris kept on filling up reassuringly
with American faces, American M.P.s, Sam Browne belts and canned
goods; and in July Major Moorehouse, who had just arrived back
from the States, came into the office with a firsthand account of
Château Thierry and announced that the war would be over in a year.

The same evening he asked Eveline to dine with him at the Café de
la Paix and to do it she broke a date she had with Jerry Burnham who
had gotten back from the Near East and the Balkans and was full of
stories of cholera and calamity. J.W. ordered a magnificent dinner, he
said Eleanor had told him to see if Eveline didn't need a little cheering
up. He talked about the gigantic era of expansion that would dawn
for America after the war. America the good samaritan healing the
wounds of wartorn Europe. It was as if he was rehearsing a speech,
when he got to the end of it he looked at Eveline with a funny depre-
catory smile and said, "And the joke of it is, it's true," and Eveline
laughed and suddenly found that she liked J.W. very much indeed.

She had on a new dress she'd bought at Paquin's with some money
her father had sent her for her birthday, and it was a relief after the
uniform. They were through eating before they had really gotten
started talking. Eveline wanted to try to get him to talk about himself. After dinner they went to Maxim's, but that was full up with
brawling drunken aviators, and the rumpus seemed to scare J.W. so
that Eveline suggested to him that they go down to her place and have
a glass of wine. When they got to the quai de la Tournelle, just as they
were stepping out of J.W.'s staffcar she caught sight of Don Stevens
walking down the street. For a second she hoped he wouldn't see
them, but he turned around and ran back. He had a young fellow
with him in a private's uniform whose name was Johnson. They all
went up and sat around glumly in her parlor. She and J.W. couldn't
seem to talk about anything but Eleanor, and the other two sat glumly
in their chairs looking embarrassed until J.W. got to his feet, went
down to his staffcar, and left.

"God damn it, if there's anything I hate it's a Cross Red Major,"
broke out Don as soon as the door closed behind J.W.

Eveline was angry. "Well, it's no worse than being a fake Quaker,"
she said icily.

"You must forgive our intruding, Miss Hutchins," mumbled the
doughboy who had a blonde Swedish look.

"We wanted to get you to come out to a café or something, but it's too late now," started Don crossly. The doughboy interrupted him, "I hope, Miss Hutchins, you don't mind our intruding, I mean my intruding . . . I begged Don to bring me along. He's talked so much about you and it's a year since I've seen a real nice American girl."

He had a deferential way of talking and a whiny Minnesota accent that Eveline hated at first, but by the time he excused himself and left she liked him and stood up for him when Don said, "He's an awful sweet guy but there's something sappy about him. I was afraid you wouldn't like him." She wouldn't let Don spend the night with her as he'd expected and he went away looking very sullen.

In October Eleanor came back with a lot of antique Italian painted panels she'd picked up for a song. In the Red Cross office there were more people than were needed for the work and she and Eleanor and J.W. took a tour of the Red Cross canteens in the east of France in a staffcar. It was a wonderful trip, the weather was good for a wonder, almost like American October, they had lunch and dinner at regimental headquarters and army corps headquarters and divisional headquarters everywhere, and all the young officers were so nice to them, and J.W. was in such a good humor and kept them laughing all the time, and they saw field batteries firing and an airplane duel and sausage balloons and heard the shriek of an arrivé. It was during that trip that Eveline began to notice for the first time something cool in Eleanor's manner that hurt her; they'd been such good friends the first week Eleanor had gotten back from Rome.

Back in Paris it suddenly got very exciting, so many people they knew turned up, Eveline's brother George who was an interpreter at the headquarters of the S.O.S. and a Mr. Robbins, a friend of J.W.'s who was always drunk and had a very funny way of talking and Jerry Burnham and a lot of newspaper men and Major Appleton who was now a Colonel. They had little dinners and parties and the main difficulty was sorting out ranks and getting hold of people who mixed properly. Fortunately their friends were all officers or correspondents who ranked as officers. Only once Don Stevens turned up just before they were having Colonel Appleton and Brigadier General Byng to dinner, and Eveline's asking him to stay made things very awkward because the General thought Quakers were slackers of the worst kind, and Don flared up and said a pacifist could be a better patriot than a staff officer in a soft job and that patriotism was a crime against humanity anyway. It would have been very disagreeable if

Colonel Appleton who had drunk a great many cocktails hadn't broken through the little gilt chair he was sitting on and the General had laughed and kidded the Colonel with a bad pun about avoir du poise that took everybody's mind off the argument. Eleanor was very sore about Don, and after the guests had left she and Eveline had a standup quarrel. Next morning Eleanor wouldn't speak to her; Eveline went out to look for another apartment.

Newsreel XXVIII

Oh the eagles they fly high
In Mobile, in Mobile

Americans swim broad river and scale steep banks of canal in brilliant capture of Dun. It is a remarkable fact that the Compagnie Generale Transatlantique, more familiarly known as the French Line, has not lost a single vessel in its regular passenger service during the entire period of the war

RED FLAG FLIES ON BALTIC

"I went through Egypt to join Allenby;" he said, "I flew in an aeroplane making the journey in two hours that it took the children of Israel forty years to make. That is something to set people thinking of the progress of modern science."

Lucky cows don't fly
In Mobile, in Mobile

PERSHING FORCES FOE FURTHER BACK

SINGS FOR WOUNDED SOLDIERS; NOT SHOT AS SPY

Je donnerais Versailles
Paris et Saint Denis
Le tours de Nôtre Dâme
Les clochers de mon pays

HELP THE FOOD ADMINISTRATION BY REPORTING WAR PROFITEERS

the completeness of the accord reached on most points by the conferees caused satisfaction and even some surprise among participants

REDS FORCE MERCHANT VESSELS TO FLEE

HUNS ON RUN

Auprès de ma blonde
Qu'il fait bon fait bon fait bon
Auprès de ma blonde
Qu'il fait bon dormir

CHEZ LES SOCIALISTES LES AVEUGLES SONT ROI

The German government requests the President of the united States of America to take steps for the restoration of peace, to notify all the belligerents of this request and to invite them to delegate plenipotentiaries for the purpose of taking up negotiations. The German Government accepts, as a basis for the peace negotiations, the programme laid down by the President of the United States in his message to Congress of January 8th, 1918, and in his subsequent pronouncements, particularly in his address of September 27th, 1918. In order to avoid further bloodshed the German government requests the President of the United States to bring about the immediate conclusion of a general armistice on land, on the water, and in the air.

Joe Williams

Joe had been hanging around New York and Brooklyn for a while, borrowing money from Mrs. Olsen and getting tanked up all the time. One day she went to work and threw him out. It was damned cold and he had to go to a mission a couple of nights. He was afraid of getting arrested for the draft and he was fed up with every goddam thing; it ended by his going out as ordinary seaman on the *Appalachian,* a big new freighter bound for Bordeaux and Genoa. It kinder went with the way he felt being treated like a jailbird again and swabbing decks and chipping paint. In the focastle there was mostly country kids who'd never seen the sea and a few old bums who weren't good for anything. They got into a dirty blow four days out and shipped a small tidal wave that stove in two of the starboard lifeboats and the convoy got scattered and they found that the deck hadn't been properly caulked and the water kept coming down into the

focastle. It turned out that Joe was the only man they had on board
the mate could trust at the wheel, so they took him off scrubbing
paint and in his four hour tricks he had plenty of time to think about
how lousy everything was. In Bordeaux he'd have liked to look up
Marceline, but none of the crew got to go ashore.

The bosun went and got cockeyed with a couple of doughboys and
came back with a bottle of cognac for Joe, whom he'd taken a shine
to, and a lot of latrine talk about how the frogs were licked and the
limeys and the wops were licked something terrible and how if it
hadn't been for us the Kaiser ud be riding into gay Paree any day and
as it was it was nip and tuck. It was cold as hell. Joe and the bosun
went and drank the cognac in the galley with the cook who was an
old timer who'd been in the Klondike gold rush. They had the ship to
themselves because the officers were all ashore taking a look at the
mademosels and everybody else was asleep. The bosun said it was the
end of civilization and the cook said he didn't give a f—k and Joe
said he didn't give a f—k and the bosun said they were a couple of
goddam bolshevikis and passed out cold.

It was a funny trip round Spain and through the Straits and up the
French coast to Genoa. All the way there was a single file of camouflaged freighters, Greeks and Britishers and Norwegians and Americans, all hugging the coast and creeping along with lifepreservers
piled on deck and boats swung out on the davits. Passing 'em was another line coming back light, transports and colliers from Italy and
Saloniki, white hospital ships, every kind of old tub out of the seven
seas, rusty freighters with their screws so far out of the water you
could hear 'em thrashing a couple of hours after they were hull down
and out of sight. Once they got into the Mediterranean there were
French and British battleships to seaward all the time and sillylooking
destroyers with their long smokesmudges that would hail you and
come aboard to see the ship's papers. Ashore it didn't look like war a
bit. The weather was sunny after they passed Gibraltar. The Spanish
coast was green with bare pink and yellow mountains back of the
shore and all scattered with little white houses like lumps of sugar
that bunched up here and there into towns. Crossing the Gulf of Lyons in a drizzling rain and driving fog and nasty choppy sea they
came within an ace of running down a big felucca loaded with barrels
of wine. Then they were bowling along the French Riviera in a howling northwest wind, with the redroofed towns all bright and shiny

and the dry hills rising rocky behind them, and snowmountains standing out clear up above. After they passed Monte Carlo it was a circus, the houses were all pink and blue and yellow and there were tall poplars and tall pointed churchsteeples in all the valleys.

That night they were on the lookout for the big light marked on the chart for Genoa when they saw a red glare ahead. Rumor went around that the heinies had captured the town and were burning it. The second mate put up to the skipper right on the bridge that they'd all be captured if they went any further and they'd better go back and put into Marseilles but the skipper told him it was none of his goddam business and to keep his mouth shut till his opinion was asked. The glare got brighter as they not nearer. It turned out to be a tanker on fire outside the breakwater. She was a big new Standard Oil tanker, settled a little in the bows with fire pouring out of her and spreading out over the water. You could see the breakwater and the lighthouses and the town piling up the hills behind with red glitter in all the windows and the crowded ships in the harbor all lit up with the red flare.

After they'd anchored, the bosun took Joe and a couple of the youngsters in the dingy and they went over to see what they could do aboard the tanker. The stern was way up out of water. So far as they could see there was no one on the ship. Some wops in a motorboat came up and jabbered at them but they pretended not to understand what they meant. There was a fireboat standing by too, but there wasn't anything they could do. "Why the hell don't they scuttle her?" the bosun kept saying.

Joe caught sight of a ropeladder hanging into the water and pulled the dingy over to it. Before the others had started yelling at him to come back he was half way up it. When he jumped down onto the deck from the rail he wondered what the hell he was doing up there. God damn it, I hope she does blow up, he said aloud to himself. It was bright as day up there. The forward part of the ship and the sea around it was burning like a lamp. He reckoned the boat had hit a mine or been torpedoed. The crew had evidently left in a hurry as there were all sorts of bits of clothing and a couple of seabags by the davits aft where the lifeboats had been. Joe picked himself out a nice new sweater and then went down into the cabin. On a table he found a box of Havana cigars. He took out a cigar and lit one. It made him feel good to stand there and light a cigar with the goddam tanks ready to blow him to Halifax any minute. It was a good cigar, too. In a tissuepaper package on the table were seven pairs of ladies' silk stockings. Swell to take home to Del, was his first thought. But then he remembered that he was through with all that. He stuffed the silk stockings into his pants pockets anyway, and went back on deck.

The bosun was yelling at him from the boat for chrissake to come along or he'd get left. He just had time to pick up a wallet on the companion way. "It ain't gasoline, it's crude oil. She might burn for a week," he yelled at the guys in the boat as he came slowly down the ladder pulling at the cigar as he came and looking out over the harbor packed with masts and stacks and derricks at the big marble houses and the old towers and porticos and the hills behind all lit up in red. "Where the hell's the crew?"

"Probably all cockeyed ashore by this time, where I'd like to be," said the bosun. Joe divvied up the cigars but he kept the silk stockings for himself. There wasn't anything in the wallet. "Hellofa note," grumbled the bosun, "haven't they got any chemicals?" "These goddam wops wouldn't know what to do with 'em if they did have," said one of the youngsters.

They rowed back to the *Appalachian* and reported to the skipper that the tanker had been abandoned and it was up to the port authorities to get rid of her.

All next day the tanker burned outside the breakwater. About nightfall another of her tanks went off like a roman candle and the fire began spreading more and more over the water. The *Appalachian* heaved her anchor and went up to the wharf.

That night Joe and the bosun went out to look at the town. The streets were narrow and had steps in them leading up the hill to broad avenues, with cafés and little tables out under the colonnades, where the pavements were all polished marble set in patterns. It was pretty chilly and they went into a bar and drank pink hot drinks with run in them.

There they ran into a wop named Charley who'd been twelve years in Brooklyn and he took them to a dump where they ate a lot of spaghetti and fried veal and drank white wine. Charley told about how they treated you like a dog in the Eyetalian army and the pay was five cents a day and you didn't even get that and Charley was all for il Presidente Veelson and the fourteen points and said soon they'd make peace without victory and bigga revoluzione in Italia and make bigga war on the Francese and the Inglese treata Eyetalian lika dirt. Charley brought in two girls he said were his cousins, Nedda and Dora, and one of 'em sat on Joe's knees and, boy, how she could eat spaghetti, and they all drank wine. It cost 'em all the money Joe had to pay for supper.

When he was taking Nedda up to bed up an outside staircase in the courtyard he could see the flare of the tanker burning outside of the harbor on the blank walls and tiled roofs of the houses.

Nedda wouldn't get undressed but wanted to see Joe's money. Joe didn't have any money so he brought out the silk stockings. She looked worried and shook her head but she was darn pretty and had big black eyes and Joe wanted it bad and yelled for Charley and Charley came up the stairs and talked wop to the girl and said sure she'd take the silk stockings and wasn't America the greatest country in the world and tutti aleati and Presidente Veelson big man for Italia. But the girl wouldn't go ahead until they'd gotten hold of an old woman who was in the kitchen, who came wheezing up the stairs and felt the stockings, and musta said they were real silk and worth money, because the girl put her arm around Joe's neck and Charley said, "Sure, pard, she sleepa with you all night, maka love good."

But about midnight when the girl had gone to sleep Joe got tired of lying there. He could smell the closets down in the court and a rooster kept crowing loud as the dickens like it was right under his ear. He got up and put on his clothes and tiptoed out. The silk stockings were hanging on a chair. He picked 'em up and shoved them in his pockets again. His shoes creaked like hell. The street door was all bolted and barred and he had a devil of a time getting it open. Just as he got out in the street a dog began to bark somewhere and he ran for it. He got lost in a million little narrow stone streets, but he figured that if he kept on going down hill he'd get to the harbor sometime. Then he began to see the pink glow from the burning tanker again on some of the housewalls and steered by that.

On some steep steps he ran into a couple of Americans in khaki uniforms and asked them the way and they gave him a drink out of a bottle of cognac and said they were on their way to the Eyetalian front and that there'd been a big retreat and that everything was cockeyed and they didn't know where the cockeyed front was and they were going to wait right there till the cockeyed front came right to them. He told 'em about the silk stockings and they thought it was goddam funny, and showed him the way to the wharf where the *Appalachian* was and they shook hands a great many times when they said goodnight and they said the wops were swine and he said they were princes to have shown him the way and they said he was a prince and they finished up the cognac and he went on board and tumbled into his bunk.

When the *Appalachian* cleared for home the tanker was still burning outside the harbor. Joe came down with dose on the trip home and he couldn't drink anything for several months and kinda steadied down when he got to Brooklyn. He went to the shoreschool run by the Shipping Board in Platt Institute and got his second mate's license and made trips back and forth between New York and St. Nazaire all through that year on a new wooden boat built in Seattle called the *Owanda,* and a lot of trouble they had with her.

He and Janey wrote each other often. She was overseas with the Red Cross and very patriotic. Joe began to think that maybe she was right. Anyway if you believed the papers the heinies were getting licked, and it was a big opportunity for a young guy if you didn't get in wrong by being taken for a proGerman or a Bolshevik or some goddam thing. After all as Janey kept writing civilization had to be saved and it was up to us to do it. Joe started a savings account and bought him a Liberty bond.

Armistice night Joe was in St. Nazaire. The town was wild. Everybody ashore, all the doughboys out of their camps, all the frog soldiers out of their barracks, everybody clapping everybody else on the back, pulling corks, giving each other drinks, popping champagne bottles, kissing every pretty girl, being kissed by old women, kissed on both cheeks by French veterans with whiskers. The mates and the skipper and the chief and a couple of naval officers they'd never seen before all started to have a big feed in a café but they never got further than soup because everybody was dancing in the kitchen and they poured the cook so many drinks he passed out cold and they all sat there singing and drinking champagne out of tumblers and cheering the allied flags that girls kept carrying through.

Joe went cruising looking for Jeanette who was a girl he'd kinder taken up with whenever he was in St. Nazaire. He wanted to find her before he got too zigzag. She'd promised to couchay with him that night before it turned out to be Armistice Day. She said she never couchayed with anybody else all the time the *Owanda* was in port and he treated her right and brought her beaucoup presents from L'Amerique, and du sucer and du cafay. Joe felt good, he had quite a wad in his pocket and, god damn it, American money was worth something these days; and a couple of pounds of sugar he'd brought in the pockets of his raincoat was better than money with the mademosels.

He went in back where there was a cabaret all red plush with mirrors and the music was playing *The Star Spangled Banner* and everybody cried Vive L'Amerique and pushed drinks in his face as he came in and then he was dancing with a fat girl and the music was playing some damn foxtrot or other. He pulled away from the fat girl because he'd seen Jeanette. She had an American flag draped over her dress. She was dancing with a big sixfoot black Senegalese. Joe saw red. He pulled her away from the nigger who was a frog officer all full of gold braid and she said, "Wazamatta cherie," and Joe hauled off and hit the damn nigger as hard as he could right on the button but the nigger didn't budge. The nigger's face had a black puzzled smiling look like he was just going to ask a question. A waiter and a coupla frog soldiers came up and tried to pull Joe away. Everybody was yelling and jabbering. Jeanette was trying to get between Joe and the waiter and got a sock in the jaw that knocked her flat. Joe laid out a couple of frogs and was backing off towards the door, when he saw in the mirror that a big guy in a blouse was bringing down a bottle on his head held with both hands. He tried to swing around but he didn't have time. The bottle crashed his skull and he was out.

Newsreel XXIX

the arrival of the news caused the swamping of the city's telephone lines

> *Y fallait pas*
> *Y fallait pas*
> *Y fallait pas-a-a-a-a-yallez*

BIG GUNS USED IN HAMBURG

at the Custom House the crowd sang The Star Spangled Banner under the direction of Byron R. Newton the Collector of the Port

MORGAN ON WINDOWLEDGE
KICKS HEELS AS HE SHOWERS
CROWD WITH TICKERTAPE

down at the battery the siren of the fireboat *New York* let out a shriek when the news reached there and in less time than it takes to say boo pandemonium broke loose all along the waterfront

> *Oh say can you see by the dawn's early light*

WOMEN MOB CROWN PRINCE FOR
KISSING MODISTE

> *Allons enfants de la patrie*
> *Le jour de gloire est arrivé*

> *It's the wrong way to tickle Mary*
> *It's the wrong place to go*

"We've been at war with the devil and it was worth all the suffering it entailed," said William Howard Taft at a victory celebration here last night

Kahakatee, beautiful Katee
She's the only gugugirl that I adore
And when the moon shines

Unipress, N. Y.
Paris urgent Brest Admiral Wilson who announced 16:00 (4 P.M.) Brest newspaper armistice been signed later notified unconfirmable meanwhile Brest riotously celebrating

TWO TROLLIES HELD UP BY GUNMEN IN QUEENS

Over the cowshed
I'll be waiting at the kakakitchen door

SPECIAL GRAND JURY ASKED TO INDICT BOLSHEVISTS

the soldiers and sailors gave the only touch of color to the celebration. They went in wholeheartedly for having a good time, getting plenty to drink despite the fact that they were in uniform. Some of these returned fighters nearly caused a riot when they took an armful of stones and attempted to break an electric sign at Broadway and Forty-second Street reading:

WELCOME HOME TO OUR HEROES

Oh say can you see by the dawn's early light
What so proudly we hailed at the twilight's last gleaming
When the rocket's red glare the bombs bursting in air
Was proof to our eyes that the flag was still there

The Camera Eye (36)

when we emptied the rosies to leeward over the side every night after the last inspection we'd stop for a moment's gulp of the November gale the lash of spray in back of your ears for a look at the spume splintered off the leaping waves shipwreckers drowners of men (in

their great purple floating mines rose and fell gently submarines travelled under them on an even keel) to glance at the sky veiled with
scud to take our hands off the greasy handles of the cans full of slum
they couldnt eat (nine meals nine dumpings of the leftover grub
nine cussingmatches with the cockney steward who tried to hold
out on the stewed apricots inspections AttenSHUN   click clack At
Ease   shoot the flashlight in everycorner of the tin pans   nine
lineups along the leaving airless corridor of seasick seascared doughboys with their messkits in their hands)

    Hay sojer tell me they've signed an armistice   tell me the wars
over   they're takin us home   latrine talk the hell you say   now
I'll tell one   we were already leading the empty rosies down three
flights of iron ladders into the heaving retching hold starting up
with the full whenever the ship rolled a little slum would trickle out
the side

Meester Veelson

    The year that Buchanan was elected president Thomas Wood-
row Wilson
        was born to a presbyterian minister's daughter
    in the manse at Staunton in the valley of Virginia; it was the old
Scotch-Irish stock; the father was a presbyterian minister too and
teacher of rhetoric in theological seminaries; the Wilsons lived in a
universe of words linked into an incontrovertible firmament by two
centuries of calvinist divines,
        God was the Word
        and the Word was God.
    Dr. Wilson was a man of standing who loved his home and his
children and good books and his wife and correct syntax and talked
to God every day at family prayers;
        he brought his sons up
        between the bible and the dictionary.

    The years of the Civil War
        the years of fife and drum and platoonfire and proclamations

the Wilsons lived in Augusta, Georgia; Tommy was a backward child, didn't learn his letters till he was nine, but when he learned to read his favorite reading was Parson Weems'
 Life of Washington.

In 1870 Dr. Wilson was called to the Theological Seminary at Columbia, South Carolina; Tommy attended Davidson college,
 where he developed a good tenor voice;
then he went to Princeton and became a debater and editor of the *Princetonian.* His first published article in the Nassau Literary Magazine was an appreciation of Bismarck.

Afterwards he studied law at the University of Virginia; young Wilson wanted to be a Great Man, like Gladstone and the eighteenth century English parliamentarians; he wanted to hold the packed benches spellbound in the cause of Truth; but lawpractice irked him; he was more at home in the booky air of libraries, lecturerooms, college chapel, it was a relief to leave his lawpractice at Atlanta and take a Historical Fellowship at Johns Hopkins; there he wrote *Congressional Government.*

At twentynine he married a girl with a taste for painting (while he was courting her he coached her in how to use the broad "a") and got a job at Bryn Mawr teaching the girls History and Political Economy. When he got his Ph.D. from Johns Hopkins he moved to a professorship at Wesleyan, wrote article, started a History of the United States,
 spoke out for Truth Reform Responsible Government Democracy from the lecture platform, climbed all the steps of a brilliant university career; in 1901 the trustees of Princeton offered him the presidency;
 he plunged into reforming the university, made violent friends and enemies, set the campus by the ears,
 and the American people began to find on the front pages the name of Woodrow Wilson.

In 1909 he made addresses on Lincoln and Robert E. Lee
 and in 1910
the democratic bosses of New Jersey, hardpressed by muckrakers and reformers, got the bright idea of offering the nomination for

governor to the stainless college president who attracted such large
audiences

by publicly championing Right.

When Mr. Wilson addressed the Trenton convention that nomi-
nated him for governor he confessed his belief in the common man,
(the smalltown bosses and the wardheelers looked at each other and
scratched their heads); he went on, his voice growing firmer:

*that is the man by whose judgment I for one wish to be guided, so
that as the tasks multiply, and as the days come when all will feel confu-
sion and dismay, we may lift up our eyes to the hills out of these dark
valleys where the crags of special privilege overshadow and darken our
path, to where the sun gleams through the great passage in the broken
cliffs, the sun of God,*

the sun meant to regenerate men,

*the sun meant to liberate them from their passion and despair and
lift us to those uplands which are the promised land of every man who
desires liberty and achievement.*

The smalltown bosses and the wardheelers looked at each other
and scratched their heads; then they cheered; Wilson fooled the wise-
acres and doublecrossed the bosses, was elected by a huge plurality;

so he left Princeton only half reformed to be Governor of New
Jersey,

and became reconciled with Bryan

at the Jackson Day dinner: when Bryan remarked, "I of course
knew that you were not with me in my position on the currency,"
Mr. Wilson replied, "All I can say, Mr Bryan, is that you are a great
big man."

He was introduced to Colonel House,

that amateur Merlin of politics who was spinning his webs at the
Hotel Gotham

and at the convention in Baltimore the next July the upshot of
the puppetshow staged for sweating delegates by Hearst and House
behind the scenes, and Bryan booming in the corridors with a handkerchief over his wilted collar, was that Woodrow Wilson was nomi-
nated for the presidency.

The bolt of the Progressives in Chicago from Taft to T.R. made
his election sure;

so he left the State of New Jersey halfreformed

(pitiless publicity was the slogan of the Shadow Lawn Campaign)

and went to the White House

our twentyeighth president.

While Woodrow Wilson drove up Pennsylvania Avenue beside Taft the great buttertub, who as president had been genially undoing T.R.'s reactionary efforts to put business under the control of the government,

J. Pierpont Morgan sat playing solitaire in his back office on Wall Street, smoking twenty black cigars a day, cursing the follies of democracy.

Wilson flayed the interests and branded privilege refused to recognize Huerta and sent the militia to the Rio Grande

to assume a policy of watchful waiting. He published *The New Freedom* and delivered his messages to Congress in person, like a college president addressing the faculty and students. At Mobile he said:

I wish to take this occasion to say that the United States will never again seek one additional foot of territory by conquest;

and he landed the marines at Vera Cruz.

We are witnessing a renaissance of public spirit, a reawakening of sober public opinion, a revival of the power of the people the beginning of an age of thoughtful reconstruction . . .

but the world had started spinning round Sarajevo.

First it was *neutrality in thought and deed,* then *too proud to fight* when the *Lusitania* sinking and the danger to the Morgan loans and the stories of the British and French propagandists set all the financial centers in the East bawling for war, but the suction of the drumbeat and the guns was too strong; the best people took their fashions form Paris and their broad "a's" from London, and T.R. and the House of Morgan.

Five months after his reelection on the slogan *He kept us out of war,* Wilson pushed the Armed Ship Bill through congress and declared that a state of war existed between the United States and the Central Powers;

Force without stint or limit, force to the utmost.

* * *

Wilson became the state (war is the health of the state), Washington his Versailles, manned the socialized government with dollar a year men out of the great corporations and ran the big parade

of men munitions groceries mules and trucks to France. Five million men stood at attention outside of their tarpaper barracks every sundown while they played *The Star Spangled Banner.*

War brought the eight hour day, women's votes, prohibition, compulsory arbitration, high wages, high rates of interest, cost plus contracts and the luxury of being a Gold Star Mother.

If you objected to making the world safe for cost plus democracy you went to jail with Debs.

Almost too soon the show was over, Prince Max of Baden was pleading for the Fourteen Points, Foch was occupying the bridgeheads on the Rhine and the Kaiser out of breath ran for the train down the platform at Potsdam wearing a silk hat and some say false whiskers.

With the help of *Almighty God, Right, Truth, Justice, Freedom, Democracy, the Selfdetermination of Nations, No indemnities no annexations,*

and Cuban sugar and Caucasian manganese and Northwestern wheat and Dixie cotton, the British blockade, General Pershing, the taxicabs of Paris and the seventyfive gun

we won the war.

On December 4th, 1918, Woodrow Wilson, the first president to leave the territory of the United States during his presidency, sailed for France on board the *George Washington,*

the most powerful man in the world.

In Europe they knew what gas smelt like and the sweet sick stench of bodies buried too shallow and the grey look of the skin of starved children; they read in the papers that Meester Veelson was for peace and freedom and canned goods and butter and sugar;

he landed at Brest with his staff of experts and publicists after a rough trip on the *George Washington.*

La France héroïque was there with the speeches, the singing schoolchildren, the mayors in their red sashes. (Did Meester Veelson see the gendarmes at Brest beating back the demonstration of dockyard workers who came to meet him with red flags?)

At the station in Paris he stepped from the train onto a wide red carpet that lead him, between rows of potted palms, silk hats, legions of honor, decorated busts of uniforms, frockcoats, rosettes, boutonnières, to a Rolls Royce. (Did Meester Veelson see the women in black, the cripples in their little carts, the pale anxious faces along the streets, did he hear the terrible anguish of the cheers as they hurried him and his new wife to the hôtel de Mûrat, where in rooms full of brocade, gilt clocks, Buhl cabinets and ormolu cupids the presidential suite had been prepared?)

While the experts were organizing the procedure of the peace conference, spreading green baize on the tables, arranging the protocols,

the Wilsons took a tour to see for themselves: the day after Christmas they were entertained at Buckingham Palace; at Newyears they called on the pope and on the microscopic Italian king at the Quirinal. (Did Meester Veelson know that in the peasants' wargrimed houses along the Brenta and the Piave they were burning candles in front of his picture cut out of the illustrated papers?) (Did Meester Veelson know that the people of Europe spelled a challenge to oppression out of the Fourteen Points as centuries before they had spelled a challenge to oppression out of the ninetyfive articles Martin Luther nailed to the churchdoor in Wittenberg?)

January 18, 1919, in the midst of serried uniforms, cocked hats and gold braid, decorations, epaulettes, orders of merit and knighthood, the High Contracting Parties, the allied and associated powers met in the Salon de l'Horloge at the quai d'Orsay to dictate the peace,

but the grand assembly of the peace conference was too public a place to make peace in

so the High Contracting Parties

formed the Council of Ten, went into the Gobelin Room and, surrounded by Rubens's History of Marie de Medici,

began to dictate the peace.

But the Council of Ten was too public a place to make peace in so they formed the Council of Four.

Orlando went home in a huff

and then there were three:

Clemenceau,

Lloyd George,

Woodrow Wilson.

Three old men shuffling the pack,
dealing out the cards:
the Rhineland, Danzig, the Polish corridor, the Ruhr, self determination of small nations, the Saar, League of Nations, mandates, the
Mespot, Freedom of the Seas, Transjordania, Shantung, Fiume and
the Island of Yap:
machine gun fire and arson
starvation, lice, cholera, typhus;
oil was trumps.

Woodrow Wilson believed in his father's God
so he told the parishioners in the little Lowther Street Congrega-
tional church where his grandfather had preached in Carlisle in Scot-
land, a day so chilly that the newspaper men sitting in the old pews all
had to keep their overcoats on.

On April 7th he ordered the *George Washington* to be held at
Brest with steam up ready to take the American delegation home;
but he didn't go.

On April 19 sharper Clemenceau and sharper Lloyd George got
him into their little cosy threecardgame they called the Council of
Four.

On June 28th the Treaty of Versailles was ready
and Wilson had to go back home to explain to the politicians
who'd been ganging up on him meanwhile in the Senate and House
and to sober public opinion and to his father's God how he'd let himself be trimmed and how far he'd made the world safe
for democracy and the New Freedom.

From the day he landed in Hoboken he had his back to the wall
of the White House, talking to save his faith in words, talking to save
his faith in the League of Nations, talking to save his faith in himself,
in his father's God.

He strained every nerve of his body and brain, every agency of
the government he had under his control; (if anybody disagreed he
was a crook or a red; no pardon for Debs).

In Seattle the wobblies whose leaders were in jail, in Seattle the
wobblies whose leaders had been lynched, who'd been shot down like

dogs, in Seattle the wobblies lined four blocks as Wilson passed, stood silent with their arms folded staring at the great liberal as he was hurried past in his car, huddled in his overcoat, haggard with fatigue, one side of his face twitching. The men in overalls, the workingstiffs let him pass in silence after all the other blocks of handclapping and patriotic cheers.

In Pueblo, Colorado, he was a grey man hardly able to stand, one side of his face twitching:

Now that the mists of this great question have cleared away, I believe that men will see the Truth, eye for eye and face to face. There is one thing the American People always rise to and extend their hand to, that is, the truth of justice and of liberty and of peace. We have accepted that truth and we are going to be led by it, and it is going to lead us, and through us the world, out into pastures of quietness and peace such as the world never dreamed of before.

That was his last speech;

on the train to Wichita he had a stroke. He gave up the speaking tour that was to sweep the country for the League of Nations. After that he was a ruined paralysed man barely able to speak;

the day he gave up the presidency to Harding the joint committee of the Senate and House appointed Henry Cabot Lodge, his lifelong enemy, to make the formal call at the executive office in the Capitol and ask the formal question whether the president had any message for the congress assembled in joint session;

Wilson managed to get to his feet, lifting himself painfully by the two arms of the chair. "Senator Lodge, I have no further communication to make, thank you . . . Good morning," he said.

In 1924 on February 3rd he died.

Newsreel XXX

MONSTER GUNS REMOVED?

Longhaired preachers come out every night
Try to tell you what's wrong and what's right
But when asked about something to eat
They will answer in accents so sweet

PRESIDENT HAS SLIGHT COLD AT SEA

Special Chef and Staff of Waiters and Kitchen Helpers Drafted from the Biltmore

Every Comfort Provided

Orchestra to Play During Meals and Navy Yard Band to Play for Deck Music

You will eat bye and bye
In that glorious land above the sky

the city presents a picture of the wildest destruction especially around the General Post Office which had been totally destroyed by fire, nothing but ruins remaining

Work and pray
Live on hay

Three truckloads of Records Gathered Here

eleven men were killed and twentythree injured, some of them seriously as the result of an explosion of fulminate of mercury in the priming unit of one of the cap works of the E. I. duPont de Nemours Powder Company; in the evening Mrs. Wilson released carrier pigeons . . . *and through it all how fine the spirit of the nation was, what unity of purpose what untiring zeal what elevation of purpose ran through all its splendid display of strength, its untiring accomplishment. I have said that those of us who stayed at home to do the work of organi-*

zation and supply would always wish we had been with the men we sustained by our labor, but we can never be ashamed . . . in the dining room music was furnished by a quartet of sailors

You'll get pie
In the sky
When you die

GORGAS WOULD PUT SOLDIERS IN HUTS

800 FIGHTING MEN CHEER BOLSHEVIKI

All the arrangements were well ordered but the crowd was kept at a distance. The people gathered on the hills near the pier raised a great shout when the president's launch steamed up. A detour was made from the Champs Elysees to cross the Seine over the Alexander III bridge which recalled another historic pageant when Paris outdid herself to honor an absolute ruler in the person of the czar.

ADDRESSED 1400 MAYORS FORM PALACE BALCONY

BRITISH NAVY TO BE SUPREME
DECLARES CHURCHILL

The Camera Eye (37)

alphabetically according to rank tapped out with two cold index fingers on the company Corona *Allots Class A & B Ins prem C & D*

Atten—SHUN snap to the hooks and eyes at my throat constricting the adamsapple bringing together the US and the Caduceus

At Ease

outside they're drilling in the purple drizzle of a winter afternoon in Ferrières en Gatinais, Abbaye founded by Clovis over the skeletons of three disciples of nôtre seigneur Jésus-Christ *3rd Lib Loan Sec of Treas* Altian Politian and Hermatian *4th Lib Loan Sec of Treas must be on CL E or other form Q.M.C. 38* now it's raining hard and the gutters gurgle   there's tinkling from all the little glassgreen streams   Alcuin was prior once   and millwheels grind behind the mossed stone walls and Clodhilde and Clodomir were buried here *promotions only marked under gains* drowsily clacked out on the rusteaten Corona in the cantonment of O'Reilly's Travelling Circus alone except for the undertaker soldiering in his bunk and the dry hack of the guy that has TB that the MO was never sober enough to examine

Iodine will make you happy
Iodine will make you well

fourthirty   the pass comes alive among the CC pills in my pocket

the acting QM Sarge and the Topkicker go out through the gate of USAAS base camp in their slickers in the lamplit rain and make their way without a cent in their OD to the Cheval Blanc where by chevrons and parleyvooing they bum drinks and omelettes avec pommes frites and kid applecheeked Madeleine may wee

in the dark hallway to the back room the boys are lined up waiting to get in to the girl in black from out of town to drop ten francs and hurry to the propho station *sol viol sk not L D viol Go 41/14 rd sent S C M*

outside it's raining on the cobbled town inside we drink vin rouge parlezvous froglegs may wee couchez avec and the old territorial at the next table drinks illegal pernod and remarks   Toute est bien fait dans la nature à la votre aux Americains

Après la guerre finee
Back to the States for me

Dans la mort il n'y a rien de terrible Quant on va mourir on pense à tout mais vite

the first day in the year dismissed after rollcall I went walking with a fellow from Philadelphia along the purple wintryrutted roads under the purple embroidery of the pleached trees full of rooks cackling overhead over the ruddier hills to a village   we're going to walk a long way get good wine full of Merovingian names millwheels glassgreen streams where the water gurgles out of old stone gargoyles Madeleine's red apples the smell of beech leaves we're going to drink wine the boy from Philadelphia's got beaucoup jack   wintry purpler wine   the sun breaks out through the clouds on the first day in the year

in the first village

we stop in our tracks

to look at a waxwork

the old man has shot the pretty peasant girl who looks like Madeleine but younger she lies there shot in the left breast in the blood in the ruts of the road pretty and plump as a little quail

The old man then took off one shoe and put the shotgun under his chin pulled the trigger with his toe and blew the top of his head off   we stand looking at the bare foot and the shoe and the foot in the shoe and the shot girl and the old man with a gunnysack over his head and the dirty bare toe he pulled the trigger with   Faut pas toucher until the commissaire comes procès verbale

on this first day
of the year the sun
is shining

Newsreel XXXI

washing and dressing hastily they came to the ground floor at the brusque call of the commissaries, being assembled in one of the rear rooms in the basement of the house. Here they were lined up in a semicircle along the wall, the young grandduchesses trembling at the unusual nature of the orders given and at the gloomy hour. They more than suspected the errand upon which the commissaries had come. Addressing the czar, Yarodsky, without the least attempt to soften his announcement, stated that they must all die and at once. The revolution was in danger, he stated, and the fact that there were still the members of the reigning house living added to that danger. Therefore to remove them was the duty of all Russian patriots. "Thus your life is ended," he said in conclusion.

"I am ready," was the simple announcement of the czar, while the czarina, clinging to him, loosed her hold long enough to make the sign of the cross, an example followed by the grandduchess Olga and by Dr. Botkin.

The czarevitch, paralyzed with fear, stood in stupefaction beside his mother, uttering no sound either in supplication or protest, while his three sisters and the other grandduchesses sank to the floor trembling.

Yarodsky drew his revolver and fired the first shot. A volley followed and the prisoners reeled to the ground. Where the bullets failed to find their mark the bayonet put the finishing touches. The mingled blood of the victims not only covered the floor of the room where the execution took place but ran in streams along the hallway

Daughter

The Trents lived in a house on Pleasant avenue that was the finest street in Dallas that was the biggest and fastest growing town in Texas that was the biggest state in the Union and had the blackest soil and the whitest people and America was the greatest country in the world and Daughter was Dad's onlyest sweetest little girl. Her real name was Anne Elizabeth Trent after poor dear mother who had died when she was a little tiny girl but Dad and the boys called her Daughter. Buddy's real name was William Delaney Trent like Dad who was a prominent attorney, and Buster's real name was Spencer Anderson Trent.

Winters they went to school and summers they ran wild on the ranch that grandfather had taken up as a pioneer. When they'd been very little there hadn't been any fences yet and still a few maverick steers out along the creekbottoms, but by the time Daughter was in highschool everything was fenced and they were building a macadam road out from Dallas and Dad went everywhere in the Ford instead of on his fine Arab stallion Mullah he'd been given by a stockman at the Fat Stock Show in Waco when the stockman had gone broke and hadn't been able to pay his lawyer's fee. Daughter had a creamcolored pony named Coffee who'd nod his head and paw with his hoof when he wanted a lump of sugar, but some of the girls she knew had cars and Daughter and the boys kept after Dad to buy a car, a real car instead of that miserable old flivver he drove around the ranch.

When Dad bought a Pierce Arrow touring car the spring Daughter graduated from highschool, she was the happiest girl in the world. Sitting at the wheel in a fluffy white dress the morning of Commencement outside the house waiting for Dad, who had just come out from the office and was changing his clothes, she had thought how much she'd like to be able to see herself sitting there in the not too hot June morning in the lustrous black shiny car among the shiny brass and nickel fixtures under the shiny paleblue big Texas sky in the middle of the big flat rich Texas country that ran for two hundred miles in every direction. She could see half her face in the little oval mirror on the mudguard. It looked red and sunburned under her sandybrown hair. If she only had red hair and a skin white like buttermilk like Susan Gillespie had, she was wishing when she saw Joe Washburn coming along the street dark and seriouslooking under his panama hat. She fixed her face in a shy kind of smile just in time to have him say, "How lovely you look, Daughter, you must excuse ma sayin' so." "I'm just waiting for Dad and the boys to go to the exercises. O Joe, we're late and I'm so excited. . . . I feel like a sight."

"Well, have a good time." He walked on unhurriedly putting his hat back on his head as he went. Something hotter than the June sunshine had come out of Joe's very dark eyes and run in a blush over her face and down the back of her neck under her thin dress and down the middle of her bosom, where the little breasts that she tried never to think of were just beginning to be noticeable. At last Dad and the boys came out all looking blonde and dressed up and sunburned. Dad made her sit in the back seat with Bud who sat up stiff as a poker.

The big wind that had come up drove grit in their faces. After she caught sight of the brick buildings of the highschool and the crowd and the light dresses and the stands and the big flag with the stripes all wiggling against the sky she got so excited she never remembered anything that happened.

That night, wearing her first evening dress at the dance she came to in the feeling of tulle and powder and crowds, boys all stiff and scared in their dark coats, girls packing into the dressing room to look at each other's dresses. She never said a word while she was dancing, just smiled and held her head a little to one side and hoped somebody would cut in. Half the time she didn't know who she was dancing with, just moved smiling in a cloud of pink tulle and colored lights, boys' faces bobbed in front of her, tried to say smarty ladykillerish things or else were shy and tonguetied, different colored faces on top of the same stiff bodies. Honestly she was surprised when Susan Gillespie came up to her when they were getting their wraps to go home and giggled, "My dear, you were the belle of the ball." When Bud and Buster said so next morning and old black Emma who'd brought them all up after mother died came in from the kitchen and said, "Lawsy, Miss Annie, folks is talkin' all over town abut how you was the belle of the ball last night," she felt herself blushing happily all over. Emma said she'd heard it from that noaccount yaller man on the milk route whose aunt worked at Mrs. Washburn's, then she set down the popovers and went out with a grin as wide as a piano. "Well, Daughter," said Dad in his deep quiet voice, tapping the top of her hand, "I thought so myself but I thought maybe I was prejudiced."

During the summer Joe Washburn, who'd just graduated from law school at Austin and who was going into Dad's office in the fall, came and spent two weeks with them on the ranch. Daughter was just horrid to him, made old Hildreth give him a mean little old oneeyed pony to ride, put horned toads in his cot, would hand him hot chile sauce instead of catsup at table or try to get him to put salt instead of sugar in his coffee. The boys got so off her they wouldn't speak to her and Dad said she was getting to be a regular tomboy, but she couldn't seem to stop acting like she did.

Then one day they all rode over to eat supper on Clear Creek and went swimming by moonlight in the deep hole there was under the bluff. Daughter got a crazy streak in her after a while and ran up and said she was going to dive from the edge of the bluff. The water looked so good and the moon floated shivering on top. They all yelled at her not to do it but she made a dandy dive right from the edge. But something was the matter. She'd hit her head, it hurt terribly. She was swallowing water, she was fighting a great weight that was pressing down on her, that was Joe. The moonlight flowed out in a swirl leaving it all black, only she had her arms around Joe's neck, her fingers were tightening around the ribbed muscles of his arms. She came to with his face looking into hers and the moon up in the sky again and warm stuff pouring over her forehead. She was trying to say, "Joe, I wanto, Joe, I wanto," but it all drained away into warm sticky black again, only she caught his voice deep, deep . . . "pretty near had me drowned too . . ." and Dad sharp and angry like in court, "I told her she oughtn't to dive off there."

She came to herself again in bed with her head hurting horribly and Dr. Winslow there, and the first thing she thought was where was Joe and had she acted like a little silly telling him she was crazy about him? But nobody said anything about it and they were all awful nice to her except that Dad came, still talking with his angry courtroom voice, and lectured her for being foolhardy and a tomboy and having almost cost Joe his life by the stranglehold she had on him when they'd pulled them both out of the water. She had a fractured skull and had to be in bed all summer and Joe was awful nice though he looked at her kinder funny out of his sharp black eyes the first time he came in her room. As long as he stayed on the ranch he came to read to her after lunch. He read her all of *Lorna Doone* and half of *Nicholas Nickleby* and she lay there in bed, hot and cosy in her fever, feeling the rumble of his deep voice through the pain in her head and fighting all the time inside not to cry out like a little silly that she was crazy about him and why didn't he like her just a little bit. When he'd gone it wasn't any fun being sick any more. Dad or Bud came and read to her sometimes but most of the time she liked better reading to herself.

She read all of Dickens, *Lorna Doone* twice, and Poole's *The Harbor*, that made her want to go to New York.

Next fall Dad took her north for a year in a finishing school in Lancaster, Pennsylvania. She was excited on the trip up on the train and loved every minute of it, but Miss Tynge's was horrid and the girls were all northern girls and so mean and made fun of her clothes and talked about nothing but Newport, and Southampton, and matinée idols she'd never seen; she hated it. She cried every night after she'd gone to bed thinking how she hated the school and how Joe Washburn would never like her now. When Christmas vacation came and she had to stay on with the two Miss Tynges and some of the teachers who lived too far away to go home either, she just decided she wouldn't stand it any longer and one morning before anybody was up she got out of the house, walked down to the station, bought herself a ticket to Washington, and got on the first westbound train with nothing but a toothbrush and a nightgown in her handbag. She was scared all alone on the train at first but such a nice young Virginian who was a West Point Cadet got on at Havre de Grace where she had to change; they had the time of their lives together laughing and talking. In Washington he asked permission to be her escort in the nicest way and took her all around, to see the Capitol and the White House and the Smithsonian Institute and set her up to lunch at the New Willard and put her on the train for St. Louis that night. His name was Paul English. She promised she'd write him every day of her life. She was so excited she couldn't sleep lying in her berth looking out of the window of the pullman at the trees and the circling hills all in the faint glow of snow and now and then lights speeding by; she could remember exactly how he looked and how his hair was parted and the long confident grip of his hand when they said goodby. She'd been a little nervous at first, but they'd been like old friends right from the beginning and he'd been so courteous and gentlemanly. He'd been her first pickup.

When she walked in on Dad and the boys at breakfast a sunny winter morning two days later, my, weren't they surprised; Dad tried to scold her, but Daughter could see that he was as pleased as she was. Anyway, she didn't care, it was so good to be home.

After Christmas she and Dad and the boys went for a week's hunting down near Corpus Christi and had the time of their lives and Daughter shot her first deer. When they got back to Dallas Daughter said she wasn't going back to be finished but that what she would like to do was go up to New York to stay with Ada Washburn, who was studying at Columbia, and to take courses where she'd really learn something. Ada was Joe Washburn's sister, an old maid but bright as a dollar and was working for her Ph.D in Education. It took a lot of arguing because Dad had set his heart on having Daughter go to a finishing school but she finally convinced him and was off again to New York.

She was reading *Les Misérables* all the way up on the train and looking out at the greyishbrownish winter landscape that didn't seem to have any life to it after she left the broad hills of Texas, pale green with winter wheat and alfalfa, feeling more and more excited and scared as hour by hour she got nearer New York. There was a stout motherly woman who'd lost her husband who got on the train at Little Rock and wouldn't stop talking about the dangers and pitfalls that beset a young woman's path in big cities. She kept such a strict watch on Daughter that she never got a chance to talk to the interesting looking young man with the intense black eyes who boarded the train at St. Louis and kept going over papers of some kind he had in a brown briefcase. She thought he looked a little like Joe Washburn. At last when they were crossing New Jersey and there got to be more and more factories and grimy industrial towns, Daughter's heart got to beating so fast she couldn't sit still but kept having to go out and stamp around in the cold raw air of the vestibule. The fat greyheaded conductor asked her with a teasing laugh if her beau was going to be down at the station to meet her, she seemed so anxious to get in. They were going through Newark then. Only one more stop. The sky was lead color over wet streets full of automobiles and a drizzly rain was pitting the patches of snow with grey. The train began to cross wide desolate saltmarshes, here and there broken by an uneven group of factory structures or a black river with steamboats on it. There didn't seem to be any people; it looked so cold over those marshes Daughter felt scared and lonely just looking at them and wished she was home. Then suddenly the train was in a tunnel, and the porter was piling all the bags in the front end of the car. She got into the fur coat Dad had bought her as a Christmas present and pulled her gloves on over her hands cold with excitement for fear that maybe Ada Washburn hadn't gotten her telegram or hadn't been able to come down to meet her.

But there she was on the platform in noseglasses and raincoat looking as oldmaidish as ever and a slightly younger girl with her who turned out to be from Waco and studying art. They had a long ride in a taxi up crowded streets full of slush with yellow and grey snowpiles along the sidewalks. "If you'd have been here a week ago, Anne Elizabeth, I declare you'd have seen a real blizzard."

"I used to think snow was like on Christmas cards," said Esther Wilson who was an interestinglooking girl with black eyes and a long face and a deep kind of tragicsounding voice. "But it was just an illusion like a lot of things." "New York's no place for illusions," said Ada sharply. "It all looks kinder like a illusion to me," said Daughter, looking out of the window of the taxicab.

Ada and Esther had a lovely big apartment on University Heights where they had fixed up the dining room as a bedroom for Daughter. She didn't like New York but it was exciting; everything was grey and grimy and the people all seemed to be foreigners and nobody paid any attention to you except now and then a man tried to pick you up on the street or brushed up against you in the subway which was disgusting. She was signed up as a special student and went to lectures about Economics and English Literature and Art and talked a little occasionally with some boy who happened to be sitting next to her, but she was so much younger than anybody she met and she didn't seem to have the right line of talk to interest them. It was fun going to matinées with Ada sometimes or riding down all bundled up on top of the bus to go to the art-museum with Esther on Sunday afternoons, but they were both of them so staid and grown up and all the time getting shocked by things she said and did.

When Paul English called up and asked her to go to a matinée with him one Saturday, she was very thrilled. They'd written a few letters back and forth but they hadn't seen each other since Washington. She was all morning putting on first one dress and then the other, trying out different ways of doing her hair and was still taking a hot bath when he called for her so that Ada had to entertain him for the longest time. When she saw him all her thrill dribbled away, he looked so stiff and stuckup in his dress uniform. First thing she knew she was kidding him, and acting silly going downtown in the subway so that by the time they got to the Astor where he took her to lunch, he looked sore as a pup. She left him at the table and went to the ladies' room to see if she couldn't get her hair to look a little better than it did and got to talking with an elderly Jewish lady in diamonds who'd lost her pocketbook, and when she got back the lunch was standing cold on the table and Paul English was looking at his wristwatch uneasily. She didn't like the play and he tried to get fresh in the taxicab driving up Riverside Drive although it was still broad daylight, and she slapped his face. He said she was the meanest girl he'd ever met and she said she liked being mean and if he didn't like it he knew what he could do. Before that she'd made up her mind that she'd crossed him off her list.

She went in her room and cried and wouldn't take any supper. She felt real miserable having Paul English turn out a pill like that. It was lonely not having anybody to take her out and no chance of meeting anybody because she had to go everywhere with those old maids. She lay on her back on the floor looking at the furniture from underneath like when she'd been little and thinking of Joe Washburn. Ada came in and found her in the silliest position lying on the floor with her legs in the air; she jumped up and kissed her all over her face and hugged her and said she'd been a little idiot but it was all over now and was there anything to eat in the icebox.

When she met Edwin Vinal at one of Ada's Sunday evening parties that she didn't usually come out to on account of people sitting around so prim and talking so solemn and deep over their cocoa and cupcakes, it made everything different and she began to like New York. He was a scrawny kind of young fellow who was taking courses in sociology. He sat on a stiff chair with his cocoacup balanced uncomfortably in his hand and didn't seem to know where to put his legs. He didn't say anything all evening but just as he was going, he picked up something Ada said about values and began to talk a blue streak, quoting all the time from a man named Veblen. Daughter felt kind of attracted to him and asked who Veblen was, and he began to talk to her. She wasn't up on what he was talking about but it made her feel lively inside to have him talking right to her like that. He had light hair and black eyebrows and lashes around very pale grey eyes with little gold specks in them. She liked his awkward lanky way of moving around. Next evening he came to see her and brought her a volume of the *Theory of the Leisure Class* and asked her if she didn't want to go skating with him at the St. Nicholas rink. She went in her room to get ready and began to dawdle around powdering her face and looking at herself in the glass. "Hey, Anne, for gosh sakes, we haven't got all night," he yelled through the door. She had never had iceskates on her feet before, but she knew how to rollerskate, so with Edwin holding her arm she was able to get around the big hall with its band playing and all the tiers of lights and faces around the balcony. She had more fun than she'd had any time since she left home.

Edwin Vinal had been a social worker and lived in a settlement house and now he had a scholarship at Columbia but he said the profs were too theoretical and never seemed to realize it was real people like you and me they were dealing with. Daughter had done churchwork and taken around baskets to poorwhite families at Christmas time and said she'd like to do some socialservicework right here in New York. As they were taking off their skates he asked her if she really meant it and she smiled up at him and said, "Hope I may die if I don't."

So the next evening he took her downtown threequarters of an hour's ride in the subway and then a long stretch on a crosstown car to a settlement house on Grand Street where she had to wait while he gave an English lesson to a class of greasylooking young Lithuanians or Polaks or something like that. Then they walked around the streets and Edwin pointed out the conditions. It was like the Mexican part of San Antonio or Houston only there were all kinds of foreigners. None of them looked as if they ever bathed and the streets smelt of garbage. There was laundry hanging out everywhere and signs in all kinds of funny languages. Edwin showed her some in Russian and Yiddish, one in Armenian and two in Arabic. The streets were awful crowded and there were pushcarts along the curb and peddlers everywhere and funny smells of cooking coming out of restaurants, and outlandish phonograph music. Edwin pointed out two tiredlooking painted girls who he said were streetwalkers, drunks stumbling out of a saloon, a young man in a checked cap he said was a cadet drumming up trade for a disorderly house, some sallowfaced boys he said were gunmen and dope peddlers. It was a relief when they came up again out of the subway way uptown where a springy wind was blowing down the broad empty streets that smelt of the Hudson River. "Well, Anne, how did you like your little trip to the underworld?"

"Allright," she said after a pause. "Another time I think I'll take a gun in my handbag. . . . But all those people, Edwin, how on earth can you make citizens out of them? We oughtn't to let all those foreigners come over and mess up our country."

"You're entirely wrong," Edwin snapped at her. "They'd all be decent if they had a chance. We'd be just like them if we hadn't been lucky enough to be born of decent families in small prosperous American towns."

"Oh, how can you talk so silly, Edwin, they're not white people and they never will be. They's just like Mexicans or somethin', or niggers." She caught herself up and swallowed the last word. The colored elevator boy was drowsing on a bench right behind her.

"If you're not the benightedest little heathen I ever saw," said Edwin teasingly. "You're a Christian, aren't you, well, have you ever thought that Christ was a Jew?"

"Well, I'm fallin' down with sleep and can't argue with you but I know you're wrong." She went into the elevator and the colored elevator boy got up yawning and stretching. The last she saw of Edwin in the rapidly decreasing patch of light between the floor of the elevator and the ceiling of the vestibule he was shaking his fist at her. She threw him a kiss without meaning to.

When she got in the apartment, Ada, who was reading in the livingroom, scolded her a little for being so late, but she pleaded that she was too tired and sleepy to be scolded. "What do you think of Edwin Vinal, Ada?" "Why, my dear, I think he's a splendid young fellow, a little restless maybe, but he'll settle down. . . . Why?"

"Oh, I dunno," said Daughter, yawning, "Good night, Ada darlin'."

She took a hot bath and put a lot of perfume on and went to bed, but she couldn't go to sleep. Her legs ached from the greasy pavements and she could feel the walls of the tenements sweating lust and filth and the smell of crowded bodies closing in on her, in spite of the perfume she still had the rank garbagy smell in her nose, and the dazzle of street lights and faces pricked her eyes. When she went to sleep she dreamed she had rouged her lips and was walking up and down, up and down with a gun in her handbag; Joe Washburn walked by and she kept catching at his arm to try to make him stop but he kept walking by without looking at her and so did Dad and they wouldn't look when a big Jew with a beard kept getting closer to her and he smelt horrid of the East Side and garlic and waterclosets and she tried to get the gun out of her bag to shoot him and he had his arms around her and was pulling her face close to his. She couldn't get the gun out of the handbag and behind the roaring clatter of the subway in her ears was Edwin Vinal's voice saying, "You're a Christian, aren't you? You're entirely wrong . . . a Christian, aren't you? Have you ever thought that Christ would have been just like them if he hadn't been lucky enough to have been born of decent people . . . a Christian, aren't you. . . ."

Ada, standing over her in a nightgown, woke her up, "What can be the matter, child?" "I was having a nightmare . . . isn't that silly?" said Daughter and sat boltupright in bed. "Did I yell bloody murder?" "I bet you children were out eating Welsh Rabbit, that's why you were so late," said Ada, and went back to her room laughing.

That spring Daughter coached a girls' basketball team at a Y.W.C.A. in the Bronx, and got engaged to Edwin Vinal. She told him she didn't want to marry anybody for a couple of years yet, and he said he didn't care about carnal marriage but that the important thing was for them to plan a life of service together. Sunday evenings, when the weather got good, they would go and cook a steak together in Palisades Park and sit there looking through the trees at the lights coming on in the great toothed rockrim of the city and talk about what was good and evil and what real love was. Coming back they'd stand hand in hand in the bow of the ferry boat among the crowd of boyscouts and hikers and picnickers and look at the great sweep of lighted buildings fading away into the ruddy haze down the North River and talk about all the terrible conditions in the city. Edwin would kiss her on the forehead when he said Goodnight and she'd go up in the elevator feeling that the kiss was a dedication.

At the end of June she went home to spend three months on the ranch, but she was very unhappy there that summer. Somehow she couldn't get around to telling Dad about her engagement. When Joe Washburn came out to spend a week the boys made her furious teasing her about him and telling her that he was engaged to a girl in Oklahoma City, and she got so mad she wouldn't speak to them and was barely civil to Joe. She insisted on riding a mean little pinto that bucked and threw her once or twice. She drove the car right through a gate one night and busted both lamps to smithereens. When Dad scolded her about her recklessness she'd tell him he oughtn't to care because she was going back east to earn her own living and he'd be rid of her. Joe Washburn treated her with the same grave kindness as always, and sometimes when she was acting crazy she'd catch a funny understanding kidding gleam in his keen eyes that would make her feel suddenly all weak and silly inside. The night before he left the boys cornered a rattler on the rockpile behind the corral and Daughter dared Joe to pick it up and snap its head off. Joe ran for a forked stick and caught the snake with a jab behind the head and threw it with all his might against the wall of the little smokehouse. As it lay wriggling on the grass with a broken back Bud took its head off with a hoe. It had six rattles and a button. "Daughter," Joe drawled, looking her in the face with his steady smiling stare, "sometimes you talk like you didn't have good sense."

"You're yaller, that's what's the matter with you," she said.

"Daughter, you're crazy . . . you apologize to Joe," yelled Bud, running up red in the face with the dead snake in his hand. She turned and went into the ranchhouse and threw herself on her bed. She didn't come out of her room till after Joe had left in the morning.

The week before she left to go back to Columbia she was good as gold and tried to make it up to Dad and the boys by baking cakes for them and attending to the housekeeping for having acted so mean and crazy all summer. She met Ada in Dallas and they engaged a section together. She'd been hoping that Joe would come down to the station to see them off, but he was in Oklahoma City on oil business. On her way north she wrote him a long letter saying she didn't know what had gotten into her that day with the rattler and wouldn't he please forgive her.

Daughter worked hard that autumn. She'd gotten herself admitted to the School of Journalism, in spite of Edwin's disapproval. He wanted her to study to be a teacher or social worker, but she said journalism offered more opportunity. They more or less broke off over it; although they saw each other a good deal, they didn't talk so much about being engaged. There was a boy named Webb Cruthers studying journalism that Daughter got to be good friends with although Ada said he was no good and wouldn't let her bring him to the house. He was shorter than she, had dark hair and looked about fifteen although he said he was twentyone. He had a creamy white skin that made people call him Babyface, and a funny confidential way of talking as if he didn't take what he was saying altogether seriously himself. He said he was an anarchist and talked all the time about politics and the war. He used to take her down to the East Side, too, but it was more fun than going with Edwin. Webb always wanted to go in somewhere to get a drink and talk to people. He took her to saloons and to Romanian rathskellers and Arabian restaurants and more places than she'd ever imagined. He knew everybody everywhere and seemed to manage to make people trust him for the check, because he hardly ever had any money, and when they'd spent whatever she had with her Webb would have to charge the rest. Daughter didn't drink more than an occasional glass of wine, and if he began to get too obstreperous, she'd make him take her to the nearest subway and go on home. Then next day he'd be a little weak and trembly and tell her about his hangover and funny stories about adventures he'd had when he was tight. He always had pamphlets in his pockets about socialism and syndicalism and copies of *Mother Earth* or *The Masses*.

After Christmas Webb got all wrapped up in a strike of textile workers that was going on in a town over in New Jersey. One Sunday they went over to see what it was like. They got off the train at a grimy brick station in the middle of the empty business section, a few people standing around in front of lunchcounters, empty stores closed for Sunday; there seemed nothing special about the town until they walked out to the long low square brick buildings of the mills. There were knots of policemen in blue standing about in the wide muddy roadway outside and inside the wiremesh gates huskylooking young men in khaki. "These are special deputies, the sons of bitches," muttered Webb between his teeth. They went to Strike Headquarters to see a girl Webb knew who was doing publicity for them. At the head of a grimy stairway crowded with greyfaced foreign men and women in faded greylooking clothes, they found an office noisy with talk and click of typewriters. The hallway was piled with stacks of handbills that a tiredlooking young man was giving out in packages to boys in ragged sweaters. Webb found Sylvia Dalhart, a longnosed girl with glasses who was typing madly at a desk piled with newspapers and clippings. She waves a hand and said, "Webb, wait for me outside. I'm going to show some newspaper guys around and you'd better come."

Out in the hall they ran into a fellow Webb knew, Ben Compton, a tall young man with a long thin nose and redrimmed eyes, who said he was going to speak at the meeting and asked Webb if he wouldn't speak. "Jeez, what could I say to those fellers? I'm just a bum of a college student, like you, Ben." "Tell 'em the workers have got to win the world, tell 'em this fight is part of a great historic battle. Talking's the easiest part of the movement. The truth's simple enough." He had an explosive way of talking with a pause between each sentence, as if the sentence took sometime to come up from someplace way down inside. Daughter sized up that he was attractive, even though he was probably a Jew. "Well, I'll try to stammer out something about democracy in industry," said Webb.

Sylvia Dalhart was already pushing them down the stairs. She had with her a pale young man in a raincoat and black felt hat who was chewing the end of a half of a cigar that had gone out. "Fellow-workers, this is Joe Biglow from the *Globe*," she had a western burr in her voice that made Daughter feel at home. "We're going to show him around."

They went all over town, to strikers' houses where tiredlooking women in sweaters out at the elbows were cooking up lean Sunday dinners of corned beef and cabbage or stewed meat and potatoes, or in some houses they just had cabbage and bread or just potatoes. Then they went to a lunchroom near the station and ate some lunch. Daughter paid the check as nobody seemed to have any money, and it was time to go to the meeting.

The trolleycar was crowded with strikers and their wives and children. The meeting was to be held in the next town because in that town the Mills owned everything and there was no way of hiring a hall. It had started to sleet, and they got their feet wet wading through the slush to the mean frame building where the meeting was going to be held. When they got to the door there were mounted police out in front. "Hall full," a cop told them at the streetcorner, "no more allowed inside."

They stood around in the sleet waiting for somebody with authority. There were thousands of strikers, men and women and boys and girls, the older people talking among themselves in low voices in foreign languages. Webb kept saying, "Jesus, this is outrageous. Somebody ought to do something." Daughter's feet were cold and she wanted to go home.

Then Ben Compton came around from the back of the building. People began to gather around him, "There's Ben . . . there's Compton, good boy, Benny," she heard people saying. Young men moved around through the crowd whispering, "Overflow meeting . . . stand your ground, folks."

He began to speak hanging by one arm from a lamppost. "Comrades, this is another insult flung in the face of the working class. There are not more than forty people in the hall and they close the doors and tell us it's full . . ." The crowd began swaying back and forth, hats, umbrellas bobbing in the sleety rain. Then she saw the two cops were dragging Compton off and heard the jangle of the patrolwagon. "Shame, shame," people yelled. They began to back off from the cops; the flow was away from the hall. People were moving quietly and dejectedly down the street toward the trolley tracks with the cordon of mounted police pressing them on. Suddenly Webb whispered in her ear, "Let me lean on your shoulder," and jumped on a hydrant.

"This is outrageous," he shouted, "you people had a permit to use the hall and had hired it and no power on earth has a right to keep you out of it. To hell with the cossacks."

Two mounted police were loping towards him, opening a lane through the crowd as they came. Webb was off the hydrant and had grabbed Daughter's hand, "Let's run like hell," he whispered and was off doubling back and forth among the scurrying people. She followed him laughing and out of breath. A trolley car was coming down the main street. Webb caught it on the move but she couldn't make it and had to wait for the next. Meanwhile the cops were riding slowly back and forth among the crowd breaking it up.

Daughter's feet ached from paddling in slush all afternoon and she was thinking that she ought to get home before she caught her death of cold. At the station waiting for the train she saw Webb. He looked scared to death. He'd pulled his cap down over his eyes and his muffler up over this chin and pretended not to know Daughter when she went up to him. Once they got on the overheated train he sneaked up the aisle and sat down next to her.

"I was afraid some dick ud recognize me at the station," he whispered. "Well, what do you think of it?"

"I thought it was terrible . . . they're all so yaller . . . the only people looked good to me were those boys guardin' the mills, they looked like white men. . . . And as for you, Webb Cruthers, you ran like a deer."

"Don't talk so loud. . . . Do you think I ought to have waited and gotten arrested like Ben."

"Of course it's none of my business."

"You don't understand revolutionary tactics, Anne."

Going over on the ferry they were both of them cold and hungry. Webb said he had the key to a room a friend of his had down on Eighth Street and that they'd better go there and warm their feet and make some tea before they went uptown. They had a long sullen walk, neither of them saying anything, from the ferry landing to the house. The room, that smelt of turpentine and was untidy, turned out to be a big studio heated by a gasburner. It was cold as Greenland, so they wrapped themselves in blankets and took off their shoes and stockings and toasted their feet in front of the gas. Daughter took her skirt off under the blanket and hung it up over the heater. "Well, I declare," she said, "if your friend comes in we sure will be compromised."

"He won't," said Webb, "he's up at Cold Spring for the weekend." Webb was moving around in his bare feet, putting on water to boil and making toast. "You'd better take your trousers off, Webb, I can see the water dripping off them from here." Webb blushed and pulled them off, draping the blanket around himself like a Roman senator.

For a long time they didn't say anything and all they could hear above the distant hum of traffic was the hiss of the gasflame and the intermittent purr of the kettle just beginning to boil. Then Webb suddenly began to talk in a nervous spluttering way. "So you think I'm yellow, do you? Well, you may be right, Anne . . . not that I give a damn . . . I mean, you see, there's times when a fellow ought to be a coward and times when he ought to do the he-man stuff. Now don't talk for a minute, let me say something. . . . I'm hellishly attracted to you . . . and it's been yellow of me not to tell you about it before, see? I don't believe in love or anything like that, all bourgeois nonsense; but I think when people are attracted to each other I think it's yellow of them not to . . . you know what I mean."

"No, I doan', Webb," said Daughter after a pause.

Webb looked at her in a puzzled way as he brought her a cup of tea and some buttered toast with a piece of cheese on it. They ate in silence for a while; it was so quiet they could hear each other gulping little swallows of tea. "Now, what in Jesus Christ's name did you mean by that?" Webb suddenly shouted out.

Daughter felt warm and drowsy in her blanket, with the hot tea in her and the dry gasheat licking the soles of her feet. "Well, what does anybody mean by anything," she mumbled dreamily.

Webb put down his teacup and began to walk up and down the room trailing the blanket after him. "S—t," he suddenly said, as he stepped on a thumbtack. He stood on one leg looking at the sole of his foot that was black from the grime of the floor. "But, Jesus Christ, Anne . . . people ought to be free and happy about sex . . . come ahead let's." His cheeks were pink and his black hair that needed cutting was every which way. He kept on standing on one leg and looking at the sole of his foot. Daughter began to laugh. "You look awful funny like that, Webb." She felt a warm glow all over her. "Give me another cup of tea and make me some more toast."

After she'd had the tea and toast she said, "Well, isn't it about time we ought to be going uptown?" "But Christ, Anne, I'm making indecent proposals to you," he said shrilly, half laughing and half in tears. "For God's sake pay attention . . . Damn it, I'll make you pay attention, you little bitch." He dropped his blanket and ran at her. She could see he was fighting mad. He pulled her up out of her chair and kissed her on the mouth. She had quite a tussle with him, as he was wiry and strong, but she managed to get her forearm under his chin and to push his face away far enough to give him a punch on the nose. His nose began to bleed. "Don't be silly, Webb," she said, breathing hard, "I don't want that sort of thing, not yet, anyway . . . go and wash your face."

He went to the sink and began dabbling his face with water. Daughter hurried into her skirt and shoes and stockings and went over to the sink where he was washing his face, "That was mean of me, Webb, I'm terribly sorry. There's something always makes me be mean to people I like." Webb wouldn't say anything for a long time. His nose was still bleeding.

"Go along home," he said, "I'm going to stay here. . . . It's all right my mistake."

She put on her dripping raincoat and went out into the shiny evening streets. All the way home on the express in the subway she was feeling warm and tender towards Webb, like towards Dad or the boys.

She didn't see him for several days, then one evening he called and asked her if she wanted to go out on the picket line next morning. It was still dark when she met him at the ferry station. They were both cold and sleepy and didn't say much going out on the train. From the train they had to run through the slippery streets to get to the mills in time to join the picket line. Faces looked cold and pinched in the blue early light. Women had shawls over their heads, few of the men or boys had overcoats. The young girls were all shivering in their cheap fancy topcoats that had no warmth to them. The cops had already begun to break up the head of the line. Some of the strikers were singing *Solidarity Forever*, others were yelling Scabs, Scabs and making funny long jeering hoots. Daughter was confused and excited.

Suddenly everybody around her broke and ran and left her in a stretch of empty street in front of the wire fencing of the mills. Ten feet in front of her a young woman slipped and fell. Daughter caught the scared look in her eyes that were round and black. Daughter stepped forward to help her up but two policemen were ahead of her swinging their nightsticks. Daughter thought they were going to help the girl up. She stood still for a second, frozen in her tracks when she saw one of the policemen's feet shoot out. He'd kicked the girl full in the face. Daughter never remembered what happened except that she was wanting a gun and punching into the policeman's big red face and against the buttons and the thick heavy cloth of his overcoat. Something crashed down on her head from behind; dizzy and sick she was being pushed into the policewagon. In front of her was the girl's face all caved in and bleeding. In the darkness inside were other men and women cursing and laughing. But Daughter and the woman opposite looked at each other dazedly and said nothing. Then the door closed behind them and they were in the dark.

When they were committed she was charged with rioting, felonious assault, obstructing an officer and inciting to sedition. It wasn't so bad in the county jail. The women's section was crowded with strikers, all the cells were full of girls laughing and talking, singing songs and telling each other how they'd been arrested, how long they'd been in, how they were going to win the strike. In Daughter's cell the girls all clustered around her and wanted to know how she'd gotten there. She began to feel she was quite a hero. Towards evening her name was called and she found Webb and Ada and a lawyer clustered around the policesergeant's desk. Ada was mad, "Read that, young woman, and see how that'll sound back home," she said, poking an afternoon paper under her nose.

TEXAS BELLE ASSAULTS COP said one headline. Then followed an account of her knocking down a policeman with a left on the jaw. She was released on a thousand dollars bail; outside the jail, Ben Compton broke away from the group of reporters around him and rushed up to her. "Congratulations, Miss Trent," he said, "that was a darn nervy thing to do . . . made a very good impression in the press." Sylvia Dalhart was with him. She threw her arms around her and kissed her: "That was a mighty spunky thing to do. Say, we're sending a delegation to Washington to see President Wilson and present a petition and we want you on it. The President will refuse to see the delegation and you'll have a chance to picket the White House and get arrested again."

"Well, I declare," said Ada when they were safely on the train for New York. "I think you've lost your mind." "You'd have done the same thing, Ada darlin', if you'd seen what I saw . . . when I tell Dad and the boys about it they'll see red. It's the most outrageous thing I ever heard of." Then she burst out crying.

When they got back to Ada's apartment they found a telegram from Dad saying *Coming at once. Make no statement until I arrive.* Late that night another telegram came; it read: *Dad seriously ill come on home at once have Ada retain best lawyer obtainable.* In the morning Daughter scared and trembling was on the first train south. At St. Louis she got a telegram saying *Don't worry condition fair double pneumonia.* Upset as she was it certainly did her good to see the wide Texas country, the spring crops beginning, a few bluebonnets in bloom. Buster was there to meet her at the depot, "Well, Daughter," he said after he had taken her bag, "you've almost killed Dad."

Buster was sixteen and captain of the highschool ball team. Driving her up to the house in the new Stutz he told her how things were. Bud had been tearing things up at the University and was on the edge of getting fired and had gotten balled up with a girl in Galveston who was trying to blackmail him. Dad had been very much worried because he'd gotten in too deep in the oil game and seeing Daughter spread all over the front page for knocking down a cop had about finished him; old Emma was getting too old to run the house for them anymore and it was up to Daughter to give up her crazy ideas and stay home and keep house for them. "See this car? A dandy ain't it. . . . I bought it myself. . . . Did a little tradin' in options up near Amarillo on my own, jus' for the hell of it, and I made five thousand bucks." "Why, you smart kid. I tell you, Bud, it's good to be home. But about the policeman you'd have done the same yourself or you're not my brother. I'll tell you all about it sometime. Believe me it does me good to see Texas faces after those mean weaselfaced Easterners." Dr. Winslow was in the hall when they came in. He shook hands warmly and told her how well she was looking and not to worry because he'd pull her Dad through if it was the last thing he did on earth. The sickroom and Dad's restless flushed face made her feel awful, and she didn't like finding a trained nurse running the house.

After Dad began to get around a little they both went down to Port Arthur for a couple of weeks for a change to stay with an old friend of Dad's. Dad said he'd give her a car if she'd stay on, and that he'd get her out of this silly mess she'd gotten into up north.

She began to play a lot of tennis and golf again and to go out a good deal socially. Joe Washburn had married and was living in Oklahoma getting rich on oil. She felt easier in Dallas when he wasn't there; seeing him upset her so. The next fall Daughter went down to Austin to finish her journalism course, mostly because she thought her being there would keep Bud in the straight and narrow. Friday afternoons they drove back home together in her Buick sedan for the weekend. Dad had bought a new Tudor style house way out and all her spare time was taken up picking out furniture and hanging curtains and arranging the rooms. She had a great many beaux always coming around to take her out and had to start keeping an engagement book. Especially after the declaration of war social life became very hectic. She was going every minute and never got any sleep. Everybody was getting commissions or leaving for officers training camps. Daughter went in for Red Cross work and organized a canteen, but that wasn't enough and she kept applying to be sent abroad. Bud went down to San Antonio to learn to fly and Buster, who'd been in the militia, lied about his age and joined up as a private and was sent to Jefferson Barracks. At the canteen she lived in a whirl and had one or two proposals of marriage a week, but she always told them that she hadn't any intention of being a war bride.

Then one morning a War Department telegram came. Dad was in Austin on business so she opened it. Bud had crashed, killed. First thing Daughter thought was how hard it would hit Dad. The phone rang; it was a long distance call from San Antonio, sounded like Joe Washburn's voice. "Is that you, Joe?" she said weakly. "Daughter, I want to speak to your father," came his grave drawl. "I know . . . O Joe."

"It was his first solo flight. He was a great boy. Nobody seems to know how it happened. Must have been defect in structure. I'll call Austin. I know where to get hold of him. . . . I've got the number . . . see you soon, Daughter." Joe rang off. Daughter went into her room and burrowed face down into the bed that hadn't been made up. For a minute she tried to imagine that she hadn't gotten up yet, that she dreamed the phone ringing and Joe's voice. Then she thought of Bud so sharply it was as if he'd come into the room, the way he laughed, the hard pressure of his long thin hand over her hands when he'd suddenly grabbed the wheel when they'd skidded going around a corner into San Antonio the last time she'd driven him down after a leave, the clean anxious lean look of his face above the tight khaki collar of the uniform. Then she heard Joe's voice again: Must have been some defect in structure.

She went down and jumped into her car. At the fillingstation where she filled up with gas and oil the garageman asked her how the boys liked it in the army. She couldn't stop to tell him about it now. "Bully, they like it fine," she said, with a grin that hurt her like a slap in the face. She wired Dad at his lawpartner's office that she was coming and pulled out of town for Austin. The roads were in bad shape, it made her feel better to feel the car plough through the muddy ruts and the water spraying out in a wave on either side when she went through a puddle at fifty.

She averaged fortyfive all the way and got to Austin before dark. Dad had already gone down to San Antonio on the train. Dead tired, she started off. She had a blowout and it took her a long time to get it fixed; it was midnight before she drew up at the Menger. Automatically she looked at herself in the little mirror before going in. There were streaks of mud on her face and her eyes were red.

In the lobby she found Dad and Joe Washburn sitting side by side with burntout cigars in their mouths. Their faces looked a little alike. Must have been the grey drawn look that made them look alike. She kissed them both. "Dad, you ought to go to bed," she said briskly. "You look all in." "I suppose I might as well . . . There's nothing left to do," he said.

"Wait for me, Joe, until I get Dad fixed up," she said in a low voice as she passed him. She went up to the room with Dad, got herself a room adjoining, ruffled his hair and kissed him very gently and left him to go to bed.

When she got back down to the lobby Joe was sitting in the same place with the same expression on his face. It made her mad to see him like that.

Her sharp brisk voice surprised her. "Come outside a minute, Joe, I want to walk around a little." The rain had cleared the air. It was a transparent early summer night. "Look here, Joe, who's responsible for the condition of the planes? I've got to know." "Daughter, how funny you talk . . . what you ought to do is get some sleep, you're all overwrought." "Joe, you answer my question." "But Daughter, don't you see nobody's responsible. The army's a big institution. Mistakes are inevitable. There's a lot of money being made by contractors of one kind or another. Whatever you say aviation is in its infancy . . . we all knew the risks before we joined up."

"If Bud had been killed in France I wouldn't have felt like this . . but here . . . Joe, somebody's directly responsible for my brother's death. I want to go and talk to him, that's all. I won't do anything silly. You all think I'm a lunatic I know, but I'm thinking of all the other girls who have brothers training to be aviators. The man who inspected those planes is a traitor to his country and ought to be shot down like a dog." "Look here, Daughter," Joe said as he brought her back to the hotel, "we're fightin' a war now. Individual lives don't matter, this isn't the time for lettin' your personal feelin's get away with you or embarrassin' the authorities with criticism. When we've licked the huns'll be plenty of time for gettin' the incompetents and the crooks . . . that's how I feel about it."

"Well, good night, Joe . . . you be mighty careful yourself. When do you expect to get your wings?" "Oh, in a couple of weeks." "How's Gladys and Bunny?" "Oh, they're all right," said Joe; a funny constraint came into his voice and he blushed. "They're in Tulsa with Mrs. Higgins."

She went to bed and lay there without moving, feeling desperately quiet and cool; she was too tired to sleep. When morning came she went around to the garage to get her car. She felt in the pocket on the door to see if her handbag was there that always had her little pearlhandled revolver in it, and drove out to the aviation camp. At the gate the sentry wouldn't let her by, so she sent a note to Colonel Morrissey who was a friend of Dad's, saying that she must see him at once. The corporal was very nice and got her a chair in the little office at the gate and a few minutes later said he had Colonel Morrissey on the wire. She started to talk to him but she couldn't think what to say. The desk and the office and the corporal began swaying giddily and she fainted.

She came to in a staffcar with Joe Washburn who was taking her back to the hotel. He was patting her hand saying, "That's all right, Daughter." She was clinging to him and crying like a little tiny girl.

They put her to bed at the hotel and gave her bromides and the doctor wouldn't let her get up until after the funeral was over.

She got a reputation for being a little crazy after that. She stayed on in San Antonio. Everything was very gay and tense. All day she worked in a canteen and evenings she went out, supper and dancing, every night with a different aviation officer. Everybody had taken to drinking a great deal. It was like when she used to go to highschool dances, she felt herself moving in a brilliantly lighted daze of suppers and lights and dancing and champagne and different colored faces and stiff identical bodies of men dancing with her, only now she had a kidding line and let them hug her and kiss her in taxicabs, in phonebooths, in people's backyards.

One night she met Joe Washburn at a party Ida Olsen was giving for some boys who were leaving for overseas. It was the first time she'd ever seen Joe drink. He wasn't drunk but she could see that he'd been drinking a great deal. They went and sat side by side on the back steps of the kitchen in the dark. It was a clear hot night full of dryflies with a hard hot wind rustling the dry twigs of all the trees. Suddenly she took Joe's hand: "Oh, Joe, this is awful."

Joe began to talk about how unhappy he was with his wife, how he was making big money through his oil leases and didn't give a damn about it, how sick he was of the army. They'd made him an instructor and wouldn't let him go overseas and he was almost crazy out there in camp. "Oh, Joe, I want to go overseas too. I'm leading such a silly life here." "You have been actin' kinder wild, Daughter, since Bud died," came Joe's soft deep drawling voice. "Oh, Joe, I wisht I was dead," she said and put her head on his knee and began to cry. "Don't cry, Daughter, don't cry," he began to say, then suddenly he was kissing her. His kisses were hard and crazy and made her go all limp against him.

"I don't love anybody but you, Joe," she suddenly said quietly. But he already had control of himself; "Daughter, forgive me," he said in a quiet lawyer's voice, "I don't know what I was thinking of, I must be crazy . . . this war is making us all crazy . . . Good night . . . Say . . . er . . . erase this all from the record, will you?"

That night she couldn't sleep a wink. At six in the morning she got into her car, filled up with gas and oil and started for Dallas. It was a bright fall morning with blue mist in the hollows. Dry cornstalks rustled on the long hills red and yellow with fall. It was late when she got home. Dad was sitting up reading the war news in pyjamas and bathrobe. "Well, it won't be long now, Daughter," he said. "The Hindenburg line is crumpling up. I knew our boys could do it once they got started." Dad's face was more lined with his hair whiter than she'd remembered it. She heated up a can of Campbell's soup as she hadn't taken any time to eat. They had a cosy little supper together and read a funny letter of Buster's from Camp Merritt where his outfit was waiting to go overseas. When she went to bed in her own room it was like being a little girl again, she'd always loved times when she got a chance to have a cosy chat with Dad all alone; she went to sleep the minute her head hit the pillow.

She stayed on in Dallas taking care of Dad; it was only sometimes when she thought of Joe Washburn that she felt she couldn't stand it another minute. The fake armistice came and then the real armistice, everybody was crazy for a week like a New Orleans mardigras. Daughter decided that she was going to be an old maid and keep house for Dad. Buster came home looking very tanned and full of army slang. She started attending lectures at Southern Methodist, doing church work, getting books out of the circulating library, baking angelcake; when young girlfriends of Buster's came to the house she acted as a chaperon.

Thanksgiving Joe Washburn and his wife came to dinner with them. Old Emma was sick so Daughter cooked the turkey herself. It was only when they'd all sat down to table, with the yellow candles lighted in the silver candlesticks and the salted nuts set out in the little silver trays and the decoration of pink and purple mapleleaves, that she remembered Bud. She suddenly began to feel faint and ran into her room. She lay face down on the bed listening to their grave voices. Joe came to the door to see what was the matter. She jumped up laughing, and almost scared Joe to death by kissing him square on the mouth. "I'm all right Joe," she said. "How's yourself?"

Then she ran to the table and started cheering everybody up, so that they all enjoyed their dinner. When they were drinking their coffee in the other room she told them that she'd signed up to go overseas for six months with the Near East Relief, that had been recruiting at Southern Methodist. Dad was furious and Buster said she ought to stay home now the war was over, but Daughter said, others had given their lives to save the world from the Germans and that she certainly could give up six months to relief work. When she said that they all thought of Bud and were quiet.

It wasn't actually true that she'd signed up, but she did the next morning and got around Miss Frazier, a returned missionary from China who was arranging it, so that they sent her up to New York that week, with orders to sail immediately with the office in Rome as her first destination. She was so widely excited all the time she was getting her passport and having her uniform fitted, she hardly noticed how glum Dad and Buster looked. She only had a day in New York. When the boat backed out of the dock with its siren screaming and started steaming down the North River, she stood on the front deck with her hair blowing in the wind, sniffing the funny steamboard harbor overseas smell and feeling like a twoyearold.

Newsreel XXXII

GOLDEN VOICE OF CARUSO SWELLS IN VICTORY SONG TO CROWDS ON STREETS

Oh Oh Oh, it's a lovely war
Oo wouldn't be a sodger, ay

from Pic Umbral to the north of the Stelvio it will follow the crest of the Rhetian alps up to the sources of the Adige and the Eisah passing thence by mounts Reschen and Brenner and the heights of Oetz and Boaller; thence south crossing Mount Toblach

As soon as reveille has gone
We feel just as 'eavy as lead
But we never git up till the sergeant
Brings us a cup of tea in bed

HYPNOTIZED BY COMMON LAW WIFE

army casualties soar to 64,305 with 318 today; 11,760 have paid the supreme sacrifice in action and 6,193 are severely wounded

Oh Oh Oh, it's a lovely war
Oo wouldn't be a sodger ay
Oh, it's a shayme to tayke the pay

in the villages in peasant houses the Americans are treated as guests living in the best rooms and courteously offered the best shining samovars or teaurns by the housewives

Le chef de gare il est cocu

in the largely populated districts a spectacular touch was given the festivities by groups of aliens appearing in costume and a carnival spirit prevailed

BRITISH SUPPRESS SOVIETS

> *Le chef de gare il est cocu*
> *Qui est cocu? Le chef de gare*
> *Sa femme elle l'a voulut*

there can be no reason to believe these officers of an established news organization serving newspapers all over the country failed to realize their responsibilities at a moment of supreme significance to the people of this country. Even to anticipate the event in a matter of such moment would be a grave imposition for which those responsible must be called to account

> *Any complaynts this morning?*
> *Do we complayn? Not we*
> *Wats the matter with lumps of onion*
> *Floatin' around in the tea?*

PEACE DOVE IN JEWELS GIVEN
MRS. WILSON

and the watershed of the Cols di Polberdo, Podlaniscam and Idria. From this point the line turns southeast towards the Schneeberg, excludes the whole basin of the Saave and its tributaries. From Schneeberg it goes down to the coast in such a way as to include Castna, Mattuglia and Volusca

The Camera Eye (38)

sealed signed and delivered   all over Tours you can smell lindens in bloom   it's hot my uniform sticks   the OD chafes me under the chin

only four days ago AWOL crawling under the freight cars at the station of St. Pierre-des-Corps   waiting in the buvette for the MP on guard to look away from the door so's I could slink out with a cigarette (and my heart) in my mouth   then in a tiny box of a hotel room changing the date on that old movement order

but today

my discharge sealed signed and delivered sends off sparks in my pocket like a romancandle

I walk past the headquarters of the SOS   Hay sojer your tunic's unbuttoned (f—k you buddy) and down the lindenshaded street to the bathhouse that has a court with flowers in the middle of it   the hot water gushes green out of brass swanheads into the whitemetal tub I strip myself naked soap myself all over with the sour pink soap slide into the warm deepgreen tub   through the white curtain in the window a finger of afternoon sunlight lengthens on the ceiling   towel's dry and warm smells of steam   in the suitcase I've got a suit of civvies I borrowed from a fellow I know   the buck private in the rear rank of Uncle Sam's Medical Corps (serial number . . . never could remember the number anyway I dropped it in the Loire) goes down the drain with a gurgle and hiss and

having amply tipped and gotten the eye from the fat woman who swept up the towels

I step out into the lindensmell of a July afternoon and stroll up to the café where at the little tables outside only officers may set their whipcord behinds   and order a drink of cognac unservable to those in uniform while waiting for the train to Paris and sit down firmly in long pants in the iron chair

an anonymous civilian

Newsreel XXXIII

CAN'T RECALL KILLING SISTER; CLAIMS

I've got the blues
I've got the blues
I've got the alcohoholic blues

SOAP CRISIS THREATENED

with the gay sunlight and the resumption of racing Paris has resumed its normal life. The thousands and thousands of flags of all nations hang on dozens of lines stretching from mast to mast making a fairylike effect that is positively astonishing

THREAT LETTERS REVEALED

I love my country indeed I do
But this war is making me blue
I like fightin fightin's my name
But fightin is the least about this fightin game

the police found an anteroom full of mysteriouslooking packages which when opened were found full of pamphlets in Yiddish Russian and English and of membership cards for the Industrial Workers of the World

HIGH WIND INCREASES DANGER OF MEN

WHILE PEACE IS TALKED OF WORLDWIDE WAR RAGES

the agents said the arrests were ordered from the State Department. The detention was so sudden neither of the men had time to obtain his baggage from the vessel. Then came a plaintive message from two business men at Lure; the consignment had arrived, the sacks had been opened and their contents was ordinary building plaster. The huge car remained suspended in some trees upside down while the passengers were thrown into the torrent twenty feet below

> *Lordy, lordy, war is hell*
> *Since he amputated my booze*

OUTRAGE PERPETRATED IN SEOUL

> *I've got the alcohohoholic blues*

The Department of Justice Has the Goods on the Packers According to Attorney General Palmer

L'Ecole du Malheur Nous Rend Optimistes

Unity of Free Peoples Will Prevent any Inequitable Outcome of Peace of Paris

it is only too clear that the league of nations lies in pieces on the floor of the Hotel Crillon and the modest alliance that might with advantage occupy its place is but a vague sketch

HOW TO DEAL WITH BOLSHEVISTS?
SHOOT THEM! POLES' WAY!

Hamburg Crowds Flock to See Ford

HINTS AT BIG POOL TO DEVELOP ASIA

> *When Mr. Hoover said to cut our eatin down*
> *I did it and I didn't ever raise a frown*
> *Then when he said to cut out coal,*
> *But now he's cut right into my soul*

Allons-nous Assister à la Panique des Sots?

stones were clattering on the roof and crashing through the windows and wild men were shrieking through the keyhole while enormous issues depended on them that required calm and deliberation at any rate the President did not speak to the leaders of the democratic movements

LIEBKNECHT KILLED ON WAY TO PRISON

Eveline Hutchins

Eveline had moved to a little place on the rue de Bussy where there was a street market every day. Eleanor to show that there was no hard feeling had given her a couple of her Italian painted panels to decorate the dark parlor with. In early November rumors of an armistice began to fly around and then suddenly one afternoon Major Wood ran into the office that Eleanor and Eveline shared and dragged them both away from their desks and kissed them both and shouted, "At last it's come." Before she knew it Eveline found herself kissing Major Moorehouse right on the mouth. The Red Cross office turned into a college dormitory the night of a football victory: it was the Armistice.

Everybody seemed suddenly to have bottles of cognac and to be singing, *There's a long long trail awinding* or *La Madellon pour nous n'est pas sévère.*

She and Eleanor and J.W. and Major Wood were in a taxicab going to the Café de la Paix.

For some reason they kept getting out of taxicabs and other people kept getting in. They had to get to the Café de la Paix but whenever they got into a taxicab it was stopped by the crowd and the driver disappeared. But when they got there they found every table filled and files of people singing and dancing streaming in and out all the doors. They were Greeks, Polish legionaires, Russians, Serbs, Albanians in white kilts, a Highlander with bagpipes and a lot of girls in Alsatian costume. It was annoying not being able to find a table. Eleanor said maybe they ought to go somewhere else. J.W. was preoccupied and wanted to get to a telephone.

Only Major Wood seemed to be enjoying himself. He was a grey-haired man with a little grizzled mustache and kept saying, "Ah, the lid's off today." He and Eveline went upstairs to see if they could find room there and ran into two Anzacs seated on a billiard table surrounded by a dozen bottles of champagne. Soon they were all drinking champagne with the Anzacs. They couldn't get anything to eat although Eleanor said she was starving and when J.W. tried to get into the phone booth he found an Italian officer and a girl tightly wedged together in it. The Anzacs were pretty drunk, and one of them was saying that the Armistice was probably just another bloody piece of lying propaganda; so Eleanor suggested they try to go back to her place to have something to eat. J.W. said yes, they could stop at the Bourse so that he could send some cables. He must get in touch with his broker. The Anzacs didn't like it when they left and were rather rude.

They stood around for a long time in front of the opera in the middle of swirling crowds. The streetlights were on; the grey outlines of the opera were edged along the cornices with shimmering gas flames. They were jostled and pushed about. There were no busses, no automobiles; occasionally they passed a taxicab stranded in the crowd like a rock in a stream. At last on a side street they found themselves alongside a Red Cross staffcar that had nobody in it. The driver, who wasn't too sober, said he was trying to get the car back to the garage and said he'd take them down to the quai de la Tournelle first.

Eveline was just climbing in when somehow she felt it was just too tiresome and she couldn't. The next minute she was marching arm in arm with a little French sailor in a group of people mostly in Polish uniform who were following a Greek flag and singing *la Brabançonne*.

A minute later she realized she'd lost the car and her friends and was scared. She couldn't recognize the streets even, in this new Paris full of arclights and flags and bands and drunken people. She found herself dancing with the little sailor in the asphalt square in front of a church with two towers, then with a French colonial officer in a red cloak, then with a Polish legionaire who spoke a little English and had lived in Newark, New Jersey, and then suddenly some young French soldiers were dancing in a ring around her holding hands. The game was you had to kiss one of them to break the ring. When she caught on she kissed one of them and everybody clapped and cheered and cried Vive l'Amerique. Another bunch came and kept on and on dancing around her until she began to feel scared. Her head was beginning to whirl around when she caught sight of an American uniform on the outskirts of the crowd. She broke through the ring bowling over a little fat Frenchman and fell on the doughboy's neck and kissed him, and everybody laughed and cheered and cried encore. He looked embarrassed; the man with him was Paul Johnson, Don Stevens' friend. "You see I had to kiss somebody," Eveline said blushing. The doughboy laughed and looked pleased.

"Oh, I hope you didn't mind, Miss Hutchins, I hope you don't mind this crowd and everything," apologized Paul Johnson.

People spun around them dancing and shouting and she had to

kiss Paul Johnson too before they'd let them go. He apologized solemnly again and said, "Isn't it wonderful to be in Paris to see the armistice and everything, if you don't mind the crowd and everything . . . but honestly, Miss Hutchins, they're awful goodnatured. No fights or nothin'. . . Say, Don's in this café."

Don was behind a little zinc bar in the entrance to the café shaking up cocktails for a big crowd of Canadian and Anzac officers all very drunk. "I can't get him out of there," whispered Paul. "He's had more than he ought." They got Don out from behind the bar. There seemed to be nobody there to pay for the drinks. In the door he pulled off his grey cap and cried, "Vive les quakers . . . à bas la guerre," and everybody cheered. They roamed around aimlessly for a while, now and then they'd be stopped by a ring of people dancing around her and Don would kiss her. He was noisy drunk and she didn't like the way he acted as if she was his girl. She began to feel tired by the time they got to the place de la Concorde and suggested that they cross the river and try to get to her apartment where she had some cold veal and salad.

Paul was embarrassedly saying perhaps he'd better not come, when Don ran off after a group of Alsatian girls who were hopping and skipping up the Champs Elysées. "Now you've got to come," she said. "To keep me from being kissed too much by strange men."

"But Miss Hutchins, you mustn't think Don meant anything running off like that. He's very excitable, especially when he drinks." She laughed and they walked on without saying anything more.

When they got to her apartment the old concièrge hobbled out from her box and shook hands with both of them. "Ah, madame, c'est la victoire," she said, "but it won't make my dead son come back to life, will it? For some reason Eveline could not think of anything to do but give her five francs and she went back muttering a singsong, "Merci, m'sieur, madame."

Up in Eveline's tiny rooms Paul seemed terribly embarrassed. They ate everything there was to the last crumb of stale bread and talked a little vaguely. Paul sat on the edge of his chair and told her about his travels back and forth with despatches. He said how wonderful it had been for him coming abroad and seeing the army and European cities and meeting people like her and Don Sevens and that he hoped she didn't mind his not knowing much about all the things she and Don talked about. "If this really is the beginning of peace I wonder what we'll all do, Miss Hutchins." "Oh, do call me Eveline, Paul." "I really do think it is the peace, Eveline, according to Wilson's Fourteen Points. I think Wilson's a great man myself in spite of all Don says, I know he's a darn sight cleverer than I am, but still . . . maybe this is the last war there'll ever be. Gosh, think of that . . ." She hoped he'd kiss her when he left but all he did was shake hands awkwardly and say all in a breath, "I hope you won't mind if I come to see you next time I can get to Paris."

For the Peace Conference, J.W had a suite at the Crillon, with his blonde secretary Miss Williams at a desk in a little anteroom, and Morton his English valet serving tea in the late afternoon. Eveline looked dropping into the Crillon late in the afternoon after walking up the arcades of the rue de Rivoli from her office. The antiquated corridors of the hotel were crowded with Americans coming and going. In J.W.'s big salon there'd be Morton stealthily handing around tea, and people in uniform and in frock coats and the cigarettesmoky air would be full of halftold anecdotes. J.W. fascinated her, dressed in grey Scotch tweeds that always had a crease on the trousers (he'd given up wearing his Red Cross major's uniform), with such an aloof agreeable manner, tempered by the preoccupied look of a very busy man always being called up on the phone, receiving telegrams or notes from his secretary, disappearing into the embrasure of one of the windows that looked out on the place de la Concorde with someone for a whispered conversation, or being asked to step in to see Colonel House for a moment; and still when he handed her a champagne cocktail just before they all went out to dinner on nights he didn't have to go to some official function, or asked if she wanted another cup of tea, she'd feel for a second in her eyes the direct glance of two boyish blue eyes with a funny candid partly humorous look that teased her. She wanted to know him better; Eleanor, she felt, watched them like a cat watching a mouse. After all, Eveline kept saying to herself, she hadn't any right. It wasn't as if there was anything really between them.

When J.W. was busy they often went out with Edgar Robbins who seemed to be a sort of assistant of J.W.'s. Eleanor couldn't abide him, said there was something insulting in his cynicism, but Eveline liked to hear him talk. He said the peace was going to be ghastlier than the war, said it was a good thing nobody ever asked his opinion about anything because he'd certainly land in jail if he gave it. Robbins' favorite hangout was Freddy's up back of Montmartre. They'd sit there all evening in the small smokycrowded rooms while Freddy, who had a big white beard like Walt Whitman, would play on the guitar and sing. Sometimes he'd get drunk and set the company up to drinks on the house. Then his wife, a cross woman who looked like a gypsy, would come out of the back room and curse and scream at him. People at the tables would get up and recite long poems about La Grand' route, La Misère, L'Assassinat or sing old French songs like Les Filles de Nantes. If it went over everybody present would clap hands in unison. They called that giving a bon. Freddy got to know them and would make a great fuss when they arrived, "Ah, les belles Américaines." Robbins would sit there moodily drinking calvados after calvados, now and then letting out a crack about the day's happenings at the peace conference. He said that the place was a fake that the calvados was wretched and that Freddy was a dirty old bum, but for some reason he always wanted to go back.

J.W. went there a couple of times, and occasionally they'd take some delegate from the peace conference who'd be mightily impressed by their knowledge of the inner life of Paris. J.W. was enchanted by the old French songs, but he said the place made him feel itchy and that he thought there were fleas there. Eveline liked to watch him when he was listening to a song with his eyes half closed and his head thrown back. She felt that Robbins didn't appreciate the rich potentialities of his nature and always shut him up when he started to say something sarcastic about the big cheese, as he called him. She thought it was disagreeable of Eleanor to laugh at things like that, especially when J.W. seemed so devoted to her.

When Jerry Burnham came back from Armenia and found that Eveline was going around with J. Ward Moorehouse all the time he was terribly upset. He took her out to lunch at the Medicis Grill on the left bank and talked and talked about it.

"Why, Eveline, I thought of you as a person who wouldn't be taken in by a big bluff like that. The guys nothing but a goddam megaphone. . . . Honestly, Eveline, it's not that I expect you to fall for me, I know very well you don't give a damn about me and why should you? . . . But Christ, a damn publicity agent."

"Now, Jerry," said Eveline with her mouth full of hors d'œuvres, "you know very well I'm fond of you . . . It's just too tiresome of you to talk like that."

"You don't like me the way I'd like you to . . . but to hell with that . . . Have wine or beer?"

"You pick out a nice Burgundy, Jerry, to warm us up a little. . . . But you wrote an article about J.W. yourself . . . I saw it reprinted in that column in the *Herald*."

"Go ahead, rub it in . . . Christ, I swear, Eveline, I'm going to get out of this lousy trade and . . . that was all plain oldfashioned bushwa and I thought you'd have had the sense to see it. Gee, this is good sole."

"Delicious . . . but Jerry, you're the one ought to have more sense."

"I dunno I thought you were different from other upperclass women, made your own living and all that."

"Let's not wrangle, Jerry, let's have some fun, here we are in Paris and the war's over and it's a fine wintry day and everybody's here. . . ."

"War over, my eye," said Jerry rudely. Eveline thought he was just too tiresome, and looked out the window at the ruddy winter sunlight and the old Medici fountain and the delicate violet lacework of the bare trees behind the high iron fence of the Luxemburg Garden. Then she looked at Jerry's red intense face with the turnedup nose and the crisp boyishly curly hair that was beginning to turn a little grey; she leaned over and gave the back of his hand a couple of little pats.

"I understand, Jerry, you've seen things that I haven't imagined . . . I guess it's the corrupting influence of the Red Cross."

He smiled and poured her out some more wine and said with a sigh:

"You're the most damnably attractive woman I ever met, Eveline . . . but like all women what you worship is power, when money's the main thing it's money, when it's fame it's fame, when it's art, you're a goddamned artlover . . . I guess I'm the same, only I kid myself more."

Eveline pressed her lips together and didn't say anything. She suddenly felt cold and frightened and lonely and couldn't think of anything to say. Jerry gulped down a glass of wine and started talking about throwing up his job and going to Spain to write a book. He said he didn't pretend to have any selfrespect, but that being a newspaper correspondent was too damn much nowadays. Eveline said she never wanted to go back to America, she felt life would be just too tiresome there after the war.

When they'd had their coffee they walked through the gardens. Near the senate chamber some old gentlemen were playing croquet in the last purplish patch of afternoon sunlight. "Oh, I think the French are wonderful," said Eveline. "Second childhood," growled Jerry. They rambled aimlessly round the streets, reading palegreen yellow and pink theatre notices on kiosks, looking into windows of antiqueshops. "We ought both to be at our offices," said Jerry. "I'm not going back," said Eveline, "I'll call up and say I have a cold and have gone home to bed . . . I think I'll do that anyway." "Don't do that, let's play hookey and have a swell time." They went to the café opposite St. Germain-des-Prés. When Eveline came back from phoning, Jerry had bought her a bunch of violets and ordered cognac and seltzer. "Eveline, let's celebrate," he said, "I think I'll cable the sonsobitches and tell 'em I've resigned." "Do you think you ought to do that, Jerry? After all it's a wonderful opportunity to see the peace conference and everything."

After a few minutes she left him and walked home. She wouldn't let him come with her. As she passed the window where they'd been sitting she looked in; he was ordering another drink.

On the rue de Bussy the market was very jolly under the gaslights. It all smelt of fresh greens, and butter and cheese. She bought some rolls for breakfast and a few little cakes in case somebody came in to tea. It was cosy in her little pink and white salon with the fire of brickettes going in the grate. Eveline wrapped herself up in a steamerrug and lay down on the couch.

She was asleep when her bell jingled. It was Eleanor and J.W. come to inquire how she was. J.W. was free tonight and wanted them to come to the opera with him to see *Castor and Pollux.* Eveline said she was feeling terrible but she thought she'd go just the same. She put on some tea for them and ran into her bedroom to dress. She felt so happy she couldn't help humming as she sat at her dressingtable looking at herself in the glass. Her skin looked very white and her face had a quiet mysterious look she liked. She carefully put on very little lipstick and drew her hair back to a knot behind; her hair worried her, it wasn't curly and didn't have any particular color: for a moment she thought she wouldn't go. Then Eleanor came in with a cup of tea in her hand telling her to hurry because they had to go down and wait while she dressed herself and that the opera started early. Eveline didn't have any real evening wrap so she had to wear an old rabbitfur coat over her eveningdress. At Eleanor's they found Robbins waiting; he wore a tuxedo that looked a little the worse for wear. J.W. was in the uniform of a Red Cross major. Eveline thought he must have been exercising, because his jowl didn't curve out from the tight high collar as much as it had formerly.

They ate in a hurry at Poccardi's and drank a lot of badly made Martinis. Robbins and J.W. were in fine feather, and kept them laughing all the time. Eveline understood now why they worked together so well. At the opera, where they arrived late, it was wonderful, glittering with chandeliers and uniforms. Miss Williams, J.W.'s secretary, was already in the box. Eveline thought how nice he must be to work for, and for a moment bitterly envied Miss Williams, even to her peroxide hair and her brisk chilly manner of talking. Miss Williams leaned back and said they'd missed it, that President and Mrs. Wilson had just come in and had been received with a great ovation, and Marshal Foch was there and she thought President Poincaré.

Between the acts they worked their way as best they could into the crowded lobby. Eveline found herself walking up and down with Robbins, every now and then she'd catch sight of Eleanor with J.W. and feel a little envious.

"They put on a better show out here than they do on the stage," said Robbins.

"Don't you like the production. . . . I think it's a magnificent production."

"Well, I suppose looked at from the professional point of view. . . ."

Eveline was watching Eleanor, she was being introduced to a French general in red pants; she looked handsome this evening in her hard chilly way. Robbins tried to pilot them in through the crowd to the little bar, but they gave it up, there were too many people ahead of them. Robbins started all at once to talk about Baku and the oil business. "It's funny as a crutch," he kept saying, "while we sit here wrangling under schoolmaster Wilson, John Bull's putting his hands on all the world's future supplies of oil . . . just to keep it from bolos. They've got Persia and the messpot and now I'll be damned if they don't want Baku." Eveline was bored and thinking to herself that Robbins had been in his cups too much again, when the bell rang.

When they got back to their box a leanfaced man who wasn't in evening clothes was sitting in the back talking to J.W. in a low voice. Eleanor leaned over to Eveline and whispered in her ear, "That was General Gouraud." The lights went out; Eveline found she was forgetting herself in the deep stateliness of the music. At the next intermission she leaned over to J.W. and asked him how he liked it. "Magnificent," he said, and she saw to her surprise that he had tears in his eyes. She found herself talking about the music with J.W. and the man without a dress suit, whose name was Rasmussen.

It was hot and crowded in the tall overdecorated lobby. Mr. Rasmussen managed to get a window open and they went out on the balcony that opened on the serried lights that dimmed down the avenue into a reddish glow of fog.

"That's the time I'd liked to have lived," said J.W. dreamily. "The court of the sun king?" asked Mr. Rasmussen. "No, it must have been too chilly in the winter months and I bet the plumbing was terrible." "Ah, it was a glorious time," said J.W. as if he hadn't heard. Then he turned to Eveline, "You're sure you're not catching cold . . . you ought to have a wrap, you know."

"But as I was saying, Moorehouse," said Rasmussen in a different tone of voice, "I have positive information that they can't hold Baku without heavy reinforcements and there's no one they can get them from except from us." The bell rang again and they hurried to their box.

After the opera they went to the Café de la Paix to drink a glass of champagne, except for Robbins who went off to take Miss Williams back to her hotel. Eveline and Eleanor sat on the cushioned bench on either side of J.W. and Mr. Rasmussen sat on a chair opposite them. He did most of the talking, taking nervous gulps of champagne between sentences or else running his fingers through his spiky black hair. He was an engineer with Standard Oil. He kept talking about Baku and Mohommarah and Mosul, how the Anglo-Persian and the Royal Dutch were getting ahead of the U.S. in the Near East and trying to foist off Armenia on us for a mandate, which the Turks had pillaged to the last blade of grass, leaving nothing but a lot of starving people to feed. "We'll probably have to feed 'em anyway," said J.W. "But my gosh, man, something can be done about it, even if the president has so far forgotten American interests to let himself be bulldozed by the British in everything, public opinion can be aroused. We stand to lose our primacy in world oil production." "Oh, well, the matter of mandates isn't settled yet." "What's going to happen is that the British are going to present a fait accompli to the Conference . . . findings keepings . . . why it would be better for us for the French to have Baku." "How about the Russians?" asked Eveline. "According to selfdetermination the Russians have no right to it. The population is mostly Turkish and Armenian," said Rasmussen. "But, by gorry, I'd rather have the reds have it than the British, of course I don't suppose they'll last long."

"No, I have reliable information that Lenine and Trotsky have split and the monarchy will be restored in Russia inside of three months." When they finished the first bottle of champagne, Mr. Rasmussen ordered another. By the time the café closed Eveline's ears were ringing. "Let's make a night of it," Mr. Rasmussen was saying.

They went in a taxicab up to Montmarte to L'Abbaye where there was dancing and singing and uniforms everywhere and everything was hung with the flags of the Allies. J.W. asked Eveline to dance with him first and Eleanor looked a little sour when she had to go off in the arms of Mr. Rasmussen who danced very badly indeed. Eveline and J.W. talked about the music of Rameau and J.W. said again that he would have liked to have lived in the times of the court at Versailles. But Eveline said what could be more exciting than to be in Paris right now with all the map of Europe being remade right under their noses, and J.W. said perhaps she was right. They agreed that the orchestra was too bad to dance to.

Next dance Eveline danced with Mr. Rasmussen who told her how handsome she was and said he needed a good woman in his life; that he'd spent all his life out in the bush grubbing around for gold or testing specimens of shale and that he was sick of it, and if Wilson now was going to let the British bulldoze him into giving them the world's future supply of oil when we'd won the war for them, he was through. "But can't you do something about it, can't you put your ideas before the public, Mr. Rasmussen?" said Eveline, leaning a little against him; Eveline had a crazy champagneglass spinning in her head.

"That's Moorehouse's job not mine, and there isn't any public since the war. The public'll damn well do what it's told, and besides like God Almighty it's far away . . . what we've got to do is make a few key men understand the situation. Moorehouse is the key to the key men." "And who's the key to Moorehouse?" asked Eveline recklessly.

The music had stopped. "Wish to heaven I knew," said Rasmussen soberly in a low voice. "You're not, are you?" Eveline shook her head with a tightlipped smile like Eleanor's.

When they'd eaten onion soup and some cold meat J.W. said, "Let's go up to the top of the hill and make Freddy play us some songs." "I thought you didn't like it up there," said Eleanor. "I don't, my dear, said J.W., "but I like those old French songs." Eleanor looked cross and sleepy. Eveline wished she and Mr. Rasmussen would go home; she felt if she could only talk to J.W. alone, he'd be so interesting.

Freddy's was almost empty; it was chilly in there. They didn't have any champagne and nobody drank the liqueurs they ordered. Mr. Rasmussen said Freddy looked like an old prospector he'd known out in the Sangre de Cristo mountains and began to tell a long story about Death Valley that nobody listened to. They were all chilly and sleepy and silent, going back across Paris in the old mouldysmelling twocylinder taxi. J.W. wanted a cup of coffee, but there didn't seem to be anywhere open where he could get it.

Next day Mr. Rasmussen called Eveline up at her office to ask her to eat lunch with him and she was hard put to it to find an excuse not to go. After that Mr. Rasmussen seemed to be everywhere she went, sending her flowers and theatre tickets, coming around with automobiles to take her riding, sending her little blue pneumatiques full of tender messages. Eleanor teased her about her new Romeo.

Then Paul Johnson turned up in Paris, having gotten himself into the Sorbonne detachment, and used to come around to her place on the rue de Bussy in the late afternoons and sit watching her silently and lugubriously. He and Mr. Rasmussen would sit there talking about wheat and the stockyards, while Eveline dressed to go out with somebody else, usually Eleanor and J.W. Eveline could see that J.W. always liked to have her along as well as Eleanor when they went out in the evenings; it was just that welldressed American girls were rare in Paris at the time, she told herself, and that J.W. liked to be seen with them and to have them along when he took important people out to dinner. She and Eleanor treated each other with a stiff nervous sarcasm now, except occasionally when they were alone together, they talked like in the old days, laughing at people and happenings together. Eleanor would never let a chance pass to poke fun at her Romeos.

Her brother George turned up at the office one day with a captain's two silver bars on his shoulders. His whipcord uniform fitted like a glove, his puttees shone and he wore spurs. He'd been in the intelligence service attached to the British and had just come down from Germany where he'd been an interpreter on General McAndrews' staff. He was going to Cambridge for the spring term and called everybody blighters or rotters and said the food at the restaurant where Eveline took him for lunch was simply ripping. After he'd left her, saying her ideas were not cricket, she burst out crying. When she was leaving the office that afternoon, thinking gloomily about how George had grown up to be a horrid little prig of a brasshat, she met Mr. Rasmussen under the arcades of the rue de Rivoli; he was carrying a mechanical canarybird. It was a stuffed canary and you wound it up underneath the cage. Then it fluttered its wings and sang. He made her stop on the corner while he made it sing. "I'm going to send that back home to the kids," he said. "My wife and I are separated but I'm fond of the kids; they live in Pasadena . . . I've had a very unhappy life." Then he invited Eveline to step into the Ritz bar and have a cocktail with him. Robbins was there with a redheaded newspaper woman from San Francisco. They sat at a wicker table together and drank Alexanders. The bar was crowded. "What's the use of a league of nations if it's to be dominated by Great Britain and her colonies?" said Mr. Rasmussen sourly. "But don't you think any kind of a league's better than nothing?" said Eveline. "It's not the name you give things, it's who's getting theirs underneath that counts," said Robbins.

"That's a very cynical remark," said the California woman. "This isn't any time to be cynical."

"This is a time," said Robbins, "when if we weren't cynical we'd shoot ourselves."

In March Eveline's two week leave came around. Eleanor was going to make a trip to Rome to help wind up the affairs of the office there, so they decided they'd go down on the train together and spend a few days in Nice. They needed to get the damp cold of Paris out of their bones. Eveline felt as excited as a child the afternoon when they were all packed and ready to go and had bought wagon lit reservations and gotten their transport orders signed.

Mr. Rasmussen insisted on seeing her off and ordered up a big dinner in the restaurant at the Gare de Lyon that Eveline was too excited to eat, what with the smell of the coalsmoke and the thought of waking up where it would be sunny and warm. Paul Johnson appeared when they were about half through, saying he'd come to help them with their bags. He'd lost one of the buttons off his uniform and he looked gloomy and mussed up. He said he wouldn't eat anything but nervously drank down several glasses of wine. Both he and Mr. Rasmussen looked like thunderclouds when Jerry Burnham appeared drunk as a lord carrying a large bouquet of roses. "Won't that be taking coals to Newcastle, Jerry?" said Eveline. "You don't know Nice . . . you'll probably have skating down there . . . beautiful figure eights on the ice." "Jerry," said Eleanor in her chilly little voice, "you're thinking of St. Moritz." "You'll be thinking of it too," said Jerry, "when you feel that cold wind."

Meanwhile Paul and Mr. Rasmussen had picked up their bags. "Honestly, we'd better make tracks," said Paul, nervously jiggling Eveline's suitcase. "It's about traintime." They all scampered through the station. Jerry Burnham had forgotten to buy a ticket and couldn't go out on the platform; they left him arguing with the officials and searching his pockets for his presscard. Paul put the bags in the compartment and shook hands hurriedly with Eleanor. Eveline found his eyes in hers serious and hurt like a dog's eyes.

"You won't stay too long, will you? There's not much time left," he said. Eveline felt she'd like to kiss him, but the train was starting. Paul scrambled off. All Mr. Rasmussen could do was hand some papers and Jerry's roses through the window and wave his hat mournfully from the platform. It was a relief the train had started. Eleanor was leaning back against the cushions laughing and laughing.

"I declare, Eveline. You're too funny with your Romeos." Eveline couldn't help laughing herself. She leaned over and patted Eleanor on the shoulder. "Let's just have a wonderful time," she said.

Next morning early when Eveline woke up and looked out they were in the station at Marseilles. It gave her a funny feeling because she'd wanted to stop off there and see the town, but Eleanor had insisted on going straight to Nice, she hated the sordidness of seaports she'd said. But later when they had their coffee in the diner, looking out at the pines and the dry hills and headlands cutting out blue patches of the Mediterranean, Eveline felt excited and happy again.

They got a good room in a hotel and walked through the streets in the cool sunshine among the wounded soldiers and officers of all the allied armies and strolled along the Promenade des Anglais under the grey palmtrees and gradually Eveline began to feel a chilly feeling of disappointment coming over her. Here was her two weeks leave and she was going to waste it at Nice. Eleanor kept on being crisp and cheerful and suggested they sit down in the big café on the square where a brass band was playing and have a little dubonnet before lunch. After they'd sat there for some time, looking at the uniforms and the quantities of overdressed women who were no better than they should be, Eveline leaned back in her chair and said, "And now that we're here, darling, what on earth shall we do?"

The next morning Eveline woke late; she almost hated to get up as she couldn't imagine how she was going to pass the time all day. As she lay there looking at the stripes of sunlight on the wall that came through the shutters, she heard a man's voice in the adjoining room, that was Eleanor's. Eveline stiffened and listened. It was J.W.'s voice. When she got up and dressed she found her heart was pounding. She was pulling on her best pair of transparent black silk stockings when Eleanor came in, "Who do you think's turned up? J.W. just motored down to see me off to Italy . . . He said it was getting too stuffy for him around the Peace Conference and he had to get a change of air . . . Come on in, Eveline, dear, and have some coffee with us."

She can't keep the triumph out of her voice, aren't women silly, thought Eveline. "That's lovely, I'll be right in, darling," she said in her most musical tones.

J.W. had on a light grey flannel suit and a bright blue necktie and his face was pink from the long ride. He was in fine spirits. He'd driven down from Paris in fifteen hours with only four hours sleep after dinner in Lyons. They all drank a great deal of bitter coffee with hot milk and planned out a ride.

It was a fine day. The big Packard car rolled them smoothly along the Corniche. They lunched at Monte Carlo, took a look at the casino in the afternoon and went on and had tea in an English tearoom in Mentone. Next day they went up to Grasse and saw the perfume factories, and the day after they put Eleanor on the rapide for Rome. J.W. was to leave immediately afterwards to go back to Paris. Eleanor's thin white face looked a little forlorn Eveline thought, looking out at them through the window of the wagonlit. When the train pulled out Eveline and J.W. stood on the platform in the empty station with the smoke swirling milky with sunlight under the glass roof overhead and looked at each other with a certain amount of constraint. "She's a great little girl," said J.W. "I'm very fond of her," said Eveline. Her voice rang false in her ears. "I wish we were going with her."

They walked back out to the car. "Where can I take you, Eveline, before I pull out, back to the hotel?" Eveline's heart was pounding again. "Suppose we have a little lunch before you go, let me invite you to lunch." "That's very nice of you . . . well, I suppose I might as well, I've got to lunch somewhere. And there's no place fit for a white man between here and Lyons."

They lunched at the casino over the water. The sea was very blue. Outside there were three sailboats with lateen sails making for the entrance to the port. It was warm and jolly, smelt of wine and food sizzled in butter in the glassedin restaurant. Eveline began to like it in Nice.

J.W. drank more wine than he usually did. He began to talk about his boyhood in Wilmington and even hummed a little of a song he'd written in the old days. Eveline was thrilled. Then he began to tell her about Pittsburgh and his ideas about capital and labor. For dessert they had peaches flambé with rum; Eveline recklessly ordered a bottle of champagne. They were getting along famously.

They began to talk about Eleanor. Eveline told about how she'd met Eleanor in the Art Institute and how Eleanor had meant everything to her in Chicago, the only girl she'd ever met who was really interested in the things she was interested in, and how much talent Eleanor had, and how much business ability. J.W. told about how much she'd meant to him during the trying years with his second wife Gertrude in New York, and how people had misunderstood their beautiful friendship that had been always free from the sensual and the degrading.

"Really," said Eveline, looking J.W. suddenly straight in the eye, "I'd always thought you and Eleanor were lovers." J.W. blushed. For a second Eveline was afraid she'd shocked him. He wrinkled up the skin around his eyes in a comical boyish way. "No, honestly not . . . I've been too busy working all my life ever to develop that side of my nature . . . People think differently about those things than they did." Eveline nodded. The deep flush on his face seemed to have set her cheeks on fire. "And now," J.W. went on, shaking his head gloomily, "I'm in my forties and it's too late."

"Why too late?"

Eveline sat looking at him with her lips a little apart, her cheeks blazing. "Maybe it's taken the war to teach us how to live," he said. "We've been too much interested in money and material things, it's taken the French to show us how to live. Where back home in the States could you find a beautiful atmosphere like this?" J.W. waved his arm to include in a sweeping gesture the sea, the tables crowded with women dressed in bright colors and men in their best uniforms, the bright glint of blue light on glasses and cutlery. The waiter mistook his gesture and slyly substituted a full bottle for the empty bottle in the champagnepail.

"By golly, Eveline, you've been so charming, you've made me forget the time and going back to Paris and everything. This is the sort of thing I've missed all my life until I met you and Eleanor . . . of course with Eleanor it's been all on the higher plane . . . Let's take a drink to Eleanor . . . beautiful talented Eleanor . . . Eveline, women have been a great inspiration to me all my life, lovely charming delicate women. Many of my best ideas have come from women, not directly, you understand, but through the mental stimulation . . . People don't understand me, Eveline, some of the newspaper boys particularly have written some very hard things about me . . . why, I'm an old newspaper man myself . . . Eveline, permit me to say that you look so charming and understanding . . . this illness of my wife . . . poor Gertrude . . . I'm afraid she'll never be herself again. . . . You see, it's put me in a most disagreeable position, if some member of her family is appointed guardian it might mean that the considerable sum of money invested by the Staple family in my business, would be withdrawn . . . that would leave me with very grave embarrassments . . . then I've had to abandon my Mexican affairs . . . what the oil business down there needs is just somebody to explain its point of view to the Mexican public, to the American public, my aim was to get the big interests to take the public in . . ." Eveline filled his glass. Her head was swimming a little, but she felt wonderful. She wanted to lean over and kiss him, to make him feel how she admired and understood him. He went on talking with the glass in his hand, almost as if he were speaking to a whole rotary club. ". . . to take the public into its confidence . . . I had to throw overboard all that . . . when I felt the government of my country needed me. My position is very difficult in Paris, Eveline. . . . They've got the President surrounded by a Chinese wall . . . I fear that his advisers don't realize the importance of publicity, of taking the public into their confidence at every move. This is a great historical moment, America stands at the parting of the ways . . . without us the war would have ended in a German victory or a negotiated peace . . . And now our very allies are trying to monopolize the natural resources of the world behind our backs. . . . You remember what Rasmussen said . . . well, he's quite right. The President is surrounded by sinister intrigues. Why, even the presidents of the great corporations don't realize that now is the time to spend money, to spend it like water. I could have the French press in my pocket in a week with the proper resources, even in England I have a hunch that something could be done if it was handled the right way. And then the people are fully behind us everywhere, they are sick of autocracy and secret diplomacy, they are ready to greet American democracy, American democratic business methods with open arms. The only way for you to secure the benefits of the peace to the world is for us to dominate it. Mr. Wilson doesn't realize the power of a modern campaign of scientific publicity . . . Why, for three weeks I've been trying to get an interview with him, and back in Washington I was calling him Woodrow, almost . . . It was at his personal request that I dropped everything in New York at great personal sacrifice, brought over a large part of my office staff . . . and now . . . but Eveline, my dear girl, I'm afraid I'm talking you to death."

Eveline leaned over and patted his hand that lay on the edge of the table. Her eyes were shining, "Oh, it's wonderful," she said. "Isn't this fun, J.W.?"

"Ah, Eveline, I wish I was free to fall in love with you."

"Aren't we pretty free, J.W.? and it's wartime . . . I think all the conventional rubbish about marriage and everything is just too tiresome, don't you?"

"Ah, Eveline, if I was only free . . . let's go out and take a little air . . . Why, we've been here all afternoon."

Eveline insisted on paying for the lunch although it took all the money she had on her. They both staggered a little as they left the restaurant, Eveline felt giddy and leaned against J.W.'s shoulder. He kept patting her hand and saying, "There, there, we'll take a little ride."

Towards sunset they were riding around the end of the bay into Cannes. "Well, well, we must pull ourselves together," said J.W. "You don't want to stay down here all alone, do you, little girl? Suppose you drive back to Paris with me, we'll stop off in some picturesque villages, make a trip of it. Too likely to meet people we know around here. I'll send back the staff car and hire a French car . . . take no chances." "All right, I think Nice is just too tiresome anyway."

J.W. called to the chauffeur to go back to Nice. He dropped her at her hotel and saying he'd call for her at ninethirty in the morning and that she must get a good night's sleep. She felt terribly let down after he'd gone; had a cup of tea that was cold and tasted of soap sent to her room; and went to bed. She lay in bed thinking that she was acting like a nasty little bitch; but it was too late to go back now. She couldn't sleep, her whole body felt jangled and twitching. This way she'd look like a wreck tomorrow, she got up and rustled around in her bag until she found some aspirin. She took a lot of the aspirin and got back in bed again and lay perfectly still but she kept seeing faces that would grow clear out of the blur of a halfdream and then fade again, and her ears buzzed with long cadences of senseless talk. Sometimes it was Jerry Burnham's face that would bud out of the mists changing slowly into Mr. Rasmussen's or Edgar Robbins' or Paul Johnson's or Freddy Seargeant's. She got up and walked shivering up and down the room for a long time. Then she got into bed again and fell asleep and didn't wake up until the chambermaid knocked on the door saying that a gentleman was waiting for her.

When she got down J.W. was pacing up and down in the sun outside the hotel door. A long lowslung Italian car was standing under the palms beside the geranium bed. They had coffee together without saying much at a little iron table outside the hotel. J.W. said he'd had a miserable room in a hotel where the service was poor.

As soon as Eveline got her bag down they started off at sixty miles an hour. The chauffeur drove like a fiend through a howling north wind that increased as they went down the coast. They were in Marseilles stiff and dustcaked in time for a late lunch at a fish restaurant on the edge of the old harbor. Eveline's head was whirling again, with speed and lashing wind and dust and vines and olivetrees and grey rock mountains whirling past and now and then a piece of slateblue sea cut out with a jigsaw.

"After all, J.W., the war was terrible," said Eveline. "But it's a great time to be alive. Things are happening at last." J.W. muttered something about a surge of idealism between his teeth and went on eating his bouillabaisse. He didn't seem to be very talkative today. "Now at home," he said, "they wouldn't have left all the bones in the fish this way." "Well, what do you think is going to happen about the oil situation?" Eveline started again. "Blamed if I know," said J.W. "We'd better be starting if we're going to make that place before nightfall."

J.W. had sent the chauffeur to buy an extra rug and they wrapped themselves up tight under the little hood in the back of the car. J.W. put his arm around Eveline and tucked her in. "Now we're snug as a bug in a rug," he said. They giggled cosily together.

The mistral got so strong the poplars were all bent double on the dusty plains before the car started to climb the winding road to Les Baux. Bucking the wind cut down their speed. It was dark when the got into the ruined town.

They were the only people in the hotel. It was cold there and the knots of olivewood burning in the grates didn't give any heat, only puffs of grey smoke when a gust of wind came down the chimney, but they had an excellent dinner and hot spiced wine that made them feel much better. They had to put on their overcoats to go up to their bedroom. Climbing the stairs J.W. kissed her under the ear and whispered, "Eveline, dear little girl, you make me feel like a boy again."

Long after J.W. had gone to sleep Eveline lay awake beside him listening to the wind rattling the shutters, yelling around the corners of the roof, howling over the desert plain far below. The house smelt of dry dusty coldness. No matter how much she cuddled against him, she couldn't get to feel really warm. The same creaky carrousel of faces, plans, scraps of talk kept going round and round in her head, keeping her from thinking consecutively, keeping her from going to sleep.

Next morning when J.W. found he had to bathe out of a basin he made a face and said, "I hope you don't mind roughing it this way, dear little girl."

They went over across the Rhone to Nîmes for lunch riding through Arles and Avignon on the way, then they turned back to the Rhone and got into Lyons late at night. They had supper sent up to their room in the hotel and took hot baths and drank hot wine again. When the waiter had taken away the tray Eveline threw herself on J.W.'s lap and began to kiss him. It was a long time before she'd let him go to sleep.

Next morning it was raining hard. They waited around a couple of hours hoping it would stop. J.W. was preoccupied and tried to get

Paris on the phone, but without any luck. Eveline sat in the dreary hotel salon reading old copies of *l'Illustration*. She wished she was back in Paris too. Finally they decided to start.

The rain went down to a drizzle but the roads were in bad shape and by dark they hadn't gotten any further than Nevers. J.W. was getting the sniffles and started taking quinine to ward off a cold. He got adjoining rooms with a bath between in the hotel at Nevers, so that night they slept in separate beds. At supper Eveline tried to get him talking about the peace conference, but he said, "Why talk shop, we'll be back there soon enough, why not talk about ourselves and each other."

When they got near Paris, J.W. began to get nervous. His nose had begun to run. At Fountainebleau they had a fine lunch. J.W. went in from there on the train, leaving the chauffeur to take Eveline home to the rue de Bussy and then deliver his baggage at the Crillon afterward. Eveline felt pretty forlorn riding in all alone through he suburbs of Paris. She was remembering how excited she'd been when they'd all been seeing her off at the Gare de Lyons a few days before and decided she was very unhappy indeed.

Next day she went around to the Crillon at about the usual time in the afternoon. There was nobody in J.W.'s anteroom but Miss Williams, his secretary. She stared Eveline right in the face with such cold hostile eyes that Eveline immediately thought she must know something. She said Mr. Moorehouse had a bad cold and fever and wasn't seeing anybody.

"Well, I'll write him a little note," said Eveline. "No, I'll call him up later. Don't you think that's the idea, Miss Williams?" Miss Williams nodded her head dryly. "Very well," she said.

Eveline lingered. "You see, I've just come back from leave . . . I came back a couple of days early because there was so much sightseeing I wanted to do near Paris. Isn't the weather miserable?"

Miss Williams puckered her forehead thoughtfully and took a step towards her. "Very . . . It's most unfortunate, Miss Hutchins, that Mr. Moorehouse should have gotten this cold at this moment. We have a number of important matters pending. And the way things are at the Peace Conference the situation changes every minute so that constant watchfulness is necessary . . . We think it is a very important moment from every point of view . . . Too bad Mr. Moorehouse should get laid up just now. We feel very badly about it, all of us. He feels just terribly about it."

"I'm so sorry," said Eveline, "I do hope he'll be better tomorrow."

"The doctor says he will . . . but it's very unfortunate."

Eveline stood hesitating. She didn't know what to say. Then she caught sight of a little gold star that Miss Williams wore on a brooch. Eveline wanted to make friends. "Oh, Miss Williams," said, "I didn't know you lost anyone dear to you." Miss Williams's face got more chilly and pinched than ever. She seemed to be fumbling for something to say. "Er . . . my brother was in the navy," she said and walked over to her desk where she started typing very fast. Eveline stood where she was a second watching Miss Williams's fingers twinkling on the keyboard. Then she said weakly, "Oh, I'm so sorry," and turned and went out.

When Eleanor got back, with a lot of old Italian damask in her trunk, J.W. was up and around again. It seemed to Eveline that Eleanor had something cold and sarcastic in her manner of speaking she'd never had before. When she went to the Crillon to tea Miss Williams would hardly speak to Eveline, but put herself out to be polite to Eleanor. Even Morton, the valet, seemed to make the same difference. J.W. from time to time gave her a furtive squeeze of the hand, but they never got to go out alone any more. Eveline began to think of going home to America, but the thought of going back to Santa Fé or to any kind of life she'd lived before was hideous to her. She wrote J.W. long uneasy notes every day telling him how unhappy she was, but he never mentioned them when she saw him. When she asked him once why he didn't ever write her a few words he said quickly, "I never write personal letters," and changed the subject.

In the end of April Don Stevens turned up in Paris. He was in civilian clothes as he'd resigned from the reconstruction unit. He asked Eveline to put him up as he was broke. Eveline was afraid of the concièrge and of what Eleanor or J.W. might say if they found out, but she felt desperate and bitter and didn't care much what happened anyway; so she said all right, she'd put him up but he wasn't to tell anybody where he was staying. Don teased her about her bourgeois ideas, said those sorts of things wouldn't matter after the revolution, that the first test of strength was coming on the first of May. He made her read *L'Humanité* and took her up to the rue du Croissant to show her the little restaurant where Jaurès had been assassinated.

One day a tall longfaced young man in some kind of a uniform came into the office and turned out to be Freddy Seargeant, who had just got a job in the Near East Relief and was all excited about going out to Constantinople. Eveline was delighted to see him, but after she'd been with him all afternoon she began to feel that the old talk about the theater and decoration and pattern and color and form didn't mean much to her any more. Freddy was in ecstasy about being in Paris, and the little children sailing boats in the ponds in the Tuileries gardens, and the helmets of the Garde Republicaine turned out to salute the King and Queen of the Belgians who happened to be going up the rue de Rivoli when they passed. Eveline felt mean and teased him about not having gone through with it as a C.O.; he explained that a friend had gotten him into the camouflage service before he knew it and that he didn't care about politics anyway, and that before he could do anything the war was over and he was discharged. They tried to get Eleanor to go out to dinner with them, but she had a mysterious engagement to dine with J.W. and some people from the quai d'Orsay, and couldn't come. Eveline went with Freddy to the Opera Comique to see *Pélléas* but she felt fidgety all through it and almost slapped him when she saw he was crying at the end. Having an orange water ice at the Café Néapolitain afterwards, she upset Freddy terribly by saying Debussy was old hat, and he took her home glumly in a taxi. At the last minute she reflected and tried to be nice to him; she promised to go out to Chartres with him the next Sunday.

It was still dark when Freddy turned up Sunday morning. They went out and got some coffee sleepily from an old woman who had a little stand in the doorway opposite. They still had an hour before train time and Freddy suggested they go and get Eleanor up. He'd so looked forward to going to Chartres with both of them, he said; it would be old times all over again, he hated to think how life was drawing them all apart. So they got into a cab and went down to the quai de la Tournelle. The great question was how to get in the house as the street door was locked and there was no concièrge. Freddy rang and rang the bell until finally the Frenchman who lived on the lower floor came out indignant in his bathrobe and let them in.

They banged on Eleanor's door. Freddy kept shouting, "Eleanor Stoddard, you jump right up and come to Chartres with us." After a while Eleanor's face appeared, cool and white and collected, in the crack of the door above a stunning blue negligée.

"Eleanor, we've got just a half an hour to catch the train for Chartres, the taxi has full steam up outside and if you don't come we'll all regret it to our dying day."

"But I'm not dressed . . . it's so early."

"You look charming enough to go just as you are." Freddy pushed through the door and grabbed her in his arms. "Eleanor, you've got to come . . . I'm off for the Near East tomorrow night."

Eveline followed them into the salon. Passing the half open door of the bedroom, she glanced in and found herself looking J.W. full in the face. He was sitting bolt upright in the bed, wearing pyjamas with a bright blue stripe. His blue eyes looked straight through her. Some impulse made Eveline pull the door to. Eleanor noticed her gesture. "Thank you, darling," she said coolly, "it's so untidy in there."

"Oh, do come, Eleanor . . . after all you can't have forgotten old times the way hardhearted Hannah there seems to have," said Freddy in a cajoling whine.

"Let me think," said Eleanor, tapping her chin with the sharp pointed nail of a white forefinger, "I'll tell you what we'll do, darlings, you two go out on the poky old train as you're ready and I'll run out as soon as I'm dressed and call up J.W. at the Crillon and see if he won't drive me out. Then we can all come back together. How's that?"

"That would be lovely, Eleanor dear," said Eveline in a singsong voice. "Splendid, oh, I knew you'd come . . . well, we've got to be off. If we miss each other we'll be in front of the cathedral at noon . . . Is that all right?"

Eveline went downstairs in a daze. All the way out to Chartres Freddy was accusing her bitterly of being absentminded and not liking her old friends any more.

By the time they got to Chartres it was raining hard. They spent a gloomy day there. The stained glass that had been taken away for safety during the war hadn't been put back yet. The tall twelfth-century saints had a wet, slimy look in the driving rain. Freddy said that the sight of the black virgin surrounded by candles in the crypt was worth all the trouble of the trip for him, but it wasn't for Eveline. Eleanor and J.W. didn't turn up; "Of course not in this rain," said Freddy. It was a kind of relief to Eveline to find that she'd caught cold and would have to go to bed as soon as she got home. Freddy took her to her door in a taxi but she wouldn't let him come up for fear he'd find Don there.

Don was there, and was very sympathetic about her cold and tucked her in bed and made her a hot lemonade with cognac in it. He had his pockets full of money, as he'd just sold some articles, and had gotten a job to go to Vienna for the *Daily Herald* of London. He was pulling out as soon after May 1 as he could . . . "unless something breaks here," he said impressively. He went away that evening to a hotel, thanking her for putting him up like a good comrade even if she didn't love him any more. The place felt empty after he'd gone. She almost wished she'd made him stay. She lay in bed feeling feverishly miserable, and finally went to sleep feeling sick and scared and lonely.

The morning of the first of May, Paul Johnson came around before she was up. He was in civilian clothes and looked young and slender and nice and lighthaired and handsome. He said Don Stevens had gotten him all wrought up about what was going to happen what with the general strike and all that; he'd come to stick around if Eveline didn't mind. "I thought I'd better not be in uniform, so I borrowed this suit from a feller," he said. "I think I'll strike too," said Eveline. "I'm so sick of that Red Cross office I could scream."

"Gee, that ud be wonderful, Eveline. We can walk around and see the excitement. . . . It'll be all right if you're with me . . . I mean I'll be easier in my mind if I know where you are if there's trouble . . . You're awful reckless, Eveline."

"My, you look handsome in that suit, Paul . . . I never saw you in civilian clothes before."

Paul blushed and put his hands uneasily into his pockets. "Lord, I'll be glad to get into civvies for keeps," he said seriously. "Even through it'll mean me goin' back to work . . . I can't get a darn thing out of these Sorbonne lectures . . . everybody's too darn restless, I guess . . . and I'm sick of hearing what bums the boche are, that's all the frog profs seem to be able to talk about."

"Well, go out and read a book and I'll get up. . . . Did you notice if the old woman across the way had coffee out?"

"Yare, she did," called Paul from the salon to which he'd retreated when Eveline stuck her toes out from under the bedclothes. "Shall I go out and bring some in?"

"That's a darling, do. . . . I've got brioches and butter here . . . take that enamelled milkcan out of the kitchen."

Eveline looked at herself in the mirror before she started dressing. She had shadows under her eyes and faint beginnings of crowsfeet. Chillier than the damp Paris room came the thought of growing old. It was so horribly actual that she suddenly burst into tears. An old hag's tearsmeared face looked at her bitterly out of the mirror. She pressed the palms of her hands hard over her eyes. "Oh, I lead such a silly life," she whispered aloud.

Paul was back. She could hear him moving around awkwardly in the salon. "I forgot to tell you . . . Don says Anatole France is going to march with the mutilays of la guerre. . . . I've got the cafay o lay whenever you're ready."

"Just a minute," she called from the basin where she was splashing cold water on her face. "How old are you, Paul?" she asked him when she came out of her bedroom all dressed, smiling, feeling that she was looking her best.

"Free, white and twenty one . . . we'd better drink up this coffee before it gets cold." "You don't look as old as that." "Oh, I'm old enough to know better," said Paul, getting very red in the face. "I'm five years older than that," said Eveline. "Oh, how I hate growing old." "Five years don't mean anything," stammered Paul.

He was so nervous he spilt a lot of coffee over his trouserleg. "Oh, hell, that's a dumb thing to do," he growled. "I'll get it out in a second," said Eveline, running for a towel.

She made him sit in a chair and kneeled down in front of him and scrubbed at the inside of his thigh with the towel. Paul sat there stiff, red as a beet, with his lips pressed together. He jumped to his feet before she'd finished. "Well, let's go out and see what's happening. I wish I knew more about what it's all about."

"Well, you might at least say thank you," said Eveline, looking up at him.

"Thanks, gosh, it's awful nice of you, Eveline."

Outside it was like Sunday. A few stores were open on the side streets but they had their iron shutters halfway down. It was a grey day; they walked up the Boulevard St. Germain, passing many people out strolling in their best clothes. It wasn't until a squadron of the Guarde Republicaine clattered past them in their shiny helmets and their tricolor plumes that they had any inkling of tenseness in the air.

Over on the other side of the Seine there were more people and little groups of gendarmes standing around.

At the crossing of several streets they saw a cluster of old men in workclothes with a red flag and a sign, L'UNION DES TRAVAILLEURS FERA LA PAIX DU MONDE. A cordon of republican guards rode down on them with their sabres drawn, the sun flashing on their helmets. The old men ran or flattened themselves in doorways.

On the Grands Boulevards there were companies of poilus in tin hats and grimy blue uniforms standing round their stacked rifles. The crowds on the streets cheered them as they surged past, everything seemed goodnatured and jolly. Eveline and Paul began to get tired; they'd been walking all morning. They began to wonder where they'd get any lunch. Then too it was starting to rain.

Passing the Bourse they met Don Stevens, who had just come out of the telegraph office. He was sore and tired. He'd been up since five o'clock. "If they're going to have a riot why the hell can't they have it in time to make the cables . . . Well, I saw Anatole France dispersed on the Place d'Alma. Ought to be a story in that except for all this damned censorship. Things are pretty serious in Germany . . . I think something's going to happen there."

"Will anything happen here in Paris, Don?" asked Paul.

"Damned if I know . . . some kids busted up those gratings around the trees and threw them at the cops on the avenue Magenta. . . . Burnham in there says there are barricades at the end of the place de la Bastille, but I'm damned if I'm going over till I get something to eat . . . I don't believe it anyway . . . I'm about foundered. What are you two bourgeois doing out a day like this?"

"Hey, fellowworker, don't shoot," said Paul, throwing up his hands. "Wait till we get something to eat," Eveline laughed. She thought how much better she liked Paul than she liked Don.

They walked around a lot of back streets in the drizzling rain and at last found a little restaurant from which came voices and a smell of food. They ducked in under the iron shutter of the door. It was dark and crowded with taxidrivers and workingmen. They squeezed into the end of a marble table where two old men were playing chess. Eveline's leg was pressed against Paul's. She didn't move; then he began to get red and moved his chair a little. "Excuse me," he said.

They all ate liver and onions and Don got to talking with the old men in his fluent bad French. They said the youngsters weren't good for anything nowadays, in the old days when they descended into the street they tore up the pavings and grabbed the cops by the legs and pulled them off their horses. Today was supposed to be a general strike and what had they done? . . . nothing . . . a few urchins had thrown some stones and one café window had been broken. It wasn't like that that liberty defended itself and the dignity of labor. The old men went back to their chess. Don set them up to a bottle of wine.

Eveline was sitting back halflistening, wondering if she'd go around to see J.W. in the afternoon. She hadn't seen him or Eleanor since that Sunday morning; she didn't care anyway. She wondered if Paul would marry her, how it would be to have a lot of little babies that would have the same young coltish fuzzy look he had. She liked it in this little dark restaurant that smelt of food and wine and caporal ordinaire, sitting back and letting Don lay down the law to Paul about the revolution. "When I get back home I guess I'll bum around the country a little, get a job as a harvest hand and stuff like that and find out about those things," Paul said finally. "Now I don't know a darn thing, just what I hear people say."

After they had eaten they were sitting over some glasses of wine, when they heard an American voice. Two M.P.'s had come in and were having a drink at the zinc bar. "Don't talk English," whispered Paul. They sat there stiffly trying to look as French as possible until the two khaki uniforms disappeared, then Paul said, "Whee, I was scared . . . they'd picked me up sure as hell if they'd found me without my uniform. . . . Then it'd have been the Roo Saint Anne and goodby Paree." "Why, you poor kid, they'd have shot you at sunrise," said Eveline. "You go right home and change your clothes at once . . . I'm going to the Red Cross for a while anyway."

Don walked over to the rue de Rivoli with her. Paul shot off down another street to go to his room and get his uniform. "I think Paul Johnson's an awfully nice boy, where did you collect him, Don?" Eveline said in a casual tone. "He's kinder simple . . . unlicked cub kind of a kid . . . I guess he's all right . . . I got to know him when the transport section he was in was billeted near us up in the Marne . . . Then he got this cush job in the Post Despatch Service and now he's studying at the Sorbonne. . . . By God, he needs it . . . no social ideas . . . Paul still thinks it was the stork."

"He must come from near where you came from . . . back home, I mean."

"Yare, his dad owns a grain elevator in some little tank town or other . . . petit bourgeois . . . bum environment . . . He's not a bad kid in spite of it . . . Damn shame he hasn't read Marx, something to stiffen his ideas up." Don made a funny face. "That goes with you too, Eveline, but I gave you up as hopeless long ago. Ornamental but not useful." They'd stopped and were talking on the streetcorner under the arcade. "Oh, Don, I think your ideas are just too tiresome," she began. He interrupted, "Well, solong, here comes a bus . . . I oughtn't to ride on a scab bus but it's too damn far to walk all the way to the Bastille." He gave her a kiss. "Don't be sore at me." Eveline waved her hand, "Have a good time in Vienna, Don." He jumped on the platform of the bus as it rumbled past. The last Eveline saw the woman conductor was trying to push him off because the bus was complet.

She went up to her office and tried to look as if she'd been there all day. At a little before six she walked up the street to the Crillon and went up to see J.W. Everything was as usual there, Miss Williams looking chilly and yellowhaired at her desk, Morton stealthily handing around tea and petit fours, J.W. deep in talk with a personage in a cutaway in the embrasure of the window, halfhidden by the heavy champagnecolored drapes, Eleanor in a pearlgrey afternoon dress Eveline had never seen before, chatting chirpily with three young staffofficers in front of the fireplace. Eveline had a cup of tea and talked about something or other with Eleanor for a moment, then she said she had an engagement and left.

In the anteroom she caught Miss Williams' eye as she passed. She stopped by her desk a moment: "Busy as ever, Miss Williams," she said.

"It's better to be busy," she said. "It keeps a person out of mischief . . . It seems to me that in Paris they waste a great deal of time . . . I never imagined that there could be a place where people could sit around idle so much of the time."

"The French value their leisure more than anything."

"Leisure's all right if you have something to do with it . . . but this social life wastes so much of our time . . . People come to lunch and stay all afternoon, I don't know what we can do about it . . . it makes a very difficult situation." Miss Williams looked hard at Eveline. "I don't suppose you have much to do down at the Red Cross any more, do you, Miss Hutchins?"

Eveline smiled sweetly. "No, we just live for our leisure like the French."

She walked across the wide asphalt spaces of the place de la Concorde, without knowing quite what to do with herself, and turned up the Champs Elysées where the horsechestnuts were just coming into flower. The general strike seemed to be about over, because there were a few cabs on the streets. She sat down on a bench and a cadaverous looking individual in a frock coat sat down beside her and tried to pick her up. She got up and walked as fast as she could. At the Rond Point she had to stop to wait for a bunch of French mounted artillery and two seventyfives to go past before she could cross the street. The cadaverous man was beside her; he turned and held out his hand, tipping his hat as he did so, as if he was an old friend. She muttered, "Oh, it's just too tiresome," and got into a horsecab that was standing by the curb. She almost thought the man was going to get in too, but he just stood looking after her scowling as the cab drove off following the guns as if she was part of the regiment. Once at home she made herself some cocoa on the gasstove and went lonely to bed with a book.

Next evening when she got back to her apartment Paul was waiting for her, wearing a new uniform and with a resplendent shine on his knobtoed shoes. "Why, Paul, you look as if you'd been through a washing machine." "A friend of mine's a sergeant in the quartermaster's stores . . . coughed up a new outfit." "You look too beautiful for words." "You mean you do, Eveline."

They went over to the boulevards and had dinner on the salmoncolored plush seats among the Pompeian columns at Noël Peters' to the accompaniment of slithery violinmusic. Paul had his month's pay and commutation of rations in his pocket and felt fine. They talked about what they'd do when they got back to America. Paul said his dad wanted him to go into a grain broker's office in Minneapolis, but he wanted to try his luck in New York. He thought a young feller ought to try a lot of things before he settled down at a business so that he could find out what he was fitted for. Eveline said she didn't know what she wanted to do. She didn't want to do anything she'd done before, she knew that, maybe she'd like to live in Paris.

"I didn't like it much in Paris before," Paul said, "but like this, goin' out with you, I like it fine." Eveline teased him, "Oh, I don't think you like me much, you never act as if you did." "But jeeze, Eveline, you know so much and you've been around so much. It's mighty nice of you to let me come around at all, honestly I'll appreciate it all my life."

"Oh, I wish you wouldn't be like that . . . I hate people to be humble," Eveline broke out angrily.

They went on eating in silence. They were eating asparagus with grated cheese on it. Paul took several gulps of wine and looked at her in a hurt dumb way she hated. "Oh, I feel like a party tonight," she said a little later. "I've been so miserable all day, Paul . . . I'll tell you about it sometime . . . you know the kind of feeling when everything you've wanted crumbles in your fingers as you grasp it." "All right, Eveline," Paul said, banging with his fist on the table, "let's cheer up and have a big time."

When they were drinking coffee the orchestra began to play polkas and people began to dance among the table encouraged by cries of Ah Polkaah aaah from the violinist. It was a fine sight to see the middleaged diners whirling around under the beaming eyes of the stout Italian headwaiter who seemed to feel that la gaité was coming back to Paree at last. Paul and Eveline forgot themselves and tried to dance it too. Paul was very awkward, but having his arms around her made her feel better somehow, made her forget the scaring loneliness she felt.

When the polka had subsided a little Paul paid the fat check and they went out arm in arm, pressing close against each other like all the Paris lovers, to stroll on the boulevards in the May evening that smelt of wine and hot rolls and wild strawberries. They felt lightheaded. Eveline kept smiling. "Come on, let's have a big time," whispered Paul occasionally as if to keep his courage up. "I was just thinking what my friends ud think if they saw me walking up the boulevard arm in arm with a drunken doughboy," Eveline said. "No, honest, I'm not drunk," said Paul. "I can drink a lot more than you think. And I won't be in the army much longer, not if this peace treaty goes through." "Oh, I don't care," said Eveline, "I don't care what happens."

They heard music in another café and saw the shadows of dancers passing across the windows upstairs. "Let's go up there," said Eveline. They went in and upstairs to the dancehall that was a long room full of mirrors. There Eveline said she wanted to drink some Rhine wine. They studied the card a long while and finally with a funny sideways look at Paul, she suggested liebefraumilch. Paul got red, "I wish I had a liebe frau," he said. "Why probably you have . . . one in every port," said Eveline. He shook his head.

Next time they danced he held her very tight. He didn't seem so awkward as he had before. "I feel pretty lonely myself, these days," said Eveline when they sat down again. "You, lonely . . . with the whole of the Peace Conference running after you, and the A.E.F. too . . . Why, Don told me you're a dangerous woman." She shrugged her shoulders, "When did Don find that out? Maybe you could be dangerous too, Paul."

Next time they danced she put her cheek against his. When the music stopped he looked as if he was going to kiss her, but he didn't. "This is the most wonderful evening I ever had in my life," he said, "I wish I was the kind of guy you really wanted to have take you out." "Maybe you could get to be, Paul . . . you seem to be learning fast. . . . No, but we're acting silly . . . I hate ogling and flirting around . . . I guess I want the moon . . . maybe I want to get married and have a baby." Paul was embarrassed. They sat silent watching the other dancers. Eveline saw a young French soldier lean over and kiss the little girl he was dancing with on the lips; kissing, they kept on dancing. Eveline wished she was that girl. "Let's have a little more wine," she said to Paul. "Do you think we'd better? All right, what the hec, we've having a big time."

Getting in the taxicab Paul was pretty drunk, laughing and hugging her. As soon as they were in the darkness of the back of the taxi they started kissing. Eveline held Paul off for a minute, "Let's go to your place instead of mine," she said. "I'm afraid of my concièrge." "All right . . . it's awful little," said Paul, giggling. "But ish geblbbel, we should worry get a wrinkle."

When they had gotten past the bitter eyes that sized them up of the old man who kept the keys at Paul's hotel they staggered up a long chilly winding stair and into a little room that gave on a court. "It's a great life if you don't weaken," said Paul, waving his arms after he'd locked and bolted the door. It had started to rain again and the rain made the sound of a waterfall on the glass roof at the bottom of the court. Paul threw his hat and tunic in the corner of the room and came towards her, his eyes shining.

They'd hardly gotten to bed when he fell asleep with his head on her shoulder. She slipped out of bed to turn the light off and open the window and then snuggled shivering against his body that was warm and relaxed like a child's. Outside the rain poured down on the glass roof. There was a puppy shut up somewhere in the building that whined and yelped desperately without stopping. Eveline couldn't get to sleep. Something shut up inside her was whining like the puppy. Through the window she began to see the dark peak of a roof and chimneypots against a fading purple sky. Finally she fell asleep.

Next day they spent together. She'd phoned in to the Red Cross that she was sick as usual and Paul forgot about the Sorbonne altogether. They sat all morning in the faint sunshine at a café near the Madeleine making plans about what they'd do. They'd get themselves sent back home as soon as they possibly could and get jobs in New York and get married. Paul was going to study engineering in his spare time. There was a firm of grain and feed merchants in Jersey City, friends of his father's he knew he could get a job with. Eveline could start up her decorating business again. Paul was happy and confident and had lost his apologetic manner. Eveline kept telling herself that Paul had stuff in him, that she was in love with Paul, that something could be made out of Paul.

The rest of the month of May they were both a little lightheaded all the time. They spent all their pay the first few days so that they had to eat at little table d'hôte restaurants crowded with students and working people and poor clerks where they bought books of tickets that gave them a meal for two francs or two fifty. One Sunday in June they went out to St. Germain and walked through the forest. Eveline had spells of nausea and weakness and had to lie down on the grass several times. Paul looked worried sick. At last they got to a little settlement on the bank of the Seine. The Seine flowed fast streaked with green and lilac in the afternoon light, brimming the low banks bordered by ranks of huge poplars. They crossed a little ferry rowed by an old man that Eveline called Father Time. Halfway over she said to Paul, "Do you know what's the matter with me, Paul? I'm going to have a baby."

Paul let his breath out in a whistle. "Well, I hadn't just planned for that . . . I guess I've been a stinker not to make you marry me before this. . . . We'll get married right away. I'll find out what you have to do to get permission to get married in the A.E.F. I guess it's all right, Eveline . . . but, gee, it does change my plans."

They'd reached the other bank and walked up through Conflans to the railroad station to get the train back to Paris. Paul looked worried. "Well, don't you think it changes my plans too?" said Eveline dryly. "It's going over Niagara Falls in a barrel, that's what it is."

"Eveline," said Paul seriously with tears in his eyes, "what can I ever do to make it up to you? . . . honest, I'll do my best." The train whistled and rumbled into the platform in front of them. They were so absorbed in their thoughts they hardly saw it. When they'd climbed into a third class compartment they sat silent bolt upright facing each other, their knees touching, looking out of the window without seeing the suburbs of Paris, not saying anything. At last Eveline said with a tight throat, "I want to have the little brat, Paul, we have to go through everything in life." Paul nodded. Then she couldn't see his face anymore. The train had gone into a tunnel.

Newsreel XXXIV

WHOLE WORLD IS SHORT OF PLATINUM

Il serait Criminel de Negliger Les Intérêts Français dans les Balkans

KILLS SELF IN CELL

the quotation of United Cigar Stores made this month of $167 per share means $501 per share for the old stock upon which present stockholders are receiving 27% per share as formerly held. Through peace and war it has maintained and increased its dividends

6 TRAPPED ON UPPER FLOOR

How are you goin' to keep 'em down on the farm
After they've seen Paree

If Wall street needed the treaty, which means if the business interests of the country properly desired to know to what extent we are being committed in affairs which do not concern us, why should it take the trouble to corrupt the tagrag and bobtail which forms Mr. Wilson's following in Paris?

ALLIES URGE MAGYAR PEOPLE TO UPSET BELA KUN REGIME

11 WOMEN MISSING IN BLUEBEARD MYSTERY

Enfin La France Achète les stocks Américains

How are you goin' to keep 'em away from Broadway
Jazzin' around
Paintin' the town

the boulevards during the afternoon presented an unwonted aspect. The café terraces in most cases were deserted and had been cleared of their tables and chairs. At some of the cafés customers were admitted one by one and served by faithful waiters, who, however, had discarded their aprons

YEOMANETTE SHRIEKS FOR FORMER SUITOR AS SHE SEEKS DEATH IN DRIVE APARTMENT

DESIRES OF HEDJAZ STIR PARIS CRITICS

in order not prematurely to show their colors a pretense is made of disbanding a few formations; in reality however, these troops are being transferred lock stock and barrel to Kolchak

I.W.W. IN PLOT TO KILL WILSON

Find 10,000 Bags of Decayed Onions

FALL ON STAIRS KILLS WEALTHY CITIZEN

the mistiness of the weather hid the gunboat from sight soon after it left the dock, but the President continued to wave his hat and smile as the boat headed towards the George Washington

OVERTHROW OF SOVIET RULE SURE

The House of Morgan

I commit my soul into the hands of my savior, wrote John Pierpont Morgan in his will, *in full confidence that having redeemed it and washed it in His most precious blood, He will present it faultless before my heavenly father, and I intreat my children to maintain and defend at all hazard and at any cost of personal sacrifice the blessed doctrine of complete atonement for sin through the blood of Jesus Christ once offered and through that alone,*

and into the hands of the House of Morgan represented by his son,

he committed,

when he died in Rome in 1913,

the control of the Morgan interests in New York, Paris and London, four national banks, three trust companies, three life insurance companies, ten railroad systems, three street railway companies, an express company, the International Mercantile Marine,

power,

on the cantilever principle, through interlocking directorates

over eighteen other railroads, U.S. Steel, General Electric, American Tel and Tel, five major industries;

the interwoven cables of the Morgan Stillman Baker combination held credit up like a suspension bridge, thirteen percent of the banking resources of the world.

The first Morgan to make a pool was Joseph Morgan, a hotelkeeper in Hartford Connecticut who organized stagecoach lines and bought up Ætna Life Insurance stock in a time of panic caused by one of the big New York fires in the 1830's;

his son Junius followed in his footsteps, first in the drygoods business, and then as partner to George Peabody, a Massachusetts banker who built up an enormous underwriting and mercantile business in London and became a friend of Queen Victoria;

Junius married the daughter of John Pierpont, a Boston preacher, poet, eccentric, and abolitionist; and their eldest son,

John Pierpont Morgan

arrived in New York to make his fortune

after being trained in England, going to school at Vevey, proving himself a crack mathematician at the University of Göttingen,

a lanky morose young man of twenty,

just in time for the panic of '57.

(war and panics on the stock exchange, bankruptcies, warloans, good growing weather for the House of Morgan.)

When the guns started booming at Fort Sumter, young Morgan turned some money over reselling condemned muskets to the U.S. army and began to make himself felt in the gold room in downtown New York; there was more in trading in gold than in trading in muskets; so much for the Civil War.

During the Franco-Prussian war Junius Morgan floated a huge bond issue for the French government at Tours.

At the same time young Morgan was fighting Jay Cooke and the German-Jew bankers in Frankfort over the funding of the American war debt (he never did like the Germans or the Jews).

The panic of '75 ruined Jay Cooke and made J. Pierpont Morgan the boss croupier of Wall Street; he united with the Philadelphia Drexels and built the Drexel building where for thirty years he sat in his glassedin office, redfaced and insolent, writing at his desk, smoking great black cigars, or, if important issues were involved, playing solitaire in his inner office; he was famous for his few words, Yes or No, and for his way of suddenly blowing up in a visitor's face and for that special gesture of the arm that meant, *What do I get out of it?*

In '77 Junius Morgan retired; J. Pierpont got himself made a member of the board of directors of the New York Central railroad and launched the first *Corsair.* He liked yachting and to have pretty actresses call him Commodore.

He founded the Lying-in Hospital on Stuyvesant Square, and was fond of going into St. George's church and singing a hymn all alone in the afternoon quiet.

In the panic of '93
at no inconsiderable profit to himself
Morgan saved the U.S. Treasury; gold was draining out, the country was ruined, the farmers were howling for a silver standard, Grover Cleveland and his cabinet were walking up and down in the blue room at the White House without being able to come to a decision, in Congress they were making speeches while the gold reserves melted in the Subtreasuries; poor people were starving; Coxey's army was marching to Washington; for a long time Grover Cleveland couldn't bring himself to call in the representative of the Wall Street moneymasters; Morgan sat in his suite at the Arlington smoking cigars and quietly playing solitaire until at last the president sent for him;
he had a plan all ready for stopping the gold hemorrhage.

After that what Morgan said went; when Carnegie sold out he built the Steel Trust.

J. Pierpont Morgan was a bullnecked irascible man with small black magpie's eyes and a growth on his nose; he let his partners work themselves to death over the detailed routine of banking, and sat in his back office smoking black cigars; when there was something to be decided he said Yes or No or just turned his bank and went back to his solitaire.

*   *   *

Every Christmas his librarian read him Dickens' *A Christmas Carol* from the original manuscript.

He was fond of canarybirds and pekinese dogs and liked to take pretty actresses yachting. Each *Corsair* was a finer vessel than the last.

When he dined with King Edward he sat at His Majesty's right; he ate with the Kaiser tête-à-tête; he liked talking to cardinals or the pope, and never missed a conference of Episcopal bishops;

Rome was his favorite city.

He liked choice cookery and old wines and pretty women and yachting, and going over his collections, now and then picking up a jewelled snuffbox and staring at it with his magpie's eyes.

He made a collection of the autographs of the rulers of France, owned glass cases full of Babylonian tablets, seals, signets, statuettes, busts,

Gallo-Roman bronzes,

Merovingian jewels, miniatures, watches, tapestries, porcelains, cuneiform inscriptions, paintings by all the old masters, Dutch, Italian, Flemish, Spanish,

manuscripts of the gospels and the Apocalypse,

a collection of the works of Jean-Jacques Rousseau,

and the letters of Pliny the Younger.

His collectors bought anything that was expensive or rare or had the glint of empire on it, and he had it brought to him and stared hard at it with his magpie's eyes. Then it was put in a glass case.

The last year of his life he went up the Nile on a dahabiyeh and spent a long time staring at the great columns of the Temple of Karnak.

The panic of 1907 and the death of Harriman, his great opponent in railroad financing, in 1909, had left him the undisputed ruler of Wall Street, most powerful private citizen in the world;

an old man tired of the purple, suffering from gout, he had deigned to go to Washington to answer the questions of the Pujo Committee during the Money Trust Investigation: Yes, I did what seemed to me to be for the best interests of the country.

So admirably was his empire built that his death in 1913 hardly caused a ripple in the exchanges of the world: the purple descended to his son, J. P. Morgan,

who had been trained at Groton and Harvard and by associating
with the British ruling class
to be a more constitutional monarch: *J. P. Morgan suggests . . .*

By 1917 the Allies had borrowed one billion, ninehundred million dollars through the House of Morgan: we went overseas for democracy and the flag;
and by the end of the Peace Conference the phrase *J. P. Morgan
suggests* had compulsion over a power of seventyfour billion dollars.

J. P. Morgan is a silent man, not given to public utterances, but
during the great steel strike, he wrote Gary: *Heartfelt congratulations
on your stand for the open shop, with which I am, as you know, absolutely in accord. I believe American principles of liberty are deeply involved, and must win if we stand firm.*

(Wars and panics on the stock exchange,
machinegunfire and arson,
bankruptcies, warloans,
starvation, lice, cholera and typhus:
good growing weather for the House of Morgan.)

Newsreel XXXV

the Grand Prix de la Victoire, run yesterday for fiftysecond time was an event that will long remain in the memories of those present, for never in the history of the classic race has Longchamps presented such a glorious scene

Keep the home fires burning
Till the boys come home

LEVIATHAN UNABLE TO PUT TO SEA

BOLSHEVIKS ABOLISH POSTAGE STAMPS

ARTIST TAKES GAS IN NEW HAVEN

FIND BLOOD ON $1 BILL

While our hearts are yearning

POTASH CAUSE OF BREAK IN PARLEY

MAJOR DIES OF POISONING

TOOK ROACH SALTS BY MISTAKE

riot and robbery developed into the most awful pogrom ever heard of. Within two or three days the Lemberg ghetto was turned into heaps of smoking debris. Eyewitnesses estimate that the Polish soldiers killed more than a thousand jewish men and women and children

LENINE SHOT BY TROTSKY
IN DRUNKEN BRAWL

you know where I stand on beer, said Brisbane in seeking assistance

Though the boys are far away
They long for home
There's a silver lining
Through the dark clouds shining

PRESIDENT EVOKES CRY OF THE DEAD

LETTER CLEW TO BOMB OUTRAGE

Emile Deen in the preceding three installments of his interview described the situation between the Royal Dutch and the Standard Oil Company, as being the beginning of a struggle for the control of the markets of the world which was only halted by the war. "The basic factors," he said, "are envy, discontent, and suspicion." The extraordinary industrial growth of our nation since the Civil War, the opening up of new territory, the development of resources, the rapid increase in population, all these things have resulted in the creation of many big and sudden fortunes. Is there a mother, father, sweetheart, relative or friend of any one of the two million boys fighting abroad who does not thank God that Wall Street contributed H. P. Davidson to the Red Cross?

BOND THIEF MURDERED

Turn the bright side inside out
Till the boys come home

The Camera Eye (39)

daylight enlarges out of ruddy quiet very faintly throbbing wanes into my sweet darkness broadens red through the warm blood weighting the lids warmsweetly then snaps on

enormously blue yellow pink

today is Paris   pink sunlight hazy on the clouds against patches of robinsegg   a tiny siren hoots shrilly traffic drowsily rumbles clatters over the cobbles taxis squawk   the yellow's the comforter through the open window the Louvre emphasizes its sedate architecture of greypink stone between the Seine and the sky and the certainty of Paris

the towboat shiny green and red chugs against the current towing three black and mahoganyvarnished barges   their deckhouse
windows have green shutters and lace curtains and pots of geraniums
in flower   to get under the bridge a fat man in blue had to let the
little black stack drop flat to the deck

Paris comes into the room in the servantgirl's eyes the warm
bulge of her breasts under the grey smock   the smell of chickory in
coffee scalded milk and the shine that crunches on the crescent rolls
stuck with little dabs of very sweet unsalted butter

in the yellow paperback of the book that halfhides the agreeable
countenance of my friend

Paris of 1919

paris-mutuel

roulettewheel that spins round the Tour Eiffel red square white
square a million dollars a billion marks a trillion roubles baisse du
franc or a mandate for Montmartre

Cirque Médrano the steeplechase gravity of cellos tuning up on
the stage at the Salle Gaveau oboes and a triangle   la musique s'en
fout de moi says the old marchioness jingling with diamonds as she
walks out on Stravinski   but the red colt took the jumps backwards
and we lost all our money

la peinture opposite the Madeleine   Cezanne   Picassso
Modigliani

Nouvelle Athènes

la poesie of manifestos always freshtinted on the kiosks and slogans scrawled in chalk on the urinals L'UNION DES TRAVAILLEURS
FERA LA PAIX DU MONDE

revolution round the spinning Eiffel Tower

that burns up our last year's diagrams the dates fly off the calen-
dar we'll make everything new today is the Year I   Today is the
sunny morning of the first day of spring   We gulp our coffee splash
water on us jump into our clothes run downstairs set out wideawake
into the first morning of the first day of the first year

Newsreel XXXVI

TO THE GLORY OF FRANCE ETERNAL

Oh a German officer crossed the Rhine
Parleyvoo

Germans Beaten at Riga Grateful Parisians Cheer Marshals of France

Oh a German officer crossed the Rhine
He liked the women and loved the wine
Hankypanky parleyvoo

PITEOUS PLAINT OF WIFE TELLS OF
RIVAL'S WILES

Wilson's Arrival in Washington Starts Trouble. Paris strikers hear harangues at picnic. Café wrecked and bombs thrown in Fiume streets. Parisians pay more for meat. Il Serait Dangereux d'Augmenter les Vivres. Bethmann Holweg's Blood Boils. Mysterious Forces Halt Antibolshevist March.

HUN'S HAND SEEN IN PLOTS

Oh Mademoiselle from Armentières
Parleyvoo
Oh Mademoiselle from Armentières
Parleyvoo .
Hasn't been——for forty years
Hankypanky parleyvoo

wrecks mark final day at La Baule; syndicated wage earners seize opportunity to threaten employers unprepared for change. LAYS WREATH ON TOMB OF LAFAYETTE. Richest Negress is Dead. Yale Dormitories stormed by Angry Mob of Soldiers. Goldmine in Kinks.

TIGHTENS SCREW ON BERLIN

Oh he took her upstairs and into bed
And there he cracked her maidenhead
Hanypanky parleyvoo

NO DROP IN PRICES TO FOLLOW PEACE SAY BUSINESS MEN

KILLS SELF AT DESK IN OFFICE

MODERN BLUEBEARD NOW VICTIM OF MELANCHOLIA

He is none other than General Minus of the old Russian Imperial General Staff, who, during the Kerensky régime, was commander of troops in the region of Minsk. Paris policemen threaten to join strike movement, allow it to send into France barrels bearing the mystic word Mistelles. One speculator is said to have netted nearly five million francs within a week

On the first three months and all went well
But the second three months she began to swell
Hankeypanky parleyvoo

large financial resources, improved appliances and abundant raw materials of America should assist French genius in restoring and increasing industrial power of France, joining hands in the charming scenery, wonderful roads, excellent hotels, and good cookery makes site of Lyons fair crossed by the 45th parallel. Favored by great mineral resources its future looms incalculably splendid. Any man who attempts to take over control of municipal functions here will be shot on sight, Major Ole Hanson remarked. He is a little man himself but has big ideas, a big brain, and big hopes. Upon first meeting him one is struck by his resemblance to Mark Twain

Richard Ellsworth Savage

Dick and Ned felt pretty rocky the morning they sighted Fire Island lightship. Dick wasn't looking forward to landing in God's Country with no money and the draft board to face, and he was worried about how his mother was going to make out. All Ned was complaining about was wartime prohibition. They were both a little jumpy from all the cognac they'd drunk on the trip over. They were already in the slategreen shallow seas off Long Island; no help for it now. The heavy haze to the west and then the low boxlike houses that looked as if they were drowned in the water and then the white strip of beach of the Rockaways; the scenicrailways of Coney Island; the full green summer trees and the grey framehouses with their white trim on Staten Island; it was all heartbreakingly like home. When the immigration tug came alongside Dick was surprised to see Hiram Halsey Cooper, in khaki uniform and puttees, clambering up the steps. Dick lit a cigarette and tried to look sober.

"My boy, it's a great relief to see you. . . . Your mother and I have been . . . er . . ." Dick interrupted to introduce him to Ned. Mr. Cooper, who was in the uniform of a major, took him by the sleeve and drew him up the deck. "Better put on your uniform to land." "All right, sir, I thought it looked rather shabby." "All the better. . . . Well, I suppose it's hell over there . . . and no chance for courting the muse, eh? . . . You're coming up to Washington with me tonight. We've been very uneasy about you, but that's all over now . . . made me realize what a lonely old man I am. Look here, my boy, your mother was the daughter of Major General Ellsworth, isn't that so?" Dick nodded. "Of course she must have been because my dear wife was his niece. . . . Well, hurry and put your uniform on and remember . . . leave all the talking to me."

While he was changing into the old Norton-Harjes uniform Dick was thinking how suddenly Mr. Cooper had aged and wondering just how he could ask him to lend him fifteen dollars to pay the bill he'd run up at the bar.

New York had a funny lonely empty look in the summer afternoon sunlight; well here he was home. At the Pennsylvania station there were policemen and plainclothes men at all the entrances demanding the registration cards of all the young men who were not in uniform. As he and Mr. Cooper ran for the train he caught sight of a dejectedlooking group of men herded together in a corner hemmed by a cordon of sweating cops. When they got in their seats in the parlorcar on the Congressional Mr. Cooper mopped his face with a handkerchief. "You understand why I said to put your uniform on. Well, I suppose it was hell?"

"Some of it was pretty bad," said Dick casually. "I hated to come back though."

"I know you did, my boy . . . . You didn't expect to find your old mentor in the uniform of a major . . . well, we must all put our shoulders to the wheel. I'm in the purchasing department of Ordnance. You see the chief of our bureau of personnel is General Sykes; he turns out to have served with your grandfather. I've told him about you, your experience on two fronts, your knowledge of languages and . . . well . . . naturally he's very much interested. . . . I think we can get you a commission right away."

"Mr. Cooper, it's . . ." stammered Dick, "it's extraordinarily decent . . . damn kind of you to interest yourself in me this way."

"My boy, I didn't realize how I missed you . . . our chats about the muse and the ancients . . . until you had gone." Mr. Cooper's voice was drowned out by the roar of the train. Well, here I am home, something inside Dick's head kept saying to him.

When the train stopped at the West Philadelphia station the only sound was the quiet droning of the electric fans; Mr. Cooper leaned over and tapped Dick's knee, "Only one thing you must promise . . . no more peace talk till we win the war. When peace comes we can put some in our poems. . . . Then'll be the time for us all to work for a lasting peace. . . . As for the little incident in Italy . . . it's nothing . . . forget it . . . nobody ever heard of it." Dick nodded; it made him sore to feel that he was blushing. They neither of them said anything until the waiter came through calling, "Dinner now being served in the dining car forward."

In Washington (now you are home, something kept saying in Dick's head) Mr. Cooper had a room in the Willard where he put Dick up on the couch as the hotel was full and it was impossible to get another room anywhere. After he'd rolled up in the sheet Dick heard Mr. Cooper tiptoe over and stand beside the couch breathing hard. He opened his eyes and grinned. "Well, my boy," said Mr. Cooper, "it's nice to have you home . . . sleep well," and he went back to bed.

Next morning he was introduced to General Sykes: "This is the young man who wants to serve his country," said Mr. Cooper with aflourish, "as his grandfather served it. . . . In fact he was so impatient that he went to war before his country did, and enlisted in the volunteer ambulance service with the French and afterwards with the Italians." General Sykes was a little old man with bright eyes and a hawk nose and extremely deaf. "Yes, Ellsworth was a great fellow, we campaigned against Hieronimo together . . . Ah, the old west . . . I was only fourteen at Gettysburg and damme I don't think he was there at all. We went through West Point in the same class after the war, poor old Ellsworth. . . . So you've smelled powder have you, my boy?" Dick colored and nodded.

"You see, General," shouted Mr. Cooper, "he feels he wants some more . . . er . . . responsible work than was possible in the ambulance service."

"Yessiree, no place for a highspirited young fellow. . . . You know Andrews, Major . . ." The General was scribbling on a pad. "Take him to see Colonel Andrews with this memorandum and he'll fix him up, has to decide on qualifications etc. . . . You understand . . . good luck, my boy." Dick managed a passable salute and they were out in the corridor; Mr. Cooper was smiling broadly. "Well, that's done. I must be getting back to my office. You go and fill out the forms and take your medical examination . . . or perhaps that'll be at the camp . . . Anyway come and lunch with me at the Willard at one. Come up to the room." Dick saluted smiling.

He spent the rest of the morning filling out blanks. After lunch he went down to Atlantic City to see his mother. She looked just the same. She was staying in a boarding house at the Chelsea end and was very much exercised about spies. Henry had enlisted as a private in the infantry and was somewhere in France. Mother said it made her blood boil to think of the grandson of General Ellsworth being a mere private, but that she felt confident he'd soon rise from the ranks. Dick hadn't heard her speak of her father since she used to talk about him when he was a child, and asked her about him. He had died when she was quite a little girl leaving the family not too well off considering their station in life. All she remembered was a tall man in blue with a floppy felt hat caught up on one side and a white goatee; when she'd first seen a cartoon of Uncle Sam she'd thought it was her father. He always had hoarhound drops in a little silver bonbonnière in his pocket, she'd been so excited about the military funeral and a nice kind army officer giving her his handkerchief. She'd kept the bonbonnière for many years but it had had to go with everything else when your poor father . . . er . . . failed.

A week later Dick received a war department envelope addressed to Savage, Richard Ellsworth, 2nd Lieut. Ord. Dept., enclosing his commission and ordering him to proceed to Camp Merritt, N.J., within 24 hours. Dick found himself in charge of a casuals company at Camp Merritt and wouldn't have known what on earth to do if it hadn't been for the sergeant. Once they were on the transport it was better; he had what had been a first class cabin with two other 2nd Lieutenants and a Major; Dick had the drop on them all because he'd been at the front. The transport was the *Leviathan*; Dick began to feel himself again when he saw the last of Sandy Hook; he wrote Ned a long letter in doggerel that began:

> His father was a jailbird and his mother had no kale
> He was much too fond of cognac and he drank it by the pail
> But now he's a Second Lieut and supported by the State.
> Sports a handsome uniform and a military gait
> And this is the most terrific fate that ever can befall
> A boy whose grandpa was a Major-General.

The other two shavetails in the cabin were nondescript youngsters from Leland Stanford, but Major Thompson was a Westpointer and stiff as a ramrod. He was a middleaged man with a yellow round face, thin lips and noseglasses. Dick thawed him out a little by getting him a pint of whiskey through his sergeant who'd gotten chummy with the stewards, when he got seasick two days out, and discovered that he was a passionate admirer of Kipling and had heard Copeland read *Danny Deever* and been very much impressed. Furthermore he was an expert on mules and horseflesh and the author of a monograph: The Spanish Horse. Dick admitted that he'd studied with Copeland and somehow it came out that he was the grandson of the late General Ellsworth. Major Thompson began to take an interest in him and to ask him questions about the donkeys the French used to carry ammunition in the trenches, Italian cavalry horses and the works of Rudyard Kipling. The night before they reached Brest when everybody was flustered and the decks were all dark and silent for the zone, Dick went into a toilet and reread the long kidding letter he'd written Ned first day out. He tore it up into small bits, dropped them in the can and then flushed it carefully: no more letters.

In Brest Dick took three majors downtown and ordered them a meal and good wine at the hotel; during the evening Major Thompson told stories about the Philippines and the Spanish war; after the fourth bottle Dick taught them all to sing *Mademoiselle from*

Armentières. A few days later he was detached from his casuals company and set to Tours; Major Thompson, who felt he needed somebody to speak French for him and to talk about Kipling with, had gotten him transferred to his office. It was a relief to see the last of Brest, where everybody was in a continual grouch from the drizzle and the mud and the discipline and the saluting and the formations and the fear of getting in wrong with the brasshats.

Tours was full of lovely creamystone buildings buried in dense masses of bluegreen late summer foliage. Dick was on commutation of rations and boarded with an agreeable old woman who brought him up his café au lait in bed every morning. He got to know a fellow in the Personnel Department through whom he began to work to get Henry transferred out of the infantry. He and Major Thompson and old Colonel Edgecombe and several other offices dined together very often; they got so they couldn't do without Dick who knew how to order a meal comme il faut, and the proper vintages of wines and could parleyvoo with the French girls and make up limericks and was the grandson of the late General Ellsworth.

When the Post Despatch Service was organized as a separate outfit, Colonel Edgecombe who headed it, got him away from Major Thompson and his horsedealers; Dick became one of his assistants with the rank of Captain. Immediately he managed to get Henry transferred from the officers' school to Tours. It was too late though to get him more than a first lieutenancy.

When Lieutenant Savage reported to Captain Savage in his office he looked brown and skinny and sore. That evening they drank a bottle of white wine together in Dick's room. The first thing Henry said when the door closed behind them was, "Well, of all the goddam lousy grafts . . . I don't know whether to be proud of the little kid brother or to sock him in the eye."

Dick poured him a drink. "It must have been Mother's doing," he said. "Honestly, I'd forgotten that granpa was a general."

"If you knew what us guys at the front used to say about the S.O.S."

"But somebody's got to handle the supplies and the ordnance and . . ."

"And the mademosels and the vin blanc," broke in Henry.

"Sure, but I've been very virtuous . . . Your little brother's minding his p's and q's, and honestly I've been working like a nigger."

"Writing loveletters for ordnance majors, I bet. . . . Hell, you can't beat it. He lands with his nose in the butter every time. . . . Anyway I'm glad there's one successful member of the family to carry on the name of the late General Ellsworth."

"Have a disagreeable time in the Argonne?"

"Lousy . . . until they sent me back to officers' school."

"We had a swell time there in the ambulance service in '17."

"Oh, you would."

Henry drank some more wine and mellowed up a little. Every now and then he'd look around the big room with its lace curtains and its scrubbed tile floor and it's big fourposter bed and make a popping sound with his lips and mutter: "Pretty soft." Dick took him out and set him up to a fine dinner at his favorite bistro and then went around and fixed him up with Minette, who was the bestlooking girl at Madame Patou's.

After Henry had gone upstairs, Dick sat in the parlor a few minutes with a girl they called Dirty Gertie who had hair dyed red and a big floppy painted mouth, drinking the bad cognac and feeling blue. "Vous triste?" she said, and put her clammy hand on his forehead. He nodded. "Fièvre . . . trop penser . . . penser no good . . . moi aussi." Then she said she'd kill herself but she was afraid, not that she believed in God, but that she was afraid of how quiet it would be after she was dead. Dick cheered her up, "Bientot guerre finee. Tout le monde content go back home." The girl burst out crying and Madame Patou came running in screaming and clawing like a seagull. She was a heavy woman with an ugly jaw. She grabbed the girl by the hair and began shaking her. Dick was flustered. He managed to make the woman let the girl go back to her room, left some money and walked out. He felt terrible. When he got home he felt like writing some verse. He tried to recapture the sweet and heavy pulsing of feelings he used to have when·he sat down to write a poem. But all he could do was just feel miserable so he went to bed. All night half thinking half dreaming he couldn't get Dirty Gertie's face out of his head. Then he began remembering the times he used to have with Hilda at Bay Head and had a long conversation with himself about love: Everything's so hellishly sordid . . . I'm sick of whores and chastity, I want to have love affairs. He began planning what he'd do after the war, probably go home and get a political job in Jersey; a pretty sordid prospect.

He was lying on his back staring at the ceiling that was livid with dawn when he heard Henry's voice calling his name down in the street outside; he tiptoed down the cold tiled stairs and let him in.

"Why the hell did you let me go with that girl, Dick? I feel like a louse . . . Oh Christ . . . mind if I have half this bed, Dick? I'll get me a room in the morning." Dick found him a pair of pyjamas and made himself small on his side of the bed. "The trouble with you, Henry," he said, yawning, "is that you're just an old Puritan . . . you ought to be more continental."

"I notice you didn't go with any of those bitches yourself."

"I haven't got any morals but I'm finnicky, my dear, Epicurus' owne sonne," Dick drawled sleepily.

"S——t, I feel like a dirty dishrag," whispered Henry. Dick closed his eyes and went to sleep.

Early in October Dick was sent to Brest with a despatch case that the Colonel said was too important to entrust to an enlisted man. At Rennes he had to wait two hours for the train, and was sitting eating in the restaurant when a doughboy with his arm in a sling came up to him saying, "Hello, Dick, for crying out loud." It was Skinny Murray. "By gosh, Skinny, I'm glad to see you . . . it must be five or six years . . . Gee, we're getting old. Look, sit down . . . no, I can't do that."

"I suppose I ought to have saluted, sir," said Skinny stiffly.

"Can that, Skinny . . . but we've got to find a place to talk . . . got any time before your train? You see it's me the M.P.'s would arrest if they saw me eating and drinking with an enlisted man . . . Wait around till I've finished my lunch and we'll find a ginmill across from the station. I'll risk it." "I've got an hour . . . I'm going to the Grenoble leave area."

"Lucky bastard . . . were you badly wounded, Skinny?" "Piece of shrapnel in the wing, captain," said Skinny, coming to attention as a sergeant of M.P.'s stalked stiffly through the station restaurant. "Those birds gimme the willies."

Dick hurried through his lunch, paid, and walked across the square outside the station. One of the cafés had a back room that looked dark and quiet. They were just settling down to chat over two beers when Dick remembered the despatch case. He'd left it at the table. Whispering breathlessly that he'd be back he ran across the square and into the station restaurant. Three French officers were at the table. "Pardon, messieurs." It was still where he'd left it under the table. "If I'd lost that I'd have had to shoot myself," he told Skinny. They chatted about Trenton and Philadelphia and Bay Head and Dr.

Atwood. Skinny was married and had a good job in a Philadelphia bank. He had volunteered for the tanks and was winged by a bit of shrapnel before the attack started, damn lucky of him, because his gang had been wiped out by a black Maria. He was just out of hospital today and felt pretty weak on his pins. Dick took down his service data and said he'd get him transferred to Tours; just the kind of fellow they needed for a courier. Then Skinny had to run for his train, and Dick, with the despatch case tightly wedged under his arm, went out to stroll around the town daintily colored and faintly gay under the autumn drizzle.

The rumor of the fake armistice set Tours humming like a swarm of bees; there was a lot of drinking and backslapping and officers and enlisted men danced snakedances in and out of the officebuildings. When it turned out to be a false alarm Dick felt almost relieved. The days that followed everybody round the headquarters of the Despatch Service wore a mysterious expression of knowing more than they were willing to tell. The night of the real armistice Dick ate supper a little deliriously with Colonel Edgecombe and some other officers. After dinner Dick happened to meet the colonel in the courtyard out back. The colonel's face was red and his moustache bristled. "Well, Savage, it's a great day for the race," he said, and laughed a great deal. "What race?" said Dick shyly. "The human race," roared the colonel.

Then he drew Dick aside: "How would you like to go to Paris, my boy? It seems that there's to be a peace conference in Paris and that President Wilson is going to attend it in person . . . seems incredible . . . and I've been ordered to put this outfit at the disposal of the American delegation that's coming soon to dictate the peace, so we'll be Peace Conference couriers. Of course I suppose if you feel you have to go home it could be arranged."

"Oh, no, sir," broke in Dick hurriedly. "I was just beginning to worry about having to go home and look for a job. . . . The Peace Conference will be a circus and any chance to travel around Europe suits me." The colonel looked at him with narrowed eyes. "I wouldn't put it just that way . . . service should be our first thought . . . naturally what I said is strictly confidential." "Oh, strictly," said Dick, but he couldn't help wearing a grin on his face when he went back to join the others at the table.

Paris again; and this time in a new whipcord uniform with silver bars at his shoulders and with money in his pockets. One of the first things he did was to go back to look at the little street behind the Pantheon where he'd lived with Steve Warner the year before. The tall chalkgrey houses, the stores, the little bars, the bigeyed children in the black smocks, the youngsters in caps with silk handkerchiefs around their necks, the Parisian drawl of the argot; it all made him feel vaguely unhappy; he was wondering what had happened to Steve. It was a relief to get back to the office where the enlisted men were moving in newly arrived American rolltop desks and yellow varnished card index cases.

The hub of this Paris was the hôtel de Crillon on the place de la Concorde, its artery the rue Royale where arriving dignitaries, President Wilson, Lloyd George and the King and Queen of the Belgians were constantly parading escorted by the garde republicaine in their plumed helmets; Dick began living in a delirium of trips to Brussels on the night express, lobster cardinal washed down with Beaune on the red plush settees at Larue's, champagne cocktails at the Ritz bar, talk full of the lowdown over a demie at the Café Weber; it was like the old days of the Baltimore convention, only he didn't give a damn any more; it all hit him cockeyed funny.

One night soon after Christmas, Colonel Edgecombe took Dick to dinner at Voisin's with a famous New York publicity man who was said to be very near to Colonel House. They stood a moment on the pavement outside the restaurant to look at the tubby domed church opposite. "You see, Savage, this fellow's the husband of a relative of mine, one of the Pittsburgh Staples . . . smooth . . . it seems to me. You look him over. For a youngster you seem to have a keen eye for character."

Mr. Moorehouse turned out to be a large quietspoken blueeyed jowly man with occasionally a touch of the southern senator in his way of talking. With him were a man named Robbins and a Miss Stoddard, a fraillooking woman with very transparent alabaster skin and a sharp chirpy voice; Dick noticed that she was stunningly welldressed. The restaurant was a little too much like an Episcopal church; Dick said very little, was very polite to Miss Stoddard and kept his eyes and ears open, eating the grandducal food and carefully tasting the mellow wine that nobody else seemed to pay any attention to. Miss Stoddard kept everybody talking, but nobody seemed to want to commit themselves to saying anything about the peace conference. Miss Stoddard told with considerable malice about the furnishings of the hôtel de Mûrat and the Wilsons' colored maid and what kind of clothes the President's wife, whom she insisted on calling Mrs. Galt, was wearing. It was a relief when they got to the cigars and liqueurs. After dinner Colonel Edgecombe offered to drop Mr. Moorehouse at the Crillon, as he staffcar had come for him. Dick and Mr. Robbins took Miss Stoddard home in a taxicab to her apartment opposite Nôtre Dâme on the left bank. They left her at her door. "Perhaps you'll come around some afternoon to tea, Captain Savage," she said.

The taximan refused to take them any further, said it was late and that he was bound home to Noisy-le-sec and drove off. Robbins took hold of Dick's arm. "Now for crissake let's go and have a decent drink. . . . Boy, I'm sick of the bigwigs." "All right," said Dick, "where'll we go?" Walking along the foggy quay, past the shadowly bulk of Nôtre Dâme, they talked scatteringly about Paris and how cold it was. Robbins was a short man with an impudent bossy look on his red face. In the café it was only a little less chilly than in the street. "This climate's going to be the death of me," said Robbins, snuggling his chin down in his overcoat. "Woolly underwear's the only answer, that's one thing I've learned in the army," said Dick laughing.

They settled on a plush bench near the stove at the end of the cigarsmoky giltornamented room. Robbins ordered a bottle of Scotch whiskey, glasses, lemon, sugar and a lot of hot water. It took a long time to get the hot water, so Robbins poured them each a quarter of a tumbler of the whiskey straight. When he'd drunk his, his face that had been sagging and tired, smoothed out so that he looked ten years younger. "Only way to keep warm in this goddam town's to keep stewed." "Still I'm glad to be back in little old Paree," said Dick, smiling and stretching his legs out under the table. "Only place in the world to be right at present," said Robbins. "Paris is the hub of the world . . . unless it's Moscow."

At the word Moscow a Frenchman playing checkers at the next table brought his eyes up from the board and stared at the two Americans. Dick couldn't make out what there was in his stare; it made him uneasy. The waiter came with the hot water. It wasn't hot enough, so Robbins made a scene and sent it back. He poured out a couple of halftumblers of straight whiskey to drink while they were waiting. "Is the President going to recognize the soviets?" Dick found himself asking in a low voice.

"I'm betting on it . . . I believe he's sending an unofficial mission. Depends a little on oil and manganese . . . it used to be King Coal, but now it's Emperor Petroleum and Miss Manganese, queen consort of steel. That's all in the pink republic of Georgia . . . I hope to get there soon, they say that they have the finest wine and the most beautiful women in the world. By God, I got to get there. . . . But the oil . . . God damn it, that's what this damned idealist Wilson can't understand, while they're setting him up to big feeds at Buckingham palace the jolly old British army is occupying Mosul, the Karun River, Persia . . . now the latrine news has it that they're in Baku . . . the future oil metropolis of the world."

"I thought the Baku fields were running dry."

"Don't you believe it . . . I just talked to a fellow who'd been there . . . a funny fellow, Rasmussen, you ought to meet him." Dick said hadn't we got plenty of oil at home. Robbins banged his fist on the table.

"You never can have plenty of anything . . . that's the first law of thermodynamics. I never have plenty of whiskey. . . . You're a young fellow, do you ever have plenty of tail? Well, neither Standard Oil or the Royal Dutch-Shell can ever have plenty of crude oil."

Dick blushed and laughed a little forcedly. He didn't like this fellow Robbins. The waiter finally came back with boiling water and Robbins made them each a toddy. For a while neither of them said anything. The checkerplayers had gone. Suddenly Robbins turned to Dick and looked in his face with his hazy blue drunkard's eyes: "Well, what do you boys think about it all? What do the fellers in the trenches think?"

"How do you mean?"

"Oh, hell, I don't mean anything. . . . But if they thought the war was lousy wait till they see the peace . . . Oh, boy, wait till they see the peace."

"Down at Tours I don't think anybody thought much about it either way . . . however, I don't think that anybody that's seen it considers war the prize way of settling international difficulties . . . I don't think Blackjack Pershing himself thinks that."

"Oh, listen to him . . . can't be more than twentyfive and he talks like a book by Woodrow Wilson . . . I'm a son of a bitch and I know it, but when I'm drunk I say what I goddam please."

"I don't see any good a lot of loud talk's going to do. It's a magnificent tragic show . . . the Paris fog smells of strawberries . . . the gods don't love us but we'll die young just the same. . . . Who said I was sober?"

They finished up a bottle. Dick taught Robbins a rhyme in French:

> *Les marionettes font font font*
> *Trois petit tours et puis s'en vont*

and when the café closed they went out arm in arm. Robbins was humming,

> *Cheer up, Napoleon, you'll soon be dead*
> *A short life and a gay one*

and stopping to talk with all the petite femmes they met on the Boul' Mich'. Dick finally left him talking to a cowlike woman in a flappy hat in front of the fountain on the Place St. Michel, and began the long walk home to his hotel that was opposite the Gare St. Lazare.

The broad asphalt streets were deserted under the pink arclights but here and there on benches along the quais, under the bare dripping trees along the bank of the Seine, in spite of the raw night couples were still sitting huddled together in the strangleholds of l'amour. At the corner of the boulevard Sébastopol a whitefaced young man who was walking the other way looked quickly into his face and stopped. Dick slackened his pace for a moment, but walked on past the string of marketcarts rumbling down the rue de Rivoli, taking deep breaths to clear the reek of whiskey out of his head. The long brightlylighted avenue that led to the opera was empty. In front of the opera there were a few people, a girl with a lovely complexion who was hanging on the arm of a poilu gave him a long smile. Almost at his hotel he ran face to face into a girl who seemed remarkably pretty, before he knew it he was asking her what she was doing out so late. She laughed, charmingly he thought, and said she was doing the same thing he was. He took her to a little hotel on the back street behind his own. They were shown into a chilly room that smelt of furniture polish. There was a big bed, a bidet, and a lot of heavy claretcolored hangings. The girl was older than he'd thought and very tired, but she had a beautiful figure and very pale skin; he was glad to see how clean her underwear was, with a pretty lace edging. They sat a little while on the edge of the bed talking low.

When he asked her what her name was, she shook her head and smiled, "Qu'est-ce que ça vous fait?"

"L'homme sans nom et la femme sans nom, vont faire l'amour a l'hotel du néant," he said. "Oh qu'il est rigolo, celui-là," she giggled. "Dis, tu n'est pas malade?" He shook his head. "Moi non plus," she said, and started rubbing up against him like a kitten.

When they left the hotel they roamed around the dark streets until they found an earlymorning coffeebar. They ate coffee and croissants together in drowsy intimate quiet, leaning very close to each other as they stood against the bar. She left him to go up the hill towards Montmartre. He asked her if he couldn't see her again sometime. She shrugged her shoulders. He gave her thirty francs and kissed her and whispered in her ear a parody of his little rhyme:

> Les petites marionettes font font font
> Un P'tit peu d'amour et puis s'en vont

She laughed and pinched his cheek and the last he heard of her was her gruff giggle and "Oh qu'il est rigolo, celui-là."

He went back to his room feeling happy and sleepy and saying to himself: what's the matter with my life is I haven't got a woman of my own. He had just time to wash and shave and put on a clean shirt and to rush down to headquarters in order to be there when Colonel Edgecombe, who was a damnably early riser, got in. He found orders to leave for Rome that night.

By the time he got on the train his eyes were stinging with sleepiness. He and the sergeant who went with him had a compartment reserved at the end of a first class coach marked Paris-Brindisi. Outside of their compartment the train was packed; people were standing in the aisles. Dick had taken off his coat and Sam Browne belt and was loosening his puttees, planning to stretch out on one of the seats and go to sleep even before the train left, when he saw a skinny American face in the door of the compartment. "I beg your pardon, is this Ca-ca-captain Savage?" Dick sat up and nodded yawning. "Captain Savage, my name is Barrow, G. H. Barrow, attached to the American delegation. . . . I have to go to Rome tonight and there's not a seat on the train. The transport officer in the station very kindly said that . . . er . . . er although it wasn't according to Hoyle you might stretch a point and allow us to ride with you . . . I have with me a very charming young lady member of the Near East Relief . . ." "Captain Savage, it certainly is mighty nice of you to let us ride with you," came a drawling Texas voice, and a pinkcheeked girl in a dark grey uniform brushed past the man who said his name was Barrow and climbed up into the car. Mr. Barrow, who was shaped like a string bean and had a prominent twitching Adam's apple and popeyes, began tossing up satchels and suitcases. Dick was sore and began to say stiffly, "I suppose you know that it's entirely against my orders . . ." but he heard his own voice saying it and suddenly grinned and said, "All right, Sergeant Wilson and I will probably be shot at sunrise, but go ahead." At that moment the train started.

Dick reluctantly scraped his things together into one corner and settled down there and immediately closed his eyes. He was much too sleepy to make the effort of talking to any damn relievers. The sergeant sat in the other corner and Mr. Barrow and the girl occupied the other seat. Through his doze Dick could hear Mr. Barrow's voice chugging along, now and then drowned out by the rattle of the express train. He had a stuttery way of talking like a badly running motorboat engine. The girl didn't say much except, "Oh my," and "I declare," now and then. It was the European situation: President Wilson says . . . new diplomacy . . . new Europe . . . permanent peace without annexations or indemnities. President Wilson says . . . new understanding between capital and labor . . . President Wilson appeals to . . . industrial democracy . . . plain people all over the world behind the president. Covenant. League of Nations . . . Dick was asleep dreaming of a girl rubbing her breasts against him purring like a kitten, of a popeyed man making a speech, of William Jennings Wilson speaking before the Baltimore conflagration, of industrial democracy in a bathhouse on the Marne in striped trunks, with a young Texas boy with pink cheeks who wanted to . . . like a string bean . . . with a twitching adamsapple . . .

He woke up with a nightmarish feeling that somebody was choking him. The train had stopped. It was stifling in the compartment. The blue shade was drawn down on the lamp overhead. He stepped over everybody's legs and went out in the passage and opened a window. Cold mountain air cut into his nostrils. The hills were snowy in the moonlight. Beside the track a French sentry was sleepily leaning on his rifle. Dick yawned desperately.

The Near East Relief girl was standing beside him, looking at him smiling. "Where are we gettin' to, Captain Savage? ... Is this Italy yet?" "I guess it's the Swiss Border ... we'll have a long wait, I guess ... they take forever at these borders."

"Oh Jimminy," said the girl, jumping up and down, "it's the first time I ever crossed a border."

Dick laughed and settled back into his seat again. The train pulled into a barny lonelylooking station, very dimly lit, and the civilian passengers started piling out with their baggage. Dick sent his papers by the sergeant to the military inspection and settled back to sleep again.

He slept soundly and didn't wake up until the Mont Cenis. Then it was the Italian frontier. Again cold air, snowy mountains, everybody getting out into an empty barn of a station.

Sleepysentimentally remembering the last time he'd gone into Italy on the Fiat car with Sheldrake, he walked shivering to the station bar and drank a bottle of mineral water and a glass of wine. He took a couple of bottles of mineral water and a fiasco of chianti back to the compartment, and offered Mr. Barrow and the girl drinks when they came back from the customs and the police looking very cross and sleepy. The girl said she couldn't drink wine because she'd signed a pledge not to drink or smoke when she joined the N.E.R., but she drank some mineral water and complained that it tickled her nose. Then they all huddled back into their corners to try to sleep some more. By the time they pulled into the Termi station in Rome they were all calling each other by their first names. The Texas girl's name was Anne Elizabeth. She and Dick had spent the day standing in the corridor looking out at the saffronroofed towns and the peasants' houses each with a blue smear on the stucco behind the grapevine over the door, and the olives and the twisted shapes of the vines in their redterraced fields; the pale hilly Italian landscape where the pointed cypresses stood up so dark they were like gashes in a canvas. She'd told him all about trying to get overseas all through the war and how her brother had been killed learning to fly at San Antonio, and how nice Mr. Barrow had been on the boat and in Paris but that he would try to make love to her and acted so silly, which was very inconvenient; Dick said well maybe it wasn't so silly. He could see that Anne Elizabeth felt fine about travelling to Rome with a real army officer who'd been to the front and could talk Italian and everything.

From the station he had to rush to the embassy with his despatch cases, but he had time to arrange to call up Miss Trent at the Near East Relief. Barrow too shook hands with him warmly and said he hoped they'd see something of each other; he was anxious to establish contacts with people who really knew what it was all about.

The only thing Dick thought of that night was to get through and get to bed. Next morning he called up Ed Schuyler at the Red Cross. They ate a big winey lunch together at an expensive restaurant near the Pincio gardens. Ed had been leading the life of Riley; he had an apartment on the Spanish Stairs and took a lot of trips. He'd gotten fat. But now he was in trouble. The husband of an Italian woman he'd been running round with was threatening to challenge him to a duel and he was afraid there'd be a row and he'd lose his job with the Red Cross. "The war was all right but it's the peace that really gets you," he said. Anyway he was sick of Italy and the Red Cross and wanted to go home. The only thing was that they were going to have a revolution in Italy and he'd like to stay and see it. "Well, Dick, for a member of the grenadine guards you seem to have done pretty well for yourself."

"All a series of accidents," said Dick, wrinkling up his nose. "Things are funny, do you know it?" "Don't I know it . . . I wonder what happened to poor old Steve? Fred Summers was joining the Polish Legion, last I heard of him." "Steve's probably in jail," said Dick, "where we ought to be." "But it's not every day you get a chance to see a show like this."

It was four o'clock when they left the restaurant. They went to Ed's room and sat drinking cognac in his window looking out over the yellow and verdigris roofs of the city and the baroque domes sparkling in the last sunlight, remembering how tremendously they'd felt Rome the last time they'd been there together, talking about what they'd be doing now that the war was over. Ed Schuyler said he wanted to get a foreign correspondent job that would take him out east; he couldn't imagine going back home to upstate New York; he had to see Persia and Afghanistan. Talking about what he was going to do made Dick feel hellishly miserable. He started walking back and forth across the tiled floor.

The bell rang and Schuyler went out in the hall. Dick heard whispering and a woman's voice talking Italian in a thin treble. After a moment Ed pushed a little longnosed woman with huge black eyes into the room. "This is Magda," he said, "Signora Sculpi, meet Captain Savage." After that they had to talk in mixed French and Italian.

"I don't think it's going to rain," said Dick. "Suppose I get hold of a girl for you and we take a drive and eat supper at Caesar's palace . . . maybe it won't be too cold."

Dick remembered Anne Elizabeth and called up the N.E.R. The Texas voice was delighted, said the relievers were awful and that she'd made a date with Mr. Barrow but would get out of it. Yes, she'd be ready if they called for her in half an hour. After a lot of bargaining between Signora Sculpi and a cabman they hired a twohorse landau, considerably elegant and decrepit. Anne Elizabeth was waiting for them at her door. "Those old hens make me tired," she said, jumping into the cab. "Tell him to hurry or Mr. Barrow'll catch us. . . . Those old hens say I have to be in by nine o'clock. I declare it worse'n Sundayschool in there. . . . It was mighty nice of you to ask me out to meet your friends, Captain Savage. . . . I was just dying to get out and see the town. . . . Isn't it wonderful? Say, where does the Pope live?"

The sun had set and it had begun to get chilly. The Palazzo dei Cesari was empty and chilly, so they merely had a vermouth there and went back into town for dinner. After dinner they went to a show at the Apollo. "My, I'll ketch it," said Anne Elizabeth, "but I don't care. I want to see the town."

She took Dick's arm as they went into the theatre. "Do you know, Dick . . . all these foreigners make me feel kinder lonesome . . . I'm glad I got a white man with me. . . . When I was at school in New York I used to go out to Jersey to see a textile strike . . . I used to be interested in things like that. I used to feel like I do now then. But I wouldn't miss any of it. Maybe it's the way you feel when you're having a really interesting time." Dick felt a little drunk and very affectionate. He squeezed her arm and leaned over her. "Bad mans shan't hurt lil' Texas girl," he crooned. "I guess you think I haven't got good sense," said Anne Elizabeth, suddenly changing her tone. "But oh lawsie, how'm I going to get along with that Methodist Board of Temperance and Public Morals I've got to live with! I don't mean I don't think their work's fine . . . It's awful to think of poor little children starving everywhere. . . . We've won the war, now it's up to us to help patch things up in Europe just like the President says." The curtain was going up and all the Italians around started shushing. Anne Elizabeth subsided. When Dick tried to get hold of her hand she pulled it away and flicked his with her fingers. "Say, I thought you were out of highschool," she said.

The show wasn't much, and Anne Elizabeth who couldn't understand a word, kept letting her head drop on Dick's shoulder and going to sleep. In the intermission when they all went to the bar for drinks, Anne Elizabeth dutifully took lemonade. Going upstairs again to their seats, there was suddenly a scuffle. A little Italian with eyeglasses and a bald head had run at Ed Schuyler screaming, "Traditore." He ran at him so hard that they both lost their balance and rolled down the redcarpeted steps, the little Italian punching and kicking and Ed holding him off at arm's length as best he could. Dick and Anne Elizabeth, who turned out to be very strong, grabbed the little Italian, picked him up off the ground and locked his arms behind him while Signora Sculpi fell on his neck sobbing. It was the husband.

Ed meanwhile got to his feet looking very red and sheepish. By the time the Italian police appeared everything had quieted down and the manager was nervously brushing the dust off Ed's uniform. Anne Elizabeth found the little Italian his eyeglasses, that were badly bent, and he led his wife out, who was sobbing. He looked so funny, when he stopped in the door with his bent eyeglasses trembling on the end of his nose to shake his fist at Ed, that Dick couldn't help laughing. Ed was apologizing profusely to the manager, who seemed to take his side, explaining to the policemen in their shiny hats that the husband was pazzo. The bell rang and they all went back to their seats. "Why, Anne Elizabeth, you're a jujutsu expert," Dick whispered, his lips touching her ear. They got to giggling so they couldn't pay attention to the show and had to go out to a café.

"Now I suppose all the wops'll think I'm a coward if I don't challenge the poor little bugger to a duel." "Sure, it'll be cappistols at thirty paces now . . . or eggplants at five yards." Dick was laughing so hard he was crying. Ed began to get sore. "It isn't funny," he said, "it's hell of a thing to have happen . . . a guy never seems to be able to have any fun without making other people miserable . . poor Magda . . . it's hellish for her. . . . Miss Trent, I hope you'll excuse this ridiculous exhibition." Ed got up and went home.

"Well, what on earth was that about, Dick?" asked Anne Elizabeth, when they'd gotten out in the street and were walking towards the N.E.R. boarding house. "Well, I suppose Signore husband was jealous on account of Ed's running around with Magda . . . or else it's a pretty little blackmail plot . . . poor Ed seems all cut up about it." "People sure do things over here they wouldn't do at home . . . I declare it's peculiar." "Oh, Ed gets in trouble everywhere. . . He's got a special knack." "I guess it's the war and continental standards and everything loosens up people's morals. . . . I never was prissy, but my goodness, I was surprised when Mr. Barrow asked me to go to his hotel the first day we landed . . . I'd only spoken to him three or four times before on the boat. . . . Now at home he wouldn't have done that, not in a thousand years." Dick looked searchingly into Anne Elizabeth's face. "In Rome do as the Romans do," he said with a funny smirk. She laughed, looking hard into his eyes as if trying to guess what he meant. "Oh, well, I guess it's all part of life," she said. In the shadow of the doorway he wanted to do some heavy kissing, but she gave him a quick peck in the mouth and shook her head. Then she grabbed his hand and squeezed it hard and said, "Let's us be good friends." Dick walked home with his head swimming with the scent of her sandy hair.

Dick had three or four days to wait in Rome. The President was to arrive on January 3 and several couriers were held at his disposition. Meanwhile he had nothing to do but walk around the town and listen to the bands practicing *The Star-Spangled Banner* and watch the flags and the stands going up.

The first of January was a holiday; Dick and Ed and Mr. Barrow and Anne Elizabeth hired a car and went out to Hadrian's Villa and then on to Tivoli for lunch. It was a showery day and there was a great deal of mud on the roads. Anne Elizabeth said the rolling Campagna, yellow and brown with winter, made her think of back home along the Middlebuster. They ate fritto misto and drank a lot of fine gold Frascati wine at the restaurant above the waterfall. Ed and Mr. Barrow agreed about the Roman Empire and that the ancients knew the art of life. Anne Elizabeth seemed to Dick to be flirting with Mr. Barrow. It made him sore the way she let him move his chair close to hers when they sat drinking their coffee on the terrace afterwards, looking down into the deep ravine brimmed with mist from the waterfall. Dick sat drinking his coffee without saying anything.

When she'd emptied her cup Anne Elizabeth jumped to her feet and said she wanted to go up to the little round temple that stood on the hillside opposite like something in an old engraving. Ed said the path was too steep for so soon after lunch. Mr. Barrow said without enthusiasm, er, he'd go. Anne Elizabeth was off running across the bridge and down the path with Dick running after her slipping and stumbling in the loose gravel and the puddles. When they got to the bottom the mist was soppy and cold on their faces. The waterfall was right over their heads. Their ears were full of the roar of it. Dick looked back to see if Mr. Barrow was coming.

"He must have turned back," he shouted above the falls. "Oh, I hate people who won't ever go anywhere," yelled Anne Elizabeth. She grabbed his hand. "Let's run up to the temple." They got up there breathless. Across the ravine they could see Ed and Mr. Barrow still sitting on the terrace of the restaurant. Anne Elizabeth thumbed her nose at them and then waved. "Isn't this wonderful?" she spluttered. "Oh, I'm wild about ruins and scenery . . . I'd like to go all over Italy and see everything. . . . Where can we go this afternoon? . . . Let's not go back and listen to them mouthing about the Roman Empire."

"We might get to Nemi . . . you know the lake where Caligula had his galleys . . . but I don't think we can get there without the car." "Then they'd come along. . . . No, let's take a walk." "It might rain on us." "Well, what if it does? We won't run."

They went up a path over the hills above the town and soon found themselves walking through wet pastures and oakwoods with the Campagna stretching lightbrown below them and the roofs of Tivoli picked out with black cypresses like exclamation points. It was a showery springfeeling afternoon. They could see the showers moving in dark grey and whitish blurs across the Campagna. Underfoot little redpurple cyclamens were blooming. Anne Elizabeth kept picking them and poking them in his face for him to smell. Her cheeks were red and her hair was untidy and she seemed to feel too happy to walk, running and skipping all the way. A small sprinkle of rain wet them a little and made the hair streak on her forehead. Then there was a patch of chilly sunlight. They sat down on the root of a big beechtree and looked up at the long redbrown pointed buds that glinted against the sky. Their noses were full of the smell of the little cyclamens. Dick felt steamy from the climb and the wet underbrush and the wine he'd drunk and the smell of the little cyclamens. He turned and looked in her eyes. "Well," he said. She grabbed him by the ears and kissed him again and again. "Say you love me," she kept saying in a strangling voice. He could smell her sandy hair and warm body and the sweetness of the little cyclamens. He pulled her to her feet and held her against his body and kissed her on the mouth; their tongues touched. He dragged her through a break in the hedge into the next field. The ground was too wet. Across the field was a little hut made of brush. They staggered as they walked with their arms around each other's waists, their thighs grinding stiffly together. The hut was full of dry cornfodder. They lay squirming together among the dry crackling cornfodder. She lay on her back with her eyes closed, her lips tightly pursed. He had one hand under her head and with the other was trying to undo her clothes; something tore under his hand. She began pushing him away. "No, no, Dick, not here . . . we've got to go back." "Darling girl . . . I must . . . you're so wonderful." She broke away from him and ran out of the hut. He sat up on the floor, hating her, brushing the dry shreds off his uniform.

Outside it was raining hard. "Let's go back; Dick, I'm crazy about you but you oughtn't to have torn my panties . . . oh, you're so exasperating." She began to laugh.

"You oughtn't to start anything you don't want to finish," said Dick. "Oh, I think women are terrible . . . except prostitutes . . . there you know what you're getting."

She went up to him and kissed him. "Poor little boy . . . he feels so cross. I'm so sorry . . . I'll sleep with you, Dick . . . I promise I will. You see it's difficult . . . In Rome we'll get a room somewhere."

"Are you a virgin?" His voice was constrained and stiff.

She nodded. "Funny, isn't it? . . . In wartime . . . You boys have risked your lives. I guess I can risk that." "I guess I can borrow Ed's apartment. I think he's going to Naples tomorrow." "But you really love me, Dick?" "Of course, . . . it's only this makes me feel terrible . . . making love's so magnificent." "I suppose it is . . . Oh, I wish I was dead."

They plodded along down the hill through the downpour that gradually slackened to a cold drizzle. Dick felt tired out and sodden; the rain was beginning to get down his neck. Anne Elizabeth had dropped her bunch of cyclamens.

When they got back the restaurant keeper said that the others had gone to the Villa d'Este, but would come back soon. They drank hot rum and water and tried to dry themselves over a brazier of charcoal in the kitchen. "We're a fine pair of drowned rats," tittered Anne Elizabeth. Dick growled, "A pair of precious idiots."

By the time the others came back they were warm but still wet. It was a relief to argue with Barrow who was saying that if the ruling classes of today knew as much about the art of life as those old Italians he wouldn't be a socialist. "I didn't think you were a socialist any more," broke in Anne Elizabeth. "I'm sure I'm not; look how the German socialists have acted in the war and now they try to crybaby and say they wanted peace all along."

"It's possible . . . to rec . . . to reconcile being a socialist with faith in our President and . . . er . . . in democracy," stammered Barrow, going close to her. "We'll have to have a long talk about that, Anne Elizabeth."

Dick noticed how his eyes goggled when he looked at her. I guess he's out after her, he said to himself. When they got into the car he didn't care whether Barrow sat next to her or not. They drove all the way back to Rome in the rain.

The next three days were very busy with President Wilson's visit to Rome. Dick got cards to various official functions, heard a great many speeches in Italian and French and English, saw a great many silk hats and decorations and saluted a great deal and got a pain in the back from holding a stiff military posture. In the Roman Forum he was near enough the President's party to hear the short man with black mustaches who was pointing out the ruins of the temple of Romulus, say in stiff English, "Everything here bears relation to the events of the great war." There was a hush as the people in the outer groups of dignitaries strained their ears to hear what Mr. Wilson would say.

"That is true," replied Mr. Wilson in a measured voice. "And we must not look upon these ruins as mere stones, but as immortal symbols." A little appreciative murmur came from the group. The Italian spoke a little louder next time. All the silk hats cocked at an angle as the dignitaries waited for the Italian's reply. "In America," he said with a little bow, "you have something greater, and it is hidden in your hearts."

Mr. Wilson's silk hat stood up very straight against all the time-eaten columns and the endless courses of dressed stone. "Yes," replied Mr. Wilson, "it is the greatest pride of Americans to have demonstrated the immense love of humanity which they bear in their hearts." As the President spoke Dick caught sight of his face past the cocksfeathers of some Italian generals. It was a grey stony cold face grooved like the columns, very long under the silk hat. The little smile around the mouth looked as if it had been painted on afterwards. The group moved on and passed out of earshot.

That evening at five, when he met Anne Elizabeth at Ed's apartment he had to tell her all about the official receptions. He said all he'd seen had been a gold replica of the wolf suckling Romulus and Remus up at the Capitol when the President had been made a Roman citizen, and his face in the forum. "A terrifying face, I swear it's a reptile's face, not warmblooded, or else the face on one of those old Roman politicians on a tomb on the Via Appia. . . . Do you know what we are, Anne Elizabeth? we're the Romans of the Twentieth Century"; he burst out laughing, "and I always wanted to be a Greek."

Anne Elizabeth who was a great admirer of Wilson was annoyed at first by what he was saying. He was nervous and excited and went on talking and talking. For this once she broke her pledge and drank some hot rum with him, as the room was terribly chilly. In the light of the street lamps on the little corner of the Spanish Stairs they could see from Ed's window, they could see the jumbled darkness of crowds continually passing and repassing. "By God, Anne Elizabeth, it's terrible to think about it. . . . You don't know the way people feel, people praying for him in peasants' huts . . . oh, we don't know anything and we're grinding them all underfoot. . . . It's the sack of Corinth . . . they think he's going to give them peace, give them back the cosy beforethewar world. It makes you sick to hear all the speeches. . . . Oh, Christ, let's stay human as long as we can . . . not get reptile's eyes and stone faces and ink in our veins instead of blood. . . . I'm damned if I'll be a Roman."

"I know what you mean," said Anne Elizabeth, ruffling up his hair. "You're an artist, Dick, and I love you very much . . . you're my poet, Dick."

"To hell with them all," said Dick, throwing his arms around her.

In spite of the hot rum, Dick was very nervous when he took his clothes off. She was trembling when he came to her on the bed. It was all right, but she bled a good deal and they didn't have a very good time. At supper afterwards they couldn't seem to find anything to say to each other. She went home early and Dick wandered desolately around the streets among the excited crowds and the flags and the illuminations and the uniforms. The Corso was packed; Dick went into a café and was greeted by a group of Italian officers who insisted on setting him up to drinks. One young fellow with an olive skin and very long black eyelashes, whose name was Carlo Hugobuoni, became his special friend and entertainer and took him around to all the tables introducing him as Il captain Salvaggio Ricardo. It was all asti spumante and Evviva gli americani and Italia irridenta and Meester Veelson who had saved civiltá and evviva la pace, and they ended by taking Dick to see the belle ragazze. To his great relief all the girls were busy at the house where they took him and Dick was able to slip away and go back to the hotel to bed.

The next morning when he came down to drink his coffee there was Carlo waiting for him in the hotel lobby. Carlo was very sleepy; he hadn't been able to find a raggaza until five in the morning but now he was at the orders of his caro amico to show him round the town. All day Dick had him with him, in spite of his efforts to get rid of him without hurting his feelings. He waited while Dick went to get his orders from the military mission, had lunch with him and Ed Schuyler; it was all Ed could do to get him away so that Dick could go to Ed's apartment to meet Anne Elizabeth. Ed was very funny about it, said that, as he'd lost Magda, he wouldn't be able to do anything worthwhile there himself and was glad to have Dick using the room for venereal purposes. Then he linked his arm firmly in Carlo's and carried him off to a café.

Dick and Anne Elizabeth were very tender and quiet. It was their last afternoon together. Dick was leaving for Paris that night, and Anne Elizabeth expected to be sent to Constantinople any day. Dick promised he'd get himself out to see her there. That night Anne Elizabeth went with him to the station. There they found Carlo waiting with a huge salami wrapped in silver paper and a bottle of chianti. The fellow that was going with him had brought the despatch cases, so there was nothing for Dick to do but get on the train. He couldn't seem to think of anything to say and it was a relief when the train pulled out.

As soon as he reported to Colonel Edgecombe he was sent off again to Warsaw. Through Germany all the trains were late and people looked deathly pale and everybody talked of a bolshevik uprising. Dick was walking up and down the snowy platform, stamping to keep his feet warm, during an endless wait at a station in East Prussia, when he ran into Fred Summers. Fred was a guard on a Red Cross supply car and invited Dick to ride with him a couple of stations. Dick fetched his despatches and went along. Fred had the caboose fitted with an oilstove and a cot and a great store of wine, cognac and Baker's chocolate. They rode all day together talking as the train joggled slowly across an endless grey frozen plain. "It's not a peace," said

Fred Summers, "it's a cockeyed massacre! Christ, you ought to see the pogroms." Dick laughed and laughed. "Jerusalem, it makes me feel good to hear you, you old bum, Fred. . . . It's like the old days of the grenadine guards."

"Jez, that was a circus," said Fred. "Out here it's too damn hellish to be funny . . . everybody starved and crazy."

"You were damn sensible not to get to be an officer . . . you have to be so damn careful about everything you say and do you can't have any kind of good time."

"Jez, you're the last man I'd ever have expected to turn out a captain."

"C'est la guerre," said Dick.

They drank and talked and talked and drank so much that Dick could barely get back to his compartment with his despatch case. When they got into the Warsaw station Fred came running up with a package of chocolate bars. "Here's a little relief, Dick," he said. "It's a fine for coucher avec. Ain't a woman in Warsaw won't coucher for all night for a chocolate bar."

When he got back to Paris, Dick and Colonel Edgecombe went to tea at Miss Stoddard's. Her drawingroom was tall and stately with Italian panels on the walls and yellow and orange damask hangings; through the heavy lace in the windows you could see the purple branches of the trees along the quai, the jade Seine and the tall stone lace of the apse of Nôtre Dâme. "What a magnificent setting you have arranged for yourself, Miss Stoddard," said Colonel Edgecombe, "and if you excuse the compliment, the gem is worthy of its setting." "They were fine old rooms," said Miss Stoddard, "all you need do with those old houses is to give them a chance." She turned to Dick: "Young man, what did you do to Robbins that night we all had supper together? He talks about nothing else but what a bright fellow you are." Dick blushed. "We had a glass of uncommonly good scotch together afterwards . . . It must have been that." "Well, I'll have to keep my eye on you . . . I don't trust these bright young men."

They drank tea sitting around an ancient wroughtiron stove. A fat major and a lanternjawed Standard Oil man named Rasmussen came in, and later a Miss Hutchins who looked very slender and welltailored in her Red Cross uniform. They talked about Chartres and about the devastated regions and the popular enthusiasm that was greeting Mr. Wilson everywhere and why Clemenceau always wore grey lisle gloves. Miss Hutchins said it was because he really had claws instead of hands and that was why they called him the tiger.

Miss Stoddard got Dick in the window: "I hear you've just come from Rome, Captain Savage . . . I've been in Rome a great deal since the war began . . . Tell me what you saw . . . tell me about everything . . . I like it better than anywhere." "Do you like Tivoli?" "Yes, I suppose so; it's rather a tourist place, though, don't you think?" Dick told her the story of the fight at the Apollo without mentioning Ed's name, and she was very much amused. They got along very well in the window watching the streetlamps come into greenish bloom along the river as they talked; Dick was wondering how old she was, la femme de trente ans.

As he and the Colonel were leaving they met Mr. Moorehouse in the hall. He shook hands warmly with Dick, said he was so glad to see him again and asked him to come by late some afternoon, his quarters were at the Crillon and there were often some interesting people there. Dick was curiously elated by the tea, although he'd expected to be bored. He began to think it was about time he got out of the service, and, on the way back to the office, where they had some work to clean up, asked the Colonel what steps he ought to take to get out of the service in France. He thought he might get a position of some kind in Paris. "Well, if you're looking for that, this fellow Moorehouse is the man for you . . . I believe he's to be in charge of some sort of publicity work for Standard Oil . . . Can you see yourself as a public relations counsel, Savage?" The Colonel laughed. "Well, I've got my mother to think of," said Dick seriously.

At the office Dick found two letters. One was from Mr. Wigglesworth saying that Blake had died of tuberculosis at Saranac the week before, and the other was from Anne Elizabeth:

DARLING:

I'm working at a desk in this miserable dump that's nothing but a collection of old cats that make me tired. Darling, I love you so much. We must see each other soon. I wonder what Dad and Buster would say if I brought a goodlooking husband home from overseas. They'd be hopping mad at first but I reckon they'd get over it. Gol darn it, I don't want to work at a desk, I want to travel around Europe and see the sights. The only thing I like here is a little bunch of cyclamens on my desk. Do you remember the cute little pink cyclamens? I've got a bad cold and I'm lonely as the dickens. This Methodist Board of Temperance and Public Morals are the meanest people I've ever seen. Ever been homesick, Dick? I don't believe you ever have. Do get yourself sent right back to Rome. I wish I hadn't been such a prissy silly little girl up there where the cyclamens bloomed. It's hard to be a woman, Dick. Do anything you like but don't forget me. I love you so.

ANNE ELIZABETH.

When Dick got back to his hotel room with the two letters in the inside pocket of his tunic he threw himself down on the bed and lay a long time staring at the ceiling. A little before midnight Henry knocked on the door. He was just in from Brussels. "Why, what's the matter, Dick, you look all grey . . . are you sick or something?"

Dick got to his feet and washed his face at the washbasin. "Nothing the matter," he spluttered through the water. "I'm fed up with this man's army, I guess."

"You look like you'd been crying."

"Crying over spilt milk," said Dick, and cleared his throat with a little laugh.

"Say, Dick, I'm in trouble, you've got to help me out. . . . You remember that girl Olga, the one who threw the teapot at me?" Dick nodded. "Well, she says she's going to have a baby and that I'm the proud parent. . . . It's ridiculous."

"Well, things like that happen," said Dick sourly.

"No, but Christ, man, I don't want to marry the bitch . . . or support the offspring . . . it's too silly. Even if she is going to have a baby it's probably not mine . . . She says she'll write to General Pershing. Some of those poor devils of enlisted men they sent up for twenty years for rape . . . it's the same story."

"They shot a couple. . . . Thank God I wasn't on that courtmartial."

"But think of how it ud upset mother. . . . Look here, you can parleyvoo better'n I can . . . I want you to come and talk to her."

"All right. . . but I'm dead tired and feel lousy . . ." Dick put on his tunic. "Say, Henry, how are you off for jack? The franc's dropping all the time. We might be able to give her a little money, and we'll be going home soon, we'll be too far away for blackmail." Henry looked low. "It's a hell of a thing to have to admit to your kid brother," he said, "but I played poker the other night and got cleaned out . . . I'm S.O.L. all down the line."

They went around to the place on Montmartre where Olga was hatcheck girl. There was nobody there yet, so she was able to come out and have a drink with them at the bar. Dick rather liked her. She was a bleached blonde with a small, hard, impudent face and big brown eyes. Dick talked her around, saying that his brother couldn't marry a foreigner on account of la famille and not having a situation and that he would soon be out of the army and back at a drafting desk . . . did she know how little a draftsman in an architect's office was paid en Amerique? Nothing at all, and with la vie chère and la chute du franc and le dollar would go next maybe and la revolution mondiale would be coming on, and the best thing she could do was to be a good little girl and not have the baby. She began to cry . . . she so wanted to get married and have children and as for an avortment . . . mais non, puis non. She stamped her foot and went back to her hatcheck booth. Dick followed her and consoled her and patted her cheek and said que voulez vous it was la vie and wouldn't she consider a present of five hundred francs? She shook her head but when he mentioned a thousand she began to brighten up and to admit that que voulez vous it was la vie. Dick left her and Henry cheerfully making a date to go home together after the boite closed. "Well, I had a couple of hundred bucks saved up, I guess it'll have to go . . . try to hold her off until we can get a good exchange . . . and Henry, the next time you play poker, for goodness' sake watch yourself."

The day before the first plenary session of the Peace Conference Dick was running into the Crillon to go up to see Mr. Moorehouse who had promised to get cards for him and Colonel Edgecombe, when he saw a familiar face in a French uniform. It was Ripley, just discharged from the French artillery school at Fontainebleau. He said he was in there trying to find an old friend of his father's to see if he could get a job connected with the peace delegations. He was broke and Marianne the Third Republic wasn't keeping him any more unless he enlisted in the foreign legion and that was the last thing he wanted to do. After Dick had phoned Major Edgecombe that Mr. Moorehouse had been unable to get them cards and that they must try again through military channels they went and had a drink together at the Ritz bar.

"Big time stuff," said Ripley, looking around at the decorations on the uniforms and the jewels on the women, "*How are you goin' to keep 'em down on the farm . . . After they've see Paree?*" Dick grunted. "I wish to hell I knew what I was going to do after I got out of this man's army." "Ask me something easy . . . oh, I guess I can get a job somewhere . . . if the worst comes to the worst I'll have to go back and finish Columbia . . . I wish the revolution ud come. I don't want to go back to the States . . . hell, I dunno what I want to do." This kind of talk made Dick feel uneasy: "Mefiez vous," he quoted. "Les oreilles enemies vous écoutent." "And that's not the half of it."

"Say, have you heard anything from Steve Warner?" Dick asked in a low voice. "I got a letter from Boston . . . I think he got a year's sentence for refusing to register . . . He's lucky . . . A lot of those poor devils got twenty years." "Well, that comes of monkeying with the buzzsaw," said Dick outloud. Ripley looked at him hard with narrowed eyes for a second; then they went on talking about other things.

That afternoon Dick took Miss Stoddard to tea at Rumpelmeyers, and afterwards walked up to the Crillon with her to call on Mr. Moorehouse. The corridors of the Crillon were lively as an anthill with scuttling khaki uniforms, marine yeomen, messenger boys, civilians; a gust of typewriter clicking came out from every open door. At every landing groups of civilian experts stood talking in low voices, exchanging glances with passersby, scribbling notes on scratchpads. Miss Stoddard grabbed Dick's arm with her sharp white fingers, "Listen . . . it's like a dynamo. . . what do you think it means?" "Not peace," said Dick.

In the vestibule of Mr. Moorehouse's suite, she introduced him to Miss Williams, the tiredlooking sharpfaced blonde who was his secretary. "She's a treasure," Miss Stoddard whispered as they went through into the drawingroom, "does more work than anybody in the whole place."

There were a great many people standing around in the blue light that filtered in through the long windows. A waiter was making his way among the groups with a tray of glasses and a valetlooking person was tiptoeing around with a bottle of port. Some people had teacups and others had glasses in their hands but nobody was paying much attention to them. Dick noticed at once from the way Miss Stoddard walked into the room and the way Mr. Moorehouse came forward a little to meet her, that she was used to running the show in that room. He was introduced to various people and stood around for a while with his mouth shut and his ears open. Mr. Moorehouse spoke to him and remembered his name, but at that moment a message came that Colonel House was on the phone and Dick had no further chance to talk to him. As he was leaving Miss Williams, the secretary, said; "Captain Savage, excuse me a moment . . . You're a friend of Mr. Robbins', aren't you?" Dick smiled at her and said, "Well, rather an acquaintance, I'd say. He seems a very interesting fellow." "He's a very brilliant man," said Miss Williams, "but I'm afraid he's losing his grip . . . as I look at it it's very demoralizing over here . . . for a man. How can anybody expect to get through their work in a place where they take three hours for lunch and sit around drinking in those miserable cafés the rest of the time?"

"You don't like Paris, Miss Williams."

"I should say not."

"Robbins does," said Dick maliciously. "Too well," said Miss Williams. "I thought if you were a friend of his you might help us straighten him out. We're very worried over him. He hasn't been here for two days at a most important time, very important contacts to be made. J.W.'s working himself to the bone. I'm so afraid he'll break down under the strain . . . And you can't get a reliable stenographer or an extra typewriter . . . I have to do all the typing beside my secretarial duties." "Oh, it's a busy time for all of us," said Dick. "Goodby, Miss Williams." She gave him a smile as he left.

In late February he came back from a long dismal run to Vienna to find another letter from Anne Elizabeth:

DICK DARLING:

Thanks for the fine postcards. I'm still at this desk job and so lonely. Try to come to Rome if you can. Something is happening that is going to make a great change in our lives. I'm terribly worried about it but I have every confidence in you. I know you're straight, Dicky boy. Oh, I've got to see you. If you don't come in a day or two I may throw up everything and come to Paris. Your girl,

ANNE ELIZABETH.

Dick went cold all over when he read the letter in the Brasserie Weber where he'd gone to have a beer with an artillery 2nd lieutenant named Staunton Wills who was studying at the Sorbonne. Then he read a letter from his mother complaining about her lonely old age and one from Mr. Cooper offering him a job. Wills was talking bout a girl he'd seen at the Theatre Caumartin he wanted to get to know, and was asking Dick in his capacity of an expert in these matters, how he ought to go about it. Dick tried to keep talking about how he could certainly get to see her by sending her a note through the ouvreuse, tried to keep looking at the people with umbrellas passing up and down the rue Royale and the wet taxis and shiny staffcars, but his mind was in a panic; she was going to have a baby; she expected him to marry her; I'm damned if I will. After they'd had their beer, he and Wills went walking down the left bank of the Seine, looking at old books and engfavings in the secondhand bookstalls and ended up having tea with Eleanor Stoddard.

"Why are you looking so doleful, Richard?" asked Eleanor. They had gone into the window with their teacups. At the table Wills was sitting talking with Eveline Hutchins and a newspaper man. Dick took a gulp of tea. "Talking to you's a great pleasure to me, Eleanor," he said.

"Well, then it's not that that's making you pull such a long face?"

"You know . . . some days you feel as if you were stagnating . . . I guess I'm tired of wearing a uniform . . . I want to be a private individual for a change."

"You don't want to go home, do you?"

"Oh, no, I've got to go, I guess, to do something about mother, that is if Henry doesn't go . . . Colonel Edgecombe says he can get me released from the service over here, that is, if I waive my right to transportation home. God knows I'm willing to do that."

"Why don't you stay over here . . . We might get J.W. to fix up something for you . . . How would you like to be one of his bright young men?"

"It ud be better than ward politics in Joisey . . . I'd like to get a job that sent me traveling . . . It's ridiculous because I spend my life on the train in this service, but I'm not fed up with it yet."

She patted the back of his hand: "That's what I like about you, Richard, the appetite you have for everything . . . J.W. spoke several times about that keen look you have . . . he's like that, he's never lost his appetite, that's why he's getting to be a power in the world . . . you know Colonel House consults him all the time . . . You see, I've lost my appetite." They went back to the teatable.

Next day orders came around to send a man to Rome; Dick jumped at the job. When he heard Anne Elizabeth's voice over the phone, chilly panic went through him again, but he made his voice as agreeable as he could. "Oh, you were a darling to come, Dicky boy," she was saying. He met her at a café at the corner of the Piazza Venezia. It made him feel embarrassed the uncontrolled way she ran up to him and threw her arms around his neck and kissed him. "It's all right," she said laughing, "they'll just think we're a couple of crazy Americans . . . Oh, Dick, lemme look at you . . . Oh, Dickybody, I've been so lonesome for you."

Dick's throat was tight. "We can have supper together, can't we?" he managed to say. "I thought we might get hold of Ed Schuyler."

She'd picked out a small hotel on a back street for them to go to. Dick let himself be carried away by her; after all, she was quite pretty today with her cheeks so flushed and the smell of her hair made him think of the smell of the little cyclamens on the hill above Tivoli; but all the time he was making love to her, sweating and straining in her arms, wheels were going round in his head: what can I do, can I do, can I do?

They were so late getting to Ed's place that he had given them up. He was all packed up to leave Rome for Paris and home the next day. "That's fine," said Dick, "we'll go on the same train." "This is my last night in Rome, ladies and gentlemen," said Ed, "let's go and have a bangup supper and to hell with the Red Cross."

They ate an elaborate supper with first class wines, at a place in front of Trajan's column, but Dick couldn't taste anything. His own voice sounded tinnily in his ears. He could see that Ed was making mighty efforts to cheer things up, ordering fresh bottles, kidding the waiter, telling funny stories about his misadventures with Roman ladies. Anne Elizabeth drank a lot of wine, said that the N.E.R. dragons weren't as bad as she had painted them, that they'd given her a latchkey when she'd told them her fiancé was in Rome for just that evening. She kept nudging Dick's knee with hers under the table and wanted them to sing *Auld Lang Syne*. After dinner they rode around in a cab and stopped to drop coins in the Trevi fountain. They ended up at Ed's place sitting on packing boxes, finishing up a bottle of champagne Ed suddenly remembered and singing *Auprès de ma blonde*.

All the time Dick felt sober and cold inside. It was a relief when Ed announced drunkenly that he was going to visit some lovely Roman ladies of his acquaintance for the last time and leave his flat to I promessi sposi for the night. After he'd gone Anne Elizabeth threw her arms around Dick: "Give me one kiss, Dickyboy, and then you must take be back to the Methodist Board of Temperance and Public Morals . . . after all, it's private morals that count. Oh, I love our private morals." Dick kissed her, then he went and looked out of the window. It had started to rain again. Frail ribbons of light from a streetlamp shot along the stone threads of the corner of the Spanish Stairs he could see between the houses. She came and rested her head on his shoulder:

"What you thinking about, Dickyboy?"

"Look, Anne Elizabeth, I've been wanting to talk about it . . . do you really think that . . . ?"

"It's more than two months now . . . It couldn't be anything else, and I have a little morning sickness now and then. I'd been feeling terrible today, only I declare seeing you's made me forgot all about it."

"But you must realize . . . it worries me terribly. There must be something you can do about it."

"I tried castor oil and quinine . . . that's all I know . . . you see I'm just a simple country girl."

"Oh, do be serious . . . you've got to do something. There are plenty of doctors would attend to it . . . I can raise the money somehow . . . It's hellish, I've got to go back tomorrow . . . I wish I was out of this goddam uniform."

"But I declare I think I'd kinda like a husband and a baby . . . if you were the husband and the baby was yours."

"I can't do it . . . I couldn't afford it . . . They won't let you get married in the army."

"That's not so, Dick," she said slowly.

They stood a long time side by side without looking at each other, looking at the rain over the dark roofs and the faint phosphorescent streaks of the streets. She spoke in a trembly frail voice, "You mean you don't love me anymore."

"Of course I do, I don't know what love is . . . I suppose I love any lovely girl . . . and especially you, sweetheart." Dick heard his own voice, like somebody else's voice in his ears. "We've had some fine times together." She was kissing him all around his neck above the stiff collar of the tunic. "But, darling, can't you understand I can't support a child until I have some definite career, and I've got my mother to support; Henry's so irresponsible I can't expect anything from him. But I've got to take you home; it's getting late."

When they got down into the street the rain had let up again. All the waterspouts were gurgling and water glinted in the gutters under the street lamps. She suddenly slapped him, shouted you're it, and ran down the street. He had to chase her, swearing under his breath. He lost her in a small square and was getting ready to give her up and go home when she jumped out at him from behind a stone phoenix on the edge of a fountain. He grabbed her by the arm, "Don't be so damn kittenish," he said nastily. "Can't you see I'm worried sick." She began to cry.

When they got to her door she suddenly turned to him and said seriously, "Look, Dick, maybe we'll put off the baby . . . I'll try horseback riding. Everybody says that works. I'll write you . . . honestly, I wouldn't hamper your career in any way . . . and I know you ought to have time for your poetry . . . You've got a big future, boy, I know it . . . if we got married I'd work too."

"Anne Elizabeth, you're a wonderful girl, maybe if we didn't have the baby we might wangle it somehow." He took her by the shoulders and kissed her on the forehead. Suddenly she started jumping up and down, chanting like a child, "Goody, goody, goody, we're going to get married."

"Oh, do be serious, kid."

"I am . . . unto death," she said slowly. "Look, don't come to see me tomorrow . . . I have a lot of supplies to check up. I'll write you to Paris."

Back at the hotel it gave him a curious feeling putting on his pyjamas and getting alone into the bed where he and Anne Elizabeth had been together that afternoon. There were bedbugs and the room smelt and he spent a miserable night.

All the way down to Paris on the train, Ed kept making him drink and talking about the revolution, saying he had it on good authority the syndicates were going to seize the factories in Italy the first of May. Hungary had gone red and Bavaria, next it would be Austria, then Italy, then Prussia and France; the American troops sent against the Russians in Archangel had mutinied: "It's the world revolution, a goddam swell time to be alive, and we'll be goddam lucky if we come out of it with whole skins."

Dick said grumpily that he didn't think so; the Allies had things well in hand. "But, Dick, I thought you were all for the revolution, it's the only possible way to end this cockeyed war." "The war's over now and all these revolutions are just the war turned inside out . . . You can't stop war by shooting all your opponents. That's just more war." They got sore and argued savagely. Dick was glad they were alone in the compartment. "But I thought you were a royalist, Ed." "I was . . . but since seeing the King of Italy I've changed my mind . . . I guess I'm for a dictator, the man on the white horse."

They settled to sleep on either side of the compartment, sore and drunk. In the morning they staggered out with headaches into the crisp air of a frontier station and drank steaming hot chocolate a freshfaced Frenchwoman poured out for them into big white cups. Everything was frosty. The sun was rising bright vermilion. Ed Schuyler talked about la belle, la douce France, and they began to get along better. By the time they reached the banlieue, they were talking about going to see Spinelli in *Plus Ça Change* that night.

After the office and details to attend to and the necessity of appearing stiff and military before the sergeants it was a relief to walk down the left bank of the Seine, where the buds were bursting pink and palest green on the trees, and the bouquinistes were closing up their stalls in the deepening lavender twilight, to the quai de la Tournelle where everything looked like two centuries ago, and to walk slowly up the chilly stone stairs to Eleanor's and to find her sitting behind the teatable in an ivorycolored dress with big pearls around her neck pouring tea and retailing, in her malicious gentle voice, all the latest gossip of the Crillon and the Peace Conference. It gave Dick a funny feeling when she said as he was leaving that they wouldn't see each other for a couple of weeks as she was going to Rome to do some work at the Red Cross office there. "What a shame we couldn't have been there at the same time," said Dick. "I'd have liked that too," she said. "A revederdci, Richard."

March was a miserable month for Dick. He didn't seem to have any friends any more and he was sick to death of everybody around the despatch service. When he was off duty his hotel room was so cold that he'd have to go out to a café to read. He missed Eleanor and going to her cosy apartment in the afternoon. He kept getting worrying letters from Anne Elizabeth; he couldn't make out from them what had happened; she made mysterious references to having met a charming friend of his at the Red Cross who had meant so much. Then too he was broke because he kept having to lend Henry money to buy off Olga with.

Early in April he got back from one of his everlasting trips to Coblenz and found a pneumatique from Eleanor for him at his hotel. She was inviting him to go on a picnic to Chantilly with her and J.W. the next Sunday.

They left at eleven from the Crillon in J.W.'s new Fiat. There was Eleanor in her grey tailored suit and a stately lady of a certain age named Mrs. Wilberforce, the wife of a vice-president of Standard Oil, and longfaced Mr. Rasmussen. It was a fine day and everybody felt the spring in the air. At Chantilly they went through the château and fed the big carp in the moat. They ate their lunch in the woods, sitting on rubber cushions. J.W. kept everybody laughing explaining how he hated picnics, asking everybody what it was that got into even the most intelligent women that they were always trying to make people go on picnics. After lunch they drove to Senlis to see the houses that the Uhlans had destroyed their in the battle of the Marne. Walking through the garden of the ruined château, Eleanor and Dick dropped behind the others. "You don't know anything about when they're going to sign peace, do you, Eleanor?" asked Dick.

"Why, it doesn't look now as if anybody would ever sign . . . certainly the Italians won't; have you seen what d'Annunzio said?"

"Because the day after peace is signed I take off Uncle Sam's livery . . . The only time in my life time has ever dragged on my hands has been since I've been in the army."

"I got to meet a friend of yours in Rome," said Eleanor, looking at him sideways. Dick felt chilly all over. "Who was that?" he asked. It was an effort to keep his voice steady. "That little Texas girl . . . she's a cute little thing. She said you were engaged!" Eleanor's voice was cool and probing like a dentist's tool.

"She exaggerated a little," he gave a little dry laugh, "as Mark Twain said when they reported his death." Dick felt that he was blushing furiously.

"I hope so . . . You see, Richard . . . I'm old enough to be, well at least your maiden aunt. She's a cute little thing . . . but you oughtn't to marry just yet, of course it's none of my business . . . an unsuitable marriage has been the ruination of many a promising young fellow . . . I shouldn't say this."

"But I like your taking an interest like that, honestly it means a great deal to me . . . I understand all about marry in haste and repent at leisure. In fact I'm not very much interested in marriage anyway . . . but . . . I don't know . . . Oh, the whole thing is very difficult."

"Never do anything difficult . . . It's never worth it," said Eleanor severely. Dick didn't say anything. She quickened her step to catch up with the others. Walking beside her he caught sight of her coldly chiselled profile jiggling a little from the jolt of her high heels on the cobbles. Suddenly she turned to him laughing, "Now I won't scold you any more, Richard, ever again."

A shower was coming up. They'd hardly got back into the car before it started to rain. Going home the gimcrack Paris suburbs looked grey and gloomy in the rain. When they parted in the lobby of the Crillon J.W. let Dick understand that there would be a job for him in his office as soon as he was out of the service. Dick went home and wrote his mother about it in high spirits:

> . . . It's not that everything isn't intensely interesting here in Paris or that I haven't gotten to know people quite close to what's really going on, but wearing a uniform and always having to worry about army regulations and saluting and everything like that, seems to keep my mind from working. Inside I'll be in the doldrums until I get a suit of civvies on again. I've been promised a position in J. Ward Moorehouse's office here in Paris; he's a dollar a year expert, but as soon as peace is signed he expects to start his business up again. He's an adviser on public relations and publicity to big corporations like Standard Oil. It's the type of work that will allow me to continue my real work on the side. Everybody tells me it's the opportunity of a lifetime. . . .

The next time he saw Miss Williams she smiled broadly and came right up to him holding our her hand. "Oh, I'm so glad, Captain Savage. J.W. says you're gong to be with us . . . I'm sure it'll be an enjoyable and profitable experience for all parties."

"Well, I don't suppose I ought to count my chickens before they're hatched," said Dick. "Oh, they're hatched all right," said Miss Williams, beaming at him.

In the middle of May Dick came back from Cologne with a hangover after a party with a couple of aviators and some German girls. Going out with German girls was strictly against orders from G.H.Q.

and he was nervous for fear they might have been seen conducting themselves in a manner unbecoming to officers and gentlemen. He could still taste the sekt with peaches in it when he got off the train at the Gare du Nord. At the office Colonel Edgecombe noticed how pale and shaky he looked and kidded him about what a tremendous time they must be having in the occupied area. Then he sent him home to rest up. When he got to his hotel he found a pneumatique from Anne Elizabeth:

I'm staying at the Continental and must see you at once.

He took a hot bath and went to bed and slept for several hours. When he woke up it was already dark. It was some time before he remembered Anne Elizabeth's letter. He was sitting on the edge of the bed sullenly buckling his puttees to go around and see her when there was a knock on his door. It was the elevatorman telling him a lady was waiting for him downstairs. The elevatorman had hardly said it before Anne Elizabeth came running down the hall. She was pale and had a red bruise on one side of her face. Something cantankerous in the way she ran immediately got on Dick's nerves. "I told them I was your sister and ran up the stairs," she said, kissing him breathlessly. Dick gave the elevatorman a couple of francs and whispered to her, "Come in. What's the matter?" He left the room door half open.

"I'm in trouble . . . the N.E.R. is sending me home."

"How's that?"

"Played hookey once too often, I guess . . . I'm just as glad; they make me tired."

"How did you hurt yourself?"

"Horse fell with me down at Ostia . . . I've been having the time of my life riding Italian cavalry horses . . . they'll take anything."

Dick was looking her hard in the face trying to make her out. "Well," he said, "is it all right? . . . I've got to know . . . I'm worried sick about it."

She threw herself face down on the bed. Dick tiptoed over and gently closed the door. She had her head stuck into her elbow and was sobbing. He sat on the edge of the bed and tried to get her to look at him. She suddenly got up and began walking around the room. "Nothing does any good . . . I'm going to have the baby . . . Oh, I'm so worried about Dad. I'm afraid it'll kill him if he finds out . . . Oh, you're so mean . . . you're so mean."

"But, Anne Elizabeth, do be reasonable . . . Can't we go on being friends? I've just been offered a very fine position when I get out of the service, but I can't take a wife and child at this stage of the game, you must understand that . . . and if you want to get married there are plenty of fellows who'd give their eyeteeth to marry you . . . You know how popular you are . . . I don't think marriage means anything anyway."

She sat down in a chair and immediately got up again. She was laughing: "If Dad or Buster was here it would be a shotgun wedding, I guess . . . but that wouldn't help much." Her hysterical laugh got on his nerves; he was shaking from the effort to control himself and talk reasonably.

"Why not G. H. Barrow? He's a prominent man and has money . . . He's crazy about you, told me so himself when I met him at the Crillon the other day . . . After all, we have to be sensible about things . . . It's no more my fault than it is yours . . . if you'd taken proper precautions. . . ."

She took her hat off and smoothed her hair in the mirror. Then she poured some water out in his washbasin, washed her face and smoothed her hair again. Dick was hoping she'd go, everything she did drove him crazy. There were tears in her eyes when she came up to him. "Give me a kiss, Dick . . . don't worry about me . . . I'll work things out somehow."

"I'm sure it's not too late for an operation," said Dick. "I'll find out an address tomorrow and drop you a line to the Continental . . . Anne Elizabeth . . . it's splendid of you to be so splendid about this."

She shook her head, whispered goodby and hurried out of the room.

"Well, that's that," said Dick aloud to himself. He felt terribly sorry about Anne Elizabeth. Gee, I'm glad I'm not a girl, he kept thinking. He had a splitting headache. He locked his door, got undressed and put out the light. When he opened the window a gust of raw rainy air came into the room and made him feel better. It was just like Ed said, you couldn't do anything without making other people miserable. A hell of a rotten world. The streets in front of the Gare St. Lazare shone like canals where the streetlamps were reflected in them. There were still people on the pavements, a man calling I'nTRANsigeant, twangy honk of taxicabs. He thought of Anne Elizabeth going home alone in a taxicab through the wet streets. He wished he had a great many lives so that he might have spent one of them with Anne Elizabeth. Might write a poem about that and send it to her. And the smell of the little cyclamens. In the café opposite the waiters were turning the chairs upside down and setting them on the tables. He wished he had a great many lives so that he might be a waiter in a café turning the chairs upside down. The iron shutters clanked as they came down. Now was the time the women came out on the streets, walking back and forth, stopping, loitering, walking back and forth, and those young toughs with skin the color of mushrooms. He began to shiver. He got into bed, the sheets had a clammy glaze on them. All the same Paris was no place to go to bed alone, no place to go home alone in a honking taxi, in the heartbreak of honking taxis. Poor Anne Elizabeth. Poor Dick. He lay shivering between the clammy sheets, his eyes were pinned open with safetypins.

Gradually he got warmer. Tomorrow. Seventhirty: shave, buckle puttees . . . café au lait, brioches, beurre. He'd be hungry, hadn't had any supper . . . deux oeux sur le plat. Bonjour m'ssieurs mesdames. Jingling spurs to the office, Sergeant Ames at ease. Day dragged out in khaki; twilight tea at Eleanor's, make her talk to Moorehouse to clinch job after the signing of the peace, tell her about the late General Ellsworth, they'll laugh about it together. Dragged out khaki days until after the signing of the peace. Dun, drab, khaki. Poor Dick got to go to work after signing of the peace. Poor Tom's cold. Poor Dickyboy . . . Richard . . . He brought his feet up to where he could rub them. Poor Richard's feet. After the Signing of the Peace.

By the time his feet were warm he'd fallen asleep.

Newsreel XXXVII

SOVIET GUARDS DISPLACED

the American commander-in-chief paid tribute to the dead and wounded, urged the soldiers to thank God for the victory and declared that a new version of duty to God and Country had come to all. When the numbers were hoisted it was found that that of M. A. Aumont's Zimzizimi was missing. The colt had been seized with a fit of coughing in the morning and was consequently withdrawn almost at the last moment

REPUBLICANS GETTING READY FOR THE HECKLING OF WILSON

MOVE TO INDICT EXKAISER IN CHICAGO

Johnny get your gun
get your gun
get your gun
We've got em on the run

we face a great change in the social structure of this great country, declared Mr. Schwab, the man who becomes the aristocrat of the future will become so not because of birth or wealth but because he has done something for the good of the country

RUTHLESS WAR TO CRUSH REDS

on the run
on the run

at the same time several columns of soldiers and sailors appeared in front of the chancellor's palace. The situation in Germany is developing into a neck and neck race between American food and Bolshevism. Find Lloyd George Taking Both Sides in Peace Disputes.

Oh that tattooed French Ladee
Tattooed from neck to knee
She was a sight to see

MACKAY OF POSTAL CALLS BURLESON BOLSHEVIK

popular demonstrations will mark the visits of the President and of the rulers of Great Britain and Belgium who will be entertained at a series of fêtes. The irony of the situation lies in the fact that the freedom of speech and the press for which the social democrats clamored is now proving the chief source of menace to the new government

Right across her jaw
Was the Royal Flying Corps
On her back was the Union Jack
Now could you ask for more?

the war department today decided to give out a guarded bulletin concerning a near mutiny of some of the American troops in the Archangel sector and their refusal to go to the front when ordered in spite of police orders comparative quiet prevailed, but as the procession moved along the various avenues, Malakoff, Henri Martin, Victor Hugo, and the Trocadèro and through the districts in the aristocratic quarter of Paris in which Jaurès lived there was a feeling of walking over mined roads where the merest incident might bring about an explosion

REINFORCEMENTS RUSHED TO REMOVE
CAUSE OF ANXIETY

All up and down her spine
Was the Kings Own Guard in line
And all around her hips
Steamed a fleet of battleships

the workers of Bavaria have overcome their party divisions and united in a mighty bloc against all domination and exploitation; they have taken over in Workers, Soldiers and Peasant's Councils entire public authority

Right above her kidney
Was a birdseye view of Sydney

But what I loved best was across her chest
My home in Tennessee

FORMER EASTSIDERS LARGELY RESPONSIBLE FOR BOLSHEVISM, SAYS DR. SIMONS

ORDERS HOUSING OF LABOR IN PALACES

UKRAINIANS FIRE ON ALLIED MISSION

it looks at present as if Landru would be held responsible for the deaths of all the women who have disappeared in France, not only for the past ten years but for many decades previously

The Camera Eye (40)

I walked all over town general strike no busses   no taxi-cabs   the gates of the Metro closed   Place de Iéna I saw red flags Anatole France in a white beard placards MUTILES DE LA GUERRE and the nutcracker faces of the agents de sûreté

Mort aux vaches

at the place de la Concorde the Republican Guards in christmastree helmets were riding among the crowd whacking the Parisians with the flat of their swords   scraps of the *International* worriedlooking soldiers in their helmets lounging with grounded arms all along the Grands Boulevards

Vive les poilus

at the Republique   à bas la guerre MORT AUX VACHES à bas la Paix des Assassins   they've torn up the gratings from around the trees and are throwing stones and bits of cast iron at the fancydressed republican guards hissing whistling poking at the horses with umbrellas   scraps of the *International*

at the Gare de l'Est they're singing the *International* entire   the gendarmerie nationale is making its way slowly down Magenta into stones whistles bits of iron the *International*   Mort Aux Vaches   Barricades we must build barricades   young kids are trying to break down the shutters of an arms shop   revolver shots an old woman in a window was hit (Whose blood is that on the cobbles?) we're all running down a side street dodging into courtyards concièrges trying to close the outside doors on cavalry charging twelve abreast firecracker faces   scared and mean behind their big moustaches under their Christmastree helmets

　　　　at a corner I run into a friend running too   Look out   They're shooting to kill and it's begun to rain hard so we dive in together just before a shutter slams down on the door of the little café   dark and quiet inside a few working men past middle age are grumblingly drinking at the bar   Ah les salops   There are no papers   Somebody said the revolution had triumphed in Marseilles and Lille   Ca va taper dure   We drink grog americain our feet are wet   at the next table two elderly men are playing chess over a bottle of white wine

　　　　later we peep out from under the sliding shutter that's down over the door into the hard rain on the empty streets only a smashed umbrella and an old checked cap side by side in the clean stone gutter and a torn handbill L'UNION DES TRAVAILLEURS FERA

Newsreel XXXVIII

C'est la lutte finale
Groupons-nous et demain
L'internationale
Sera le genre humain

FUSILLADE IN THE DIET

Y.M.C.A. WORKERS ARRESTED FOR STEALING FUNDS

declares wisdom of people alone can guide the nation in such an enterprise SAYS U.S. MUST HAVE WORLD'S GREATEST FLEET *when I was in Italy a little limping group of wounded Italian soldiers sought an interview with me. I could not conjecture what they were going to say to me, and with the greatest simplicity, with a touching simplicity they presented me with a petition in favor of the League of Nations.* Soldiers Rebel at German Opera

ORDERED TO ALLOW ALL GREEKS TO DIE

CANADIANS RIOT IN BRITISH CAMP

Arise ye pris'ners of starvation
Arise ye wretched of the earth
For justice thunders condemnation
A qui la Faunte se le Beurre est Cher?

GAINS RUN HIGH IN WALL STREET

MANY NEW RECORDS

NE SOYONS PAS LES DUPES DU TRAVESTI BOLCHEVISTE

the opinion prevails in Washington that while it might be irksome to the American public to send troops to Asia Minor people would be more willing to use an army to establish order south of the

Rio Grande. Strikers menace complete tieup of New York City. Order restored in Lahore. Lille undertakers on strike

THREAT OF MUTINY BY U. S. TROOPS

CALIFORNIA JURY QUICKLY RENDERS VERDICT AGAINST SACRAMENTO WORKERS

> 'Tis the final conflict
> Let each stand in his place
> The international party
> Shall be the human race

BOLSHEVISM READY TO COLLAPSE SAYS ESCAPED GENERAL

the French Censor will not allow the Herald to say what the Chinese Delegation has done but that there is serious unrest it would be idle to deny. Men who have been deprived of the opportunity to earn a living, who see their children crying for food, who face an indefinite shutdown of industries and a possible cessation of railway traffic with all the disorganization of national life therein implied, can hardly be expected to view the situation calmly and with equanimity

BRITISH TRY HARD TO KEEP PROMISE TO HANG KAISER

it is declared the Coreans are confident President Wilson will come in an aeroplane and listen to their views. A white flag set up on Seoul Hill is presumed to indicate the landingplace

Daughter

She wasn't sick a bit and was popular on the crossing that was very gay although the sea was rough and it was bitter cold. There was a Mr. Barrow who had been sent on a special mission by the President who paid her a great deal of attention. He was a very interesting man and full of information about everything. He'd been a socialist and very close to labor. He was so interested when she told him about her experiences in the textile strike over in Jersey. In the evenings they'd walk around and around the deck arm in arm, now and then being almost thrown off their feet by an especially heavy roll. She had a little trouble with him trying to make love to her, but managed to argue him out of it by telling him what she needed right now was a good friend, that she'd had a very unhappy love affair and couldn't think of anything like that any more. He was so kind and sympathetic, and said he could understand that thoroughly because his relation with women had been very unsatisfactory all his life. He said people ought to be free in love and marriage and not tied by conventions or inhibitions. He said what he believed in was passionate friendship. She said she did too, but when he wanted her to come to his room in the hotel the first night they were in Paris, she gave him a terrible tonguelashing. But he was so nice to her on the trip down to Rome that she began to think that maybe if he asked her to marry him she might do it.

There was an American officer on the train, Captain Savage, so good looking and such a funny talker, on his way to Rome with important despatches. From the minute she met Dick, Europe was wonderful. He talked French and Italian, and said how beautiful the old tumbledown towns were and screwed up his mouth so funnily when he told stories about comical things that happened in the war. He was a little like Webb only so much nicer and more selfreliant and betterlooking. From the minute she saw him she forgot all about Joe and as for G. H. Barrow, she couldn't stand the thought of him. When Captain Savage looked at her it made her all melt up inside; by the time they'd gotten to Rome she'd admitted to herself she was crazy about him. When they went out walking together the day they all made an excursion to the ruins of the Emperor Hadrian's villa, and the little town where the waterfall was, she was glad that he'd been drinking. She wanted all the time to throw herself in his arms; there was something about the rainy landscape and the dark lasciviouseyed people and the old names of the towns and the garlic and oil in the food and the smiling voices and the smell of the tiny magenta wildflowers he said were called cyclamens that made her not care about anything anymore. She almost fainted when he started to make love to her. Oh, she wished he would, but No, No, she couldn't just then, but the next day she'd drink in spite of the pledge she'd signed with the N.E.R. and shoot the moon. It wasn't so sordid as she'd expected but it wasn't so wonderful either; she was terribly scared and cold and sick, like when she'd told him she hadn't ever before. But the next day he was so gentle and strong, and she suddenly felt very happy. When he had to go back to Paris and there was nothing but office work and a lot of dreary old maids to talk to, it was too miserable.

When she found she was going to have a baby she was scared, but she didn't really care so much; of course he'd marry her. Dad and Buster would be sore at first but they'd be sure to like him. He wrote poetry and was going to be a writer when he got out of the army; she was sure he was going to be famous. He didn't write letters very often and when she made him come back to Rome he wasn't nearly as nice about it as she expected; but of course it must have been a shock to him. They decided that perhaps it would be better not to have the baby just then or get married till he got out of the service, though there didn't seem to be any doubt in his mind about getting married then. She tried several things and went riding a great deal with Lieutenant Grassi, who had been educated at Eton and spoke perfect English and was so charming to her and said she was the best woman rider he'd ever known. It was on account of her going out riding so much with Lieutenant Grassi and getting in so late that the old cats at the N.E.R. got sore and sent her home to America.

Going to Paris on the train, Daughter really was scared. The horseback riding hadn't done any good, and she was sore all over from a fall she'd had when one of Lieutenant Grassi's cavalry horses fell with her and broke his leg when she took him over a stone wall. The horse had to be shot and the Lieutenant had been horrid about it; these foreigners always showed a mean streak in the end. She was worried about people's noticing how she looked because it was nearly three months now. She and Dick would have to get married right away, that's all there was to it. Perhaps it would even be better to tell people they'd been married in Rome by a fat little old priest.

The minute she saw Dick's face when she was running down the corridor towards him in his hotel, she knew it was all over; he didn't love her the least bit. She walked home to her hotel hardly able to see where she was going through the slimywet Paris streets. She was surprised when she got there because she expected she'd lose her way. She almost hoped she'd lose her way. She went up to her room and sat down in a chair without taking off her dripping wet hat and coat. She must think. This was the end of everything.

The next morning she went around to the office; they gave her her transportation back home and told her what boat she was going on and said she must sail in four days. After that she went back to the hotel and sat down in a chair again and tried to think. She couldn't go home to Dallas like this. A note from Dick came around giving her the address of a doctor.

Do forgive me, he wrote. You're a wonderful girl and I'm sure it'll be all right.

She tore the thin blue letter up in little tiny pieces and dropped it out the window. Then she lay down on the bed and cried till her eyes burned. Her nausea came on and she had to go out in the hall to the toilet. When she lay down again she went to sleep for a while and woke up feeling hungry.

The day had cleared; sunlight was streaming into the room. She walked downstairs to the desk and called up G. H. Barrow in his office. He seemed delighted and said if she'd wait for him a half an hour, he'd come and fetch her out to lunch in the Bois; they'd forget everything except that it was spring and that they were beautiful pagans at heart. Daughter made a sour face, but said pleasantly enough over the phone that she'd wait for him.

When he came he wore a sporty grey flannel suit and a grey fedora hat. She felt very drab beside him in the darkgray uniform she hated so. "Why, my dearest little girl . . . you've saved my life," he said. "Su-su-spring makes me think of suicide unless I'm in lu-lu-love . . . I was feeling . . . er . . . er . . . elderly and not in love. We must change all that." "I was feeling like that too." "What's the matter?" "Well, maybe I'll tell you and maybe I won't." She almost liked his long nose and his long jaw today. "Anyway, I'm too starved to talk." "I'll do all the talking . . ." he said laughing. "Alwawaways do anywawaway . . . and I'll set you up to the bububest meal you ever ate."

He talked boisterously all the way out in the cab about the Peace Conference and the terrible fight the President had had to keep his principles intact. "Hemmed in by every sinister intrigue, by all the poisonous ghosts of secret treaties, with two of the cleverest and most unscrupulous manipulators out of oldworld statecraft as his opponents . . . He fought on . . . we are all of us fighting on . . . It's the greatest crusade in history; if we win, the world will be a better place to live in, if we lose, it will be given up to Bolshevism and despair . . . you can imagine, Anne Elizabeth, how charming it was to have your pretty little voice suddenly tickle my ear over the telephone and call me away if only for a brief space from all this worry and responsibility . . . why, there's even a rumor that an attempt has been made to poison the President at the hôtel Mûrat . . . it's the President alone with a few backers and wellwishers and devoted adherents who is standing out for decency, fairplay and good sense, never forget that for an instant. . . ." He talked on and on as if he was rehearsing a speech. Daughter heard him faintly like through a faulty telephone connection. The day too, the little pagodas of bloom on the horsechestnuts, the crowds, the overdressed children, the flags against the blue sky, the streets of handsome houses behind trees with their carved stonework and their iron balconies and their polished windows shining in the May sunshine; Paris was all little and bright and far away like a picture seen through the wrong end of a field glass. When the luncheon came on at the big glittery outdoor restaurant it was the same thing, she couldn't taste what she was eating.

He made her drink quite a lot of wine and after a while she heard herself talking to him. She'd never talked like this to a man before. He seemed so understanding and kind. She found herself talking to him about Dad and how hard it had been giving up Joe Washburn, and how going over on the boat her life had suddenly seemed all new . . . "Somethin' funny's happened to me, I declare . . . I always used to get along with everybody fine and now I can't seem to. In the N.E.R. office in Rome I couldn't get along with any of those old cats, and I got to be good friends with an Italian boy, used to take me horseback riding an' I couldn't get along with him, and you know Captain Savage on the train to Italy who let us ride in his compartment, we went out to Tivoli with him," her ears began to roar when she spoke of Dick. She was going to tell Mr. Barrow everything. "We got along so well we got engaged and now I've quarreled with him."

She saw Mr. Barrow's long knobbly face leaning towards her across the table. The gap was very wide between his front teeth when he smiled. "Do you think, Annie girl, you could get along with me a little?" He put his skinny puffyveined hand towards her across the table. She laughed and threw her head to one side, "We seem to be gettin' along all right right now."

"It would make me very happy if you could . . . you make me very happy, anyway, just to look at you . . . I'm happier at this moment than I've been for years, except perhaps for the mumumoment when the Covenant for the League of Nations was signed."

She laughed again, "Well, I don't feel like any Peace Treaty, the fact is I'm in terrible trouble." She found herself watching his face carefully; the upper lip thinned, he wasn't smiling any more.

"Why, what's the mamamatter . . . if there was any wawaway I could . . . er . . . be of assistance . . . I'd be the happiest fellow in the world."

"Oh, no . . . I hate losing my job though and having to go home in disgrace . . . that's about the size of it . . . it's all my fault for running around like a little nitwit." She was going to break down and cry, but suddenly the nausea came on again and she had to hurry to the ladies' room of the restaurant. She got there just in time to throw up. The shapeless leatherfaced woman there was very kind and sympathetic; it scared Daughter how she immediately seemed to know what was the matter. She didn't know much French but she could see that the woman was asking if it was Madame's first child, how many months, congratulating her. Suddenly she decided she'd kill herself. When she got back Barrow had paid the bill and was walking back and forth on the gravel path in front of the tables.

"You poor little girl," he said. "What can be the matter? You suddenly turned deathly pale."

"It's nothing . . . I think I'll go home and lie down . . . I don't think all that spaghetti and garlic agreed with me in Italy . . . maybe it's that wine."

"But perhaps I could do something about finding you a job in Paris. Are you a typist or stenographer?"

"Might make a stab at it," said Daughter bitterly. She hated Mr. Barrow. All the way back in the taxi she couldn't get to say anything. Mr. Barrow talked and talked. When she got back to the hotel she lay down on the bed and gave herself up to thinking about Dick.

She decided she'd go home. She stayed in her room and although Mr. Barrow kept calling up asking her out and making suggestions about possible jobs she wouldn't see him. She said she was having a bilious attack and would stay in bed. The night before she was to sail he asked her to dine with him and some friends and before she knew it she said she'd go along. He called for her at six and took her for cocktails at the Ritz Bar. She'd gone out and bought herself an evening dress at the Galleries Lafayette and was feeling fine, she was telling herself as she sat drinking the champagne cocktail, that if Dick should come in now she wouldn't bat an eyelash. Mr. Barrow was talking about the Fiume situation and the difficulties the President was having with Congress and how he feared that the whole great work of the League of Nations was in danger, when Dick came in looking very handsome in his uniform with a pale older woman in grey and a tall stoutish lighthaired man, whom Mr. Barrow pointed out as J. Ward Moorehouse. Dick must have seen her but he wouldn't look at her. She didn't care anymore about anything. They drank down their cocktails and went out. On the way up to Montmartre she let Mr. Barrow give her a long kiss on the mouth that put him in fine spirits. She didn't care; she had decided she'd kill herself.

Waiting for them at the table at the Hermitage Mr. Barrow had reserved, was a newspaper correspondent named Burnham and a Miss Hutchins who was a Red Cross worker. They were very much excited about a man named Stevens who had been arrested by the Army of Occupation, they thought accused of Bolshevik propaganda; he'd been courtmartialed and they were afraid he was going to be shot. Miss Hutchins was very upset and said Mr. Barrow ought to go to the President about it as soon as Mr. Wilson got back to Paris. In the meantime they had to get the execution stayed. She said Don Stevens was a newspaper man and although a radical not connected with any kind of propaganda and anyway it was horrible to shoot a man for wanting a better world. Mr. Barrow was very embarrassed and stuttered and hemmed and hawed and said that Stevens was a very silly young man who talked too much about things he didn't understand, but that he supposed he'd have to do the best he could to try to get him out but that after all, he hadn't shown the proper spirit. . . . That made Miss Hutchins very angry, "But they're going to shoot him . . . suppose it had happened to you . . ." she kept saying. "Can't you understand that we've got to save his life?"

Daughter couldn't seem to think of anything to say as she didn't know what they were talking about; she sat there in the restaurant looking at the waiters and the lights and the people at the tables. Opposite there was a party of attractive looking young French officers. One of them, a tall man with a hawk nose, was looking at her. Their eyes met and she couldn't help grinning. Those boys looked as if they were having a fine time. A party of Americans dressed up like plush horses crossed the floor between her and the Frenchman. It was Dick and the pale woman and J. Ward Moorehouse and a big middleaged woman in a great many deep pink ruffles and emeralds. They sat down at the table next to Daughter's table where there had been a sign saying Reservée all evening. Everybody was introduced and she and Dick shook hands very formally, as if they were the merest acquaintances. Miss Stoddard, whom she'd been so friendly with in Rome, gave her a quick inquisitive cold stare that made her feel terrible.

Miss Hutchins immediately went over and began talking about Don Stevens and trying to get Mr. Moorehouse to call up Colonel House right away and get him to take some action in his case. Mr. Moorehouse acted very quiet and calm and said he was sure she need have no anxiety, he was probably only being held for investigation and in any case he didn't think the courtmartial in the Army of Occupation would take extreme measures against a civilian and an American citizen. Miss Hutchins said all she wanted was a stay because his father was a friend of La Follette's and would be able to get together considerable influence in Washington. Mr. Moorehouse smiled when he heard that. "If his life depended on the influence of Senator La Follette, I think you would have cause to be alarmed, Eveline, but I think I can assure you that it doesn't." Miss Hutchins looked very cross when she heard that and settled back to glumly eating her supper. Anyway the party was spoiled. Daughter couldn't imagine what it was that had made everybody so stiff and constrained; maybe she was imagining it on account of her and Dick. Now and then she gave him a sideways glance. He looked so different from the way she'd known him sitting there so prim and prissylooking, talking to the stout woman in pink in a low pompous whisper now and then. It made her want to throw a plate at him.

It was a relief when the orchestra started playing dance music. Mr. Barrow wasn't a very good dancer and she didn't like the way he kept squeezing her hand and patting her neck. After they were through dancing they went into the bar to have a gin fizz. The ceiling was hung with tricolor decoration; the four French officers were in there; there were people singing *La Madelon de la Victoire* and all the tough little girls were laughing and talking loud shrill French. Mr. Barrow was whispering in her ear all the time, "Darling girl, you must let me take you home tonight. . . . You mustn't sail . . . I'm sure I can arrange everything with the Red Cross or whatever it is. . . . I've led such an unhappy life and I think I'd kill myself if I had to give you up . . . couldn't you love me just a little . . . I've dedicated my life to unattainable ideals and here I am getting old without grasping true happiness for a moment. You're the only girl I've ever known who seemed really a beautiful pagan at heart . . . appreciate the art of life." Then he kissed her wetly in the ear.

"But, George, I can't love anybody now . . . I have everybody."

"Let me teach you . . . just give me a chance."

"If you knew about me, you wouldn't want me," she said coldly. She caught again a funny scared look on his face and a thinning of his lips over his widely spaced teeth.

They went back to the table. She sat there fidgeting while everybody talked carefully, with long pauses, about the Peace Treaty, when it was going to be signed, whether the Germans would sign. Then she couldn't stand it any longer and went to the ladies' room to powder her nose. On the way back to the table she peeped into the bar to see what was going on in there. The hawknosed French officer caught sight of her, jumped to his feet, clicked his heels together, saluted, bowed and said in broken English, "Charming lady, will you not stay a moment and drink once with your umble servant?" Daughter went to their table and sat down. "You boys looked like you were having such a good time," she said. "I'm with the worst old set of plush horses . . . They make me tired." "Permettez, mademoiselle," he said, and introduced her to his friends. He was an aviator. They were all aviation officers. His name was Pierre. When she told them her brother had been an aviator and had been killed, they were very nice to her. She couldn't help letting them think Bud had been killed at the front. "Mademoiselle," said Pierre solemnly, "allow me, with all possible respect, to be your brother." "Shake," she said. They all shook hands solemnly, they were drinking little glasses of cognac, but after that they ordered champagne. She danced with them all. She was very happy and didn't care what happened. They were young goodlooking boys, all the time laughing and nice to her. They had clasped their hands and were dancing ring around the rosy in the middle of the floor while everybody around was clapping, when she saw Mr. Barrow's face red and indignant in the door. Next time the doorway spun around she yelled over her shoulder. "Be back in a minute, teacher." The face disappeared. She was dizzy but Pierre caught her and held her tight; he smelt of perfume but still she liked having him hold her tight.

He suggested they go somewhere else, "Mademoiselle Sistair," he whispered, "allow us to show you the mystères de Paree . . . afterwards we can come back to your plus orsairs. They will probably become intoxicate . . . plus orsairs invariably intoxicate." They laughed. He had grey eyes and light hair, he said he was a Norman. She said he was the nicest Frenchman she'd ever met. She had a hard time getting her coat from the checkroom because she didn't have any check, but she went in and picked it out while Pierre talked French to the checkgirl. They got into a long low grey car; Daughter had never seen such speeding. Pierre was a fine driver though; he had a game of running full speed towards a gendarme and swerving just enough at the right moment. She said supposing he hit one; he shrugged his shoulders and said, "It does not mattair . . . they are . . . ow do you call it? . . . bloody cows." They went to Maxims, where it was too quiet for them, then to a little tough dancehall way across Paris. Daughter could see that Pierre was wellknown everywhere and an Ace. The other aviators met girls in different places and dropped away. Before she realized it she and Pierre were alone in the long grey car. "Primo," he was explaining, "we will go to Les Halles to eat soupe à l'oignon . . . and then I shall take you a little tour en avion." "Oh, please do. I've never been up in a plane . . . I'd like to go up and loop the loop . . . promise you'll loop the loop." "Entendu," he said.

They sat a little sleepily in a small empty eatingplace and ate onion soup and drank some more champagne. He was still very kind and considerate but he seemed to have exhausted his English. She thought vaguely about going back to the hotel and catching the boattrain, but all she seemed to be able to say was, "Loop the loop, promise me you'll loop the loop." His eyes had gotten a little glazy, "With Mademoiselle Sistair," he said, "I do not make love . . . I make the loop the loop."

It was a long drive out to the aviation field. A little greyness of dawn was creeping over everything. Pierre couldn't drive straight any more, so that she had to grab the wheel once or twice to steady him. When they drew up with a jerk at the field she could see the row of hangars and three planes standing out in deepest blue and beyond, rows of poplartrees against the silver rim of the plain. Overhead the sky sagged heavily like a wet tent. Daughter got out of the car shivering. Pierre was staggering a little. "Perhaps you will go instead to bed . . . to bed it is very good," he said yawning. She put her arm around him, "You promised you'd take me up and loop the loop." "Allright," he said angrily and walked towards one of the planes. He fumbled with the engine a while and she could hear him swearing in French. Then he went into the hangar to wake up a mechanic. Daughter stood there shivering in the growing silvery light. She wouldn't think of anything. She wanted to go up in a plane. Her head ached but she didn't feel nauseated. When the mechanic came back with Pierre she could make out that he was arguing with him trying to make him give up the flight. She got very sore: "Pierre, you've got to take me up," she yelled at the two men sleepily arguing in French. "Aw-right, Mademoiselle Sistair." They wrapped a heavy armycoat around her and strapped her very carefully in the observer's seat. Pierre climbed into the pilot seat. It was a Bleriot monoplane, he said. The mechanic spun the propeller. The engine started. Everything was full of the roar of the engine. Suddenly she was scared and sober, thought about home and Dad and Buster and the boat she was going to take tomorrow, no it was today. It seemed an endless time with the engine roaring. The light was brighter. She started to fumble with the straps to unstrap them. It was crazy going up like this. She had to catch that boat. The plane had started. It was bouncing over the field, bouncing along the ground. They were still on the ground rumbling bouncing along. Maybe it wouldn't go up. She hoped it wouldn't go up. A row of poplars swept past below them. The motor was a settled roar now, they were climbing. It was daylight; a cold silver sun shone in her face. Underneath them was a floor of thick white clouds like a beach. She was terribly cold and stunned by the roar of the motor. The man in goggles in front of her turned around and yelled something. She couldn't hear. She'd forgotten who Pierre was. She stretched her hand out towards him and waved it around. The plane went on climbing steadily. She began to see hills standing up in the light on either side of the white beach of clouds, must be the valley of the Seine full of fog; where was Paris? They were plunging into the sun, no, no, don't, don't, now it's the end. The white clouds were a ceiling overhead, the sun spun around once first fast then slowly then the plane was climbing again. She felt terribly sick, she was afraid she was going to faint. Dying must be like this. Perhaps she'd have a miscarriage. Her body was throbbing with the roar of the engine. She had barely strength enough to stretch her hand toward him again and make the same motion. The same thing again. This time she didn't feel so bad. They were climbing again into the blue sky, a wind must have come up because the plane was lunging a little, took an occasional sickening drop into a pocket. The face in the goggles turned around and swayed from side to side. She thought the lips formed the words, No good; but now she could see Paris like an embroidered pincushion, with all the steeples and the Eiffel Tower and the towers of the Trocadèro sticking up through a milky haze. The Sacré Cœur on Montmartre was very white and cast a shadow clear to the garden that looked like a map. Then it was behind them and they were circling over green country. It was rough and she began to feel sick again. There was a ripping sound of some kind. A little wire waving loose and glistening against the blue began to whine. She tried to yell to the man in the goggles. He turned and saw her waving and went up into another dive. This time. No. Paris, the Eiffel Tower, the Sacré Cœur, the green fields spun. They were climbing again. Daughter saw the shine of a wing gliding by itself a little way from the plane. The spinning sun blinded her as they dropped.

Newsreel XXXIX

spectacle of ruined villages and tortured earth "the work of fiends" wrings heart of Mr. Hugh C. Wallace during his visit to wasted and shelltorn regions

WHIPPET TANKS ON FIFTH AVENUE STIR LOAN ENTHUSIASM

U. S. MOBILIZES IN ORIENT AGAINST
JAP MENACE

Rule Britannia, rule the waves
Britains never never shall be slaves

YOUNG WOMAN FOUND STRANGLED IN YONKERS

the socialrevolutionaries are the agents of Denekine, Kolchak and the Allied Imperial Armies. I was one of the organizers of the Soldiers, Sailors and Workmen's council in Seattle. There is the same sentiment in this meeting that appeared at our first meeting in Seattle when 5000 men in uniform attended. EX-KAISER SPENDS HOURS IN WRITING. Speaking broadly their choice is between revolutionary socialism and anarchy. England already has plunged into socialism, France hesitates, Belgium has gone, Italy is going, while Lenine's shadow grows stronger and stronger over the conference.

TEN SHIPS LAID BARRIER OF SUDDEN DEATH FROM ORKNEYS TO SKAGGERAK

NO COAL? TRY PEAT

If you want to find the generals
I know where they are
If you want to find the generals
I know where they are

masses still don't know how the war started, how it was conducted or how it ended, declared Maximilian Harden. The war ministry was stormed by demonstrators who dragged our Herr Neuring and threw him into the Elbe where he was shot and killed as he tried to swim to the bank

VICIOUS PRACTICES RESPONSIBLE FOR HIGH LIVING
COST, WILSON TELLS CONGRESS

I saw them
I saw them
Down in the
Deep dugout

The Camera Eye (41)

arent you coming to the anarchist picnic   there's going to be an anarchist picnic sure you've got to come to the anarchist picnic this afternoon it was way out at Garches in a kind of park it took a long time to get out there we were late there were youngsters and young girls with glasses and old men with their whiskers and long white zits and everybody wore black artist ties   some had taken off their shoes and stockings and were wandering around in the long grass   a young man with a black artist tie was reading a poem   Voilà said a voice c'est plûtot le geste proletaire it was a nice afternoon we sat on the grass and looked around le geste proletaire

But God damn it they've got all the machineguns in the world all the printingpresses linotypes tickerribbon curling irons plushhorses Ritz and we   you   I?   barehands a few songs not very good songs plûtot le geste proletaire

Les bourgeois à la lanterne nom de dieu

et l'humanité la futurité la lutte des classes l'inépuisible angoisse des foules la misère du travailleur tu sais mon vieux sans blague

it was chilly early summer gloaming among the eighteenthcenturyshaped trees when we started home   I sat on the impériale of the third class car with the daughter of the Libertaire (that's Patrick

Henry ours after all give me or death) a fine girl her father she said never let her go out alone never let her see any young men it was like being in a convent she wanted liberty fraternity equality and a young man to take her out in the tunnels the coalgas made us cough and she wanted l'Amérique la vie le theatre le feev o'clock le smoking le foxtrot she was a nice girl we sat side by side on the roof of the car and looked at the banlieue de Paris a desert of little gingerbread brick maisonettes flattening out under the broad gloom of evening she and I tu sais mon ami but what kind of goddam management is this?

Newsreel XL

CRIMINAL IN PYJAMAS SAWS BARS;
SCALES WALLS; FLEES

Italians! against all and everything remember that the beacon is lighted at Fiume and that all harangues are contained in the words: Fiume or Death.

Criez au quatre vents que je n'accepte aucune transaction. Le reste ici contre tout le monde et je prépare de très mauvais jours.

Criez cela je vous prie a tû-tête

the call for enlistments mentions a chance for gold service stripes, opportunities for big game hunting and thrilling watersports added to the general advantages of travel in foreign countries

> *Chi va piano*
> *Va sano*
> *Chi va forte*
> *Va 'la morte*
> *Evviva la libertá*

EARTHQUAKE IN ITALY DEVASTATES
LIKE WAR

only way Y.M.C.A. girls can travel is on troop ships; part of fleet will go seaward to help Wilson

DEMPSEY KNOCKS OUT WILLARD
IN THIRD ROUND

Ils sont sourds.
Je vous embrasse.
Le cœur de Fiume est à vous.

Joe Hill

A young Swede name Hillstrom went to sea, got himself cal-
loused hands on sailingships and tramps, learned English in the
focastle of the steamers that make the run from Stockholm to Hull,
dreamed the Swede's dream of the west;

when he got to America they gave him a job polishing cuspidors
in a Bowery saloon.

He moved west to Chicago and worked in a machineshop.

He moved west and followed the harvest, hung around employ-
ment agencies, paid out many a dollar for a job in a construction
camp, walked out many a mile when the grub was too bum, or the
boss too tough, or too many bugs in the bunkhouse;

read Marx and the I.W.W. Preamble and dreamed about forming the structure of the new society within the shell of the old.

He was in California for the S.P. strike (*Casey Jones, two locomotives, Casey Jones*), used to play the concertina outside the bunkhouse
door, after supper, evenings (*Longhaired preachers come out every
night*), had a knack for setting rebel words to tunes (*And the union
makes us strong*).

Along the coast in cookshacks flophouses jungles wobblies ho-
boes bindlestiffs began singing Joe Hill's songs. They sang 'em in the
county jails of the State of Washington, Oregon, California, Nevada,
Idaho, in the bullpens in Montana and Arizona, sang 'em in Walla
Walla, San Quentin and Leavenworth,

forming the structure of the new society within the jails of the
old.

At Bingham, Utah, Joe Hill organized the workers of the Utah
Construction Company in the One Big Union, won a new wage-
scale, shorter hours, better grub. (The angel Moroni didn't like
labororganizers any better than the Southern Pacific did.)

The angel Moroni moved the hearts of the Mormons to decide it
was Joe Hill shot a grocer named Morrison. The Swedish consul and
President Wilson tried to get him a new trial but the angel Moroni
moved the hearts of the supreme court of the State of Utah to sustain

the verdict of guilty. He was in jail a year, went on making up songs. In November 1915 he was stood up against the wall in the jail yard in Salt Lake City.

"Don't mourn for me organize," was the last word he sent out to the workingstiffs of the I.W.W. Joe Hill stood up against the wall of the jail yard, looked into the muzzles of the guns and gave the word to fire.

They put him in a black suit, put a stiff collar around his neck and a bow tie, shipped him to Chicago for a bangup funeral, and photographed his handsome stony mask staring into the future.

The first of May they scattered his ashes to the wind.

Ben Compton

The history of all hitherto existing society is the history of class struggles. . . .

The old people were Jews but at school Benny always said no he wasn't a Jew he was an American because he'd been born in Brooklyn and lived at 2531 25th Avenue in Flatbush and they owned their home. The teacher in the seventh grade said he squinted and sent him home with a note, so Pop took an afternoon off from the jewelry store where he worked with a lens in his eye repairing watches, to take Benny to an optician who put drops in his eyes and made him read little teeny letters on a white card. Pop seemed tickled when the optician said Benny had to wear glasses, "Vatchmaker's eyes . . . takes after his old man," he said and patted his cheek. The steel eyeglasses were heavy on Benny's nose and cut into him behind the ears. It made him feel funny to have Pop telling the optician that a boy with glasses wouldn't be a bum and a baseball player like Sam and Isidore but would attend to his studies and be a lawyer and a scholar like the men of old. "A rabbi maybe," said the optician, but Pop said rabbis were loafers and lived on the blood of the poor, he and the old woman still ate kosher and kept the sabbath like their fathers but synagogue and the rabbis . . . he made a spitting sound with his lips. The optician laughed and said as for himself he was a freethinker but religion was good for the commonpeople. When they got home momma said the glasses made Benny look awful old. Sam and Izzy yelled, "Hello, foureyes," when they came in from selling papers, but at school next day they told the other kids it was a statesprison offence to roughhouse a feller with glasses. Once he had the glasses Benny got to be very good at his lessons.

In highschool he made the debating team. When he was thirteen Pop had a long illness and had to give up work for a year. They lost the house that was almost paid for and went to live in a flat on Myrtle Avenue. Benny got work in a drugstore evenings. Sam and Izzy left home, Sam to work in a furrier's in Newark; Izzy had gotten to loafing in poolparlors so Pop threw him out. He'd always been a good athlete and palled around with an Irishman named Pug Riley who was going to get him into the ring. Momma cried and Pop forbade any of the kids to mention his name; still they all knew that Gladys, the oldest one, who was working as a stenographer over in Manhattan, sent Izzy a five dollar bill now and then. Benny looked much older than he was and hardly ever thought of anything except making money so the old people could have a house of their own again. When he grew up he'd be a lawyer and a business man and make a pile quick so that Gladys could quit work and get married and the old people could buy a big house and live in the country. Momma used to tell him about how when she was a young maiden in the old country they used to go out in the woods after strawberries and mushrooms and stop by a farmhouse and drink milk all warm and foamy from the cow. Benny was going to get rich and take them all out in the country for a trip to a summer resort.

When Pop was well enough to work again he rented half a twofamily house in Flatbush where at least they'd be away from the noise of the elevated. The same year Benny graduated from highschool and won a prize for an essay on The American Government. He'd gotten very tall and thin and had terrible headaches. The old people said he'd outgrown himself and took him to see Dr. Cohen who lived on the same block but had his office downtown near Borough Hall. The doctor said he'd have to give up night work and studying too hard, what he needed was something that would keep him outdoors and develop his body. "All work and no play makes Jack a dull boy," he said, scratching the grizzled beard under his chin. Benny said he had to make some money this summer because he wanted to go to New York University in the fall. Dr. Cohen said he ought to eat plenty of milkdishes and fresh eggs and go somewhere where he could be out in the sun and take it easy all summer. He charged two dollars. Walking home the old man kept striking his forehead with the flat of his hand and saying he was a failure, thirty years he had worked in America and now he was a sick old man all used up and couldn't provide for his children. Momma cried. Gladys told them not to be silly, Benny was a clever boy and a bright student and what was the use of all his booklearning if he couldn't think up some way of getting a job in the country. Benny went to bed without saying anything.

A few days later Izzy came home. He rang the doorbell as soon as the old man had gone to work one morning. "You almost met Pop," said Benny who opened the door. "Nutten doin'. I waited round the corner till I seen him go. . . . How's everybody?" Izzy had on a light grey suit and a green necktie and wore a fedora hat to match the suit. He said he had to get to Lancaster, Pennsylvania, to fight a Filipino featherweight on Saturday. "Take me with you," said Benny. "You ain't tough enough, kid . . . too much the momma's boy." In the end Benny went with him. They rode on the L to Brooklyn Bridge and then walked across New York to the ferry. They bought tickets to Elizabeth. When the train stopped in a freightyard they sneaked forward into the blind baggage. At West Philadelphia they dropped off and got chased by the yard detective. A brewery wagon picked them up and carried them along the road as far as West Chester. They had to walk the rest of the way. A Mennonite farmer let them spend the night in the barn, but in the morning he wouldn't let them have any breakfast until they'd chopped wood for two hours. By the time they got to Lancaster Benny was all in. He went to sleep in the lockerroom at the Athletic Club and didn't wake up until the fight was over. Izzy had knocked out the Filipino featherweight in the third round and won a purse of twentyfive dollars. He sent Benny over to a lodginghouse with the shine who took care of the lockerroom and went out with the boys to paint the town red. Next morning he turned up with his face green and got his eyes bloodshot; he'd spent all his money, but he'd gotten Benny a job helping a feller who did a little smalltime fightpromoting and ran a canteen in a construction camp up near Mauch Chunk.

It was a road job. Ben stayed there for two months earning ten dollars a week and his keep. He learned to drive a team and to keep books. The boss of the canteen, Hiram Volle, gypped the construction workers in their accounts, but Benny didn't think much about it because they were most of 'em wops, until he got to be friends with a young fellow named Nick Gigli who worked with the gang at the gravelpit. Nick used to hang around the canteen before closingtime in the evening; then they'd go out and smoke a cigarette together and talk. Sundays they'd walk out in the country with the Sunday paper and fool around all afternoon lying in the sun and talking about the articles in the magazine section. Nick was from north Italy and all the men in the gang were Sicilians, so he was lonely. His father and elder brothers were anarchists and he was too; he told Benny about Bakunin and Malatesta and said Benny ought to be ashamed of himself for wanting to get to be a rich businessman; sure he ought to study and learn, maybe he ought to get to be a lawyer, but he ought to work for the revolution and the working class, to be a business man was to be a shark and a robber like that son of a bitch Volle. He taught Benny to roll cigarettes and told him about all the girls that were in love with him; that girl in the boxoffice of the movie in Mauch Chunk; he could have her anytime he wanted, but a revolutionist ought to be careful about the girls he went with, women took a classconscious working man's mind off his aims, they were the main seduction of capitalist society. Ben asked him if he thought he ought to throw up his job with Volle, because Volle was such a crook, but Nick said any other capitalist would be the same, all they could do was wait for the Day. Nick was eighteen with bitter brown eyes and a skin almost as dark as a mulatto's. Ben thought he was great on account of all he'd done; he'd shined shoes, been a sailor, a miner, a dishwasher and had worked in textile mills, shoefactories and a cement factory and had had all kinds of women and been in jail for three weeks in the Paterson strike. Round the camp if any of the wops saw Ben going anywhere alone he'd yell at him, "Hey, kid, where's Nick?"

On Friday evening there was an argument in front of the window where the construction boss was paying the men off. That night, when Ben was getting into his bunk in the back of the tarpaper shack the canteen was in, Nick came around and whispered in his ear that the bosses had been gypping the men on time and that they were going on strike tomorrow. Ben said if they went out he'd go out too. Nick called him a brave comrade in Italian and hauled off and kissed him on both cheeks. Next morning only a few of the pick and shovel men turned out when the whistle blew. Ben hung around the door of the cookshack not knowing what to do with himself. Volle noticed him and told him to hitch up the team to go down to the station after a box of tobacco. Ben looked at his feet and said he couldn't because he was on strike. Volle burst out laughing and told him to quit his kidding, funniest thing he'd ever heard of a kike walking out with a lot of wops. Ben felt himself go cold and stiff all over: "I'm not a kike any more'n you are. . . . I'm an American born . . . and I'm goin' to stick with my class, you dirty crook." Volle turned white and stepped up and shook a big fist under Ben's nose and said he was fired and that if he wasn't a little f—g shrimp of a foureyed kike he'd knock his goddam block off, anyway his brother sure would give him a whaling when he heard about it.

Ben went to his bunk and rolled his things into a bundle and went off to find Nick. Nick was a little down the road where the bunkhouses were, in the center of a bunch of wops all yelling and waving their arms. The superintendent and the gangbosses all turned out with revolvers in black holsters strapped around their waists and one of them made a speech in English and another one Sicilian saying that this was a squareshooting concern that had always treated laborers square and if they didn't like it they could get the hell out. They'd never had a strike and didn't propose to begin now. There was big money involved in this job and the company wasn't going to work and see it tied up by any goddam foolishness. Any man who wasn't on his job next time the whistle blew was fired and would have to get a move on and remember that the State of Pennsylvania had vagrancy laws. When the whistle blew again everybody went back to work except Ben and Nick. They walked off down the road with their bundles. Nick had tears in his eyes and was saying, "Too much gentle, too much patient . . . we do not know our strength yet."

That night they found a brokendown schoolhouse a little off the road on a hill above a river. They'd bought some bread and peanut butter at a store and sat out in front eating it and talking about what they'd do. By the time they'd finished eating it was dark. Ben had never been out in the country alone like that at night. The wind rustled the woods all around and the rapid river seethed down in the valley. It was a chilly August night with a heavy dew. They didn't have any covering so Nick showed Ben how to take his jacket off and put it over his head and how to sleep against the wall to keep from getting sore lying on the bare boards. He'd hardly gotten to sleep when he woke up icycold and shaking. There was a window broken; he could see the frame and the jagged bits of glass against the cloudy moon-light. He lay back, musta been dreaming. Something banged on the roof and rolled down the shingles over his head and dropped to the ground. "Hay, Ben, for chrissake wassat?" came Nick's voice in a hoarse whisper. They both got up and stared out through the broken windowframe.

"That was busted before," said Nick. He walked over and opened the outside door. They both shivered in the chilly wind up the valley that rustled the trees like rain, the river down below made a creaking grinding noise like a string of carts and wagons.

A stone hit the roof above them and rolled off. The next one went between their heads and hit the cracked plaster of the wall behind. Ben heard the click of the blade as Nick opened his pocketknife. He strained his eyes till the tears came but he couldn't make out anything but the leaves stirring in the wind.

"You come outa there . . . come up here . . . talk . . . you son of a bitch," yelled Nick.

There was no answer.

"What do you think?" whispered Nick over his shoulder to Ben.

Ben didn't say anything; he was trying to keep his teeth from chat-tering. Nick pushed him back in and pulled the door to. They piled the dusty benches against the door and blocked up the lower part of the window with boards out of the floor.

"Break in. I keell one of him anyhow," said Nick. "You don't believe in speerits?"

"Naw, no such thing," said Ben. They sat down side by side on the floor with their backs to the cracked plaster and listened. Nick had put the knife down between them. He took Ben's fingers and made him feel the catch that held the blade steady. "Good knife . . . sailor knife," he whispered. Ben strained his ears. Only the spattering sound of the wind in the trees and the steady grind of the river. No more stones came.

Next morning they left the schoolhouse at first day. Neither of them had had any sleep. Ben's eyes were stinging. When the sun came up they found a man who was patching up a broken spring on a truck. They helped him jack it up with a block of wood and he gave them a lift into Scranton where they got jobs washing dishes in a hashjoint run by a Greek.

. . . all fixed fastfrozen relations, with their train of ancient and venerable prejudices and opinions, are swept away, all newformed ones become antiquated before they can ossify. . . .

Pearldiving wasn't much to Ben's taste, so at the end of a couple of weeks, as he'd saved up the price of the ticket, he said he was going back home to see the old people. Nick stayed on because a girl in a candystore had fallen for him. Later he'd go up to Allentown, where a brother of his had a job in a steelmill and was making big money. The last thing he said when he went down and put Ben on the train for New York was, "Benny, you learn and study . . . be great man for workingclass and remember too much girls bad business."

Ben hated leaving Nick but he had to get home to find a job for the winter that would give him time to study. He took the exams and matriculated at the College of the City of New York. The old man borrowed a hundred dollars from the Morris Plan to get him started and Sam sent him twentyfive from Newark to buy books with. Then he made a little money himself working in Kahn's drugstore evenings. Sunday afternoons he went to the library and read Marx's *Capital*. He joined the Socialist Party and went to lectures at the Rand School whenever he got a chance. He was working to be a wellsharpened instrument.

The next spring he got sick with scarlet fever and was ten weeks in the hospital. When he got out his eyes were so bad it gave him a headache to read for an hour. The old man owed the Morris Plan another hundred dollars besides the first hundred dollars and the interest and the investigation fees.

Ben had met a girl at a lecture at Cooper Union who had worked in a textile mill over in Jersey. She'd been arrested during the Paterson strike and had been blacklisted. Now she was a salesgirl at Wanamaker's, but her folks still worked in the Botany Mill at Passaic. Her name was Helen Mauer; she was five years older than Ben, a pale blonde and already had lines in her face. She said there was nothing in the socialist movement; it was the syndicalists had the right idea. After the lecture she took him to the Cosmopolitan Café on 2nd Avenue to have a glass of tea and introduced him to some people she said were real rebels; when Ben told Gladys and the old people about them the old man said, "Pfooy . . . radical jews," and made a spitting sound with his lips. He said Benny ought to cut out these monkeyshines and get to work. He was getting old and now he was in debt, and if he got sick it would be up to Benny to support him and the old woman. Ben said he was working all the time but that your folks didn't count, it was the workingclass that he was working for. The old man got red in the face and said his family was sacred and next to that his own people. Momma and Gladys cried. The old man got to his feet; choking and coughing, he raised his hands above his head and cursed Ben and Ben left the house.

He had no money on him and was still weak from the scarlet fever. He walked across Brooklyn and across the Manhattan Bridge and up through the East Side, all full of ruddy lights and crowds and pushcarts and vegetables that smelt of the spring, to the house where Helen lived on East 6th Street. The landlady said he couldn't go up to her room. Helen said it wasn't any of her business but while they were arguing about it his ears began to ring and he fainted on the hall settee. When he came to with water running down his neck Helen helped him up the four flights and made him lie down on her bed. She yelled down to the landlady who was screaming about the police, that she would leave first thing in the morning and nothing in the world could make her leave sooner. She made Ben some tea and they sat up all night talking on her bed. They decided that they'd live in free union together and spent the rest of the night packing her things. She had mostly books and pamphlets.

Next morning they went out at six o'clock, because she had to be at Wanamaker's at eight, to look for a room. They didn't exactly tell the next landlady they weren't married, but when she said, "So you're bride and groom?" they nodded and smiled. Fortunately Helen had enough money in her purse to pay the week in advance. Then she had to run off to work. Ben didn't have any money to buy anything to eat so he lay on the bed reading *Progress and Poverty* all day. When she came back in the evening she brought in some supper from a delicatessen. Eating the rye bread and salami they were very happy. She had such large breasts for such a slender little girl. He had to go out to a drugstore to buy some safeties because she said how could she have a baby just now when they had to give all their strength to the movement. There were bedbugs in the bed, but they told each other that they were as happy as they could be under the capitalist system, that some day they'd have a free society where workers wouldn't have to huddle in filthy lodginghouses full of bedbugs or row with landladies and lovers could have babies if they wanted to.

A few days later Helen was laid off from Wanamaker's because they were cutting down their personnel for the slack summer season. They went over to Jersey where she went to live with her folks and Ben got a job in the shipping department of a worsted mill. They rented a room together in Passaic. When a strike came he and Helen were both on the committee. Ben got to be quite a speechmaker. He was arrested several times and almost had his skull cracked by a policeman's billy and got six months in jail out of it. But he'd found out that when he got up on a soapbox to talk he could make people listen to him, that he could talk and say what he thought and get a laugh or a cheer out of the massed upturned faces. When he stood up in court to take his sentence he started to talk about surplus value. The strikers in the audience cheered and the judge had the attendants clear the courtroom. Ben could see the reporters busily taking down what he said; he was glad to be a living example of the injustice and brutality of the capitalist system. The judge shut him up by saying he'd give him another six months for contempt of court if he didn't keep quiet, and Ben was taken to the county jail in an automobile full of special deputies with riot guns. The papers spoke of him as a wellknown socialist agitator.

In jail Ben got to be friends with a wobbly named Bram Hicks, a tall youngster from Frisco with light hair and blue eyes who told him if he wanted to know the labormovement he ought to get him a red card and go out to the Coast. Bram was a boilermaker by profession but had shipped as a sailor for a change and landed in Perth Amboy broke. He'd been working on the repairshift of one of the mills and had gone out with the rest. He'd pushed a cop in the face when they'd broken up a picketline and been sent up for six months for assault and battery. Meeting him once a day in the prison yard was the one thing kept Ben going in jail.

They were both released on the same day. They walked along the street together. The strike was over. The mills were running. The streets where there'd been picketlines, the hall where Ben had made speeches looked quiet and ordinary. He took Bram around to Helen's. She wasn't there, but after a while she came in with a little redfaced ferretnosed Englishman whom she introduced as Billy, an English comrade. First thing Ben guessed that he was sleeping with her. He left Bram in the room with the Englishman and beckoned her outside. The narrow upper hall of the old frame house smelt of vinegar. "You're through with me?" he asked in a shaky voice.

"Oh, Ben, don't act so conventional."

"You mighta waited till I got outa jail."

"But can't you see that we're all comrades? You're a brave fighter and oughtn't to be so conventional, Ben. . . . Billy doesn't mean anything to me. He's a steward on a liner. He'll be going away soon."

"Then I don't mean anything to you either." He grabbed Helen's wrist and squeezed it as hard as he could. "I guess I'm all wrong, but I'm crazy about you. . . . I thought you . . ."

"Ouch, Ben . . . you're talkin' silly, you know how much I like you." They went back in the room and talked about the movement. Ben said he was going west with Bram Hicks.

. . . he becomes an appendage of the machine and it is only the most simple, most monotonous, most easily required knack that is required of him. . . .

Bram knew all the ropes. Walking, riding blind baggage or on empty gondolas, hopping rides on delivery wagons and trucks, they got to Buffalo. In a flophouse there Bram found a guy he knew who got them signed on as deckhands on a whaleback going back light to Duluth. In Duluth they joined a gang being shipped up to harvest wheat for an outfit in Saskatchewan. At first the work was very heavy for Ben and Bram was scared he'd cave in, but the fourteen hour days out in the sun and the dust, the copious grub, the dead sleep in the lofts of the big barns began to toughen him up. Lying flat on the straw in his sweat clothes he'd still feel through his sleep the tingle of the sun on his face and neck, the strain in his muscles, the whir of the reapers and binders along the horizon, the roar of the thresher, the grind of gears of the trucks carrying the red wheat to the elevators. He began to talk like a harvest stiff. After the harvest they worked in a fruitcannery on the Columbia River, a lousy steamy job full of the sour stench of rotting fruitpeelings. There they read in *Solidarity* about the shingleweavers' strike and the free speech fight in Everett, and decided they'd go down and see what they could do to help out. The last day they worked there Bram lost the forefinger of his right hand repairing the slicing and peeling machinery. The company doctor said he couldn't get any compensation because he'd already given notice, and, besides, not being a Canadian . . . A little shyster lawyer came around to the boarding house where Bram was lying on the bed in a fever, with his hand in a big wad of bandage, and tried to get him to sue, but Bram yelled at the lawyer to get the hell out. Ben said he was wrong, the working class ought to have its lawyers too.

When the hand had healed a little they went down on the boat from Vancouver to Seattle. I.W.W. headquarters there was like a picnic ground, crowded with young men coming in from every part of the U.S. and Canada. One day a big bunch went down to Everett on the boat to try to hold a meeting at the corner of Wetmore and Hewitt Avenues. The dock was full of deputies with rifles, and revolvers. "The Commercial Club boys are waiting for us," some guy's voice tittered nervously. The deputies had white handkerchiefs around their necks. "There's Sheriff McRae," said somebody. Bram edged up to Ben. "We better stick together. . . . Looks to me like we was goin' to get tamped up some." The wobblies were arrested as fast as they stepped off the boat and herded down to the end of the dock. The deputies were drunk most of them, Ben could smell the whisky on the breath of the redfaced guy who grabbed him by the arm. "Get a move on there, you son of a bitch . . ." He got a blow from a riflebutt in the small of the back. He could hear the crack of saps on men's skulls. Anybody who resisted had his face beaten to a jelly with a club. The wobblies were made to climb up into a truck. With the dusk a cold drizzle had come on. "Boys, we got to show 'em we got guts," a redhaired boy said. A deputy who was holding on to the back of the truck aimed a blow at him with his sap but lost his balance and fell off. The wobblies laughed. The deputy climbed on again, purple in the face. "You'll be laughin' outa the other side of your dirty mugs when we get through with you," he yelled.

Out in the woods where the county road crossed the railroad track they were made to get out of the trucks. The deputies stood around them with their guns leveled while the sheriff who was reeling drunk, and two welldressed middleaged men talked over what they'd do. Ben heard the word gauntlet. "Look here, sheriff," somebody said, "we're not here to make any kind of disturbance. All we want's our constitutional rights of free speech." The sheriff turned towards them waving the butt of his revolver, "Oh, you do, do you, you c——s. Well, this is Snohomish county and you ain't goin' to forget it . . . if you come here

again some of you fellers is goin' to die, that's all there is about it. . . .
All right, boys, let's go."

The deputies made two lines down towards the railroad track.
They grabbed the wobblies one by one and beat them up. Three of
them grabbed Ben. "You a wobbly?" "Sure I am, you dirty yellow . . ."
he began. The sheriff came up and hauled off to hit him. "Look out,
he's got glasses on." A big hand pulled the glasses off. "We'll fix that."
Then the sheriff punched him in the nose with his fist. "Say you ain't."
Ben's mouth was full of blood. He set his jaw. "He's a kike, hit him
again for me." "Say, you ain't a wobbly." Somebody whacked a rifle-
barrel against his shins and he fell forward. "Run for it," they were
yelling. Blows with clubs and riflebutts were splitting his ears.

He tried to walk forward without running. He tripped on a rail and
fell, cutting his arm on something sharp. There was so much blood in
his eyes he couldn't see. A heavy boot was kicking him again and
again in the side. He was passing out. Somehow he staggered forward.
Somebody was holding him up under the arms and was dragging him
free of the cattleguard on the track. Another fellow began to wipe his
face off with a handkerchief. He heard Bram's voice way off somewhere, "We're over the county line, boys." What with losing his glasses
and the rain and the night and the shooting pain all up and down his
back Ben couldn't see anything. He heard shots behind them and yells
from where other guys were running the gauntlet. He was the center
of a little straggling group of wobblies making their way down the
railroad track. "Fellow workers," Bram was saying in his deep quiet
voice, "we must never forget this night."

At the interurban trolley station they took up a collection among
the ragged and bloody group to buy tickets to Seattle for the guys
most hurt. Ben was so dazed and sick he could hardly hold the ticket
when somebody pushed it into his hand. Bram and the rest of them
set off to walk the thirty miles back to Seattle.

Ben was in hospital three weeks. The kicks in the back had affected
his kidneys and he was in frightful pain most of the time. The mor-
phine they gave him made him so dopey he barely knew what was
happening when they brought in the boys wounded in the shooting
on the Everett dock on November 5th. When he was discharged he
could just walk. Everybody he knew was in jail. At General Delivery
he found a letter from Gladys enclosing fifty dollars and saying his father wanted him to come home.

The Defense Committee told him to go ahead; he was just the man to raise funds for them in the east. An enormous amount of money would be needed for the defense of the seventyfour wobblies held in the Everett jail charged with murder. Ben hung around Seattle for a couple of weeks doing odd jobs for the Defense Committee, trying to figure out a way to get home. A sympathizer who worked in a shipping office finally got him a berth as supercargo on a freighter that was going to New York through the Panama canal. The sea trip and the detailed clerical work helped him to pull himself together. Still there wasn't a night he didn't wake up with a nightmare scream in his throat sitting up in his bunk dreaming the deputies were coming to get him to make him run the gauntlet. When he got to sleep again he'd dream he was caught in the cattleguard and the teeth were tearing his arms and heavy boots were kicking him in the back. It got so it took all his nerve to lie down in his bunk to go to sleep. The men on the ship thought he was a hophead and steered clear of him. It was a great day when he saw the tall buildings of New York shining in the brown morning haze.

... when in the course of development class distinctions have disappeared and all production has been concentrated in the hands of a vast association of the whole nation, the public power will lose its political character....

Ben lived at home that winter because it was cheaper. When he told Pop he was going to study law in the office of a radical lawyer named Morris Stein whom he'd met in connection with raising money for the Everett boys, the old may was delighted. "A clever lawyer can protect the workers and the poor Jews and make money too," he said, rubbing his hands. "Benny, I always knew you were a good boy." Momma nodded and smiled. "Because in this country it's not like over there under the warlords, even a lazy bum's got constitootional rights, that's why they wrote the constitootion for." It made Ben feel sick talking to them about it.

He worked as a clerk in Stein's office on lower Broadway and in the evenings addressed protest meetings about the Everett massacre. Morris Stein's sister Fanya, who was a thin dark wealthy woman about thirtyfive, was an ardent pacifist and made him read Tolstoy and Kropotkin. She believed that Wilson would keep the country out of the European war and sent money to all the women's peace organizations. She had a car and used to run him around town sometimes when he had several meetings in one evening. His heart would always be thumping when he went into the hall where the meeting was and began to hear the babble and rustle of the audience filing in, garment workers on the East Side, waterfront workers in Brooklyn, workers in chemical and metalproducts plants in Newark, parlor socialists and pinks at the Rand School or on lower Fifth Avenue, the vast anonymous mass of all classes, races, trades in Madison Square Garden. His hands would always be cold when he shook hands with the chairman and other speakers on the platform. When his turn came to speak there'd be a moment when all the faces looking up at him would blur into a mass of pink, the hum of the hall would deafen him, he'd be in a panic for fear he'd forgotten what he wanted to say. Then all at once he'd hear his own voice enunciating clearly and firmly, feel its reverberance along the walls and ceiling, feel ears growing tense, men and women leaning forward in their chairs, see the rows of faces quite clearly, the groups of people who couldn't find seats crowding at the doors. Phrases like *protest, massaction, united workingclass of this country and the world, revolution,* would light up the eyes and faces under him like the glare of a bonfire.

After the speech he'd feel shaky, his glasses would be so misted he'd have to wipe them, he'd feel all the awkwardness of his tall gangling frame. Fanya would get him away as soon as she could, tell him with shining eyes that he'd spoken magnificently, take him downtown, if the meeting had been in Manhattan, to have some supper in the Brevoort basement or at the Cosmopolitan Café before he went home on the subway to Brooklyn. He knew that she was in love with him, but they rarely talked about anything outside of the movement.

When the Russian revolution came in February, Ben and the Steins bought every edition of the papers for weeks, read all the correspondents' reports with desperate intentness; it was the dawning of The Day. There was a feeling of carnival all down the East Side and in the Jewish sections of Brooklyn. The old people cried whenever they spoke of it. "Next Austria, then the Reich, then England . . . freed peoples everywhere," Pop would say. "And last, Uncle Sam," Ben would add, grimly setting his jaw.

The April day Woodrow Wilson declared war, Fanya went to bed with a hysterical crying fit. Ben went up to see her at the apartment

Morris Stein and his wife had on Riverside Drive. She'd come back from Washington the day before. She'd been up there with a women's peace delegation trying to see the President. The detectives had run them off the White House lawn and several girls had been arrested. "What did you expect? . . . of course the capitalists want war. They'll think a little different when they find what they're getting's a revolution." She begged him to stay with her, but he left saying he had to go see them down at *The Call.* As he left the house, he found himself making a spitting noise with his lips like his father. He told himself he'd never go there again.

He registered for the draft on Stein's advice, though he wrote *conscientious objector* on the card. Soon after that he and Stein quarrelled. Stein said there was nothing to it but to bow before the storm; Ben said he was going to agitate against it until he was put in jail. That meant he was out of a job and it was the end of his studying law. Kahn wouldn't take him back in his drugstore because he was afraid the cops would raid him if it got to be known he had a radical working for him. Ben's brother Sam was working in a munition factory at Perth Amboy and making big money; he kept writing Ben to stop his foolishness and get a job there too. Even Gladys told him it was silly to ram his head against a stone wall. In July he left home and went back to live with Helen Mauer over in Passaic. His number hadn't been called yet, so it was easy to get a job in the shipping department of one of the mills. They were working overtime and losing hands fast by the draft.

The Rand School had been closed up, *The Call* suspended, every day new friends were going around to Wilson's way of looking at things. Helen's folks and their friends were making good money, working overtime; they laughed or got sore at any talk of protest strikes or revolutionary movements; people were buying washing machines, liberty bonds, vacuum cleaners, making first payments on houses. The girls were buying fur coats and silk stockings. Helen and Ben began to plan to go out to Chicago, where the wobblies were putting up a fight. September 2nd came the roundup of I.W.W. officials by government agents. Ben and Helen expected to be arrested, but they were passed over. They spent a rainy Sunday huddled on the bed in their dank room, trying to decide what they ought to do. Everything they trusted was giving way under their feet. "I feel like a rat in a trap," Helen kept saying. Every now and then Ben would jump up and walk up and down hitting his forehead with the palm of his hand. "We gotta do something here, look what they're doing in Russia."

One day a warworker came around to the shipping department to sign everybody up for a Liberty Bond. He was a cockylooking young man in a yellow slicker. Ben wasn't much given to arguments during working hours, so he just shook his head and went back to the manifest he was making out. "You don't want to spoil the record of your department, do you? It's one hundred percent perfect so far." Ben tried to smile. "It seems too bad, but I guess it'll have to be." Ben could feel the eyes of the other men in the office on him. The young man in the slicker was balancing uneasily from one foot to the other. "I don't suppose you want people to think you're a pro-German or a pacifist, do you?" "They can suppose what they damn like, for all I care." "Let's see your registration card, I bet you're a slacker." "Look here, get me," said Ben, getting to his feet, "I don't believe in capitalist war and I'm not going to do anything I can help to support it." The young man in the slicker turned his back, "Oh, if you're one of them yellow bastards I won't even talk to you." Ben went back to work. That evening when he was punching the timeclock a cop stepped up to him. "Let's see your registration card, buddy." Ben brought the card out from his inside pocket. The cop read it over carefully, "Looks all right to me," he said reluctantly. At the end of the week Ben found he was fired; no reason given.

He went to the room in a panic. When Helen came back he said he was going to Mexico. "They could get me under the espionage act for what I told that guy about fighting capitalism." Helen tried to calm him down, but he said he wouldn't sleep in that room another night, so they packed their bags and went over to New York on the train. They had about a hundred dollars saved up between them. They got a room on East 8th Street under the name of Mr. and Mrs. Gold. It was the next morning that they read in the *Times* that the Maximalists had taken over the government in Petrograd with the slogan All Power to the Soviets. They were sitting in a small pastry shop on 2nd Avenue drinking their morning coffee, when Ben, who had run around to the newsstand for a paper, came back with the news. Helen began to cry: "Oh, darling, it's too good to be true. It's the world revolution. . . . Now the workers 'll see that they were being deceived by false good times, that the war's really aimed at them. Now the other armies 'll start to mutiny." Ben took her hand under the table and squeezed it hard. "We gotto work now, darling. . . . I'll go to jail here before I'll run away to Mexico. I'd acted like a yellow bastard if it hadn't been for you, Helen. . . . A man's no good alone."

They gulped their coffee and walked around to the Ferbers' house on 17th Street. Al Ferber was a doctor, a short stout man with a big paunch; he was just leaving the house to go to his office. He went back into the hall with them and yelled upstairs to his wife: "Molly, come down . . . Kerensky's run out of Petrograd with a flea in his ear . . . dressed as a woman he ran." Then he said in Yiddish to Ben that if the comrades were going to hold a meeting to send greetings to the soldiers' and peasants' government, he'd give a hundred dollars toward expenses, but his name would have to be kept out of it or else he'd lose his practice. Molly Ferber came downstairs in a quilted dressing gown and said she'd sell something and add another hundred. They spent the day going around to find comrades they had the addresses of; they didn't dare use the phone for fear of the wires being tapped.

The meeting was held at the Empire Casino in the Bronx a week later. Two Federal agents with beefsteak faces sat in the front row with a stenographer who took down everything that was said. The police closed the doors after the first couple of hundred people had come in. The speakers on the platform could hear them breaking up the crowd outside with motorcycles. Soldiers and sailors in uniform were sneaking into the gallery by ones and twos and trying to stare the speakers out of countenance.

When the old whitehaired man who was chairman of the meeting walked to the front of the stage and said, "Comrades, gentlemen of the Department of Justice and not forgetting our young wellwishers up in the gallery, we have met to send a resolution of greetings from the oppressed workers of America to the triumphant workers of Russia," everybody stood up and cheered. The crowd milling around outside cheered too. Somewhere they could hear a bunch singing the *International*. They could hear policewhistles and the dang dang of a patrol wagon. Ben noticed that Fanya Stein was in the audience; she looked pale and her eyes held onto him with a fixed feverish stare. When his turn came to speak he began by saying that on account of the kind sympathizers from Washington in the audience, he couldn't say what he wanted to say but that every man and woman in the audience who was not a traitor to their class knew what he wanted to say. . . . "The capitalist governments are digging their own graves by driving their people to slaughter in a crazy unneccessary war that nobody can benefit from except bankers and munition makers. . . . The American working class, like the working classes of the rest of the world, will learn their lesson. The profiteers are giving us instruction in the use of guns; the day will come when we will use it." "That's enough, let's go, boys," yelled a voice from the gallery. The soldiers and sailors started hustling the people out of the seats. The police from the entrances converged on the speakers. Ben and a couple of others were arrested. The men in the audience who were of conscription age were made to show their registration cards before they could leave. Ben was hustled out into a closed limousine with the blinds drawn before he could speak to Helen. He'd hardly noticed who it was had clicked the handcuffs on his wrists.

They kept him for three days without anything to eat or drink in a disused office in the Federal building on Park Row. Every few hours a new bunch of detectives would stamp into the room and question him. His head throbbing, and ready to faint with thirst, he'd face the ring of long yellow faces, jowly red faces, pimply faces, boozers' and hopheads' faces, feel the eyes boring into him; sometimes they kidded and cajoled him, and sometimes they bullied and threatened; one bunch brought in pieces of rubber hose to beat him up with. He jumped up and faced them. For some reason they didn't beat him up, but instead brought him some water and a couple of stale ham sandwiches. After that he was able to sleep a little.

An agent yanked him off his bench and led him out into a well-appointed office where he was questioned almost kindly by an elderly man at a mahogany desk with a bunch of roses on the corner of it. The smell of the roses made him feel sick. The elderly man said he could see his lawyer and Morris Stein came into the room.

"Benny," he said, "leave everything to me . . . Mr. Watkins has consented to quash all charges if you'll promise to report for military training. It seems your number's been called."

"If you let me out," Ben said in a low trembling voice, "I'll do my best to oppose capitalist war until you arrest me again." Morris Stein and Mr. Watkins looked at each other and shook their heads indulgently. "Well," said Mr. Watkins, "I can't help but admire your spirit and wish it was in a better cause." It ended by his being let out on fifteen thousand dollars bail on Morris Stein's assurance that he would do no agitating until the date of his trial. The Steins wouldn't tell him who put up the bail.

Morris and Edna Stein gave him a room in their apartment; Fanya was there all the time. They fed him good food and tried to make him drink wine with his meals and a glass of milk before going to bed. He didn't have any interest in anything, slept as much as he could, read all the books he found on the place. When Morris would try to talk to him about his case he'd shut him up, "You're doing this, Morris . . . do anything . . . why should I care. I might as well be in jail as like this." "Well, I must say that's a compliment," Fanya said laughing.

Helen Mauer called up several times to tell him how things were going. She'd always say she had no news to tell that she could say over the telephone, but he never asked her to come up to see him. About as far as he went from the Steins' apartment was to go out every day to sit for a while on a bench on the Drive and look out over the grey Hudson at the rows of frame houses on the Jersey side and the grey palisades.

The day his case came up for trial the press was full of hints of German victories. It was spring and sunny outside the broad grimy windows of the courtroom. Ben sat sleepily in the stuffy gloom. Everything seemed very simple. Stein and the Judge had their little jokes together and the Assistant District Attorney was positively genial. The jury reported "guilty" and the judge sentenced him to twenty years' imprisonment. Morris Stein filed an appeal and the judge let him stay out on bail. The only moment Ben came to life was when he was allowed to address the court before being sentenced. He made a speech about the revolutionary movement he'd been preparing all these weeks. Even as he said it it seemed silly and weak. He almost stopped in the middle. His voice strengthened and filled the courtroom as he got to the end. Even the judge and the old snuffling attendants sat up when he recited for his peroration, the last words of the communist manifesto:

In place of the old bourgeois society, with its classes and class antagonisms, we shall have an association, in which the free development of each is the condition for the free development of all.

The appeal dragged and dragged. Ben started studying law again. He wanted to work in Stein's office to pay for his keep, but Stein said it would be risky, he said the war would be over soon and the red scare would die down, so that he could get him off with a light sentence. He brought lawbooks up for him to study and promised to take him into partnership if he passed his bar exam, once he could get his citizenship restored. Edna Stein was a fat spiteful woman and rarely spoke to him; Fanya fussed over him with nervous doting attentions that made him feel sick. He slept badly and his kidneys bothered him. One night he got up and dressed and was tiptoeing down the carpeted hall towards the door with his shoes in his hand, when Fanya with her black hair down her back came out of the door of her room. She was in a nightdress that showed her skinny figure and flat breasts. "Benny, where are you going?"

"I'm going crazy here . . . I've got to get out." His teeth were chattering. "I've got to get back into the movement. . . . They'll catch me and send me to jail right away . . . it will be better like that."

"You poor boy, you're in no condition." She threw her arms round his neck and pulled him into her room.

"Fanya, you gotto let me go. . . . I might make it across the Mexican border . . . other guys have."

"You're crazy . . . and what about your bail?"

"What do I care . . . don't you see we gotto do something."

She'd pulled him down on her bed and was stroking his forehead. "Poor boy . . . I love you so, Benny, couldn't you think of me a little bit . . . just a little teeny bit . . . I could help you so much in the movement. . . . Tomorrow we'll talk about it . . . I want to help you, Benny." He let her untie his necktie.

The armistice came, and news of the peace conference, revolutionary movements all over Europe, Trotsky's armies driving the whites out of Russia. Fanya Stein told everybody she and Ben were married and took him to live with her at her studio apartment on 8th Street, where she nursed him through the flu and double pneumonia. The first day the doctor said he could go out she drove up the Hudson in her Buick sedan. They came back in the early summer gloaming to find a special delivery letter from Morris. The circuit court had denied the appeal, but reduced the sentence to ten years. The next day at noon he'd have to report to be delivered by his bondsmen to the custody of the U.S. District Court. He'd probably go to Atlanta. Soon after the letter Morris himself turned up. Fanya had broken down and was crying hysterically. Morris looked pale. "Ben," he said, "we're beaten . . . You'll have to go to Atlanta for a while . . . you'll have good company down there . . . but don't worry. We'll take your case to the President. Now that the war's over they can't keep the liberal press muzzled any more."

"That's all right," said Ben, "it's better to know the worst."

Fanya jumped up from the couch where she'd been sobbing and started screaming at her brother. When Ben went out to walk around the block he left them quarreling bitterly. He found himself looking carefully at the houses, the taxicabs, the streetlights, people's faces, a funny hydrant that had a torso like a woman's, some bottles of mineral oil stacked in a drugstore window, Nujol. He decided he'd better go over to Brooklyn to say goodbye to the old people. At the subway station he stopped. He hadn't the strength; he'd write them.

Next morning at nine he went down to Morris Stein's office with his suitcase in his hand. He'd made Fanya promise not to come. He had to tell himself several times he was going to jail, he felt as if he was going on a business trip of some kind. He had on a new suit of English tweed Fanya had bought him.

Lower Broadway was all streaked red, white and blue with flags; there were crowds of clerks and stenographers and officeboys lining both pavements where he came up out of the subway. Cops on motorcycles were keeping the street clear. From down towards the Battery came the sound of a military band playing *Keep the Home Fires Burning*. Everybody looked flushed and happy. It was hard to keep from walking in step to the music in the fresh summer morning that smelt of the harbor and ships. He had to keep telling himself: those are the people who sent Debs to jail, those are the people who shot Joe Hill, who murdered Frank Little, those are the people who beat us up in Everett, who want me to rot for ten years in jail.

The colored elevatorboy grinned at him when he took him up in the elevator, "Is they startin' to go past yet, mister?" Ben shook his head and frowned.

The lawoffice looked clean and shiny. The telephone girl had red hair and wore a gold star. There was an American flag draped over the door of Stein's private office. Stein was at his desk talking to an upperclasslooking young man in a tweed suit. "Ben," Stein said cheerily, "meet Stevens Warner . . . He's just gotten out of Charlestown, served a year for refusing to register."

"Not quite a year," said the young man, getting up and shaking hands. "I'm out on good behavior."

Ben didn't like him, in his tweed suit and his expensive looking necktie; all at once he remembered that he was wearing the same kind of suit himself. The thought made him sore. "How was it?" he asked coldly.

"Not so bad, they had me working in the greenhouse . . . They treated me fairly well when they found out I'd already been to the front."

"How was that?"

"Oh, in the ambulance service. . . . They just thought I was mildly insane. . . . It was a damned instructive experience."

"They treat the workers different," said Ben angrily.

"And now we're going to start a nationwide campaign to get all the other boys out," said Stein, getting to his feet and rubbing his hands, "starting with Debs . . . you'll see, Ben, you won't be down there long . . . people are coming to their senses already."

A burst of brassy music came up from Broadway, and the regular tramp of soldiers marching. They all looked out of the window. All down the long grey canyon flags were streaming out, uncoiling tickertape and papers glinted all through the ruddy sunlight, squirmed in the shadows; people were yelling themselves hoarse.

"Damn fools," said Warner, "it won't make the doughboys forget about K.P."

Morris Stein came back into the room with a funny brightness in his eyes. "Makes me feel maybe I missed something."

"Well, I've got to be going," said Warner, shaking hands again. "You certainly got a rotten break, Compton . . . don't think for a minute we won't be working night and day to get you out . . . I'm sure public sentiment will change. We have great hopes of President Wilson . . . after all, his labor record was fairly good before the war."

"I guess it'll be the workers will get me out, if I'm gotten out," said Ben.

Warner's eyes were searching his face. Ben didn't smile. Warner stood before him uneasily for a moment and then took his hand again. Ben didn't return the pressure. "Good luck," said Warner and walked out of the office.

"What's that, one of these liberalminded college boys?" Ben asked of Stein. Stein nodded. He'd gotten interested in some papers on his desk. "Yes . . . great boy, Steve Warner . . . you'll find some books or magazines in the library . . . I'll be with you in a few minutes."

Ben went into the library and took down a book on Torts. He read and read the fine print. When Stein came to get him he didn't know what he'd been reading or how much time had passed. Walking up Broadway the going was slow on account of the crowds and the bands and the steady files of marching soldiers in khaki with tin hats on their heads. Stein nudged him to take his hat off as a regimental flag passed them in the middle of a fife and drum corps. He kept it in his hand so as not to have to take it off again. He took a deep breath of the dusty sunny air of the street, full of girls' perfumerysmells and gasoline from the exhaust of the trucks hauling the big guns, full of laughing and shouting and shuffle and tramp of feet; then the dark doorway of the Federal Building gulped them.

It was a relief to have it all over, alone with the deputy on the train for Atlanta. The deputy was a big morose man with bluish sacks under his eyes. As the handcuffs cut Ben's wrist he unlocked them except when the train was in a station. Ben remembered it was his birthday; he was twentythree years old.

Newsreel XLI

in British Colonial Office quarters it is believed that Australian irritation will diminish as soon as it is realized that the substance is more important than the shadow. It may be stated that press representatives who are expeditious in sending their telegrams at an early hour, suffer because their telegrams are thrown into baskets. Others which come later are heaped on top of them and in the end the messages on top of the basket are dealt with first. But this must not be taken as an insult. Count von Brochdorf-Ranzau was very weak and it was only his physical condition that kept him from rising

PRIVATES HOLD UP CABMAN

Hold the fort for we are coming
Union men be strong;
Side by side we battle onward,
Victory will come.

New York City Federation Says Evening Gowns Are Demoralizing Youth of the Land

SOLDIERS OVERSEAS FEAR LOSS OF GOLD V

CONSCRIPTION A PUZZLE

Is there hostile propaganda at work in Paris?

We meet today in Freedom's cause
And raise our voices high
We'll join our hands in union strong
To battle or to die

FRANCE YET THE FRONTIER OF FREEDOM

provision is made whereby the wellbeing and development of backward and colonial regions are regarded as the sacred trust of civilization over which the league of nations exercises supervising care

REDS WEAKENING WASHINGTON HEARS

Hold the fort for we are coming
Union men be strong

the marine workers affiliation meeting early last night at no. 26 Park Place voted to start a general walkout at 6 A.M. tomorrow

BURLESON ORDERS ALL POSTAL TELEGRAPH NEWS SUPPRESSED

his reply was an order to his followers to hang these two lads on the spot. They were placed on chairs under trees, halters fastened on the boughs were placed around their necks, and then they were maltreated until they pushed the chair away from them with their feet in order to finish their torments

The Camera Eye (42)

four hours we casuals pile up scrapiron in the flatcars and four hours we drag the scrapiron off the flatcars and pile it on the side of the track   KEEP THE BOYS FIT TO GO HOME is the slogan of the YMCA   in the morning the shadows of the poplars point west and in the afternoon they point out east where Persia is the jagged bits of old iron cut into our hands through the canvas gloves a kind of grey slagdust plugs our noses and ears stings eyes   four hunkies   a couple of wops   a bohunk   dagoes   guineas   two little dark guys with blue chins nobody can talk to

spare parts no outfit wanted to use

mashed mudguards busted springs old spades and shovels entrenching tools twisted hospital cots   a mountain of nuts and bolts of all sizes   four million miles of barbedwire chickenwire rabbitfence   acres of tin roofing square miles of parked trucks   long parades of locomotives strung along the yellow rails of the sidings

KEEP THE BOYS FIT TO GO up in the office the grumpy sergeants doing the paperwork dont know where home is lost our outfits our service records our aluminum numberplates no spika de Engliss no entiendo comprend pas no capisco nyeh panimayoo

   day after day the shadows of the poplars point west northwest north northeast east   When they desoit they always heads south the corporal said   Pretty tough but if he aint got a soivice record how can we make out his discharge KEEP OUR BOYS FIT for whatthehell the war's over

   scrap

Newsreel XLII

it was a gala day for Seattle. Enormous crowds not only filled the streets on the line of march from the pier but finally later in the evening machineguns were placed in position, the guardsmen withstanding a shower of missles until their inaction so endangered them the officers gave the order to fire. WOULD CUT OFF LIGHT. President Lowell of Harvard University has urged the students to serve as strikebreakers. "In accordance with its tradition of public service, the university desires at this time of crisis to maintain order and support the laws of the Commonwealth."

THREE ARMIES FIGHT FOR KIEW

Calls Situation a Crime against Civilization

TO MAKE US INVULNERABLE

during the funeral services of Horace Traubel, literary executor and biographer of Walt Whitman, this afternoon, a fire broke out in the Unitarian Church of the Messiah. Periodicals, tugboats and shipyards were effected. 2000 passengers held up at Havre from which Mr. Wilson embarked to review the Pacific fleet, but thousands were massed on each side of the street seemingly satisfied merely to get a glimpse of the President. As the *George Washington* steamed slowly to her berth in Hoboken through the crowded lower bay, every craft afloat gave welcome to King Albert and Queen Elizabeth by hoarse blasts of their whistles

CRUCIBLE STEEL CONTINUES TO LEAD MARKET

> *My country 'tis of thee*
> *Sweet land of libertee*
> *Of thee I sing*

Paul Bunyan

When Wesley Everest came home from overseas and got his discharge from the army he went back to his old job of logging. His folks were of the old Kentucky and Tennessee stock of woodsmen and squirrelhunters who followed the trail blazed by Lewis and Clark into the rainy giant forests of the Pacific slope. In the army Everest was a sharpshooter, won a medal for a crack shot.

(Since the days of the homesteaders the western promoters and the politicians and lobbyists in Washington had been busy with the rainy giant forests of the Pacific slope, with the result that:

ten monopoly groups aggregating only one thousand eight hundred and two holders, monopolized one thousand two hundred and eight billion, eight hundred million,

[1,208,800,000,000]

square feet of standing timber, . . . enough standing timber . . . to yield the planks necessary [over and above the manufacturing wastage] to make a floating bridge more than two feet thick and more than five miles wide from New York to Liverpool; —

wood for scaffolding, wood for jerrybuilding residential suburbs, billboards, wood for shacks and ships and shantytowns, pulp for tabloids, yellow journals, editorial pages, advertising copy, mailorder catalogues, filingcards, army paperwork, handbills, flimsy.)

Wesley Everest was a logger like Paul Bunyan.

The lumberjacks, loggers, shingleweavers, sawmill workers were the helots of the timber empire; the I.W.W. put the idea of industrial democracy in Paul Bunyan's head; wobbly organizers said the forests ought to belong to the whole people, said Paul Bunyan ought to be paid in real money instead of in company scrip, ought to have a decent place to dry his clothes, wet from the sweat of a day's work in zero weather and snow, an eight hour day, clean bunkhouses, wholesome grub; when Paul Bunyan came back from making Europe safe for the democracy of the Big Four, he joined the lumberjack's local to help make the Pacific slope safe for the workingstiffs. The wobblies were reds. Not a thing in this world Paul Bunyan's ascared of.

(To be a red in the summer of 1919 was worse than being a hun or a pacifist in the summer of 1917.)

The timber owners, the sawmill and shinglekings were patriots; they'd won the war (in the course of which the price of lumber had gone up from $16 a thousand feet to $116; there are even cases where the government paid as high as $1200 a thousand for spruce); they set out to clean the reds out of the logging camps;

free American institutions must be preserved at any cost;

so they formed the Employers Association and the Legion of Loyal Loggers, they made it worth their while for bunches of ex-soldiers to raid I.W.W. halls, lynch and beat up organizers, burn subversive literature.

On Memorial Day 1918 the boys of the American Legion in Centralia led by a group from the Chamber of Commerce wrecked the I.W.W. hall, beat up everybody they found in it, jailed some and piled the rest of the boys in a truck and dumped them over the county line, burned the papers and pamphlets and auctioned off the fittings for the Red Cross; the wobblies' desk still stands in the Chamber of Commerce.

The loggers hired a new hall and the union kept on growing. Not a thing in this world Paul Bunyan's ascared of.

Before Armistice Day, 1919, the town was full of rumors that on that day the hall would be raided for keeps. A young man of good family and pleasant manners, Warren O. Grimm, had been an officer with the American force in Siberia; that made him an authority on labor and Bolsheviks, so he was chosen by the business men to lead the 100% forces in the Citizens Protective League to put the fear of God into Paul Bunyan.

The first thing the brave patriots did was pick up a blind newsdealer and thrash him and drop him in a ditch across the county line.

The loggers consulted counsel and decided they had a right to defend their hall and themselves in case of a raid. Not a thing in this world Paul Bunyan's ascared of.

Wesley Everest was a crack shot; Armistice Day he put on his uniform and filled his pockets with cartridges. Wesley Everest was not much of talker; at a meeting in the Union Hall the Sunday before the raid, there'd been talk of the chance of a lynching bee; Wesley Everest had been walking up and down the aisle with his O.D. coat on over a suit of overalls, distributing literature and pamphlets; when the boys said they wouldn't stand for another raid, he stopped in his tracks with the papers under his arm, rolled himself a brownpaper cigarette and smiled a funny quiet smile.

Armistice Day was raw and cold; the mist rolled in from Puget Sound and dripped from the dark boughs of the spruces and the shiny storefronts of the town. Warren O. Grimm commanded the Centralia section of the parade. The exsoldiers were in their uniforms. When the parade passed by the union hall without halting, the loggers inside breathed easier, but on the way back the parade halted in front of the hall. Somebody whistled through his fingers. Somebody yelled, "Let's go . . . at 'em, boys." They ran towards the wobbly hall. Three men crashed through the door. A rifle spoke. Rifles crackled on the hills back of the town, roared in the back of the hall.

Grimm and an exsoldier were hit.

The parade broke in disorder but the men with rifles formed again and rushed the hall. They found a few unarmed men hiding in an old icebox, a boy in uniform at the head of the stairs with his arms over his head.

Wesley Everest shot the magazine of his rifle out, dropped it and ran for the woods. As he ran he broke through the crowd in the back of the hall, held them off with a blue automatic, scaled a fence, doubled down an alley and through the back street. The mob followed. They dropped the coils of rope they had with them to lynch Britt Smith the I.W.W. secretary. It was Wesley Everest's drawing them off the kept them from lynching Britt Smith right there.

Stopping once or twice to hold the mob off with some scattered shots, Wesley Everest ran for the river, started to wade across. Up to his waist in water he stopped and turned.

Wesley Everest turned to face the mob with a funny quiet smile on his face. He'd lost his hat and his hair dripped with water and sweat. They started to rush him.

"Stand back," he shouted, "if there's bulls in the crowd I'll submit to arrest."

The mob was at him. He shot from the hip four times, then his gun jammed. He tugged at the trigger, and taking cool aim shot the foremost of them dead. It was Dale Hubbard, another exsoldier, nephew of one of the big lumber men of Centralia.

Then he threw his empty gun away and fought with his fists. The mob had him. A man bashed his teeth in with the butt of a shotgun. Somebody brought a rope and they started to hang him. A woman elbowed through the crowd and pulled the rope off his neck.

"You haven't the guts to hang a man in the daytime," was what Wesley Everest said.

They took him to the jail and threw him on the floor of a cell. Meanwhile they were putting the other loggers through the third degree.

That night the city lights were turned off. A mob smashed in the outer door of the jail. "Don't shoot, boys, here's your man," said the guard. Wesley Everest met them on his feet, "Tell the boys I did my best," He whispered to the men in the other cells.

They took him off in a limousine to the Chehalis River bridge. As Wesley Everest lay stunned in the bottom of the car a Centralia business man cut his penis and testicles off with a razor. Wesley Everest gave a great scream of pain. Somebody has remembered that after a while he whispered, "For God's sake, men, shoot me . . . don't make me suffer like this." Then they hanged him from the bridge in the glare of the headlights.

The coroner at his inquest thought it was a great joke.

He reported that Wesley Everest had broken out of jail and run to the Chehalis River bridge and tied a rope around his neck and jumped off, finding the rope too short he'd climbed back and fashioned on a longer one, had jumped off again, broke his neck and shot himself full of holes.

They jammed the mangled wreckage into a packing box and buried it.

Nobody knows where they buried the body of Wesley Everest, but the six loggers they caught they buried in the Walla Walla Penitentiary.

Richard Ellsworth Savage

The pinnacles and buttresses of the apse of Nôtre Dâme looked crumbly as cigarash in the late afternoon sunshine. "But you've got to stay, Richard," Eleanor was saying as she went about the room collecting the teathings on a tray for the maid to take out. "I had to do something about Eveline and her husband before they sailed . . . after all, she's one of my oldest friends . . . and I've invited all her wildeyed hangerson to come in afterwards." A fleet of big drays loaded with winebarrels rumbled along the quay outside. Dick was staring out into the grey ash of the afternoon. "Do close that window, Richard, the dust is pouring in. . . . Of course, I realize that you'll have to leave early to go to J.W.'s meeting with the press. . . . If it hadn't been for that he'd have had to come, poor dear, but you know how busy he is." "Well, I don't exactly find the time hanging on my hands . . . but I'll stay and greet the happy pair. In the army I'd forgotten about work." He got to his feet and walked back into the room to light a cigarette.

"Well, you needn't be so mournful about it."

"I don't see you dancing in the streets yourself."

"I think Eveline's made a very grave mistake . . . Americans are just too incredibly frivolous about marriage."

Dick's throat got tight. He found himself noticing how stiffly he put the cigarette to his mouth, inhaled the smoke and blew it out. Eleanor's eyes were on his face, cool and searching. Dick didn't say anything, he tried to keep his face stiff.

"Were you in love with that poor girl, Richard?"

Dick blushed and shook his head.

"Well, you needn't pretend to be hard about it . . . it's just young to pretend to be hard about things."

"Jilted by army officer, Texas belle killed in a plane wreck . . . but most of the correspondents know me and did their best to kill that story. . . . What did you expect me to do, jump into the grave like Hamlet? The Hon. Mr. Barrow did all of that that was necessary. It was a frightfully tough break . . ." He let himself drop into a chair. "I wish I was hard enough so that I didn't give a damn about anything. When history's walking on all our faces is no time for pretty sentiments." He made a funny face and started talking out of the corner of his mouth. "All I asked sister is to see de woild with Uncle Woodrow

. . . le beau monde sans blague tu sais." Eleanor was laughing her little shrill laugh when they heard Eveline's and Paul Johnson's voices outside on the landing.

Eleanor had bought them a pair of little blue parakeets in a cage. They drank Montracher and ate roast duck cooked with oranges. In the middle of the meal Dick had to go up to the Crillon. It was a relief to be out in the air, sitting in an open taxi, running past the Louvre made enormous by the late twilight under which the Paris streets seemed empty and very long ago like the Roman forum. All the way up past the Tuileries he played with an impulse to tell the taxidriver to take him to the opera, to the circus, to the fortifications, anywhere to hell and gone. He set his pokerface as he walked past the doorman at the Crillon.

Miss Williams gave him a relieved smile when he appeared in the door. "Oh, I was afraid you'd be late, Captain Savage." Dick shook his head and grinned. "Anybody come?" "Oh, they're coming in swarms. It'll make the front pages," she whispered. Then she had to answer the phone.

The big room was already filling up with newspaper men. Jerry Burnham whispered as he shook hands, "Say, Dick, if it's a typewritten statement you won't leave the room alive." "Don't worry," said Dick with a grin. "Say, where's Robbins?" "He's out of the picture," said Dick dryly, "I think he's in Nice drinking up the last of his liver."

J.W. had come in by the other door and was moving around the room shaking hands with men he knew, being introduced to others. A young fellow with untidy hair and his necktie crooked put a paper in Dick's hand. "Say, ask him if he'd answer some of these questions." "Is he going home to campaign for the League of Nations?" somebody asked in his other ear.

Everybody was settled in chairs; J.W. leaned over the back of his and said that this was going to be an informal chat, after all, he was an old newspaper man himself. There was a pause. Dick glanced around at J.W.'s pale slightly jowly face just in time to catch a flash of his blue eyes around the faces of the correspondents. An elderly man asked in a grave voice if Mr. Moorehouse cared to say anything about the differences of opinion between the President and Colonel House. Dick settled himself back to be bored. J.W. answered with a cool smile that they'd better ask Colonel House himself about that. When somebody spoke the word oil everybody sat up in their chairs. Yes, he could say definitely an accord, a working agreement had been reached between certain American oil producers and perhaps the Royal Dutch-Shell, oh, no, of course not to set prices but as proof of a new era of international cooperation that was dawning in which great aggregations of capital would work together for peace and democracy, against reactionaries and militarists on the one hand and against the bloody forces of bolshevism on the other. And what about the League of Nations? "A new era," went on J.W. in a confidential tone, "is dawning."

Chairs scraped and squeaked, pencils scratched on pads, everybody was very attentive. Everybody got it down that J.W. was sailing for New York on the *Rochambeau* in two weeks. After the newspapermen had gone off to make their cable deadline, J.W. yawned and asked Dick to make his excuses to Eleanor, that he was really too tired to get down to her place tonight. When Dick got out on the streets again there was still a little of the violet of dusk in the sky. He hailed a taxi; goddam it, he could take a taxi whenever he wanted to now.

It was pretty stiff at Eleanor's, people were sitting around in the parlor and in one bedroom that had been fitted up as a sort of boudoir with a tall mirror draped with lace, talking uncomfortably and intermittently. The bridegroom looked as if he had ants under his collar. Eveline and Eleanor were standing in the window talking with a gauntfaced man who turned out to be Don Stevens who'd been arrested in Germany by the Army of Occupation and for whom Eveline had made everybody scamper around so. "And any time I get in a jam," he was saying, "I always find a little Jew who helps get me out . . . this time he was a tailor."

"Well, Eveline isn't a little Jew or a tailor," said Eleanor icily, "but I can tell you she did a great deal."

Stevens walked across the room to Dick and asked him what sort of a man Moorehouse was. Dick found himself blushing. He wished Stevens wouldn't talk so loud. "Why, he's a man of extraordinary ability," he stammered.

"I thought he was a stuffed shirt . . . I didn't see what those damn fools of the bourgeois press thought they were getting for a story . . . I was there for the *D.H.*"

"Yes, I saw you," said Dick.

"I thought maybe, from what Steve Warner said, you were the sort of guy who'd be boring from within."

"Boring in another sense, I guess, boring and bored."

Stevens stood over him glaring at him as if he was going to hit him. "Well, we'll know soon enough which side a man's on. We'll all have to show our faces, as they say in Russia, before long."

Eleanor interrupted with a fresh smoking bottle of champagne. Stevens went back to talk to Eveline in the window. "Why, I'd as soon have a Baptist preacher in the house," Eleanor tittered.

"Damn it, I hate people who get their pleasure by making other people feel uncomfortable," grumbled Dick under his breath. Eleanor smiled a quick V-shaped smile and gave his arm a pat with her thin white hand, that was tipped by long nails pointed and pink and marked with halfmoons. "So do I, Dick, so do I."

When Dick whispered that he had a headache and thought he'd go home and turn in, she gripped his arm and pulled him into the hall. "Don't you dare go home and leave me alone with this frost." Dick made a face and followed her back into the salon. She poured him a glass of champagne from the bottle she still held in her hand: "Cheer up Eveline," she whispered squeakily. "She's about ready to go down for the third time."

Dick stood around for hours talking to Mrs. Johnson about books, plays, the opera. Neither of them seemed to be able to keep track of what the other was saying. Eveline couldn't keep her eyes off her husband. He had a young cubbish look Dick couldn't help liking; he was standing by the sideboard getting tight with Stevens, who kept making ugly audible remarks about parasites and the lahdedah boys of the bourgeoisie. It went on for a long time. Paul Johnson got sick and Dick had to help him find the bathroom. When he came back into the salon he almost had a fight with Stevens, who, after an argument about the Peace Conference, suddenly hauled off with his fists clenched and called him a goddam fairy The Johnsons hustled Stevens out. Eleanor came up to Dick and put her arm around his neck and said he'd been magnificent.

Paul Johnson came back upstairs after they'd gone to get the parakeets. He looked pale as a sheet. One of the birds had died and was lying on its back stiff with his claws in the air at the bottom of the cage.

At about three o'clock Dick rode home to his hotel in a taxi.

Newsreel XLIII

the placards borne by the radicals were taken away from them, their clothing torn and eyes blackened before the service and ex-service men had finished with them

34 Die After Drinking Wood Alcohol   Trains in France May Soon Stop

Gerard Throws His Hat into the Ring

SUPREME COURT DASHES LAST HOPE OF MOIST MOUTH

LIFE BOAT CALLED BY ROCKET SIGNALS SEARCHES IN VAIN FOR SIXTEEN HOURS

America I love you
You're like a sweetheart of mine

LES GENS SAGES FUIENT LES REUNIONS POLITIQUES

WALLSTREET CLOSES WEAK: FEARS TIGHT MONEY

From ocean to ocean
For you my devotion
Is touching each boundary line

LITTLE CARUSO EXPECTED

his mother, Mrs. W. D. McGillicudy said: "My first husband was killed while crossing tracks in front of a train, my second husband was killed in the same way and now it is my son

Just like a little baby
Climbing its mother's knee

MACHINEGUNS MOW DOWN MOBS IN KNOXVILLE

America I love you

Aviators Lived for Six Days on Shellfish

the police compelled the demonstrators to lower these flags and ordered the convention not to exhibit any red emblems save the red in the starry banner of the United States; it may not be indiscreet to state, however, in any case it cannot dim his glory, that General Pershing was confined to his stateroom through seasickness when the message arrived. Old Fellow of 89 Treasures Chewinggum as Precious Souvenir Couldn't Maintain His Serenity In Closing League Debates

And there's a hundred million others like me

The Body of an American

Whereasthe Congressoftheunitedstates byaconcurrentresolutionadoptedon the4thdayofmarch lastauthorizedthe Secretaryofwar to cause to be brought to theunitedstatesthe body of an American whowasamemberoftheamericanexpeditionaryforcesineuropewholosthis lifeduringtheworldwarandwhoseidentityhasnot beenestablished for burial inthememorialamphitheatreofthe nationalcemeteryatarlingtonvirginia

In the tarpaper morgue at Chalons-sur-Marne in the reek of chloride of lime and the dead, they picked out the pine box that held all that was left of

enie menie minie moe plenty other pine boxes stacked up there containing what they'd scraped up of Richard Roe

and other person or persons unknown. Only one can go. How did they pick John Doe?

Make sure he aint a dinge, boys,

make sure he aint a guinea or a kike,

how can you tell a guy's a hundredpercent when all you've got's a gunnysack full of bones, bronze buttons stamped with the screaming eagle and a pair of roll puttees?

. . . and the gagging chloride and the puky dirtstench of the yearold dead . . .

The day withal was too meaningful and tragic for applause. Silence, tears, songs and prayer, muffled drums and soft music were the instrumentalities today of national approbation.

John Doe was born (thudding din of blood in love into the shuddering soar of a man and a woman alone indeed together lurching into

and ninemonths sick drowse waking into scared agony and the pain and blood and mess of birth). John Doe was born

and raised in Brooklyn, in Memphis, near the lakefront in Cleveland, Ohio, in the stench of the stockyards in Chi, on Beacon Hill, in an old brick house in Alexandria Virginia, on Telegraph Hill, in a halftimbered Tudor cottage in Portland the city of roses,

in the Lying-In Hospital old Morgan endowed on Stuyvesant Square,

across the railroad tracks, out near the country club, in a shack cabin tenement apartmenthouse exclusive residential suburb;

scion of one of the best families in the social register, won first prize in the baby parade at Coronado Beach, was marbles champion of the Little Rock grammarschools, crack basketballplayer at the Booneville High, quarterback at the State Reformatory, having saved the sheriff's kid from drowning in the Little Missouri River was invited to Washington to be photographed shaking hands with the President on the White House steps; —

though this was a time of mourning, such an assemblage necessarily has about it a touch of color. In the boxes are seen the court uniforms of foreign diplomats, the gold braid of our own and foreign fleets and armies, the black of the conventional morning dress of American statesmen, the varicolored furs and outdoor wrapping garments of mothers and sisters come to mourn, the drab and blue of soldiers and sailors, the glitter of musical instruments and the white and black of a vested choir

—busboy harveststiff hogcaller boyscout champeen corn-shucker of Western Kansas bellhop at the United States Hotel at Saratoga Springs office boy callboy fruiter telephone lineman long-shoreman lumberjack plumber's helper,

worked for an exterminating company in Union City, filled pipes in an opium joint in Trenton, N. J.

Y.M.C.A. secretary, express agent, truckdriver, fordmechanic, sold books in Denver Colorado: Madam would you be willing to help a young man work his way through college?

President Harding, with a reverence seemingly more significant because of his high temporal station, concluded his speech:

We are met today to pay the impersonal tribute;
the name of him whose body lies before us took flight
with his imperishable soul . . .
as a typical soldier of this representative democracy he
fought and died believing in the indisputable justice of his
country's cause . . .

by raising his right hand and asking the thousands within the sound of his voice to join in the prayer:

Our Father which art in heaven hallowed be thy name . . .

Naked he went into the army;
they weighed you, measured you, looked for flat feet, squeezed your penis to see if you had clap, looked up your anus to see if you had piles, counted your teeth, made you cough, listened to your heart and lungs, made you read the letters on the card, charted your urine and your intelligence,

gave you a service record for a future (imperishable soul)

and an identification tag stamped with your serial number to hang around your neck, issued O D regulation equipment, a condiment can and a copy of the articles of war.

Atten'SHUN suck in your gut you c———r wipe that smile off your face eyes right wattja tink dis is a choirch-social? Forwar-D'ARCH.

* * *

John Doe

and Richard Roe and other person or persons unknown

drilled hiked, manual of arms, ate slum, learned to salute, to soldier, to loaf in the latrines, forbidden to smoke on deck, overseas guard duty, forty men and eight horses, shortarm inspection and the ping of shrapnel and the shrill bullets combing the air and the sorehead woodpeckers the machineguns mud cooties gasmasks and the itch.

Say feller tell me how I can get back to my outfit.

John Doe had a head

for twentyodd years intensely the nerves of the eyes the ears the palate the tongue the fingers the toes the armpits, the nerves warmfeeling under the skin charged the coiled brain with hurt sweet warm cold mine must dont sayings print headlines:

Thou shalt not the multiplication table long division, Now is the time for all good men knocks but once at a young man's door, It's a great life if Ish gebibbel, The first five years'll be the Safety First, Suppose a hun tried to rape your my country right or wrong, Catch 'em young, What he dont know wont treat 'em rough, Tell 'em nothin, He got what was coming to him he got his, This is a white man's country, Kick the bucket, Gone west, If you dont like it you can croaked him

Say buddy cant you tell me how I can get back to my outfit?

Cant help jumpin when them things go off, give me the trots them things do. I lost my identification tag swimmin in the Marne, roughhousin with a guy while we was waitin to be deloused, in bed with a girl named Jeanne (Love moving picture wet French postcard dream began with saltpeter in the coffee and ended at the propho station); —

Say soldier for chrissake cant you tell me how I can get back to my outfit?

John Doe's

heart pumped blood:

alive thudding silence of blood in your ears

down in the clearing in the Oregon forest where the punkins were punkincolor pouring into the blood through the eyes and the fallcolored trees and the bronze hoopers were hopping through the dry grass, where tiny striped snails hung on the underside of the blades and the flies hummed, wasps droned, bumblebees buzzed, and the woods smelt of wine and mushrooms and apples, homey smell of fall pouring into the blood,

and I dropped the tin hat and the sweaty pack and lay flat with the dogday sun licking my throat and adamsapple and the tight skin over the breastbone.

The shell had his number on it.

The blood ran into the ground.

The service record dropped out of the filing cabinet when the quartermaster sergeant got blotto that time they had to pack up and leave the billets in a hurry.

The identification tag was in the bottom of the Marne.

The blood ran into the ground, the brains oozed out of the cracked skull and were licked up by the trenchrats, the belly swelled and raised a generation of bluebottle flies,

and the incorruptible skeleton,

and the scraps of dried viscera and skin bundled in khaki

they took to Chalons-sur-Marne
and laid it out neat in a pine coffin
and took it home to God's Country on a battleship
and buried it in a sarcophagus in the Memorial Amphitheater in the Arlington National Cemetery
and draped the Old Glory over it
and the bugler played taps
and Mr. Harding prayed to God and the diplomats and the generals and the admirals and the brasshats and the politicians and the handsomely dressed ladies out of the society column of the *Washington Post* stood up solemn
and thought how beautiful sad Old Glory God's Country it was to have the bugler play taps and the three volleys made their ears ring.

Where his chest ought to have been they pinned
the Congressional Medal, the D.S.C., the Medaille Militaire, the

Belgian Croix de Guerre, the Italian gold medal, the Vitutea Militara sent by Queen Marie of Rumania, the Czechoslovak war cross, the Virtuti Militari of the Poles, a wreath sent by Hamilton Fish, Jr., of New York, and a little wampum presented by a deputation of Arizona redskins in warpaint and feathers. All the Washingtonians brought flowers.

Woodrow Wilson brought a bouquet of poppies.

COURTESY OF LUCY DOS PASSOS COGGIN

ABOUT THE AUTHOR Born in Chicago on January 14, 1896, John Dos Passos is one of the most well known writers of our time. He graduated cum laude from Harvard College in 1916 and went on to serve in the United States Medical Corps during the remainder of World War I. Upon his return Dos Passos began writing for several newspapers and magazines. His first novel, *One Man's Initiation,* published in 1920, was inspired by his involvement in World War I. Dos Passos went on to publish more than forty books, fiction and nonfiction, focusing on social and political issues and customarily taking an extreme leftist approach. He was one of the most adept chroniclers in the twentieth century of the difficulties of the American working class and the decadence of the well-to-do. While his political views eventually grew more conservative, in his writing he still strove to create an accurate reflection of American culture throughout his career. Some consider Dos Passos's most important work to be the *U.S.A.* trilogy. Among his other well-known titles are *Three Soldiers, Manhattan Transfer,* and *District of Columbia.* In his later years he made his home with his wife on a Westmoreland County, Virginia, property previously owned by his father. John Dos Passos died in 1970 at the age of seventy-four.

ALSO BY JOHN DOS PASSOS

U.S.A.

The 42nd Parallel

"Powerfully instructive, a bold work of fiction." — *New York Times*

In *The 42nd Parallel*, through stories artfully spliced together, the lives and fortunes of five characters unfold. Mac, Janey, Eleanor, Ward, and Charley are caught on the storm track of this parallel and blown New Yorkward. ISBN 0-618-05681-5

1919

"*1919* is literally what so many books are erroneously called, a 'slice of life.' It is the kind of book a reader never forgets."
— *Chicago Daily Tribune*

In *1919*, we find America and the world at war. A low-caste sailor, a minister's daughter, a young poet, a radical Jew, and a wide-eyed Texas girl are thrown into the snarl. ISBN 0-618-05682-3

The Big Money

"To find the equivalent of Dos Passos' nationalism, one must look abroad to Tolstoy's *War and Peace*, Balzac's *Comédie Humaine*, James Joyce's *Ulysses*." — *Time*

The Big Money completes this three-volume "fable of America's materialistic success and moral decline" (*American Heritage*), returning from the war to a nation on the upswing. It is an America taking the turns too fast, speeding toward the crash of 1929.
ISBN 0-618-05683-1

Manhattan Transfer

"A novel of the very first importance." — Sinclair Lewis

Against the backdrop of towering skyscrapers and filthy tenements, Dos Passos reveals the lives of wealthy power brokers and struggling immigrants alike, and unveils their efforts to become a part of modernity before they are destroyed by it. ISBN 0-395-57423-4

AVAILABLE FROM MARINER BOOKS